SONGS OF BLUE AND GOLD

After reading English at Trinity College, Cambridge, Deborah Lawrenson worked as a journalist on the *Kentish Times*, the *Daily Mail* and the *Mail on Sunday*. She was also the London Section editor of *Woman's Journal* magazine. She has written four other novels: *The Art of Falling*, published by Arrow in 2005, *The Moonbathers* (1998) and the newspaper satires *Hot Gossip* (1994) and *Idol Chatter* (1995).

Visit www.deborah-lawrenson.co.uk

Deborah Lawrenson

Songs of Blue and Gold

arrow books

Published in Great Britain in 2008 by Arrow Books

Copyright © Deborah Lawrenson, 2008

Deborah Lawrenson has asserted her right, in accordance with the Copyright,
Designs and Patents Act 1988, to be identified as the author of this work.

This is a work of fiction. Please refer to the author's acknowledgements on page v
for details of any resemblance to actual persons.

First published in Great Britain in 2008 by Arrow Books
Random House, 20 Vauxhall Bridge Road,
London SW1V 2SA

www.rbooks.co.uk

Addresses for companies within The Random House Group Limited can be found at:
www.randomhouse.co.uk/offices.htm

The Random House Group Limited Reg. No. 954009

A CIP catalogue record for this book
is available from the British Library

ISBN 9780099505198

The Random House Group Limited makes every effort to ensure that the papers used in its books are
made from trees that have been legally sourced from well-managed
and credibly certified forests. Our paper procurement policy can be
found at: www.rbooks.co.uk/environment

The Random House Group Limited supports The Forest Stewardship
Council (FSC), the leading international forest certification organisation. All our
titles that are printed on Greenpeace approved FSC certified paper carry the FSC logo. Our paper
procurement policy can be found at www.rbooks.co.uk/environment

Typeset by Palimpsest Book Production Limited, Grangemouth, Stirlingshire

Printed and bound in the UK by
CPI Bookmarque Ltd, Croydon, CR0 4TD

Acknowledgements

This story is infused with the spirit of Lawrence Durrell. Many – although not all – biographical details are his, but Julian Adie is a separate, fictional creation. Most importantly, I would like to make it clear that Lawrence Durrell was never implicated in a suspicious drowning, although accidents at sea were a recurrent theme in his novels.

Durrell *aficionados* might be disconcerted by the way I've played fast and loose with his chronology, compressing and altering his travels and his wives' biographies to give an impression of the author's life without providing in any way an accurate portrayal. In this, the book has more in common with his fictional characters, his use of dualism and reinterpretation than with real people. 'All these writers [in my books] are variations of myself,' he said a few years before he died. I wish to acknowledge that some of Julian Adie's words come close to Lawrence Durrell's own, both written and spoken.

I have been far more faithful to the settings of the book. The White House in Kalami, Corfu, is and was, as described. It is still owned by the Athinaios family, who were Durrell's landlords in the 1930s, and I am grateful to Tassos and Daria Athinaios for permission to make of it what I will. It is crucial to emphasise that the Kiotzas family in this book is imaginary and none of the characters or events is based on fact.

In the South of France, the arts centre – L'Espace Lawrence Durrell – in Sommières is more or less as described, as are the town and the house across the river where he lived for more than twenty years.

Looking for Julian: A Search for the Truth about Adie

Melissa Norden

[Thames Press: 2008]

Introduction

Julian Adie's life and strange demise had many mythic qualities. The traveller and writer, who loved the light and made his reputation on the shores of the Mediterranean but whose world grew increasingly dark, still exerts a powerful fascination, all the more so since recent revelations.

Adie's critical reappraisal in the new biography by Martin Braxton has rightly focused on the controversial facts newly uncovered. When I was first approached by Dr Braxton, I had little idea of the full story, and my instincts – not unnaturally – were to be wary. I certainly had no expectation that our meeting would result in this book, and no inkling where our separate investigations would lead.

This is not another biography. It is a personal memoir which stands beside Dr Braxton's version of the past, casting light from a different angle on a small but intriguing episode. It is also an account of my own journey chasing the shadow of Julian Adie across his sunny places, from the Greek Islands to the South of France.

It grew from the detailed notes I kept as I found out more about my mother Elizabeth Norden's connection to Adie, a relationship which was unknown to me until the very end of her life. What began as a private quest became a defence of her reputation.

While I have rewritten in parts and smoothed my notes of conversations for ease of reading, this is at heart a record of my own experience of the story; its disclosures remain in the order in which I discovered them, and my reactions to events substantially as they were at the time.

Chapter 1

By the time I reached Corfu, the season was in its last gasp.

Evening hung early over the bay when I walked the stony beach at Kalami and found the White House. It was just as he described: defiant on a rock, the sea clawing at its feet. On the headland behind, cypress trees pointed into a curdling sky. Pebbles crunched under my feet as I went closer, and waves sighed on grey stones. A brackish smell of nets and seaweed prickled in the air.

This was how my search began. Looking for someone I didn't know, many years too late. And looking, at the same time, for someone I had always known, but trying to place her in a strange setting, reconfigured in some new history.

It was late October. My summer had disappeared, hour by hour, into the oppressive sun and rain of an English

3

heat wave that drained suddenly into autumn while it was still August. Here, though, warmth lingered. I'd fallen asleep for an hour, late afternoon, to the weary hum of ageing insects and woke with the drumming thought: time present is only a breath, a heartbeat, and then it's gone. So I went out quickly, clutching the book. My knuckles were white around it, I noticed, as if my hands belonged to someone else.

I don't mind admitting it: I was nervous, frightened of what I might find and how much it might alter my old certainties when so many of the recent ones had already gone. In retrospect, it was the perfect frame of mind in which to begin what I was trying to do; alive to changes and misinterpretations, I trusted nothing.

This was a new way of thinking for me. It still felt odd, to have no trust in the world. But thanks to Richard, there was deceit and duplicity everywhere. It was like a cold knife in the flesh, this newly minted cynicism, sharpened by my own small deceptions to cover the wound.

The lies had started as soon as I arrived alone at the boat hire office where I picked up the key to the Prospero Apartments.

'Unfortunately my husband couldn't come with me,' I told Manolis Kiotzas. He was frowning at the print out of my booking, clearly made for a married couple: Richard and Melissa Quiller.

Manolis, a jovial, wide-faced man in his forties, was sympathetic and eager to offer help. He was also waiting for more. The Greeks are tactful as well as hospitable; for all that, they are unembarrassed in their curiosity about other people's lives, especially on this island. I had learned that much already from Julian Adie.

'Work . . . his business, he couldn't get away,' I said.

Manolis pulled down the corners of his mouth, with a wry twist this time. He nodded sagely, acknowledging a wise decision not to have cancelled in the circumstances. 'Is good you have come. You will have a nice time. Still sunny for a few days, nice rest, nice food . . .'

'I'm sure I will.'

'You come to the Prospero Taverna this evening, you have some wine . . .'

I smiled, without committing myself.

He handed over two large keys and gave me directions to the apartment, about a hundred metres further up the road. It was on the first floor of a modern house overlooking the sea, a few steps up a path on the hill side of the road. I found the outside stairs at one side, and carried my bags up feeling suddenly exhausted. There was no evidence that any of the other apartments in the property were occupied. The door opened easily. Inside, it was clean and white: a bedroom, a shower room and a sitting room with a basic kitchen along one wall.

I sluiced off the grime of travel, the early morning start on the motorway, the sweat of penned-in airport queues, then lay down wrapped in a dry towel on the double bed.

I could cry now if I wanted. It didn't matter. I knew no one here in Corfu. No need for any pretence. The stupid lie to Manolis apart, I was feeling all right. Or as well as could be expected. There was relief in simply being away, a guilty relief, that the worst had happened and I could stop fearing it. I didn't intend to sleep, but my eyes closed and oblivion took over.

That first evening, thoughts of my mother came easily as I sat on the rocks below the White House. How she had always loved the sun and sea, the spiciness of southern air. Her sense of fun, but also the self-containment that sometimes made her distant. Her delight in colour and history. The Greek myths she would retell. My own sense, successfully sublimated for years, that she had made light of her struggles and did not want her subsequent decisions to be scrutinised too closely.

When my mother was young, she made a minor name for herself as a seascape painter and exhibited several times at a well-known London gallery. My father Edward helped in that; an art historian and writer, he always claimed to have promoted her. But equally, later on, he made it more difficult for her to work. Gradually, she stopped painting, though there was a brief resurgence after he left. Afterwards she became an interior decorator. She made a good living by using her eye for colour and form in other people's houses. And given that she was a woman on her own with a child to support, it may have been as simple as making the best use of a talent. She had always had a practical streak.

'Try to live in the moment,' she would say.

It was certainly possible to imagine her in this place.

A lilac veil was poised to drop over the water between the island and the mountainous Albanian coast so close by. Julian Adie's description of its hulking nearness was more accurate than I had expected.

The Gates of Paradise was his account of an idyllic sojourn by the Ionian Sea, first published at a time when Britain was 'a place of thin greasy soup and shrivelled lips' and most people could only dream of sensuous escape, of unbroken sunshine and the freedom to swim each day in cobalt-blue seas, to eat fresh figs and drink wine, make love and write poetry under the sun. Sixty years ago, it was the book that made Julian Adie famous.

Near the end he writes of this very place, this fabled white house, after he and his first wife Grace had reluctantly sailed away in the teeth of imminent war: 'It is never mentioned. The house is destroyed, and the lovely boat lies holed and upturned, a ribcage rotting in the sun. Only the shrine and the sacred pool are unchanged.'

Disingenuous, of course. All the biographical sources note, usually in a spirit of indulgence, that Adie was not to be trusted with the truth when it came to spinning his literary web. Better to mesmerise with prose studded with poetic jewels, to conjure a yearning nostalgia by smashing up the beautiful landscape, setting it out of reach like a myth, than to tell it how it was.

Maybe the house was damaged, but it was never destroyed, for all that the Germans cruelly bombed the island. It still stands, solid as it ever was, at the southern end of the horseshoe bay. The boat had been sold before they left, according to other accounts, and if Grace and Julian never spoke of their idyll it was because by the time he came to write the words, she had left him, taking their baby daughter with her. By 1945 she was back in England, while he was rampaging through parties in Cairo.

Time and truth are elastic. I could feel that strongly here, sitting on the rocks where they once sat and which he described so alluringly, peeling away the layers of the present and the past. The slippage of years is like a strong undertow of the sea over steeply shelving beach. Could Julian Adie have been right all along, in his romantic claims? Was it possible to escape from the English way of death, and emerge in the blue light of a Greek island to collect and restructure the past, current and recurrent?

Between the bay's twin headlands where tall cypresses blackened into dark fringes, the sea was glassy. The looming foreign coastline was a bulge of rocky muscle, indigo-ridged on the horizon, as I strained the sinews of my own memory for the clues I must have missed.

There was no doubt in my mind that she had sent me here deliberately when she gave me the book of poetry and with it all the unanswered questions.

Collected Poems by Julian Adie, published 1980. On the title page is an inscription by the author: '*To Elizabeth, always remembering Corfu, what could have been and what we must both forget.*'

To Elizabeth, my mother.

Part One: Garden of England

I

I t was a photograph of a white house: dice-square, built low on a rocky shore. Behind it was a promontory speared by cypresses and in front, a dark blue sea glinting with sun diamonds.

Elizabeth traced the outline of the house with a finger. The picture was trembling in her hand. She had picked it out from a pile on the floor, tipped from a battered brown envelope — yet another diversion from the awful business in hand but one Melissa had allowed because it was too draining to argue over everything.

'What have you got there?' asked Melissa.

'His home.'

'Whose home, Mum?'

She opened her mouth to reply but no words came. Her eyes filled as the silent seconds stretched. The expressive green-grey eyes sharpened with tears and the pupils shrank like a wince. The answer remained frozen.

Melissa stroked her mother's shoulder.

Home. It was a word they had been using tentatively.

For months it had been offered and retracted, reinterpreted and recast, until it was hard to know what it meant any more.

A hard, old-fashioned suitcase lay open, half-filled, on the bed. Melissa smoothed the top layer of clothes inside. It had taken hours to get this far.

Elizabeth eyed the suitcase suspiciously. She was putting the oddest things in it, and Melissa was taking them out. A cracked green vase, a Chinese doll, a camping saucepan and garden secateurs lay in limbo on the counterpane. Feeling sad and traitorous, as if by admitting she could not care for her she was failing both of them, Melissa removed a paintbrush and replaced it with three pressed nightdresses.

'We're not packing everything,' Melissa said. 'Only enough for a week or so. You know you can come back here if . . . if you don't like it.'

The nursing home was only an experiment. To see if she liked it enough to stay. It had to be her decision, even in this condition. Elizabeth Norden was still a strongminded, independent woman, no matter what was happening to her, the holes in her consciousness, the child-like panics and the words that remained frustratingly out of reach.

She wandered off down the corridor again. Melissa followed and waited more patiently than she felt. When Elizabeth emerged from a cupboard on the landing she was waving a screwdriver that Melissa was sure should have been in the kitchen tool drawer.

Elizabeth was smiling. The screwdriver was in her left hand, but she was hunched over to the right, holding something else with her elbow under the side of her cardigan.

'What have you got there?'

No answer.

'Do you want to put that in?'

Elizabeth shook her head. Her hair was still bright and thick, with streaks of the old blonde. Her lovely face was hardly lined. The devastation was all inside.

'Let's get on then, Mum.'

Back in the bedroom there were several minutes of lucidity, during which Elizabeth sensibly decided that she would take her hairdryer and embroidered dressing gown and found them immediately, despite still having one shoulder hitched up to hold whatever it was she had hidden under her arm.

'What have you got under there?'

Silence.

'You can put it in, if you want.'

The stare again. 'Is Richard here?'

Melissa shook her head.

'Why not?' Elizabeth asked. 'I thought he was downstairs.'

Clearly disappointed, she wrapped her arms tighter round her thin waist. She and Richard had always enjoyed each other's company. He had a knack of treating her as a friend, which she made easy, being as little like a mother-in-law as it's possible to imagine. They even flirted a little, which took Melissa by surprise at first. But there again, underneath the layers of self-containment, and with certain people, Elizabeth had always been rather gauchely young at heart.

'No, Mum. He's at work.'

'Later then.'

'He's not coming. He's in London.'

Elizabeth looked at her shyly. Her hands were shaking as she unwrapped the object she had twisted into the inside of her cardigan. Then she held it out. It was a book, a hardback with a glossy dust jacket.

Melissa put it into the suitcase. But this time it was Elizabeth who threw the look of astonishment and pulled it out. 'You need this,' she emphasised, and bustled out of the room.

It was a book of poetry. Melissa barely gave it a glance as she quickly put it on the chest of drawers with the paintbrush and all the other incongruous items. Taking some deep breaths she turned back to the work in hand.

The words 'Alzheimer's disease' had finally been used. The doctor called it 'AD', as though it were a new beginning and not a dreadful end. At first he would talk of 'the loss of cognitive function' as though they were at a seminar. Perhaps it wasn't correct to call it dementia any more.

In any case it was only 'probable AD'. He put it this way: 'AD is defined by specific abnormalities of the brain, but these can only be ascertained by direct examination, that is, after death by means of an autopsy.' He was a nice man, the doctor. He seemed too young though, as if he could not possibly understand the emotional impact of what he was saying. But perhaps that was a misjudgement on her part, yet another one, Melissa conceded silently.

They had passed through the early symptoms: mild memory loss and occasional disorientation. Clearly these had not manifested themselves worryingly enough. In any case, who was she to judge what was normal? Over the past few months, Melissa had felt like that herself all too often.

'Disorientation, changes in personality and judgement, moving on to anxiety, agitation, pacing and wandering, difficulty recognising family and friends, sleep disturbance,' Dr Stewart went on.

Steeling herself, she had asked.

'You have to start thinking about what is going to be for the best – for both of you.'

Melissa said nothing.

'Try the nursing home for a week.'

II

With Elizabeth away — only twelve miles away, but far enough for her to have screamed that she would not go abroad again when they drove past the station at Tunbridge Wells — the house seemed eerily empty, the life sucked out of it.

Built of rose brick and weatherboarded in white, Bell Cottage was medieval at its heart, a large cottage sunk in a tousled garden. Elizabeth's daybed vacant by the window, the house hunkered down under the storm-grey seas of the sky.

Beyond the house, paths and bridleways crossed a landscape of quiet legends: no chalk giants strode over the roll of the hills here; no dragon bones stirred under the fields; nor the swords and cries of clashing chain-mailed battle. This was a country-side of calmer beauties: the medieval house and its royal ghosts; the furry apricots espaliered against garden walls; the blasted oak around which a Tudor queen had once danced; the gentle mounds and dips of cultivation; the skeletons of hop gardens; the confluence of two snaking and babbling rivers far upstream from their eventual grandeur at Rochester and Chatham.

Melissa stayed on. She told herself it was so that she could visit her mother more easily, which was true. Also that she could not go back to London, which was not, necessarily. 'I need some time to think,' she told Richard.

When she was not sitting with Elizabeth in her room at the home, she worked in the garden, trying to tidy it and cut back as best she could, to imitate what she imagined Elizabeth would be doing this time of year. Or she walked through the countryside, striding out strenuously.

The soil smelt of decay after heavy rains as the earth closed in on itself. It clogged the boots Melissa had found in the garden shed and weighed them down.

Ferns were already rusting under the trees, the acorns browning. The throaty sawing of pheasants croaked from the undergrowth. At every turn on Melissa's solitary marches there was evidence of other lives and incidents: a soggy woollen glove hanging from a branch at chest height by the path, lost and waiting to be claimed; the disembowelled badger which sprawled across the woodland path; the flurry of feathers where a struggle had taken place.

To the rhythm of her steps as she walked, old conversations, transcripts of arguments with Richard, filled Melissa's head. The words were lodged there, primed as always for any chance to demand a rerun.

'I can't un-know what I know!'

'Relationships change; you could change your perspective!'

'See it from my point of view!'

'It's like an ache that won't go away . . .'

'You can't let go, you mean.'

One afternoon she stopped under the arch into the church-yard. On its crumbling plaster ceiling was a treasure trove of pencilled graffiti, some dating back to the nineteenth century.

Much of it was dated from the last war, though. Land-girls had once been billeted in the Guild House (an article in the parish magazine had stuck in her mind). It was a rickety construction with its origins in Tudor times, now dark and derelict. Scraps of dirty cotton curtains sagged at the diamond-paned windows. Plaster had fallen off leaving the skeleton of lath clearly exposed. Even a creeper growing up from the forgotten patch of garden to the side had died, suckers holding fast to black wormholes in the timber.

'Roll on a long time' implored one message dated 16 September 1939. Whose stories were these, and what happened next?

By nightfall she was often physically tired, but that did not always help.

'Imagine you are lying in a wooden boat on the sea, feeling it sway, feeling the pull from the currents in deep water underneath . . .' Elizabeth used to murmur, lightly stroking her forehead.

The child Melissa would float in blue, above and below: all shades of indigo and cobalt, turquoise, sky and aquamarine.

'Imagine all the blues, catching the sunlight, changing and lightening. Feel the warmth on your skin. Feel yourself sinking down into the blue and the sun. Feel how magical it is, how your arms and legs seem to float . . .'

Melissa could visualise the scene so vividly she could make the mattress rock with the waves and feel drowsy in the heat. It would not take long before she fell asleep.

In the past weeks, it was a technique to which she had returned more and more often in the sleepless reaches of the night.

*

'It's like being in no-man's-land – I can't go forward and I can't go back.'

Leonie listened, kindly, intently, head bent over the teapot. She filled their mugs again. It was Saturday afternoon, in her creamy, stone-flagged kitchen. Sunlight slanted in through floor-to-ceiling windows, brushing bronze and copper through her thick brown hair. Elizabeth had settled well enough for Melissa to allow herself a trip up to London.

'I'm dragging my heels,' said Melissa. 'But how can I make any decision about Richard when Mum is so ill?'

'So you would go back to him then?'

'Part of me wants to,' Melissa said slowly. 'We were together a long time – ten years, married for six. It certainly wasn't all bad.'

Leonie put cling film over the salads they had assembled in Mediterranean bowls for dinner with friends. A vast potato gratin sat on the counter ready to go into the oven.

Outside was a patchwork of suburban gardens overlooked by the backs of other substantial Victorian houses in the comfortable grids of Fulham. Leonie's husband and six-year-old daughter were in the garden raking leaves. Autumn was already tightening its hold on the senses as pervasively as smoke from bonfires.

'Marriages do survive affairs,' said Leonie carefully. 'But you need to be sure that you are taking him back for the right reasons.'

Melissa reached out for another biscuit. It fractured into grainy crumbs between her fingers.

'Make certain you aren't just going back into a situation where you're suspicious and on edge every time he's a bit late home. Every time he mentions another woman's name.

That's what will destroy you, it'll be even worse than before.'

She was perceptive as usual, thought Melissa. She has an instinct I lack. Even at university, when we were young enough not to be taking very much too seriously, Leonie had a knack of understanding, of seeing underneath the surface to what was really going on.

Melissa was formulating a reply when a small, muddy tornado whirled into the kitchen, scrappy plaits flying.

'Emily!' cried Leonie. 'Look at the state of you!'

'We've been doing archaeology at the end of the garden. Look!' She held out a short stick. 'Dad says it's a clay pipe.'

Leonie raised an eyebrow.

'Let's see,' asked Melissa. 'It is as well. It's clogged with earth, but there's the hole in the middle. Did you find it?'

'I did, while I was helping. But I got bored. And there are some bits of smashed plate too!'

Through the window, Ted was heaving two bags of garden waste up the side path.

Leonie followed Melissa's gaze. 'Don't be too impressed,' she said. 'First time since June he's been out there with anything more useful than a can of beer.'

She acknowledged that with a warm smile, then turned to Emily. 'You know that book I kept forgetting to give you? I managed to remember today. It's on the hall table.'

'Thanks. Did you know that a banana isn't yellow?' said Emily.

'Isn't it?'

'No, it's red and green. It's your brain that makes it seem yellow.'

'Where did you get that from?'

'Oh, it was on the Internet.'

'She asks so many questions,' said Leonie. 'You wouldn't believe how many questions, all the time.'

'Fantastic questions, though.'

'Well . . . not always. I was trying to get something done the other day when she interrupted, just would not leave it for a moment. I had to stop what I was doing . . . and the question was, "Mummy, who invented the bread bin?"'

They all laughed.

'You still didn't tell me,' said Emily. She grabbed a biscuit and wandered off.

'You are lucky,' Melissa told Leonie.

'I know.'

'Melissa, you are going to the christening, aren't you?' Leonie asked. 'Mattie was worried you hadn't replied to the invitation.'

The cream card casually and belatedly forwarded from London and left in a pile. Melissa realised, mortified, that she hadn't even read it properly.

'Oh, God, I must call them. How could I have forgotten? I'm godmother! At least I hope I still am . . . ' said Melissa, flustered. 'They asked me as soon as Tamasin was born. I wouldn't miss it, no matter what!' She was indignant anyone would doubt that.

'Call them now,' said Leonie.

After the cosiness of the afternoon, it was harder than she'd anticipated when the guests began to arrive.

'Still living in Victoria?' asked Paul, a medic she had once shared a house with for six months. He was studiously not mentioning Richard. Either Leonie or Ted must have told him.

'I've been in Kent. At my mother's house – she hasn't been well.'

He was saved from any comment on that by the arrival of a couple who looked vaguely familiar. 'Melissa, you remember Johnny and Caroline?'

'Oh, yes . . . yes, of course. Hi!'

'Great to see you! What have you been up to?' said Caroline. She was short and big-breasted, dressed in a matronly flowered ensemble.

'Still working in that library?' asked Johnny, ruddy-faced from the first glasses of wine.

'Archive,' Melissa corrected automatically. 'No . . . bit of a career break at the moment.'

'The party at the Hurlingham,' Caroline reminded her. 'Some idiot trod on my dress and ripped it. You mended it with one of those hotel kits. It was so clever of you. Do you remember?'

So that's who she was.

'And where's your lovely husband?' she asked, craning round.

'He couldn't make it.'

They all agreed it was a shame.

*D*on't ask me any more polite questions. That was all she could think after about an hour. She was raw with smiling. There was a sweet moment when Andy Temple, an old flame from college, grabbed her from behind and whispered in her ear, 'Still got it.' She took it in the spirit it was meant, and wiggled her hips. But apart from that, all seemed sacred to the concept of the couple. Most of the guests had children now. Emily was busy handing around bowls of nuts and crisps.

Jools arrived late as always, and alone.

She shrugged off her coat. 'It's more off than on with Ben at the moment. For a man who can't commit even a dinner party is scary.' She tried ineffectually to smooth down her head of curls, a style (in the loosest of senses) she had had as long as Melissa had known her. 'What about you?'

There was no need for preamble.

'Richard says he's sorry. He wants to try again.'

'It's all over with . . . her, then?'

'Seems so.'

'And what do you want?'

'Part of me thinks, Right, that's the end. There are no children involved. I'll never be able to trust him again.'

Jools rested her chin on a defiantly ring-less hand. 'And the other part?'

'Maybe I'm just angry with him. I can't help but worry what will happen next. I mean, what happens to a woman coming up for forty—'

'Forty's a while off yet!'

'Believe me, it doesn't feel like it. You think you're settled – you never plan for this one. Do you ever meet anyone else? And if you do, might it not end up even worse?'

'You can't think like that. It's just not the right basis for a good decision. Of course you'd meet someone else.'

Melissa sighed.

'But you're gorgeous!'

'Be serious.'

'I am,' said Jools. 'I still remember that party you arrived at, first year at college. Blonde hair. Great legs. You stood in the doorway . . . and there were tongues on the floor.'

Melissa shook her head.

'Obviously I thought you looked like a stuck-up cow and I would sooner have stuck nails up my nose than make friends with you,' said Jools, dead-pan.

'Now you tell me . . . .'

A burst of raucous laughter across the room seemed to make her serious, suddenly. Jools leaned in.

'What?' Melissa asked.

'Don't do it, Mel. Don't take him back. You're worth more than that.'

The directness took her aback.

'I know you. I can sense that underneath it all you want to be won round.'

'I don't know – I—'

'Just be careful, that's all.'

Melissa nodded.

'I've said enough. Let's have another drink.'

They put the world to rights over several.

III

'I hate it here, I want to go to France,' Elizabeth said when she woke up the next afternoon.

Melissa, sitting with her, waiting for her to come round, felt an uneasy mixture of empathy and frustration. According to a friendly and patently capable nurse, Elizabeth had been sleeping for hours on end every day.

'They don't talk to me,' went on Elizabeth. She squeezed the words out and started to cough.

Melissa took her hand, feeling agonies of guilt, wondering how she would cope with her back at home. 'I don't know, Mum. Perhaps we should see what Dr Stewart thinks. He said this was a good place.'

A shake of the head and a blaze of the eyes in response seemed to exhaust her. Elizabeth's head sank back on the pillows. Her cheekbones stood out prominently. The sight of her greying hair and pale cosmetic-free complexion cut Melissa to the core. Up until six months ago, her mother had always taken such care of her appearance, carefully replicating her old hair colour and discreetly painting her eyes and mouth. Despite the feathered lines, she was still beautiful.

It was hard to think of her as prematurely old, the glowing outdoor cheeks faded to milk white.

'I'll see what the doctor says,' whispered Melissa.

She seemed to have slipped further away in the day Melissa had spent in London. It was hard to know how long the disease had been there. When did the connections in her brain weaken and begin to fail? What had been normal forgetfulness in a person who was getting older, and what was more sinister? Melissa felt guilty for not knowing, for not sensing before. Perhaps it could have been halted. Perhaps she could have realised in time and done more to slow the decline. Was it too late now?

'I brought something for you.'

Melissa passed her a couple of photographs – from the same stack they had looked at in her bedroom: pictures of sea and rocky beaches, the colours gaudy under the glossy membrane. If they had sparked her interest so clearly before, perhaps they might do so again.

She stared down at them with no sign of recognition. Melissa sat quietly, giving it time. There was a worrying wheeze in Elizabeth's chest as she began to cough again. But after the fit had passed, she seemed to rally.

Astonishingly, Elizabeth nodded enthusiastically at the sunny pictures and said, 'Lovely . . . Corfu.'

Corfu? Melissa had never heard her talk about Corfu before. Was that where the photographs were taken?

'Did you like it there?' Melissa prompted eagerly.

She handed her the picture of the sea taken outside the white house, the one Elizabeth had said was someone's home.

'When did you go to Corfu, Mum?'

As before, Elizabeth ran a finger across the surface, then

looked up and brightened, her face curiously young.

'Julian,' she rasped.

'Julian?' Melissa wanted to keep this lucid moment going, keep her mother in it for as long as possible before she disappeared back into her mysterious new inner world. 'Who's Julian, Mum?'

Elizabeth considered the question, staring at a low cupboard in the room, on which stood the wherewithal to make a cup of tea or coffee. What pictures were forming in her mind? Had any gauze lifted from her injured memory? Or was she making this up, latching on to names that she had once heard and reproducing the sounds?

'That kettle never used to be green,' she said.

Melissa sat back in her seat fighting not to feel deflated. It had been weeks since anything she had tried had inspired such a positive reaction in her mother as these photographs. It had been hard not to hope they might unlock part of her mind for longer. A clutch of pictures slid off the bed and hit the floor with a sharp patter but Elizabeth did not react.

It was getting harder and harder to find lines of communication. During the two months she had been staying with Elizabeth at Bell Cottage, Melissa had been consciously probing, asking questions, trying to determine how the illness was progressing, how far it was eating up her reserves. And there had been times when she had almost seemed her normal self, remembering people and events from the past.

So where had these photographs and the memories come from – if that was indeed what they were? Who was Julian and why had she never mentioned him before? It was odd, this feeling that she did not know her mother as well as she had thought, when it had been just the two of them for so long.

But as Melissa kissed her goodbye a couple of hours later, it occurred to her that it might not be so unlikely that her mother had had her secrets. She had always held something of herself in reserve. As Melissa grew up, Elizabeth became not distant, exactly, but preoccupied somehow. More and more so. She had a quiet determination, too, which some mistook for dreaminess but which Melissa recognised in herself occasionally as a self-effacing, rather embarrassing kind of doggedness. When the demands of everyday grew too much she would retreat into a world of books, when reading and thinking was time suspended in which she recharged her inner resources. That was another trait Melissa had either inherited or learned early on to imitate.

But in remembering episodes from the past Melissa had to remind herself to be careful not to re-evaluate her mother's expressions, her words and actions in the light of the person she – Melissa – had become, instead of the child for whom they were intended.

Elizabeth had rarely been critical. 'I've made too many mistakes to tell anyone else how to live their life,' she'd said more than once over the years. It was only recently that Melissa had thought to wonder, what mistakes were they?

Melissa called Dr Stewart, who duly visited and diagnosed a lung infection. He recommended that she stay for at least another week at the nursing home where her condition could be monitored.

'Lack of appetite means weight loss – which leads to vulnerability to infection such as pleurisy. That's what I'm most concerned about now. We need to keep her where she is. Better than that draughty old house.'

'And all the meals I've cooked that she hasn't eaten.'

'Best plan, I think.'

Melissa, feeling guilty again at her relief, concurred.

IV

The doorbell rang, echoing around the cold dead air of the hall. A chill rose from the flagstones.

An elderly man stood tall on the doorstep.

'Bill Angell,' he reminded Melissa.

As soon as he said it, she recognised him. He was a widower, an old friend of her mother's. They went to the theatre together, Melissa seemed to remember, the occasional dinner out. He was good company, Elizabeth always said, but there was nothing more to it than that. Bill was a good man, a good decent man. Melissa had met him a couple of times over the years, and saw no reason to disagree.

'I was passing,' he said. 'I thought I'd drop in and see Elizabeth. Is she here?'

'You'd better come in.'

He was tall enough to have to duck to get through the ancient door, and he did so automatically as if he was used to it. He was neatly turned out, immaculately so but for a moth hole in the sleeve of his green tweed coat. His grey hair was thin, but he had not gone bald. He held himself upright as if he was ageing with dignity but no relish of the process.

He followed her into the sitting room, a slight stiffness in his walk. Melissa closed the book she had been reading and told him what had happened.

'I had been a bit concerned – for a while now,' he admitted. 'And then when she hadn't been in touch . . . I'm so sorry, I didn't realise it was all so serious . . .'

'I don't think anyone realised . . .'

Neither of them really knew what to say.

'Looks like you're busy. I hope I'm not disturbing you too much.'

Melissa shook her head. 'You're not.'

'If there's anything I can do,' said Bill. His lively grey eyes told her he meant it.

'The thing is,' said Melissa, feeling her composure slip and having to recover, wanting to talk to someone who would understand. 'It's as if I'm losing her – as the person she is, if that makes sense. The person I've always known. She can't remember anything properly, from what happened yesterday, to what she said five minutes ago.'

Bill nodded. The news had clearly upset him.

'And now she's been showing me stuff that I never knew she had. The other day she came up with some photographs I'm sure I've never seen before. Pictures of the sea and a shore – taken somewhere Mediterranean, was my guess. Anyway, she suddenly said it was Corfu, but I don't think she's ever been there. Or if she has, she's certainly never mentioned it before. But she was more animated than she'd been for ages, so I went along with it.'

Bill frowned in a gesture of sympathy. There was much

that was quietly impressive about him: his height and bearing, the soft tweed jacket and tie; his well-chosen words and concern to put others at their ease.

'It's not easy,' he said.

'And who is Julian? She was saying the name Julian.'

'I've no idea.' A pause. 'Not being much help, am I?'

Melissa smiled. 'It is a help actually, just to talk to someone who knows her well.'

'Do you want to show me the photos?' asked Bill.

They examined them together over strong coffee in the kitchen where it was warm by the old black Rayburn.

'These could well be of Corfu, couldn't they?' she said. 'I've never been but I'm sure the landscape fits – the cypress trees and the shape of the buildings, the colour of the water.'

'I'm sure you're right.'

'But when were they taken? When was she there?'

Bill exhaled with a whistle. 'I'd say these were taken in the nineteen . . . sixties,' he ventured.

'How can you tell?'

'From the development and the way the colour sits. I'm a professional photographer, or was.'

'I didn't know that.'

'Oh, yes. Not a news photographer, mind. The thought of having to take pictures of terrible accidents, people suffering, wars and unrest, anger . . . well, let's say that had no appeal. I wanted to make proper pictures of tiny things. Things that could not be seen by the human eye, like a drop of water falling into a puddle, a snowflake in flight . . .'

He paused, angling one of the pictures towards the

window and examining it minutely if dispassionately. 'I started work at sixteen at C. and A. James, the camera and photographic equipment shop on the old High Street. Learned the trade. Saved up and bought my first professional camera. A Leica, it was, lovely to the touch. I bought books and I taught myself to be a proper photographer. When Cyril James retired, I bought him out. Mary – my wife – and I ran it together.'

'I know it,' said Melissa. 'It's a bookshop as well as a studio, isn't it?'

'That was Mary's part. Art and photographic books. She ran that side – but then when she died, I had to keep on. We'd become known for that, and I didn't like to disappoint people.'

Bill stared critically at the photographs.

'They're only snapshots,' said Melissa defensively.

But he did not seem to hear her. 'Kodak paper . . . I'd say mid to late nineteen sixties . . .'

'You can be that sure?'

'Pretty much. Did you know, the world's oldest surviving photograph was taken by a man called Nicéphore Niépce, in France in 1827? It needed an exposure time of eight and a half hours, by the end of which the roofs he had captured were lit by two suns, one from the east and one from the west. He must have given up hope of producing a picture of a living person. No one could possibly have sat still for that long. But at least the print he produced was stable, as good today as it was then which is more than you can say for these.

'The way things are, there will be better records of Victorians in their rigid black-and-white poses than there will be of the second half of the twentieth century. Modern colour processing has not been all it was cracked up to be. It seemed wonderful at the time, but it's not permanent. It begins to fade after only about twenty years because the dyes break down, or rather the three colours of dye used break down at different rates so there's a noticeable shift in colour.'

They both looked back at the random mosaic of photographs on the table between them. There was a yellowing tinge to the rocks and the water on some of them that she had not noticed before.

The clock on the wall ticked loudly.

'That's how I first met Elizabeth,' said Bill. 'She came into the shop one day.'

Maybe Melissa did know that. The information was there but had to be teased out, having lain dormant for so long.

He told her how it had taken years to overcome their mutual shyness and to meet at a gallery for an exhibition. How that had progressed to a regular Thursday matinee at the repertory theatre. Their mutual dislike of stage musicals and secret passion for Ayckbourn and the sly intimacies of Alan Bennett.

All the while, Melissa was thinking how strange it was that she had never realised they were such good friends.

But then, how well did she know her mother as she had grown older? Understanding the wider story was going to be a matter of connecting disparate pieces of seemingly unrelated, almost forgotten knowledge. Just as, at the same time, an infinite number of her mother's thoughts and experiences and unconscious perceptions were fragmenting into a jumble of impressions.

They made an arrangement to visit Elizabeth at the home.

She was not sure of the rules regarding visitors, but was sure her mother would be pleased to see Bill.

Melissa was convinced she was doing the right thing, trying to stimulate Elizabeth's mind with the familiar, the friendly face, the happy memory.

Bill agreed readily.

'You don't want to take that ivy down,' he said as he paused on the doorstep where she was seeing him off. Some long dark strands of it curled by the garden wall where she had made a few half-hearted attempts to chop into it, fresh from wielding the shears in vengeance against the rambling rose which had fallen so spectacularly.

'It will only kill a tree if it's allowed to run riot all over it and reaches the crown. And over a wall a good thick mess of ivy like this gives food and shelter to all sorts of creatures . . . birds and bats and butterflies.'

'I thought it was supposed to damage brickwork.'

'Or maybe it protects the old walls from damage from wind and rain. You could be doing more harm by pulling it away. You might think about that.'

She did. It was nice to feel there was someone looking out for them, her mother and her.

Melissa did not like the idea of searching through her mother's private belongings. But she had to keep trying. She had it in her mind that if she could keep her mother talking it still might make a difference.

The photograph albums were easy to find. They were in the dining room cupboard where they had always been kept. The photographs of them as a family — such as it was —

were fading now, coming loose from the pages. Her father Edward, handsome, bulky, cigarette in hand. Melissa as a baby, as a child. And always her mother's character behind the lens: busy, no-nonsense, the practical balanced by the creative.

But the adhesive had browned and slackened its hold; the plastic film which held them flat was brittle now. Bill was right. Their colours had already begun to degenerate into strange olive greens and tan yellows, no longer a true reflection of life. The images were slipping silently away, pressed in books in the dark of cupboards and drawers. Ultimately they would be nothing but colourless compound and some ghostly outlines.

Searching for anything unfamiliar, she found nothing. Neither was there anything more in the cupboard on the landing.

She wandered into her mother's bedroom.

The book of poems was still where she had left it on the chest of drawers. *Collected Poems* by Julian Adie. A hardback copy in beautiful, almost unread condition.

Melissa read a few lines, then closed and turned it over. Why had her mother said that she needed this? Or was it just nonsense, like all the other sad peculiarities? There was so much Melissa did not know, and she was conscious that the time for explanations was running out.

Julian. It was an odd coincidence. She opened the book again at the title page, and this time the handwritten lines in black ink leapt off the page: '*To Elizabeth, always remembering Corfu, what could have been and what we must both forget.*' The signature was clear and wellformed. '*Julian Adie*'. It physically startled her. Whatever did it mean, with its unmistakably intimate tone that was suddenly negated by the use of his surname?

She flipped to the biographical note on the inside of the dust jacket. Julian Adie was born in Darjeeling, India, in 1914 where his father was a railway engineer. He was educated at Sherborne School. In London, he worked variously as a photographer's runner, a publisher's proofreader and a jazz pianist, before publishing his first novel and spending five years in Corfu, from 1935 to 1939. He lived and worked subsequently in Egypt, Rhodes, Cyprus and France. He was married four times.

A bare outline that told her next to nothing about the man. What was Julian Adie like as a person? Did he have a run of marital bad luck – or would a tally of four wives tend to indicate that he was the one who created the problems?

'*To Elizabeth, always remembering Corfu, what could have been and what we must both forget.*'

The cruel irony of the words struck her. At first glance they had seemed merely romantic and intriguing. And what, specifically, was Elizabeth supposed to forget?

M elissa took the book along with some photographs when she went to the nursing home that afternoon. Elizabeth smiled in her new enigmatic way but ignored the book and claimed she did not know anyone in the pictures. Her cough had improved, and so had her opinion of the nursing home. She was quite enjoying herself, she said, although the tigers in the garden could be fierce.

And Melissa was aware that she kept her own secrets. She still had not told her mother about Richard.

The next day, Bill Angell was waiting for her at reception. They went in together. Melissa led the way, confident she had brought a happy surprise, sure that an old friend would provide a welcome stimulus. But Elizabeth stared at Bill wide-eyed as if she was frightened, and Melissa felt guilty once again, this time for not considering her mother's need for privacy. While he was there, Elizabeth would say nothing, only shake her head. She was thinner, depleted by the chest infection as by her lack of interest in food.

'I thought you might like this.' Bill handed her a postcard. 'I've been keeping it to give you.'

Elizabeth hardly looked at the vibrant swirl of colour on the front. It slipped like water from her fingers.

After half an hour, Bill left them alone. 'I'll wait in the car park,' he said.

She joined him twenty minutes later. Elizabeth had closed her eyes and gone to sleep, her breath whining and wheezing. Touched that he had cared enough to come, and wanting in some way to make up for her mother's reaction, Melissa asked Bill, 'Shall we have a drink?'

Melissa remembered there was a cosy pub on the way back into town. She suggested it, but he said, 'I'm not much for pubs these days. Too noisy and full of machines. But if you'll risk it I could make you a cup of coffee at mine if you want to follow me back.'

'If it's no trouble, that would be nice.'

They made for their separate cars, Bill to a well-maintained blue saloon of some Japanese design and Melissa to her mother's small white Fiat. Windscreen wipers flapping against the intermittent drizzle, they headed into a gusty wind towards Tunbridge Wells.

Skirting the common, maples were shedding bark in thin shavings of coppery curlicues. A witch hazel dangled flowers of orange sea creatures and spiders. Melissa followed Bill to a house hidden in an enclave of its northern side. Edwardian, spacious and detached, with a hotchpotch of timbering apparently designed to add a rustic touch, it was set on a lawn ringed with dense shrubs. They drew up on gravel, just enough space for two cars.

Standing in the tidy hall, Melissa felt an airy hollowness stretching up the stairs. He led the way into a high-ceilinged sitting room. All was neat in there too, the furniture old but comfortable, the shelves crammed with books and a collection of unexpectedly vibrant paintings on the walls.

A room leading off was evidently a study. Here walls were entirely lined with books and a handsome desk stood in a bay window overlooking the garden. An angle-poise light had been left on by a photograph of a war memorial. The statue of a soldier, his stone form grey and lichen-mottled, half kneeling, bayonet ready, was framed by a fire of red and gold foliage behind it, as if the imaginary guns and grenades were bursting into crimson leaf and flowers.

'I'm sorry about . . . how she was. It was so kind of you to come. What was it you had been keeping for her?'

Bill picked a printed card off the desk and handed it over. It was a notice advertising an art exhibition in Brighton.

'I was sent some of these. Thought we might take a trip together, make a day of it. I didn't realise she was as bad as she is, you see. I'd ring and she didn't sound like herself. I was getting so worried . . . that was when I decided to knock on her door.'

'I'm glad you did.'

'Obviously she can't go now. But she might like it anyway for the picture on the front. I think she will.'

'Thanks.'

The clouds darkened outside, weighted by rain.

'She didn't react to anything I took her yesterday,' said Melissa.

Bill went over to one of the bookshelves. Many of the books, she saw now, were volumes of art history; serious publications on photography, large slabs of printed pages. He pulled out one: it was a huge tome titled Art of the 20th Century. It had an index which took up almost a quarter of its pages. He dragged a slightly tremulous finger down a column and began flipping pages.

'There,' he said. 'That's the picture. Do you know it?'

She drew close enough to see where he was pointing.

An abstract picture of the sea was captioned with the artist's name and dated 1967.

'No,' said Melissa.

Bill picked up the gallery invitation. She looked at the card more carefully this time. The painting on the front was very similar to the picture in the book. And there, in small print below, was the name along with two other artists for whom the gallery was putting on a joint retrospective.

'Grace Heald,' said Bill, with satisfaction.

The picture was loose and sensuous, a swirl of deep blues. 'I don't think I know her. This is good, though.'

Bill was puzzled by her reaction. A frown pinched the bridge of his nose. 'You knew Elizabeth was interested in

Grace Heald's work, the paintings as well as the photography?'

'Not really, to be honest. She had so many interests. It was hard to keep up with her!'

'Oh.' He hesitated. 'Well, that's how we met in the first place. We got talking one day in the shop and she asked if I could find some books for her.'

'Books about Grace Heald?'

'Yes.'

'I don't think I've ever heard of her,' said Melissa.

'She is quite well known, in a rather small and specialised market.'

Melissa studied the pictures. Their bold style showed certain similarities with Elizabeth's own paintings. 'Do you think my mother was influenced by her?'

'I don't know – maybe. Although this would have been long after Elizabeth gave up painting, so I'm not sure that was relevant . . . unless, of course, she was thinking of starting again.'

'She never said *why* she wanted the books?'

Bill rubbed his chin, and considered. 'I can't say that she did,' he said. 'Only that she wanted me to find anything I could about Grace Heald for her.'

The exhibition had only a few more days left to run. Brighton was sullen under damp skies. No wind ruffled the cold so that the grey sea barely breathed as it reached the pebbles on the beach. Away from the promenade, the monochrome hardly lifted, apart from a struggling kind of jauntiness in the out-of-season shop windows.

The art gallery was a brisk walk from the multi-storey car park. Holding a map printed out from the Internet, Melissa threaded a way past cafés and funky shops, past the tawdry daytime faces of the bars and clubs that came alive at night, tatty purple paint peeled away here and bodged drain pipes there.

A world away from the town which held happy memories with Richard: the sunny weekends down from London, the funfair at the end of the pier, the antiquarian bookshops, the antique-hunting, the tipsy lunches, the glitter of diamonds in the jewellers' windows of the Lanes.

East Street was a row of Victorian shops and cafés on one side, and an industrial building divided into trendy units on the other, one of which was the Chafford Gallery. A wall of glass was set in the chocolate bricks of the old warehouse or factory, through which she could see bright canvasses mounted on dazzling white walls. An expanse of polished wooden floor stretched away, muddily reflecting the reds and yellows and blues of the paintings. Against the far wall was a desk, where a young woman in black sat reading.

Melissa went in.

All along one wall, she looked for the name. Some of the work was terrible, some magnificent. The girl at the desk smiled and asked if she could help.

'I'm just looking, thank you.'

'If you need any help . . .'

There was one: signed GH. It was a huge landscape, with beautiful iridescence – blues and greens.

'Stunning, isn't it.'

It was. 'Does it have a title?'

'She gave them numbers, not names. That one is 1970.'

'That must be a year, surely?'

'Yes. I suppose so.'

A red sold sticker.

'Oh, well. I'm not surprised it's sold. It's gorgeous.'

'There are some more over there.'

She indicated a large abstract that dominated the rear section of the gallery. From ten feet away Melissa realised it was a snow-covered hillside, and shivered involuntarily. Her head had begun to hurt.

'I liked the other better,' she said at last. 'Do you have any information about Grace Heald?'

The assistant's eyes flickered over her. Maybe she was trying to assess the likelihood that Melissa was a buyer. 'We kept some photocopies of information we acquired with the pictures. Details of past exhibitions, that kind of thing. I'll see what I can do.'

'Is she still alive?'

'No. She died some time ago, I think.'

The assistant disappeared into a back room. Melissa looked around for a while longer, admiring some smaller canvasses, the generous brushstrokes and singing colours.

'This is all I can find.'

The girl held out a photocopy of a brief résumé of Grace Heald's career. One sentence sprang off the page and made Melissa's head swim: *Married to the writer and traveller Julian Adie, 1935–1942.*

V

On the day before the christening, the train to London was crowded. In a clammy corner of the carriage, Melissa felt the damp rising from thick coats as too much hot air pumped from shin-level heaters. Grey rain streaked the windows outside, condensation inside. As the dull mud of the countryside gave way to tightly packed suburban wastes, her nerves began to tighten. The concourse at Charing Cross was a hard expanse of noise and slipperiness and people. Beyond it, the rude fierce wetness churned up by traffic glittered orange in the city lights.

By the time she had walked up from St James's Park tube station, and turned left off Victoria Street into Morpeth Terrace, her feet were soaked and she wished she had worn boots. *If I really had to come and do this.*

She had to.

Outside the entrance to the mansion block, she hesitated. Should she ring the doorbell? It was late on a Saturday afternoon. Richard might well be there. What if Sarah was with him? Her hand shook as she pushed the key into the lock before she could argue herself to a standstill. The door clicked and she was striding towards the lift. In the two months since she'd been here, the building had become subtly unfamiliar: the green of the carpet was more garish, the curve of the staircase around the lift shaft more cramped.

Perhaps she should have warned Richard she was coming. But no. She had made the decision. It was better to arrive unannounced to see for herself how he was living, whether he was alone. If he was there, she told herself, she would face him calmly, whatever the circumstances.

The lift rose to the second floor.

Out of the lift, she turned right and listened. There was no light visible behind the front door keyhole. After another hesitation, she let herself in, closed the door and flicked on the hall light.

A surge of unhappiness kicked in as she worked her way quietly along the corridor. Not a sound indicated anyone else was there. Still cautious, she peered into the dark kitchen, and then the sitting room. It was odd to see all her books again, the pictures and CDs. The furniture they had bought together.

The television's red eye glowed. But that meant nothing. Richard always left it on standby. A mug and two dirty plates lay on the floor by the sofa, its cushions mangled and flecked with crumbs. She resisted the urge to sigh and start clearing up.

Across to the main bedroom. Her heart was pounding.

Still not a sound.

She pushed the door open, tensing herself for what she might see. But no one was there. The bed was unoccupied, unmade as Richard always left it. Only now did she switch the light on. His worn shirts were draped over an overflowing laundry basket. Books, newspapers and crumpled tissues, jeans littered the floor. It certainly did not look as if he was keeping the place in a state with which to impress anyone.

Relief was short-lived. All that meant was that they spent their time at Sarah's place.

She could not look at the bed, neither to remember herself there, nor to overlay those memories with thoughts of him and Sarah.

Feeling shaky, she opened her wardrobe. It did not look as if it had been touched. She reached in and pulled out a smart jacket and dress for the christening, folding them over her arm as she looked around, sure she had missed something.

So where was Richard? Perhaps the answers were all here, printed on crumpled pieces of paper: notes, telephone numbers, visa bills, receipts. This is my chance, she thought. *I should take the chance to put myself in a position of strength for once.*

She hooked the hanger over the wardrobe door, and made for the bedside table. She began to sift through the mess. *I'm an intruder in my own home.* Then she stopped. A tiny sound, something jangled. How many times had she heard that noise – or was she imagining it? She strained to hear.

Out in the passage, she listened again. From the kitchen the fridge gave a watery whine and gurgle.

Then the front door slammed. Footsteps padded down the corridor, along with a soft rustle.

She took a deep breath and prayed he was alone.

He turned into the kitchen. There was a thud on the worktop.

Idiotically, she contemplated making a run for it, past

the kitchen, down the corridor and out the front door. Instead, she took a deep breath and went over to the kitchen doorway. Richard was grimly unpacking a lone bag of supermarket shopping.

'Hello, Richard,' she said.

Her voice made him jump.

He was weekend scruffy in frayed jeans and a blue sailing sweater with holes in the arms. He needed a haircut and had not bothered to shave that morning.

He looked stricken.

'Melissa!'

Neither of them knew where to start.

'Why didn't you—?'

'I needed to collect—'

Dark shadows ringed his eyes. He looked as though he had lost weight. It could mean he had been miserable. *Equally, it might indicate he's been having a raucous time with me gone,* she thought.

'How are you?' he asked at last.

'OK.' A pause. 'You?'

A shrug. 'Not so good.'

She said nothing.

'Are you coming back – I mean has anything happened to –?'

'No.'

'So are you—?'

'That's no to both questions,' Melissa said firmly.

He leaned against the worktop, arms folded. It seemed an effort for him to look her in the eye. 'How is your mum?'

'She's gone into a nursing home.'

'Is she . . . improving?' He was as awkward as she was.

'She's not going to get better, Richard.'

'No . . . right.'

He picked up the kettle and filled it, as if he was trying to fill the space between them. 'Tea?'

She shook her head. He flicked it on to boil anyway. Standing there in the kitchen with him, it could have been any cosy Saturday afternoon. Gone was the aggressive self-defensive shield, on both sides. He seemed gentle and sad. A large part of her wished suddenly that she could wipe out everything bad that had led up to this point, forget about the betrayal and the hurt. She wanted to put her head on his shoulder and cling on, feel his hand stroking her hair and telling her it would all be all right again.

The kettle, overfilled, gave a snort and wobbled, bubbling from the spout.

She felt the waste of it all, the desolation.

He did look at her directly then. 'I am so, so sorry, Melissa.'

She stared back defiantly, holding tears in check.

'I've been so stupid! It was over with Sarah as soon as you left. Please believe me! I know I don't deserve it, but if you could give me another chance, I will never – ever – do anything to hurt you.'

He was so sincere, so abject. She could feel herself softening. After all the long weeks when she had tried to rationalise her own emotions, keep herself from going under, this was the hardest part.

'Why did you do it then?'

'Because . . . because I'm an idiot! I've been a bastard, a stupid bastard.' He held both arms out, half in supplication, half in honesty.

There was a moment when she could so easily have closed

the distance between them and reached out too. She longed to feel his arms around her, the softness of his lips. Seconds elapsed and she stayed where she was.

Her mobile rang.

She answered it, listened and hardly spoke. When the conversation was over, Richard came closer.

'What's wrong?' he asked.

VI

Elizabeth died suddenly of pneumonia in the nursing home on 5 October.

The following afternoon, Melissa stood on the bridge where the two rivers met not far from her mother's house. A turquoise kingfisher darted like a bullet down the river. A few flashy seconds and it was gone, leaving only a stab of remembered brilliance.

Julian Adie: A Biography
Stephen R. Mason
[*New Century, 1993*]

Julian Adie could hardly believe his luck when he met Grace Heald at a party in Soho, still less when she swiftly became his partner. She was tall and languid, angular and with jutting cheekbones, considered a beauty. Ever ambitious, sexually as much as socially, he set out to win her and succeeded in less than four hours. He was twenty to her twenty-two.

What was Adie's appeal to Grace? Like him, she was trying to kick against convention, though she was gentle where he could be bombastic. She was surprisingly shy for all the attention she received. Perhaps she admired his self-confidence, the way he stood up so straight in company and held forth in such torrents of wit and amusing stories that his small stature was irrelevant.

They were an unlikely couple. She towered over him by almost a foot when she wore heels. But they shared the same passions and bohemian ideals. Both were rebelling against solidly middle-class backgrounds in a social circle where creative ambition burned. Grace was an aspiring painter, who had studied at the Slade.

Soon they had set up home together: a bedsit in a house off the King's Road in Chelsea that was owned by one of her wealthy old school friends, the actress Jill Mayhew. Through Jill they socialised with the rich, and occasionally the talented, of their generation, like the then aspiring playwright Brian Gibbs, and actor Henderson Spinks.

But Adie was making little money. He supplemented his small private income by the tutoring he attempted in the late afternoons when he would rather have been at his typewriter, or preparing for a stint at the piano in one of the jazz clubs. He had also started to write seriously: mainly poetry and a novel. He made intensive studies of the Elizabethans, in particular Marlowe and Bacon. There was always a disciplined side to Adie. During the days when he was not working, he would spend up to ten hours at the British Library, reading and making notes. He felt keenly his lack of a formal university education and was determined to make up the shortfall. It was around this time that he forged what was to be a life-long friendship with Peter Commin, then an assistant at the prestigious bookshop Sandwood's in Chelsea, later to be his bibliographer.

In January 1935, Adie and Grace moved to the country, to the rural hamlet of Poundsbridge near Tunbridge Wells in Kent where he imagined they would both be able to work in peace. Despite the glorious walks to nearby Penshurst with all its Elizabethan resonances and associations with Ben Jonson and Philip Sidney, even here, the young couple felt constrained, constantly suffering from colds, surrounded by the damp claustrophobia of their cottage walls. The experiment was not a success.

A friend had gone to Corfu, an island so far off the north-west coast of Greece that part of it faced Albania. Edward Lear had lived and worked in the light and heat there in the mid-1800s. 'Come,' urged the letters. So they did.

They took a packet boat from Tilbury, ploughing across the Bay of Biscay in the first week of March 1935. Grace's parents were horrified at how far their beautiful and clever daughter had thrown in her lot with the louche and prospect-less Adie. The situation was barely improved by the news that this was a respectable passage: the Adies had been pronounced man and wife on 28 February by the registrar at Bournemouth, where his family had set up home. They had not been invited to the ceremony. It was not so much a secret wedding, as a fuss-free occasion, in the same manner as the passports had been arranged and tickets purchased with the last of that month's allowance from their respective families.

In Italy, there was a delay. A letter to the family back in Wimborne Road, Bournemouth reads, '*We are stuck on the docks with nothing but pennies for cigarettes and wine, waiting for some mischief-makers in Brindisi to settle their differences with the ship owner before we can board for the final push across the Ionian . . . we are short-tempered but managing to ration our arguments along with any unrealistic hopes. Our first marital test — G. wants either a bed for the night or an immediate divorce. I told her this is a Catholic country and she has Burned Her Bridges!!'*

When they finally arrived in Corfu they stayed for three weeks with Paddy and Bridget Williams at the Villa Limoni near Perama — it was Paddy's letters that had lured them — then struck out north to find somewhere wild and remote in which to write and paint.

At Kalami, they found rooms to rent in a fisherman's house. It was always known while they lived there as Prospero's House, but he called it the White House in his first major literary success, *The Gates of Paradise*.

Adie was to write ever after that he lived a peasant's life in Corfu: he fished with the fishermen; he toiled in the olive groves; he was a picker of oranges and kumquats. If that was not strictly true (he soon made friends with the island aristocracy and caroused in convincing imitation of a leisured and wealthy expatriate in Corfu Town) this was a time of simple pleasures and sunshine.

Photographs of the time show his blond hair bleached almost white, his beguiling grin triumphant above an octopus caught on a trident, or fish grilling on a beach fire; while Grace is almost always serene, smiling thoughtfully at the horizon from a jetty or a balcony as if she is keeping a delicious secret to herself.

The sea was the bluest he had ever seen, shot through

with veins of gold. '*We plunge into lapis lazuli, molten by the sun,*' he wrote to his old friend Peter Commin back at the bookshop in Chelsea, '*and emerge dripping with bright diamonds.*' He and Grace developed a passion for nude swimming. Adie was working hard, brimming with ideas; Grace was painting confident gaudy canvasses inspired by the lushness, the rocks, the cobalts and aquamarines of the Ionian. It was an idyll which neither ever forgot – nor from which he ever recovered, according to some who knew him in that 'period of perfection'.

And why should he not have presumed he had reached the gates of paradise? (It was typical Adie that he just hedged his bets: he was at the gates, but not quite inside . . .) He was young, lusty, fired with enthusiasm and ambition, heady with his first serious attempts at writing both poetry and prose, and perhaps most importantly, he was deeply in love with a beautiful young wife who shared his ideals.

Part Two: Wreck of Paradise

I

A lone small boat skimmed into Kalami bay from the south. The splutter of its outboard motor grew louder. Soon it was close enough to make the two men on board visible. As they nosed towards the stone landing stage at the White House, the younger stood up with a rope and ran off the front of the craft and on to the mooring with no break in his stride. He tied the boat up, amid shouting. The other gesticulated at Melissa. She turned away. In another life she might have tossed back a choice remark. It was a moment before she realised the older man was Manolis, her temporary landlord. The men unloaded some boxes from the boat, and threw some soft bags on to the stone landing stage.

Manolis shouted something else unintelligible, this time directed at her.

She closed the book and walked a few steps closer. 'Sorry?'

'How is the apartment? Is OK?'

'Oh . . . yes. Fine, thank you.'

'You are coming to the taverna? Tonight is very good swordfish!' He grinned engagingly.

She couldn't decide. What if her need for kindness had

become too great, if her friends had been right, that it was too soon after the funeral to be making this trip? Perhaps it was better to remain alone, to read and sleep through the pain, until she could accept it with a degree of self-control. The last thing she wanted was to draw attention to herself by a tear slipping down at a friendly smile or a glass of undrinkable retsina on the house.

'Where is it?' she asked eventually.

He frowned then raised his hands to encompass the front of the White House. 'Here, of course!'

'Here?'

'Yes!' shaking his head at her idiocy.

Water slurped at the rocks between them. There was no way forward on foot.

'Take the little path,' he shouted, pointing behind. 'Come round that way!'

How could she not go after that?

At the side of the house was a small paved area, where some washing still hung. A few beach toys lay abandoned in a corner, along with fishing nets and a pile of old wooden planks that seemed to suggest some renovations were under way. At the front, a short flight of stairs led up to a front door on the storey above. As she walked round she could see that to the right of this was a grey marble plaque. In Greek, then English, the engraved words announced: '*In this house lived the famous writer Julian Adie, 1935–39.*' She could not see any lights on inside. She stood for a few minutes trying to let imagination take over, to picture him as a young man bounding up those steps, but no magic happened.

A sign for Prospero's Taverna beckoned her round the far corner and down towards the rocks and sea again.

The restaurant's vine-covered canopy had been reinforced by a covering of stout canvas, and plastic sheeting had been let down all along the sea wall to take the chill off outdoor dining. She knew from the books – Adie's biography, as well as his own account – that this was the old terrace garden. She was actually in the place she had come to see, immediately and effortlessly. Only two tables were occupied. She began to see why Manolis was so keen to lure her in to eat.

A young waiter with a quiff of curly hair and a loud patterned jumper gave her a choice of any table along the sea wall. She took the one furthest away in the corner, ordered a small carafe of white wine, and chose the swordfish.

She ate listening to the waves as the night closed in and a fat moon rose. Now and then, ships passed beyond the bay, decks blazing like illuminated honeycomb. With no lights shining from the dark country opposite to provide a reference point, they might as well have been flying though the black sky.

Apart from the waiter when he served her order, she spoke to no one. It was a relief. She did not want to be drawn into any conversation, to have to pull a curtain over the truth, nor to find herself lying to strangers. It was good to be there without having to provide explanations and justifications. Not to find herself replaying her circumstances, nor why she was here alone.

How would you ever make idle chit-chat of it? *No, my husband will not be joining me, work or no work. And my mother, who loved me and could once have explained everything, has gone for ever. When I needed to go away, this was the one place that crept into my mind, that made any sense.*

Melissa stared out into the infinite-night sea and sky. There were so many questions, and she was oddly grateful for that, for the harness they provided to contain the sadness which was of such intensity she could hardly let herself feel it.

It was better to be on her own. Richard had been kind the past few weeks, but it had been a bad idea to agree to his suggestion of coming with her. She had changed her mind as soon as his name was on the booking form.

All she wanted was some time alone.

As she was leaving, the waiter took up a look-out position at the edge of the restaurant and trained a pair of binoculars on to a point on the beach. Whatever it was he could make out, he was studying it intently.

The next morning dawned yellow and peach. Sky fire was rising behind the hills across the bay. The headlands reached out dark arms to embrace it, a miraculous stillness all around. From the narrow balcony of the Prospero Apartments, Melissa watched the sun come over the lumpy red horizon until a glittering golden path led across the water to her hand on the rail. When at last she looked away and blinked, spangled circles were imprinted on her vision like a slew of gold coins.

Below, the village was a necklace of low buildings along the narrow shore road. To the left was an ugly hotel complex on the hillside. On that side the headland was colonised by large villas. But to the right, the steep slope up was verdant and untouched, the headland a mass of olive and cypress. There, where the green joined the blue, secured together by rock and beach, the White House was still the most prominent building. The village of the past was still embedded there despite the cruel disfigurements of modern development. It could have been much worse — certainly, Melissa had been prepared for far worse.

But in this craggy northern part of the island the road corkscrewed tightly down from the main highway, cutting into the side of Mount Pantokrator. There were three beach tavernas but not much else to lure the coaches of mass tourism.

Maybe in high summer the crowds and the heat and the raucous drunken mating calls of the young would make it less than the paradise it seemed that morning, but just then she was happy and glad to be there, with no past or future thoughts, standing now on the balcony, gazing at the sea as its colours deepened into azure and cobalt. She had never seen such blue.

Only one of the two small supermarkets was open. Even there the stock was being run down, but there was enough on the shelves for her to pick up coffee and milk, honey and yoghurt, bread and cheese, some fruit, water and a couple of bottles of wine. The honey held almonds and pistachio nuts in its sticky amber.

According to the guidebook which she consulted over breakfast, it was possible to walk to the Shrine of St Arsenius. Julian Adie had written about it time and again, his special bathing place: a tiny chapel at the foot of the cliffs beyond the next bay. He and his wife would take the sea route, in their little cutter, but a way existed down through the trees from the cliff path.

Melissa decided to go. She was curious. Having read the

poetry and his lyrical prose descriptions, she wanted to see the places for herself, to see if anything remained that still resonated today. If she wanted to know more about Julian Adie, it was the obvious place to start.

The air was still cool for all the brightness. Perhaps it wasn't going to be warm enough for swimming, but she put a few books, purse, towel and swimsuit in a bag anyway. She wanted to be able to take the chance if it came.

Few other people were out and about. An elderly woman dressed in two cardigans gave her a weary half-smile. A party of German walkers, most of them middle-aged in heavy leather boots, with telescopic steel sticks and rucksacks, were peeling off fleece sweatshirts. A teenage girl, ordered on the expedition by her parents, perhaps, lagged slightly behind, a fistful of wild flowers in her shirt pocket and trailing an air of resentment.

Melissa couldn't help but remember the time when she hated walking; the leg-aching boredom, while Elizabeth strode ahead, tall and narrow, hair bouncing on the resolute set of her shoulders, always seeking the wind and sun on her face.

The door of the boat hire office was open. Inside, Manolis was at his desk handing over some paperwork to a couple in shorts. She had half-expected him to appear at the taverna the previous night, and in a way she was disappointed that he had not. It would have been a good opportunity to ask him who owned the White House now, and whether there was anyone still in the village who remembered Julian Adie first hand.

Across the road the White House was shuttered. No sign of life there, not even at the taverna to the side. A few metres further on, the road disintegrated into a knobbly concrete path, and began to climb into olive groves. The way was pitted by brown spots, the mouldering stones of previous crops. Through silver-green trees was the sea. Under the olives the grass was studded with rocks and luxuriant drifts of tiny pink cyclamen. Despite reading the accounts of the lush beauty of this coastline, and staring again and again at the photographs Elizabeth had unearthed, nothing could have prepared her for the sheer exuberance of the reality. It was so unexpected; she had to let her eyes rest for a while as the words and pictures magically transposed into the reality at her feet.

The path wound down into the next bay, across the headland. Between the olives on this side, as the land tumbled away, were great rolls of black netting, twisted and slumped round the gnarled trees like so many monstrous sea snakes exhausted by writhing from cold depths. It was yet another indication that the year was on the turn, and the winter harvest would soon begin.

The beach down here was composed of grey-white stones, like the one at Kalami. A bank of prickly pear cacti grew robustly behind it, threaded here and there with wild mint which released its perfume when her feet brushed past. On the far side, an expanse of flat rock shelving into the sea looked perfect for sunbathing and swimming. A fig tree grew out of a crack where it joined the cliff wall behind. She made a mental note to return and test out her instincts. Pressing on, she followed another steep stony path up again and across fissured golden and marble-like rocks to a further cove. According to the guidebook, this was Agni.

She struck a path across the stones as instructed by the

guidebook, past several simple wooden jetties where restaurant customers could moor their boats, and then across the forecourt of the far taverna.

Two men were arguing fiercely as she walked up. Their voices rose and they stabbed fingers at each other.

'*Kalimera*,' one said, smiling brightly. Melissa jumped as she realised he was speaking to her.

'*Kalimera*,' she returned the greeting.

Then, as she passed, they gave each other a friendly bang on the back, and drew apart, still shouting. It was extraordinary how a normal Greek conversation always sounded like a ferocious verbal duel.

Leaving the men behind, she went up again into more olives and holm oak, firs and cypresses, the blue of the sea always to her left. Somewhere along here would be the footpath down to the shrine.

Twenty minutes later and breathing fast, she realised she must have gone too far. The path was now high above the sea and too close to the main coast road. The book described a fork off down to the left, a precipitous drop down but negotiable with care. She should have bought a map, of course, and not relied on a few vague paragraphs in a tourist guide.

She started back in the direction she'd come, feeling hot and a little frustrated. Clearly she was close but hadn't quite found it. For the first time since her arrival she wished she wasn't on her own. If she'd had someone with her they might have put their heads together and worked it out.

What looked as though it might be the path turned out to be a false trail. The cliff had no stone edifice at its foot.

Back on the marked way, a couple in their late fifties stopped to let her past.

'Morning,' said the man. Even had he not spoken, there was no doubt that they were British, in their faintly absurd leisure clothes and sandals. He had a boyish face that was running to beefiness, and an impressive thatch of wiry grey hair. His companion was as slight as he was broad and tall.

'Morning,' Melissa nodded. It's always a tricky moment when you run into your compatriots abroad. She was about to trudge on through, head down, when she noticed they did have a map. Swallowing her pride, not about asking for directions but for consorting with her own kind, she said, hearing the words come out stiltedly, 'Excuse me, you don't know whether I'm on the right track for the St Arsenius shrine, do you?'

They looked blank. Clearly it meant nothing to them.

'A shrine?' said the woman. 'We haven't seen a shrine, have we?'

'Is it marked on the map?' he asked.

'I don't have one. I don't suppose I could have a quick look at yours, could I?'

But there was nothing marked. Melissa thanked them and set off even faster than before.

That afternoon, she went back to the flat rock with the wild fig tree at the edge of the second bay. Hardly anyone was there, and it was perfection. Over the sloping stone moss unrolled like a soft carpet into the sea. The water was clear and surprisingly warm. She swam, lay in the sun, and read, and simply looked all around. By the time she returned to the apartment, she was relaxed and more content than she had felt in a long while.

She should have known it wouldn't last.

Every hour seemed to make her eyes open wider, her senses more acute. Each time she walked the tiny main road, effectively barely more than a lane, she noticed more: the powerful scent of jasmine escaping over a wall; bright globes in orange and lemon trees; the violet trumpets of morning glory winding through wire fencing; and everywhere the ancient gnarled olive tree, each composites of several intertwining trunks, some so holed and intricately braided you could see right through them.

From the balcony of her apartment, she watched the sun set. The mountains across the water, in a reverse of the morning's display, burned red and peach, then pink to purple. Isolated wisps of cloud made brushstrokes of black on the evening canvas.

She decided to try dinner at one of the two tavernas on the beach.

The air was warmer than the previous night, and the proprietor of Thomas's Place had planted a line of his green wooden tables outside drawn-back curtains of heavy-duty plastic sheeting. Here too they were squeezing out a last few weeks of business before autumn closed in.

Inside, candles were already lit, and willow baskets served as light fittings hung by their handles from the rush ceiling. The atmosphere was cosy. It was also more crowded than Prospero's Taverna. A young slight waiter with a sparse, possibly experimental moustache, showed her to a corner table. She was hungry, having not eaten since breakfast. The waiter recommended a local dish of prawns and feta cheese, so she ordered that and made a greedy assault on the bread basket.

Mesmerised by the waves playing on the beach, the hushing sounds of water on stone, she was trying to imagine Elizabeth here. When had she come to Corfu – when Melissa was too young to remember, or before she was born? It must have been at the same time as Julian Adie visited. So logically, if she could take a list of the dates he was here from his biography, she might be able to narrow down the possibilities. Always providing the biography was detailed enough, or indeed accurate.

A woman's voice cut through her thoughts. 'Hello again. Did you find what you were looking for?'

Melissa looked up with a start.

It was a moment before she registered who they were. Then she realised it was the couple she'd asked for directions on her walk. She hadn't spoken to anyone else all day, apart from in the supermarket and here.

'Oh . . . no. No, I didn't in the end.'

'Ah, well. Tomorrow's another day.' This was the man.

They had been shown to the empty table next to hers. The taverna was filling up.

Melissa smiled to be polite.

'All on your own?' asked the woman, taking a rather beady inventory of her table settings. It may have been her long thin nose that gave the impression of a busy little bird.

And perfectly happy, Melissa tried to convey with a nod.

'Do join us! We can't have you sitting here, eating on your own, can we?'

'Oh, no . . . really – '

They insisted. There was no way out. If she did not accept, there would be the awkwardness of continuing to sit there next to them, having rudely turned them down. Groaning inwardly, she took the chair he had pulled out at their table.

'David and Sheila Robbins,' he said, the aptness of which made Melissa smile inwardly. They stopped short of shaking hands to seal the formal introductions.

Sheila was a bank manager. 'My business is people, not money!' she trilled.

'I'm a retired police officer,' said David. That made sense; the broadness of the shoulders and the easy, slightly authoritative manner with a stranger.

'What about you – what do you do, Melissa?'

She took a deep gulp of wine. Typical of the British abroad, wanting to place you, get the measure of you, even though they might never set eyes on you again. Exactly why Julian Adie had chosen to live here all those years ago, when it was remote and the only road was impassable in winter: to escape the expatriates and their social investigations.

'I'm an archivist,' she said.

'That sounds interesting,' prompted Sheila, eager for more.

'What kind of archivist?' asked David.

'Well . . . ' Melissa hesitated, wishing this had never started. 'Most recently, government work.' From the rapt expressions on their faces this was the wrong thing to say. 'Nothing exciting, I'm afraid,' she assured them. 'I've been working for the National Archives – reams of boring minutes being transferred out of government offices to make room for more reams of boring minutes, mostly.'

'I'm sure it's fascinating,' said Sheila, giving Melissa the full benefit of her professional people skills. 'Don't you think so, David?'

'Oh, it must be.'

'We're from Bucks,' she volunteered. 'Just outside Chesham.'

They waited expectantly for her to pat the conversational ball back.

'London,' she said eventually.

Was there a flicker of suspicion in her husband's eye, as if he'd caught her hesitation and was wondering what to read into it?

'Are you staying in Kalami?' Melissa rallied with an attempt at brightness.

She stood on the beach, letting the tension go. The bay was black. The curious iron street lamps along the broadwalk cast shifting columns of light, gold and silver, on to the dark water.

She was relieved to be alone again. Sheila and David, friendly and well-meaning though they were, brought it home that for the past few days she had been living in a kind of limbo reality. It was hard to explain, but since she had arrived here she had pushed real life away, perhaps because it was so painful. She didn't want to talk to anyone. There was a haunted quality to the island because every time she looked around, she was searching for signs of the past not the present and she wanted to immerse herself in that past, hoping always that would lead her to some kind of understanding. Or perhaps it was all just a channel to be able to think about her mother as she had once been, not as she was at the end.

Melissa let herself into the apartment, and quickly put on another sweater. It was only nine-thirty, but the night air already had a chilly edge and there did not seem to be any means of heating the rooms. She moved a table lamp to the small dining table, and raised it on a pile of books and information leaflets from various holiday letting companies. Then she fetched her own books from where they were scattered around the sofa. The thick biography of Julian Adie by Stephen Mason was open with a coffee mug resting on the pages, making her slightly shocked at her own slovenliness. It was now frilled with strips of paper marking relevant passages, some with scribbled notes on.

'To Elizabeth, always remembering Corfu, what could have been and what we must both forget.'

The words were constantly in her head like the nagging refrain of a song. And still the same questions. What must be forgotten? The sense of regret in the words was overwhelming. *Why* had she never said anything about Julian Adie before? She had obviously known him, and, the inscription implied, shared an intimate understanding. But Melissa could not find one mention of Elizabeth in the biography, nor in Adie's own autobiographical accounts of his life and travels.

The nineteen sixties, the photographs had probably been taken, Bill had said. The biography certainly placed Adie on Corfu at various times from the mid-thirties right up to the seventies. So it was possible, but no more than that. It was as though their connection really had been forgotten, excised from both lives.

Although, had Elizabeth really never mentioned Julian Adie before? Melissa's initial reaction was to be sure she had not, but had she simply never heard her, switching off from the flow because she thought she knew all the stories of her mother's life? So why then, when Elizabeth was only so intermittently lucid, when she seemed barely to know who Melissa was, let alone anyone else, did she press the book of poems on her so urgently?

Why was this so important? What was Elizabeth's connection with Julian Adie and what was Melissa supposed to do with it if she found it? How did Elizabeth fit into his story? So far it was all impressions and conjecture. She needed to clear it all from her mind, in the only way she knew, before it overwhelmed her.

Melissa opened the new notebook she had brought, and started to write.

II

The sea and the light constantly moving together, inter-weaving and patterning, made Melissa aware of being alive, of blood coursing around the body, sun on her arms as she stood at the open window. It had been a good night; she had only woken twice. There seemed to be a slight easing of the spiritual numbness which had become habitual.

Perhaps putting her thoughts down on paper had helped. That had preserved them but put a stop to their noise in her mind.

She was at the tourist office when it opened at nine.

'Do you have a detailed map of this area?' she asked the man at the desk. He was dark, with well-muscled shoulders and a four-day beard which did nothing to diminish his good looks.

'A map of the island?'

'Just this part. I'd like as many details as possible. The biggest scale you have.'

He came round to the front of the desk, and led her past stands of hanging shell and bead necklaces and displays of snorkelling equipment. The way he moved implied he was well used to being cock of the walk. He pulled a couple of maps off a book rack. 'We have these. The whole island – we don't have a special one for here.'

'Can I see inside?'

He opened both. They were road maps, showing few landmarks smaller than mountains.

'Do you have a walking map?'

He shook his head. 'I'm sorry, no. We've sold them all.'

'And you won't get any more now until next year?' she guessed.

'That's right.'

'Oh, well.'

She hesitated, wondering whether it was worth asking him about Julian Adie. He waited, seemingly amused that she was lingering – or perhaps he was just pleased with himself.

'Yes?'

Something around his mouth reminded her of Richard, and she felt herself blushing.

'I – I think I'll take one of these.' She pulled out a snorkel mask.

'Anything else?'

Don't push it. 'Just this, thank you.'

But as she turned to go, she reminded herself she had nothing to lose. If she couldn't find the path to the shrine, the only option was to follow Adie and Grace, and go by sea.

'Are there any boat trips still running?' she asked. She had a vision in her mind of an organised day long sail and picnic that might go somewhere close.

He shook his head. 'Not now. It is too late.' He gave a lovely smile. 'Sorry.'

'Oh, well. It was worth asking.'

'It's always worth asking.' He paused. 'Possibly there are a few boats coming north from Kerkyra.'

'I'm sorry?'

'Kerkyra – from Corfu Town. You could maybe take a trip from there. They bring bigger boats for tours of the coast. I can find out if you are interested.'

'I could . . . but . . .' The idea didn't appeal. If all else failed, then perhaps she might, but it seemed unlikely she would be able to see anything she wanted from a boat carrying a hundred or so tourists, far less achieve what she really wanted, which was to climb on to the rocks by the shrine as Adie and Grace once did.

He thought for a moment. 'You know the boat hire office near the White House?'

'Yes.'

'Why don't you ask for your own boat?'

'I'd thought of that – but . . . I decided not to.'

'You don't like little boats?'

'Well . . .' She gave what she hoped was a wry smile. 'I'm not an experienced sailor.'

'Nervous?'

'A bit.'

'Go and see. Ask for Manolis. Tell him Christos sent you.'

'All roads lead to Manolis . . . !'

'You know him already?'

'I'm renting one of his apartments.'

'Then ask him – he might give you a special deal.'

Melissa thought about it, but then when she reached the boat hire office, she went on past. She was going to have to work up some confidence for that one. Instead she returned to the wide swimming rock on the curve of the next bay, and tried out the new snorkel. It leaked a bit (it was really nothing more than a cheap toy) but it was certainly usable if you could get used to the invasive trickle of thick salty water.

In the clear shallows, the seal-brown boulders which had broken away from the cliffs were covered in algae like a dusting of mauve chalk. Brightly coloured fish darted over part of an ammonite the size of a car wheel and off into forests of black sea grass in the bowl of the bay.

She swam around, entranced, for almost an hour, amazed that the water was so warm. Then, just as Adie described in the poem titled 'Plunge', dated 1937, she surfaced to birdsong.

Sun-dazed, Melissa made her way back into the village. She had left her watch behind that morning, deliberately wanting to cut loose. But from the tightness and reddening of her skin, she knew she must have sat for hours on the rock, staring at the sea.

A white pick-up van pulled up in front of her, just where the lane became a path too narrow for vehicles. The driver executed a dazzling three-point turn in front of her, then stopped, calling out. Melissa ignored him and carried on walking.

He shouted again before she registered what it was he was saying, and that he knew who she was. 'Mrs Quiller?'

It was only then she looked up properly and saw it was Manolis.

'I hear you want a boat! Why do you not come first to me?'

'Oh!' It was as if she'd been caught out.

'Christos says you were asking about boats!'

'Yes . . . yes I was, at the tourist office . . .'

'Many fine boats at Manolis Boat Hire,' he laughed.

'I'm sure there are,' she said. 'But they probably don't come equipped with someone who knows how to drive it.'

He spread his palms. 'Is easy! Easy boats for tourists . . . I give a lesson to everyone who takes one!'

Melissa was beginning to shake her head, knowing that would make little difference to her confidence or seaworthiness, when she found herself saying, 'All right then. I'll give it a go.'

The hills opposite were rusting in early evening when she took a wobbly step on to the boat, a basic fibreglass craft about ten feet long with a steering wheel and outboard motor. She had never thought of herself as a brave person physically, but she had a stubborn streak that could be called on to override her qualms if she wanted something badly enough. Sometimes that surprised people who saw her only as the quiet, thoughtful one who loved maps and books, and worked as a keeper of secrets, locking away information in order for it to be found again.

Richard saw her as his sweet, sensible little wife, who was happy to fall in with his plans; who had once wanted to move to Dorset to take up the job at the maritime museum and live in a house with a garden, but who made do with growing herbs on a grimy kitchen windowsill instead; who enjoyed a comfortable life that gave her no right to complain when he worked late so many nights.

What would he think if he could see me now?

She lurched into Manolis's boat. It rocked alarmingly.

'You can drive a car?' he asked.

'Yes.' Her legs were trembling.

'Then . . . no problem. First, the ignition.' He pushed a button and the engine gurgled to life. 'This here . . . neutral . . . forward . . . back . . .' He went through the controls. 'Now, we go one hundred metres forward – you are driving.'

And soon, she was.

O ut on the wind-wrinkled sea, Albania was merely the other side of a large lake. Heading south, she held a steady speed, not too fast, as Manolis had advised. Within minutes, confidence rising, she was round the headland and across the bay where she had snorkelled (it was called Yaliscary, Manolis informed her), then puttering past Agni and the cliffs where she had looked in vain for the path going down. If it hadn't been for the mention in the guidebook, it would have been all too easy to believe the shrine was another of Julian Adie's personal myths. Would she be able to see it, even from the sea?

It was there.

A small square grey-rendered building was perched just above the shoreline. Just as he described it, the shrine seemed to sail on the crest of storm-flung waves, tossed up on the very edge of the island, the moment frozen in stone when it was caught between a sweeping bowl of fractured rock and taller stacks which leant away at a mad tipsy angle. Proud straight cypresses stood watch above, while a curious light turquoise pool glowed below. She nudged the boat in as close as she could, worried all the time that it might snag on submerged rocks if she ignored Manolis's warnings.

There was no one else in sight, neither on land nor sea. She was as close as she would ever be to seeing it as Adie and Grace would have done in the nineteen thirties, before the Ionian was churned by pleasure craft full of brightly dressed tourists.

She gazed at the narrow chamber of water that gleamed below the drunken fissures and the shrine. Was that the pool where he described her diving for cherries? It must have been, though the rocks looked too jagged and hard to lie down or even stand on. It was an odd moment, entrancing yet unsettling. There were elements of obsession here. Or should that be possession, by the spirits of the past?

H er trial hour with the boat was up. On the way back she was glowing deep inside. It was hard to explain. She had done it, though it was such a little thing. There was definitely a sense that she had conquered some fear, perhaps that of taking a risk on her own.

But I am on my own. This is it, from now on.

From her shifted perspective, as she guided the boat back into Kalami the bay was a wider expanse, the village sparser and more vulnerable in contrast to the looming rise of the green mountain behind.

Manolis was waiting. She cut the engine as he had shown her when she approached the mooring, let down the anchor, then threw the rope for him to catch. He caught it with one hand and reached out the other to help her on to the landing.

'How was that – good?'

'Fantastic!'

'I said it was easy.'

'Well . . . good boat, good teacher!' She was full of her achievement.

A few waves away were the rocks where Adie and Grace had sat and talked and gazed and swum, where they had laughed and argued on summer nights with literary friends from London and Paris, splashing into silver and eating grapes at midnight.

'Who owns the White House now?' Melissa asked.

He gave his look of slightly absurd surprise. 'We do. We've always owned it.'

'You mean your family rented it to Julian Adie?'

'Of course.'

She was taken aback by the simplicity of the facts.

'I don't suppose . . . does anyone still remember when he lived here?'

'My father was a boy when Julian Adie lived here, but he remembers him well.'

'Did he come back to Kalami, after he had moved away?'

'Yes, many times.'

Melissa's heart jumped.

Was it possible that he had ever brought Elizabeth here too? 'Do you think I might be able to talk to your father about him sometime?'

'You like the books?'

'I do.'

Was any further explanation going to be required? It seemed not.

'I will tell him,' said Manolis.

M anolis, kindness pleating the corners of his eyes as he smiled, was slotting a note under the door to her apartment when Melissa returned with breakfast the next morning.

'Ah! Mrs Quiller! A little invitation for you – '

She smiled warily, suspecting some kind of special tourist deal on a boat, an ever-so-gentle hard sell. 'Thanks.'

'My mother says it is the perfect time for you to come, so you must! She is the wise woman of the village!' He laughed, wagging a finger to suggest that she should take him up on whatever offer was being made. 'She says she can tell you like tea, and not the cocktail drinks in the colours of the rainbow!'

'Right . . .'

He gestured at the door with an open palm, so Melissa put the key in the lock and opened it. On the floor was a folded piece of paper, which read:

We hope you can come to tea at the house called Seraphina on the hill behind the boat office at five o'clock today. Manos and Ekaterina Kiotzas.

'You can ask them about Julian Adie,' said Manolis.

'That's lovely! Thank you so much . . . will you thank them, and say yes, please!' She was burbling, she knew, embarrassed by her ungracious misreading of the situation.

He nodded. 'I'll tell them you are coming.'

It was warm enough, if wrapped up, to lie reading on the egg-shaped stones of Kalami beach. There were few other people on its wide crescent that morning. None of them braved the sea. A stiff wind had brewed up a few grey clouds to which were thrown upward, indignant glances.

At lunchtime Melissa wondered about trying to find the shrine path again after trying one of the three promising-looking tavernas at Agni, but in the end she packed up her bag and wandered in the other direction. The road rose up over the northern headland, and swiftly dipped down again to Kouloura.

It was enchanting: another deserted blue bay, clearly still mainly used for fishing. Brightly coloured wooden boats lay upturned on the shingle and bobbed in the tiny harbour. The only buildings were clustered around the toy port, capped by the Byzantine roundels of a solitary white villa. She sat in sunshine by the wall, feeling relaxed. One day at a time, she'd told herself. If every day could have been like that blue afternoon, just as Julian Adie experienced it when he was on the island, she too would have felt like the king of the world.

The path to the house called Seraphina twisted up through an orchard of oranges and lemons. Here, too, were blankets of pink cyclamen that grew so profusely in the olive groves that she was having to pick her way through carefully to avoid crushing them underfoot. Notes of music threaded down through the trees from a house to one side.

The idyll was rudely interrupted as Melissa drew closer.

'Ay-ooo! Po-po-po! Aaayyyy-oooooo!'

'Po-po-po!'

The terrace of the modest stone house was abandoned for all that there was a sewing box and some mending on the table along with a glass of water. Uncertain what to do, she followed the wails towards an open door into the house, where a bead curtain was partially pulled back. She wondered whether it was not, after all, a good time and she should melt away again. She was about to turn back when a hand pulled the clinking beads back further and Manolis sauntered out.

'Ah! Hello!' he greeted her as the noise intensified. 'Come in!'

As if nothing untoward was happening, he ushered her into a wide white room with a shiny tiled floor. The screams echoed slightly. They came from an older man with a sweating forehead who was waving a large white handkerchief as if in surrender to his fate.

'He's got a clove in his tooth,' explained Manolis. 'This is Eleni, my wife.'

A plump woman with smooth golden skin and a prominent mole above her lip stepped forward. She too was smiling warmly, following the rules of hospitality.

They shook hands. 'Lovely to meet you,' said Melissa, ridiculously, trying to follow their lead and keep a sociable tone against the background roars of pain.

An elderly woman she took to be the older man's wife launched a stream of withering invective.

'Ay-ooooo . . . .'

The older man was clutching his jaw, bobbing until he was bending double, and pulling an agonised face. The wife, a tiny woman with a helmet of short grey hair, crossed her arms and stood by, nodding grimly.

'My father . . . Manos. He's got a toothache but he won't go to the dentist.'

'Nasty,' Melissa agreed.

There was another outburst to which they listened politely. Melissa glanced quizzically at Manolis and Eleni.

'My mother is saying, "You stupid man, brains of a donkey, when we said clove, we meant oil of cloves, not a hard brown clove from the kitchen. To wedge it into the hole – you've probably cracked it further open and done some damage more terrible than the first!"' said Manolis.

The man then counter-attacked in a furious eruption.

Manolis cocked his head, listening. 'Hmm,' he said, and pulled down the sides of his mouth.

Melissa couldn't help herself. 'What now?'

'My father has said my mother is surely the most in-effective wise woman in the whole of the Ionian Islands, one who could not tell the difference between a goat's bottom and a bee sting, and if she can cure headaches by telephone then why cannot she lift her own loyal husband's dreadful suffering . . .'

'Or something like that,' said Eleni, as Manos's cries rose to a blood-curdling pitch. His eyes rolled in his head, then at last he seemed to realise Melissa was in the room. Manos sank suddenly into a chair with a surprising change of tone.

'Ah!' he said, in English. 'Time for tea.'

'Greeks like to shout a lot,' said Manolis. 'It makes us feel better.'

The cup and saucer rattled slightly in Melissa's hand. 'I'll remember that.'

The second surprise, obviously on a more minor scale, was that when Eleni helped her mother-in-law from the kitchen it was with a tray of Indian tea with milk and sugar, and a plate of ginger biscuits. The elder Mrs Kiotzas had taken off her apron to reveal a flower-patterned dress.

'This is what we always have, for visitors,' explained

Manolis. 'My father's father, old Manos, he learned it from the Adies. It's a family tradition now. Like the way we speak English. We passed that on too, in the traditional way.'

'My father taught Julian and his wife to speak Greek, and in return they learned English from them,' said Manos, in confident and unmistakably cultured tones. Were they an echo from Adie's own voice? It was possible.

'They brought us good business, and they gave us the language to build on it with the foreigners,' said Manolis, dunking a biscuit in his tea.

'So . . . you would put it that strongly? Julian Adie really did bring you prosperity?' asked Melissa.

There was a chorus of consent.

'Julian Adie paid for the building of the apartment at the top of the White House,' said Manolis. 'It was his idea. He wanted to live there for ever. But—'

'After Julian wrote his book the tourists began to come,' Manos took over. 'Slowly at first, then more and more of them, looking for his paradise. Always before we had lived by fishing and cultivating our olives, working in the fields. But now the boats from Kerkyra stop in the bay and let the visitors come to the taverna for lunch. They all want to see where he lived. And people still do, although maybe not so many now as before.'

'A book he wrote that none of them could read . . . what a world!' Ekaterina Kiotzas shook her head.

'Except he didn't write the book here, did he?'

'Didn't he?' Manolis frowned.

'He wrote it about five years after he left – I think he was living in Egypt by then. Not that it matters,' Melissa added swiftly.

'He was writing something,' said Manos. 'He liked to look over the sea when he was working. We would hear the noise from his writing machine like the fire from an army of guns!' He drummed his fingers on the edge of the table at maniacal speed.

'My father could not read very well,' Manos went on. 'He had never learned in school, and he did not need to for his life here. It was a tiny place, only a beach and a wide rock and a few other houses – maybe only ten families in the village. But after Julian came, it changed the way he looked at the world. Before it was just the seas and the mountains of Albania he could see. He had never been to Athens.'

'Julian was a big talker,' said Ekaterina. She had fetched her sewing from the table outside, and stabbed a needle into a linen square.

'He would sit in the family room at the White House and talk and talk – in English and Greek – about England and India and . . . Paris and Tibet . . . ' nodded Manos. 'I was a child, but it was wonderful to hear him. Always full of descriptions and ideas and plans. And laughing, too. I remember him always laughing, and wanting to know things. How do we do this? What happens here?'

'He had bright yellow hair and blue, blue eyes,' put in Ekaterina. 'I thought he looked so strange at first, but later I thought he looked like a god. I was—' she broke off, searching for the right word, and spoke rapidly in Greek to Manolis.

'Quiet . . . shy,' he answered.

'I was shy when he was there.'

'You remember him from that time too?' Melissa asked her.

'Oh, yes. Manos and I . . . we were friends as children. My family also lived in the village.'

'Do you remember his wife Grace too?'

'Yes – she was very beautiful and very gentle. Her hair was light too, and she was kind to all the children.'

'She was the one who gave us tea and biscuits from tins that were sent from England,' said Manos. 'Tins with pictures of funny little houses, and roses . . .'

'Do you think they were as happy in real life as they were in the book?'

The elder pair exchanged comments which no one translated.

'Later on, they used to shout at each other,' said Manos, rubbing his cheek and wincing. 'So we thought everything was fine.'

The conversation switched to the question of when Manos would see sense and visit the dentist up the coast in Kassiope.

A fierce exchange in Greek threatened to reopen cathartic hostilities between the old couple, before Manolis stepped in with some soothing words.

Eleni caught Melissa's eye. 'Ekaterina is what we call the wise woman of the village. But this toothache is too big for her,' she shrugged.

'What does it mean, to be a wise woman?'

'She can make the cures. No one likes going to see the doctor.'

'Really? So . . . people come to her instead of the doctor then?' Melissa tried hard to hide her scepticism.

'For small problems, yes. She can cure headaches by speaking a cure.'

'So, they just come to the house when they think she can help?'

'Or she can do it by telephone.'

'How extraordinary.'

'She has the power of vision, too,' Eleni went on.

Melissa frowned. 'You mean second sight – she can see into the future?'

'Mmm, not so much that. She can tell all about a person, what kind of person they are.'

'Psychic, you mean?'

'Yes! I think that is right.'

As if to demonstrate, Ekaterina gave her persuasive powers one final flourish. She was clearly miming an explosion of the lower jaw as a warning to Manos of what horrors lay in store for him if he did not consult a specialist on this one. At any rate there was no more shouting as she went over to the phone and fixed him with a no-nonsense stare as she spoke to someone at the other end, presumably a dentist's receptionist.

Manos raised his hands and slumped in mock despair, beaten, both by tooth and reason.

After another animated discussion, Manolis came over and announced he was driving his father to Kassiope straight away. 'I'm sorry it was not a very good day to talk about Julian Adie after all. Perhaps be better another time?'

S he wanted to sit alone, with the books and her thoughts. It wasn't clear what more she had actually learned about Adie from tea with the exuberant Kiotzas family. There were so many questions she wanted to ask, but they had flown out of her head while so much else was going on. For Melissa, it had been strange being in the middle of a family again, with all the talk and unspoken connections; another indicator of how much time she had spent alone the past few months.

Funny how, no sooner do you wake up to something than it seems to trigger confirmation everywhere. That evening she had a phone call from Richard. Or, strictly speaking, a voice message on her mobile which had been switched off for days.

'Just wanted to see how you are,' he said. *'Give me a ring soon.'*

Even now, at this distance, she could hardly bear to think about Richard; the way nothing was as she had imagined it to be. The way, when he said he'd been with Sarah, she had thought nothing of it. He was always with Sarah; they worked together and had done for a couple of years.

Melissa had met her, had even liked her as a friend, as far as it went, the few times they were introduced at work-related events: a day at Ascot, a client dinner, an evening at Glyndebourne. It wasn't as if Sarah was markedly more lovely to look at than her, or even downright ugly, downright stupid, as you sometimes read men perversely opting for in the other woman.

Naturally they had drinks after work in the City. They *had* to do it, because it was a meeting, you see. It wasn't just bottles of wine in a candlelit cellar, a man and a woman.

The reality of being betrayed is that you begin to question your own judgement, and that leads to the possibility that everything you once believed was a lie.

He was caught out. Caught out, note, rather than sorry

and aware that he was doing something that hurt her deeply. He came out with all the clichés about wanting to put it behind them and start again, but with little about why he did it and certainly with nothing approaching shame about his behaviour or any concept of how it had made her feel.

It seemed, for him, it was all about making things *look* right, rather than really making things right. But going through the motions is not the same and it made her feel angry as well as sad. For Melissa had seen it all before, from a different perspective.

Her parents separated when she was nine. It didn't come as a bolt from the blue. The only surprise was that it had taken so long, given that the atmosphere of restrained argument which could erupt at any moment into hissed recriminations was alleviated only by her father's lengthy absences.

It was only years later – and at least here she did come to know the truth – that she realised that he had other women in London, and that even when he wasn't with one of them, he was out drinking to drown the guilt. Elizabeth was short-tempered and easily provoked into snapping at her. She wasn't angry with Melissa; she was on edge and simmering with suppressed rage at him. But how could Melissa have known that at the time?

Only now, I do know how she felt.

While Elizabeth had slept in the afternoons and Melissa walked in the lush summer valleys around Bell Cottage, she stupidly hardly thought of Richard. She was her mother's only child. She was the only one to look after her. She thought he would understand that.

She went back to the flat in London thinking he would come home after work and they would have dinner together in one of the neighbourhood restaurants. It was a classic, really. Melissa remembered thinking it would be a surprise, but she meant for him, not herself.

That was where she caught them.

She didn't call Richard back.

Instead, she spread the various books around on the sofa and got a pen for notes. Julian Adie was a womaniser, an 'emotional expeditionary' he called himself once. But did he pin his own life out like a butterfly on a board when he wrote? Or did he allow only glimpses of himself for others to interpret in the light of their own experience?

Watching, listening, snooping outside the door of Julian Adie's life, she was seeing light occasionally like the twinkle of a supernova, millennia after the explosion.

She read some more of the poems, and passages she'd marked in the biography. Maybe it was not words but a mathematical flow, a mysterious algebra that had to be solved in order to answer the question. Why do men behave the way they do?

III

Eleni was carrying two large empty baskets when Melissa bumped into her the next morning on the village road.

After a broken night full of unwelcome thoughts, the worst night since she'd arrived, she was intending to swim again while the sun was warm in a windless sky. Heading over to the bay with the rock, hoping the sea would calm her as it had before, she was staring down at the suede of dust and pine needles on the path. Melissa didn't see her before she called a friendly greeting.

Eleni had come out of the turning by the boat office, her broad smooth face alight with purpose. Wrapped around her buxom body was a vast and unflattering form of apron in green canvas, which was badged with a huge array of pockets in differing sizes. Her dark hair was tied back with a purple scarf.

A boy was with her, aged about seven, thin with big grazed knees and dirty hands. In that way that sometimes happens on holiday, Melissa had all but lost track of the days. It struck her that it must be Saturday because he was not at school.

'How is Manos's tooth?' she asked.

'He is fixed, but still he complains,' Eleni laughed. 'But it is normal – he is a man.'

They exchanged smiles.

'I'm going to collect some herbs. Then we will make him some natural cures and make sure he uses them properly this time.'

'Are you in training to be a wise woman too then?' Melissa was teasing her gently, but Eleni took it entirely seriously. 'No. That is a gift. But with some help from Manolis's mother I have become interested in a different kind of helping. You have heard of aromatherapy?'

Melissa nodded.

'It is very old, here in Greece. But now the people who come here have heard of it. This year I have started a little business for the tourists in summer. They like it very much, especially when the sun is very strong and they need some cooling for the skin. It's very natural.'

'You collect wild herbs?'

'Sometimes, of course. But I have a special place where I grow what I want from seeds. And we have some secrets that give us success.'

Melissa was intrigued.

'You want to come and see?'

The day seemed set fair, another October glory. There would be plenty of time for swimming.

'Why not?' she said.

The boy ran ahead impatiently as they crossed the iron bridge over a dried-up stream bed coming down from the mountain.

'He is Nikolaos,' said Eleni proudly, 'The other one is Petros. He is already with Alexandros. I can't keep them away from his place.'

It seemed unlikely that two boys would be that fascinated by the growing of herbs, but Melissa fell into step with her. They bore left by an olive tree so twisted and gnarled it could have been hundreds of years old, and took a dusty track upwards.

'It's the animals,' said Eleni, walking at a pace. 'Alexandros always has so many he is looking after, and Petros loves animals,' Eleni went on. 'Now he's saying that he wants to be a doctor for animals when he is older. That would be many years of study, but a good job, yes?'

'Very good.'

'He says Alexandros will teach him! He doesn't quite realise . . .'

Melissa wondered what awaited them at the top of the path, remembering the day before with the Kiotzas family. An eccentric old shepherd, or perhaps an old-style hippy with views on alternative lifestyles. She wondered whether he had been here long enough to remember Julian and Grace, whether there would be any chance of asking him, with Eleni translating.

They approached the house through olive trees, some with the familiar black nets curled against them, others with small hammocks of brighter colours. The land was terraced, but the top two strips of land had been made into what looked like crowded vegetable gardens. Despite the luxuriant growth, there was a sense of rigid order, and many plants were tagged with small white labels.

The substantial two-storey stone house was divided into

two parts, each differently configured. It looked like a great domino balanced on its side. At a blue-painted door which was open on to a patio, Eleni listened, then put her head inside.

'Alexandros?'

All was quiet.

She put her baskets down by the patio wall where pots of pink and red geraniums were still blooming. 'Come, we will find them.'

Leading the way, Eleni pointed out a great pitted millstone propped against the side of the house. 'This was once used to press the olives on this farm.'

'Is Alexandros a farmer?'

'No, he is a . . . a history man.'

Melissa didn't have a chance to ask what she meant because at that moment Eleni pointed at three figures lying face down in the scrubby grass, three dark heads together. Nikolaos was one of them, another was an older boy she presumed was Petros, and the third was a man with a magnifying glass.

Eleni put a finger to her lips.

The man was handing the instrument to the younger boy when he became aware of visitors. 'Ah!' he said, looking up. Then, in excellent English, 'We may be having a . . . er, breakthrough!' before murmuring something in Greek to the boys who were still rapt in whatever it was they were studying on the ground. 'Nikolaos told me you were coming up.'

He sat back on his knees and then stood up, unwinding a tall spare frame as Eleni made the introductions. Patches of dusty earth clung to his shirt. 'This is Melissa,' said Eleni, 'and here is Alexandros.'

They shook hands formally.

Alexandros held her gaze, steadily but shyly, with dark brown eyes. Deep laughter lines scored his face, but his expression was earnest now, the smile polite rather than wide.

'Melissa – a . . . Greek name,' he said.

'Is it?' For some reason she felt awkward, wrong-footed by imagination which had made him a grey-haired sage.

'Melitta is another form, I think. And it is the name of a herb, too, the lemon balm.'

'Melissa for memory,' added Eleni.

'I thought that was rosemary,' said Melissa.

'That is a stimulant version. Melissa can be used when the body and mind need to be calmed. It is supposed to have, ah, sedative qualities, so can be used as a cure for . . . er, nervous tension, insomnia, that kind of thing,' said Alexandros, hesitantly but warming to his theme. 'It would free the mind in certain circumstances, perhaps . . . um, allowing memories to surface where they had been suppressed . . .'

'Funnily enough, that's—' she began, then stopped herself.

'What?' prompted Alexandros.

Melissa shook her head. 'What are you doing there?' she said instead, nodding over to the boys. 'It looks interesting.'

Alexandros visibly relaxed.

'Ah, well, yes, it is. We are working on trying to find some . . . er, organic solution to the olive fly problem, to detect a smell or a parasite that will keep the flies from laying their eggs. In the same way that it's well known that marigolds will keep slugs away from vegetables due to their very powerful and particular scent, or that certain lice . . . er, recoil at the smell of geranium oil, I have been trying to find a herb or plant essence that will deter this pest, or even attract a fly-eating predator. And thanks to the herbs that Eleni is growing here—'

'For the aromatherapy,' she interjected.

'—we find we have plenty of variety to experiment. As a matter of fact,' he frowned in concentration, 'the . . . ah, citronella component of the lemon balm might well be a valuable addition that we haven't tried as yet . . . This morning we have been painting some leaves with a distillation of pelargonium and bitter orange, and several species of insect have turned away in disgust!'

He laughed, and began to brush the crumbs of earth from his chest, as if he had only just realised he was dirty. His enthusiasm made him suddenly ageless despite the silvery glints in his black-brown hair, a mop long enough to curl with a wildness that implied there was more to him than seriousness under the nervy exterior.

He and Eleni exchanged a few words in Greek.

'I am going to cut my plants now,' she said, producing a pair of secateurs from a skirt pocket. 'Beautiful plants – thanks to the ladybirds and moths Alexandros has lured into them to eat the aphids. And of course, they are never treated with chemicals.'

They followed her round to the gardens at the front.

'You speak incredibly good English,' Melissa said to Alexandros.

'I, ah, spent a few years studying in London.'

'I see.'

'Also, I love to read in English. But mostly, I travel a lot for my job. Quite often my work is done in English too.' She was about to ask him more, but he turned the subject away from himself. 'We are having . . . um . . . real problems here with the olive harvest,' he began, waving his arms to indicate a state of generality.

'Chemical spraying has been . . . er, banned by the European Union – it was always sprayed from planes to control the olive fly. It lays its eggs in the developing olive which is then consumed by the growing grub, thus destroying the fruit. If more than one per cent of olives in a grove are infested, then the olives cannot be used as table olives, and if more than ten per cent are gone, then the crop cannot be made into olive oil.'

'Why did they ban it?'

'The chemical that was used is also a . . . um, mosquito deterrent, which has recently been banned in the USA. Personally, I feel there must be a better solution than that one anyway. We have to find a new one, at least, or the farmers, and the families who have always cultivated these groves, will simply think it is not worth their efforts – it is back-breaking work to tend and harvest a good crop of olives, and to nurture the trees. They simply will not do it any more. As it is there is little enough money in these tiny groves.'

'Would it matter, if they just left the trees?'

'It matters in that they might feel that they would get a better return by selling their groves for building development. That is something hardly anybody in the village wants and neither, I think, do the tourists.'

'I'm sure you're right,' she said.

'There are various scientific studies around the world that I have been following that might have an application here. It is a question of understanding the climate, and the land and vegetation. It's a delicate balance. But there is a method which I am quietly rather hopeful will prove useful here, involving a parasitic wasp . . . the wasp larva will live inside the fly larva and hatch out of the pupa after killing it. I must say that early signs are more than encouraging . . .'

His voice trailed off. 'Sorry, I must be . . . er, boring you with all this.'

'No. Not at all.' She meant it. His intelligent melodious voice was easy to listen to when he found a topic he was comfortable with.

But he suddenly seemed embarrassed. 'It has been nice to meet you,' he said abruptly.

He held out his hand, and they shook again. Then he loped across the patio and into the house without another word.

Feeling as if she had been summarily dismissed, Melissa wandered over to where Eleni was filling her baskets, and sat on the wall to wait. The sea was Indian sapphire between the trees, but incongruously, a warm breeze was wafting winter scents of wood smoke over the hill. In the olive groves on the headland she had already seen farmers pruning, cutting the branches for winter fuel. Now they were burning the dead twigs and leaves. One of the old olive stumps on a lower terrace was alight; red flames flickered inside the lacy trunk like a Halloween lantern.

It was peaceful in this warm garden with autumn coming: the late grapes puckering on the vines, shrubs bolting after the early rains. Eleni went about her business rustling and clipping. It made Melissa think of the garden she would have loved to have made in England. She closed her eyes and pushed that aside.

So she thought about Alexandros instead, and the disconcerting extent to which her imagination had pulled her in the wrong direction, had made her expect a much older man. For all the old-fashioned manners, he was probably in his late thirties, maybe early forties. He wore a wedding ring and Melissa wondered idly what his wife was like, where she was this Saturday morning.

'You like Alexandros!'

Melissa started round, caught off guard.

Eleni had come up silently. 'Yes?'

She had meant it as a question, or so Melissa took it.

'He is very nice – seems a very interesting man,' she replied.

The difference between Alexandros in reality and the image which had immediately sprung into her mind was a timely reminder not to jump to conclusions. It was one thing to make a mistake that could be so easily rectified but quite another when there was no way of proving how much about a person was fact and how much conjecture. She would have to draw on all the professional detachment she possessed if she was to draw a picture of Julian Adie and her mother with any accuracy.

Eleni pulled at bunches of leaves so they were not so tightly packed in the baskets. Then she looked up.

'He is sad too,' she said simply.

It took a while for Melissa to realise she was talking about Alexandros. Unsure how to react to that, she kept quiet.

But Eleni did not elaborate, and perhaps she had not intended any comparative judgement of her in any case. Melissa was just too raw, and over-sensitive.

Instead, Eleni shouted into the trees – an angry-sounding tirade which was most likely nothing more than a parting shot to let her sons know she was leaving and when they should come home for lunch – and they set off back down towards the village road. Melissa took one of the sweet-smelling baskets and listened as Eleni told her which herbs she had picked and what she intended to do with them.

'Come to the beauty shop tomorrow morning,' said Eleni. 'I will show you.'

That afternoon Melissa lost herself in the water at the flat rock where the fig tree grew. She cleared her mind of everything but the present and the sea-silk against her skin. Wavelets unfurled on her shoulders from a mazarine sea and delicate plumes of smoke rose from the headland to make signals across the bay.

IV

For the first morning since she had arrived in Kalami, the weather had closed in. The water in the bay was black, ruffled by a near-horizontal wind into a sheet of crepe. The yellow buoys that normally bobbed calmly by the White House were drowning in long pipeline waves that gathered strength as they neared the shore. Against the rocky headland cliffs the swell splashed in great white plumes. Any lingering heat had gone. Melissa stared out of the balcony door for a long time.

Clouds scowled across the water as she left the apartment. Out in the open she could see a massed invasion of cumulonimbus thunderheads, tumbling ponderously down from Mount Pantokrator. It was mid-morning but the resort had the air of a stormy winter evening.

Eleni's directions took her into the village centre, down by the side of the largest of the two small supermarkets, to a hairdresser's salon under a sign reading *Filoxenia*. A light was on inside but the salon was empty and the door was locked.

She rang the bell.

Eleni was wearing a professional white starched tunic and

trousers, her exuberant hair tamed into a tight bun at the back of her neck.

'You didn't give me an exact time – is now all right?' asked Melissa.

'Of course. Any time is all right.'

Melissa wondered how that could be. Eleni was usually so busy, constantly working whether at home, at her business or in the gardens. She showed Melissa to a side room, explaining how lucky she had been to be able to rent this room after a beauty therapist had left the previous year. It was important for the business to be central and easy to find, and reciprocal recommendations between her and Lia the hairdresser were helping.

'What kind of treatment would you like?' She handed over a laminated list in English. 'Rejuvenating? Relaxing and calming? Detox? Somehow I think not the after-sun soothing today . . . !'

'I think I need all of them!'

Eleni laughed. 'In that case . . . I think for you I will suggest the lavender with a tiny amount of geranium oil and berga-mot . . . with perhaps a touch . . . ' she put her head on one side with a smile to assess her client's reaction, '. . . of melissa to make it very special.'

'Sounds lovely.'

For an hour, Melissa was soothed and pummelled, surrounded by sensuous scents. Eleni left her cocooned in a warm white towel. She drifted for a while.

'Is good?' Eleni asked when she came back.
'Very. That was wonderful.'

'Get up slowly. There is a cup of mint tea for you in the salon.'

When Melissa went through, there were two cups on the tray.

'No other ladies today so we can sit in here,' said Eleni, already perched in the reception area. She looked grimly towards the window and dark skies.

'Not a day for perfect hair,' Melissa agreed.

'Your husband is not coming?'

'No.'

'He always works very hard?'

'Yes.'

They sipped tea.

'Is this your mint too?'

Eleni nodded.

Melissa seized her chance both to change the subject and try to learn some more. She wondered about Alexandros. The history man, Eleni had said. Did that mean that he might be the one person who could help? And how could she contrive to see him again?

'From Alexandros's garden?'

'Yes. He has the gift, he really does. Everything he plants grows good. The herbs, the vegetables! He has the best vegetable garden in the village, thanks to his strange ideas.'

'He's very impressive, but quite shy . . . isn't he?'

She looked at Melissa oddly. 'What makes you say that?'

'Well, I mean . . . obviously I don't know him at all, but . . . the other day, the way he was talking to us one moment, and then he suddenly went into himself and walked away.'

'Did he?'

Melissa hesitated. Had she completely misjudged the

situation, not only here in the salon but what happened with Alexandros too?

Eleni's face was hard to read.

'No, he is not shy,' she said eventually.

Her mind ran through the obvious possibilities. 'Oh. I hope I didn't do or say something to offend him?'

'No . . . not at all.'

'What then?'

Eleni sighed.

'Is there something wrong?' asked Melissa cack-handedly, before she could stop herself. She had already become too used to rifling through the pockets of other people's lives. Perhaps it could become a habit, commonly known as nosiness, or worse.

She thought Eleni was going to tell her, too. She opened her mouth, but then looked away. 'It's not for me to say.'

They sipped in silence for a few moments.

'I've been trying to find the St Arsenius shrine – the path down, I mean. I've managed to see it from one of Manolis's boats.'

'I know.'

Of course she did.

'Does anyone still go inside it?'

'Sometimes. Not very often.'

'Is it locked, or – ?'

'Alexandros goes soon, to take oil for the saint,' she said, making out a bill. 'Now the autumn storms are starting. His father and his grandfather always did it, and now it is his turn.'

Melissa ignored all the questions that raised and asked directly. 'Do you think he might let me go with him?'

A pause. 'I'm not sure. Perhaps not.'

She stood up and went over to the desk and fetched a flimsy white paper from a small ledger. Melissa paid the thirty euros they had agreed. It was a slightly awkward parting. Melissa had the distinct feeling she saw a gleam in Eleni's eye that said she was well aware of what she had wanted all along. In her over-sensitive state, it was enough to send Melissa's spirits plummeting.

Then, as Eleni was opening the door, she said, 'I can ask him. Just . . . don't expect. Do you have a telephone, a mobile?'

Melissa gave her the number.

She spent the rest of the day reading on the sofa in the apartment, her legs under a blanket she found in a wardrobe. The ache of loneliness and hurt whenever she thought about her mother and Richard had not subsided, but she was managing to push it a little further away. It helped to have other people, other lives, none of them perfect, to occupy her thoughts. It really did.

When her mobile shrilled into life a few hours later, she almost jumped out of her skin.

'Hello?'

'Hello, is that Melissa?' A man's voice, but not Richard's. The surge of anxiety cooled to the uneasy blend of relief and a disappointment she wished she did not feel.

'Ye-es.'

'This is Alexandros Catzeflis.'

'Oh . . . yes. Hello!'

'Eleni tells me you have been asking about the St Arsenius shrine.' He sounded brusque.

'Yes . . . that's right.'

'Why are you so interested?'

'I – I thought . . . it seems important if I'm visiting places that Julian Adie wrote about . . . He wrote about it so often.'

Silence.

'This is part of your literary research?'

So he knew about the questions she had already asked.

She crossed her fingers. 'Well, yes . . .'

He was clearly reluctant. Under pressure from Eleni and Manolis too, maybe.

But then, a sigh. 'I suppose, in that case . . . I am going there tomorrow. To take oil for the . . . er, saint,' he said, in the diffident way that was already becoming familiar. 'If you would like to come along, I would be pleased to take you there for your . . . literary researches.'

Was that an unnecessary emphasis, verging on sarcasm? Melissa decided to ignore it.

'I would like that very much. Thank you.'

He hesitatingly ventured the news that the weather would change for the better by the next afternoon. In the light of that they made halting, mutually polite arrangements.

V

The sun did not rise the next morning until a quarter past eight. In strange citrus light, a vast flock of birds wheeled in silhouette around the bay, clustered in *pointillism* into the shape of a fish one moment, stretched into a sword the next. A lone black cloud smudged the sky's fragile freshness.

There was a cheerful scent of honeysuckle in the lane as Melissa went down to the shop to buy breakfast, hoping for fresh rolls.

'*Kalimera!*'

She started. It was Christos, the Adonis of the tourist office. He stopped at the entrance to the shop, making it impossible for her to avoid him.

'How are you liking it here? What did you do last night?'

'I stayed in, reading.'

'Oh, no. That is not right.'

'It's perfectly right. I'm having a lovely time.'

Clearly it was his idea of hell. 'Have dinner with me tonight.'

'Oh, no . . . thank you, but really I – '

He put his head on one side and pressed his palms together

in supplication. Melissa laughed and he winked. 'You are a beautiful woman on your own. I am on my own. It's very sad.'

She shook her head, still laughing.

'Why not?' he persisted.

Now there was a question.

'I know a very, very good restaurant. Nice food. Wonderful views . . . the real Corfu – the old Corfu . . .'

How could she resist? Melissa let the eye meet run on for a while. Then she said, 'All right, then. I'll come.'

He was incorrigible. And also the youngest and most handsome man that she had flirted with for a long time. Sitting reading on the balcony later she couldn't help but smile, not in anticipation but amusement.

Impossible to pretend the thought of Richard and Sarah had nothing to do with it. Could she find it in herself to give Richard another chance? One last chance? Or did the person she loved no longer exist, the good times overwritten by hurt and betrayal?

The sea was bright jade as she passed by the White House, on her way to meet Alexandros at four. His weather predictions had proved accurate, and the sun had returned, bringing several more degrees of warmth.

The water was so clear now that the rock shelf jutting from under the house was visible two or three feet down. It ended abruptly over deep water, and she understood with a single glance how Adie and Grace had lounged at its edge as if it were their own vast natural lido. The bottom of their pool was a swirl of sea grass, black streaks of which now littered the stony beach, along with oranges wrenched from their branches by the storm and flung down where salty tongues of sea water licked inside their split skins.

The roaring of waves in the bay had gone now. Only mermaid whispers teased the shingle.

She left the beach behind and climbed into the first olive grove. The quietness had the effect of making her feel distanced from her surroundings. It lasted until the descent into the neighbouring bay and a waft of homely scent, one that had felt familiar from the very beginning, stole into her senses: the wild mint growing at the base of a vigorous patch of prickly pear.

Yaliscary was deserted, apart from a boatman packing up his summer hideaway. Time after time he walked the makeshift jetty in the far corner, shifting plastic chairs and a table, umbrellas, crates, and finally the white-painted car tyres which acted as bumpers on the side of the wooden walkway. All was piled at the end, and then he began to load his boat.

She went on towards the tavernas at Agni, where Alexandros had specified the middle one of the three. And there he was, waiting in the courtyard, standing rather rigidly by two old trees, their gnarled and whitewashed trunks intertwined like the mythical trees formed from the bodies of Philemon and Baucis after they entertained the gods unawares.

His greeting was polite but serious, old-world courtesy. He had not taken a seat; they were clearly not staying for a cup of coffee or social diversion. He said something to the waiter, whose response and parting shot implied they knew each other well, and walked off straight away leaving her to skitter after his long loping strides.

He let her chatter nervously, inconsequentially, for a few minutes until she managed to match his pace and let the breeze in the trees and the rhythm of their footsteps fill the silence between them.

The serpent path rose again into untended olives and scrub. Alexandros led the way as if this procession held in deep thought was part of the ceremony. Melissa shrank back into herself, not wanting to be an irritation or encumbrance.

Above them hung the winding road to the north of the island. Now and then the sound of a truck or bus rumbling by confirmed its existence, but silence predominated. No cicadas, no birdsong, only soles crunching over the path. She looked for landmarks she might have passed before, wanting to see where she had gone wrong and missed the tiny trail down to the shrine. The sea glistened far below to the left.

Melissa stumbled, experiencing a moment of disorientation, a sense of electric foreignness all around, the purple sound of words not understood, a warning ripple of madness. Here she was, with the history man (she still had no idea what that meant, and had missed all chances to ask), on an island where they kissed the feet bones of St Spyridon in his casket. Dead since the fourteenth century, yet his blackened mummy was still being paraded in the streets and routinely asked for protection and advice. Centuries were no time at all. It put her own tiny quest into context, tiptoe-ing across the dusty footprints laid down by someone else only a matter of decades ago. But did those faint traces still exist?

Then she calmed herself. It was, as Adie had written, '*A day when the flowers trembled and the blue reached down from Heaven*'. This was a place of beauty and hope. A land of heroes and stories.

Alexandros stopped a few feet in front, and turned. 'Not far now. Are you all right?'

His expression was distant.

She nodded.

'It's down here, but steep. Be careful.'

The turning was unmarked. There was no way she would have found it on her own. You simply had to know where it was. Grabbing at bushes and large stones on the way, she half slithered down the precipitous grass and ochre dust.

From this approach the shrine was unprepossessing. Dwarfed by its guards of cypress, rather more of them than shown in the photographs in the biography, it was little more than a hut cut into the foot of the rocky slope.

Alexandros took a small key from his pocket. There was no ornate weathered lock on the door to the shrine, but a modern padlock. It snapped open, and he tugged on the peeling wooden door.

It was dark inside, with only a feeble shaft of light from an ineffectual seaward window high up in the wall. Alexandros placed his rucksack on the floor by the door and switched on a torch. He then drew out a thick glass bottle of olive oil and took it over to the far wall where a narrow altar stood.

Goosebumps prickled Melissa's bare arms. It was not only the sudden gloom and drop in temperature. It was a sense of trespass. The strange thrill of re-enacting a scene from the past that did not belong to her.

'There's a description Julian Adie wrote, of going to the shrine with his landlord, old Manos. Do you know it?' asked Alexandros, so quietly and presciently she shivered even as she strained to hear him against a crash of waves outside. He propped the torch on the altar and began to pour oil into a battered tin lamp. The delicate stream of liquid shone like a line of burnished gold in the half-light, catching a metal cross set in a turned wooden base.

'Actually going into the shrine? No . . . I'm sure I haven't.' She could only recall reading about him being outside it, below it, bathing and diving, its magical lure for him. The pool below was where he had felt himself reborn. 'In *The Gates of Paradise*?'

'It was not in *The Gates of Paradise*. It was published in a magazine, many years later. But the odd thing was that he wrote it as if the years had never intervened, and he was still living at the White House with his wife.'

'Strange.'

'Perhaps, yes. That's what he did, anyway.'

'I'd be fascinated to read it,' she said.

'I can find it for you if you like.'

With the lamps lit they stood quietly taking in the interior. The walls were bare and damp. The dark icon on the altar was in a poor state too. The venerable, bearded face was barely visible in its frame, as if caught staring out of an unlit window.

'St Arsenius, I presume?' asked Melissa.

It was hard to make out any of his features. This was no museum piece, but a homely relic of faith. They lingered a while, each wrapped in private contemplations.

Then Alexandros left the bottle of oil on the floor by the side of the altar, and they left the saint to his lonely flame.

'Why *are* you so interested?' he asked again, knowing she had still not given him a satisfactory answer. The hesitancy in his speech seemed to have gone.

They were standing on the ledge above the pool. From here

the water was pale green, so clear the stony outlines of its curious perfection seemed man-made, a calculated, precision-cut fairy bath.

'That part in the book, where he and Grace lie baking here on the rocks, and she dives for cherries,' Melissa said, deliberately misunderstanding. 'You wonder if you stare hard enough you'll be able to see them by sheer force of imagination and will.'

He gave a little laugh at this romantic absurdity.

A couple of small brown fish broke surface with a tiny ripple.

'Did you ever meet Julian Adie?' she asked.

'Of course I did.'

'So that would have been — when? When he returned to the island in the nineteen-sixties? You must have been very young then.' How much would a very young boy remember anyway? Almost certainly nothing of relevance to an adult's life.

'I was a child when he first came back. But he continued to visit, right into the late seventies. He would take a villa in Paleokastritsa, or here, or once an apartment in Corfu Town.'

'But would he come to Kalami and see his old friends?'

'Always.'

'You seem very certain.'

'I am. He was a friend of my parents.'

Melissa was unsure how to proceed.

'He always took an interest in what I was doing,' continued Alexandros, sparing her the onus of finding a suitable prompt. If anything he sounded defensive, as if she might not believe him. 'When I was old enough to read his books, he was always happy to discuss literature and science with me. He always wanted to talk.'

'What about his other friends on the island – the ones he wrote about in *The Gates of Paradise*: the man who kept his dead mistress's skull on his writing desk, the Count B, the mad expatriates, and the visitors from England and France? Did you ever meet any of them?'

'The old Count B was dead long before I was born, as were quite a few of the colourful characters of the book. Some were composites of several people.'

'What about people who knew him later, in the nineteen sixties – I'm thinking about the expatriates? Are any of them still here?'

He frowned, and asked again, 'Why are you so interested in all this?'

She could not ignore the question a third time. But seconds passed before she replied.

'Funnily enough, I discovered I have a family connection to him as well.'

There was something about Alexandros that made it impossible to lie, or even obfuscate. He made no response beyond giving his full concentration, eyes fixed and receptive.

'My mother knew him here,' she said, stumbling on, not knowing how much to say or how to explain that the obsession had taken root now. 'I only recently found out.'

Alexandros was looking out to sea. A Minoan Lines ferry was cutting across the straits. She felt the light wind and watched as it caught the olives in a silver frenzy, the undersides of leaves dancing and whispering.

'He loved it here, didn't he – Adie?' she said softly to break the silence, sensing it was wiser to stay on neutral ground, at least for the moment. 'He must have done, the way he reproduced it so sensuously.'

Alexandros turned and started back up the elusive rocky path towards Agni. She followed.

'All those heady scents he's surrounded by, the voluptuousness of everything from sirens to figs, "the symphonies of wave on rock, the land where miracles might occur" . . .' she quoted.

'You've fallen for it then,' he said at last.

Was there an edge behind his words? She decided to take them at face value. 'Completely! But there's something more that I can't put my finger on—'

Alexandros slowed. 'An ingenious kind of despair, I think,' he said unexpectedly.

'What do you mean?'

They walked on, faces set to the breeze.

'In winter, the mud pours down these hillsides,' he said. 'It's a . . . er, great oozing brown slide into the sea. It goes into the water like a path of sludge. It's a strange sight – as if it is polluting the blue. But at least it's blue. For weeks on end, before that, the rains will have closed in and everything has been brown. It's hard to believe then that all will be . . . er . . . bright again.'

Was he talking about more than just winter on the island? The hesitancy in his speech was beginning to reappear.

She wanted to let him know he was not the only one who was struggling emotionally, but was also sufficiently self-aware to see the dangers in that. She settled for safer ground.

'He and Grace were young and healthy, living in what seemed like paradise. No wonder it seemed like the summer lasted for ever,' she said.

'I agree,' said Alexandros. 'He was trying to capture a kind of . . . immortality. There *was* a strong possibility that their lives might be cut short. The war didn't break out suddenly, catching everyone by surprise in 1939. Throughout the whole of . . . ah, Europe, they had known it was coming for years. It was only ever a question of when. Living here was not quite the escape people in Britain may have thought. Don't forget how close the Italians are, and their military activities at that time were hardly reassuring.'

Now they had fallen comfortably into step.

'Tell me about your mother,' he said abruptly. 'Why is finding out about Julian Adie so important to you?'

They were almost on the main path. The mountains opposite were lined like an ageing face in the slanting afternoon light. He did not prompt her, simply waited.

'My mother's name is Elizabeth Norden. She was an artist. It seems she met Julian Adie in Corfu. Most probably in the nineteen sixties. That's all I know. That, and the feeling that she wanted me to know something.' It sounded so lame.

'You can't ask her?' His kind tone neutralised the question's sting.

'She died earlier this month.'

He cleared his throat, as if slightly embarrassed. 'I'm very sorry to hear that.'

She swallowed hard.

'The nineteen sixties? There is someone I might be able to ask.'

'That – that would be great. Eleni told me you're a historian. Is that right?'

'Historian of . . . er, sorts. I'm thinking of Theodora. I could introduce you to her.'

He did not elaborate. It was only afterwards that she had the feeling he had chosen an effective way of closing down the conversation while giving every impression of helpfulness.

They parted on the iron bridge over the dry river bed.

'Now I understand why this is needed,' she said in an attempt at lightness, pointing down at the deep dry channel which cut through the hillside.

He looked blank.

'The winter rains and all the mud?'

'Oh, yes . . .' His mind was already elsewhere. He offered to walk her back to the apartment, but she said it wasn't necessary. The truth was, she too needed to be on her own. As he walked away, she felt slightly detached, light-headed, as if the intensity of the expedition and his company had been too much. She passed no one in the lane, which only heightened the sense of unreality.

A long hot bath, a glass of wine, a book and her own thoughts: that's what she needed. It was only when she was turning on the taps for a soak that she remembered Christos. Talking to him that morning already seemed like days ago.

She looked at her watch, still on the table where she had left it. Nearly half past six, and he would be picking her up at seven thirty.

Leaden-limbed, she showered quickly and changed into clean clothes, trying to recapture the amusement she'd felt that morning at the prospect of dinner with an attractive younger man. But there was nothing amusing left in it. She had brought no clothes appropriate for the occasion and the visit to the shrine had filled her head with ghosts. She wished she had never agreed to go.

VI

Christos knocked on the door only ten minutes late. He had donned a smart but slightly crumpled jacket and trousers which he filled with the fluid movements and grace of a practised predator. With the lion confidence of his dark hair, stubble, wide mouth and good teeth, the contrast in body language between him and Alexandros could not have been greater.

On the street, he led her to a shiny black Mercedes, with a cock-eyed number plate hanging off, a badge of honour perhaps, marking some perilous victory on the highway. Rock music filled the car, a fraction too loud.

He took a road into the sky. It was dark now. His headlights were bright around the switchback road winding up to the northernmost parts of the island, scraping round corners where the angles of a house or *kafeneion* jutted sharply into the thoroughfare. If there had been tables still outside, they would have been caught and tossed out of the way by the wings of the car.

Christos turned and grinned at one particularly close call. Melissa thought better of engaging him in any conversation that might detract from his concentration. After about ten minutes, they drew up outside a small restaurant way up in the hills.

'Where are we?' she asked.

'This is near Loutses.'

Inside were simple white walls, one of which was filled with framed black-and-white photographs of old Corfu. A seductive aroma of herbs and baking meats stole from the direction of the kitchen. She bucked herself up with the thought that if nothing else, she was about to eat well.

A corpulent man in his fifties emerged from the kitchen, slapped Christos on the back and showed them to a cosy corner table. She suspected Christos had been bringing different women for dinner here for a long time. There were few other tables occupied, and from those that were, the conversation bubbled and rose volubly in Greek.

'You will drink some *ouzo*?' Christos asked.

'Not for me, if you don't mind.'

'Some wine, then.'

'Yes, please,' she said, making a mental note to go very easy on it.

Their orders placed, he settled back and gave her a long appraising stare. It had been so long since she had been on the receiving end of anything like it, that she dropped her eyes, which made her feel even more ridiculous and gauche.

She had felt awkward ever since she got in the car, sad and self-conscious. She should never have come. It was so long since she had been out with a man she had forgotten how to behave on a date – if that was even what this was.

Determined to get over it, she asked him about his summer, how the season had gone.

Good, he said. It was a very long season on Corfu, with

the first visitors arriving in April and May for the spring flowers. 'But by the end of next week, it will be finished.'

'What will you do for the winter?'

'I will go to Athens. Rest, see friends, work a while for my brother . . .'

'What does he do?'

'He designs computer websites. I do some of that too.'

'That sounds good.'

'It's OK. I prefer being in Corfu – I love the sun and the sea.'

'And all the tourists . . .' she raised an eyebrow.

But he did not react in the way she expected. 'I like meeting people who come here. They are on holiday, happy, they want to have a nice time. It's very good that they like to come to Corfu. Especially the English. They fall in love with the island, and come back and back again.'

'I can certainly see why people would come back to Kalami.'

'Kalami, especially.'

But when she asked, he didn't know much about Adie, nor did he seem very interested.

'Not so many tourists ask about him. I don't think they know him any more,' he shrugged, leaning back as he did so to ask the waiter for more wine.

'Not even to find the White House?'

Christos chewed the corner of his mouth.

'I found the St Arsenius shrine,' she said, reminding him about the first time they'd talked. 'And I managed to take a look inside it this afternoon.'

'So, are you another one looking for information about the woman who drowned?' he asked.

*

'What?'

A shrug. 'There was a drowning at the shrine. That's what most people in the village remember about it now.'

'But that's awful . . . ! I had no idea.'

'More than that. They thought it was a killing—'

'A murder?' Melissa was incredulous.

'Yes, a murder. But nothing could be proved.'

'What happened?' This was a whole new angle, as if the light had suddenly shifted through the prism holding Julian Adie and the past.

'There was a woman who drowned there – or who was made to drown.'

'So . . .' Melissa struggled to reconcile this with the conversation she had had there only a few hours before. She felt a sudden dizziness, as if the wine had hit her behind her eyes. 'So it's a place which has a dark feeling about it, a mystery . . . something unpleasant . . . ?'

'Oh, yes,' said Christos, raising his eyebrows. 'When something terrible has happened in a place, it never leaves.'

Why had Alexandros let her blather on about Julian Adie and the perfection of the pool without even thinking to mention this?

Christos grinned, relishing the tale. 'A woman was last seen on the rocks below the shrine one evening. She never returned home. Her drowned body was found some days later. It was a big event, for a while. Some people even thought it would happen again, that another woman would disappear from there and be found dead in the sea like the first one.'

'When . . . exactly did this happen – can you remember?'

He frowned as he thought hard. 'I don't know exactly. Quite a long time ago. I heard the stories when I was a child.'

'So . . . twenty years ago then?'

He shrugged. 'Longer, I think. Before I was born. I don't remember it. I only remember my mother and father talking about it – it was a village story, people talked about it for a long time afterwards.'

'So they didn't think it was an accident then?'

Christos blew out a sigh. 'I don't know. A little tragedy – or maybe not. There was a feeling of . . . something not right about it.'

'Why?'

'Maybe the woman had been meeting a man she should not have been seeing. Maybe someone wanted to kill her. There was something like that, I think.'

'So in that case, why did some people think it might happen again? How could they suspect she was attacked – and that whoever did it might try to do the same to another woman?'

He shook his head. 'I only know what I remember being said. Stories start in villages; then they grow bigger.'

'I should ask Manolis.'

Christos let out a dry laugh.

'What?' she asked.

'Manolis is the last person who would tell you.'

She had to admit that she was puzzled.

'The Kiotzas family, and their very clever friend—'

She assumed he was referring to Alexandros.

'—they think they are the keepers of the shrine – like the little maids of the gods,' he waved his hands dismissively.

'But was this something to do with their family?'

'Not exactly.'

This was intriguing. 'Then what?'

'A scandal is a shame for the whole family. Never forget that in Greece.'

'I don't know what you are trying to say.'

He offered only another aphorism. 'All Greeks are story-tellers.'

'As in liars?'

'Sometimes. Or they will offer you a story first told by Homer, and make it sound like it happened yesterday, really happened.'

This perplexing exchange was cut short by the arrival of the first course. Christos explained the origins of the dishes, showing off all his skills as a tour guide. Melissa was deflated by the thought that he would have used all the same words on similar evenings through so many summers.

She smiled and nodded, while wondering whether what he had just told her explained Alexandros's insistence on knowing why she was so interested in the shrine.

'So . . . was there ever another suspicious drowning, after the first?'

'No.'

'What was the end of the story?'

But this time he closed that conversation down straight away.

'I don't know,' he said, leaning back and looking over her shoulder to ask the waiter for another carafe of wine.

'Don't worry so much! You are very, very serious . . .'

'I'm not worried,' said Melissa.

Christos pulled a disbelieving face. 'Relax, enjoy yourself! You're not my kind of woman anyway.'

That pulled her up short. He could not have said anything

more calculated to make her feel even more awkward and tense. And how dare he assume she found him irresistible! 'Well, that's a relief. I can assure you you're not mine,' she countered.

'I only like ugly women.'

He sat back in his chair and raised his palms.

'Ugly . . .' Melissa took a few seconds to realise his eyes were crinkling at the corners. 'Interesting . . .'

'Hairy legs. Big spotty noses. Terrible teeth . . . ah! That's something wonderful for me . . .'

'Perhaps there is more to you than meets the eye . . .' She raised her glass.

'You are not right for me, not at all.'

'I'm glad to hear it.'

'Although . . .'

'What?'

'Smile at me?'

She obliged, with a sarcastic expression.

'Actually, I am finding you quite attractive.'

'Great, thanks.'

'You have spinach on your teeth.'

She had to admit it, Christos was good company. The teasing continued, and the jokes kept coming. But he was attentive, too, making sure she was comfortable, had all that she needed. The evening might not have meant anything to either of them – it was the dregs of the season and he didn't have his usual choice of foreign women to play around with – but there was a relief in that, for her. None of it mattered. It didn't matter if he wasn't honest with her. He was nothing to her, so therefore she could relax and enjoy herself. And she was beginning to. In the flicker of the candlelight, across the table from his wicked smile and sharp twinkling eyes, she forgot her concerns. Perhaps she had not lost every scrap of confidence after all.

It was an oddly exhilarating experience. One it might even have been tempting to take further, in other circumstances.

'You know, old Manos won the money to set up the boat hire business,' he was telling her with relish. 'One night at the casino in Corfu Town. The story is he was playing roulette for the first and only time. He backed two numbers twice and they came up both times. "I heard a voice in my ear," he said when he returned to the village the next morning with a leather sack of banknotes. "Whose voice?" everyone asked. You know what he said? "No one I recognised." There was always something strange about it.'

'Why?'

'Because normally, a person would say it had been the voice of a saint.'

'But he didn't ... so?'

'It is unlikely to be true.'

It did not make sense to her, but she was not about to push the point. At heart Christos was a Greek country boy. He certainly liked a good story.

It occurred to her he might be just the person to clear up just one more mystery, though. He would probably relish doing so, if his dismissive tone earlier was anything to go by.

She took a breath, feeling disloyal but rationalising that it would be better to know so that she could avoid any crass remarks in the future. 'You know Alexandros ... ?'

A curt nod.

'What is he so unhappy about?'

He did not ask why she wanted to know. Without hesitation, he said: 'His wife left him. She ran off with someone else. Can't say I blame her – he's a strange man.'

'Strange? In what way?'

'Just . . .' Christos shrugged. 'He's like a crazy professor, all that science stuff he does. Not much fun to be with, is he?'

She sipped her wine and said nothing.

They lingered over coffees and a bright orange kumquat liqueur he persuaded her to try. He gallantly refused her offer to pay half the bill. When they got up to leave, he draped her woollen wrap over her shoulders, and left a hand there casually. She let it be, but made no move closer.

Her slight stiffness probably told him all he needed to know. She wasn't ready for any kind of involvement, not even a passing fling. When they arrived back at the steps of her apartment, he kissed her on both cheeks when she thanked him for the evening.

'Maybe some time?' He gave her another sweet grin and touched a strand of her hair. 'But not now?'

'Maybe some time,' she said.

She went inside alone.

In the middle of the night Melissa woke from a dreamscape of Adie's blue pool made ice cold by the vision of a woman falling through the water, hair drifting like seaweed, white limbs stiff and waxy.

Julian Adie, Behind the Myth
Martin Braxton
[Northern Universities Press: 2008]

Julian Adie would not return to Corfu until 1964. For the first time since his hurried flight from the island with Grace in wartime, he gazed upon the long-remembered, long-idealised inlets and headlands of his own Corcyra. From the deck of the night ferry from Brindisi, re-creating his very first sight of the island, he passed through the straits where its north-eastern point almost nudged the mountainous coast of Albania, smudged purple-brown in the day's first light.

He was holding his breath (he wrote) as the ship cut across the water to breach the last finger of cliff and cypress before Kalami, waiting for his first sight of the White House. '*For the hours leading to it, mind flying ahead to the bay, the house, I had prepared myself for disappointment, for the emblematic dribbles of rust down a grey façade; but there it was on the rocky promontory, pristine and proud. After many years, many adventures and hardships, I had returned. Just for a second, I was Odysseus, and ahead was Ithaca,*' he wrote in *Vacation* magazine (December 1964).

The trouble with this account (apart from its vanity of conferring heroic status upon himself) is arrogance of Adie's usual kind: here was a poignant homecoming purporting to be fact when it was nothing of the sort. At best the piece, which appeared not in a collection of literary memoirs but in an American magazine for those planning European holidays, was a composite of the 'imaginary truths' in which he excelled.

The touching image he presents is of the lonely wanderer returning, full of bitter nostalgia and fear that he will not regain the paradise he has carried so long in his psyche. Will memory prove to be closer to imagination than reality? In a few strokes, he has us with him on his voyage as he strains his eyes across the sea for a lost world, and (a clue to what he is up to) a mythical land.

The reality was this: on the boat from Brindisi he was accompanied by his third wife Simone, her teenage son and daughter Bryan and Jane, his sixteen-year-old daughter Hero, and a new French camper van complete with inflatable boat and outboard motor lashed to the roof rack.

For the next few years, he arrived every summer with Simone and their extended family. In the long holidays, her children would live with them. Adie's younger daughter Hero soon did the same, and Simone and Hero grew fond of one another. His elder daughter, Artemis, was also enthusiastically welcomed for holidays whenever she could join them, despite her mother Grace's coolness to the idea.

Adie enjoyed marriage to Simone. 'She suits me well. It is important to find a woman who gives you freedom,' Adie wrote to his confidant and fellow author Don Webber when the latter was going through one of his own periodic matrimonial upheavals. The two had been close since meeting in Paris before the war, though Webber had long since retreated to his native California. (Webber believed in changing wives according to mood and circumstance, at which times Adie took a position on the sidelines proffering what he considered helpful advice.)

'Simone is a Frenchwoman. She understands my needs in a way the others did not,' he informed Webber. By which he meant that their domestic happiness did not preclude sex with other women when it pleased him. Their rows could be visceral, but were never terminal.

This was the kind of woman Don appreciated too. 'You have your life well-organised,' he replied. 'I am envious and still searching for my Simone. Meanwhile I have met an eighteen-year-old nightclub dancer called Kiyo – Japanese. I'm satisfied for now.'

Julian Adie hadn't changed since, at twenty-five, he had tired of being 'an old married man' as he put it. Three summers in paradise on Corfu with Grace had enchanted and inspired him but after that he was restless, eager to explore new horizons – and that included as many adventures with other women as he could manage.

In August 1938 several of the visitors who arrived in Corfu from London and Paris sensed the tension between him and his wife. Between the sailing expeditions, the lavish beach picnics, the parties in tavernas as well as at the country villas of Corfu's fading aristocracy, the long nights arguing about writing and art and philosophy, cracks were showing in the marriage. There was brittleness to their exchanges.

Some, like Rosemary Barton, one of Grace's old friends from the Slade, put it down simply to the storm clouds that were gathering everywhere across Europe: the threat of war looming that would make their island life unsustainable. Others, like Peter Commin the trusty bookseller and caretaker of Adie's crated library, were more perspicacious. He recognised as soon as he arrived that Adie was straining at the leash. All reported hearing violent arguments between the pair, which left Grace white-faced and tearful, barely speaking to her husband, who merely cranked up the gramophone in response, along with his consumption of red wine and brandy.

He could be cruel, too, even if it was unthinkingly so. One evening he met two young ballerinas at a party in Corfu Town. For the rest of the summer, these girls were regular guests in Kalami, and he would cavort openly with either one or both on the rock below the

White House, uncaring who saw him, especially if it should happen to be Grace.

It was all a journey to Julian Adie. *'I want to swim in the great flow,'* he stated in his essay 'The Discrete Universe', written during that following autumn, and it was the one path from which he never deviated. It was also the beginning of a pattern of behaviour, which, while it may have brought him the joy of experience and the illusion of freedom, also brought great unhappiness in its wake.

Part Three: Ashore

I

Corfu, 1968

I n 1968, Elizabeth was twenty-three.

Arriving in Corfu in mid-June, she described the villa where she stayed at Kouloura as 'the perfect place to get over the awfulness of it all'. It was high on a drowsy hillside above the wide silent smile of the sea. During the day, the sound of the cicadas was a rapid pulse in the olive groves. A path led down to a stony beach where she lay out and closed her eyes. The cold waves of early summer tickled her legs like melting ice.

'I am coming back to life at last,' Elizabeth wrote. 'The past months have wrung me out. The hardest and worst thing I have ever done.'

The villa belonged to Clive and Mary Stilwell, friends of her parents. Clive was her godfather, though the fact was never mentioned between them, as if it were an embarrassment, just as the decision to cancel the life she would have led (and worse) had not been discussed. A tall, thin man, with a stoop but a kindly manner, he had become an author of well-received but poorly selling books since his retirement from teaching history at various eminent public schools. He had a particular interest in the archaeologists Heinrich Schliemann and Sir Arthur Evans, excavators of Troy and Knossos, delighting in their reckless pragmatism – the dramatic streak that saw Evans build red pillars and a throne room above the rubble of the minotaur's lair on Crete – while remaining, himself, ever the meticulous schoolmaster.

The villa, converted from two old cottages and linked with glass, was Mary's achievement, bought through a family trust years before. Her grandparents had been Corfiot, but her mother was born in Athens and was destined to expand the family horizons even further by marrying an American industrialist from Pittsburgh. Mary herself was a round-bodied force of nature, with coarse black hair, a ready wit and a determination that no problem was insoluble.

If there were times that summer when Elizabeth felt she herself might be Mary's latest project, she dismissed the suspicion, preferring to focus on her hostess's ebullient kindness and the island's healing sun.

On the ground floor of the stone and glass house were light marble floors laid with bright rugs from Turkey. On white walls hung wild swirls of paint on canvas from some local with a good deal more enthusiasm than talent. It was cool within the thick walls even when the temperature outside climbed over a hundred degrees Fahrenheit.

From the open doors, the view was of olive groves flickering black and silver down to the dark blue sea. The only other building visible was the pink fortress across the strait that guarded the Albanian coast. Elizabeth would sit for hours in the long low library, reading through midday heat, sketching and writing. What began as a record of her activities and the people she met in the closed island circle, (to avoid the humiliation, she noted, of forgetting names and basic details at a time when she was upset) soon became a repository for her thoughts. It grew by pages every day – sometimes five or six pages, illustrated by drawings, some beautifully detailed, a few tiny watercolours, tickets for boat rides, or a theatre programme.

The Stilwells gave a party a week or so after Elizabeth arrived. It was an evening of sultry stillness. Across the water the fort was half obscured in a dusty peach cloud. The mountains glowed violet. The air was almost too heavy to breathe.

Guests arriving on the wide stone terrace as the sun began to flame were soon equally red-faced. Wet patches appeared on shirts, in rings under arms. Women dabbed at their faces with white handkerchiefs. Stiffly lacquered hair congealed into perspiring hanks.

It was dark, but not noticeably cooler when Julian Adie arrived. In an open-necked white shirt and light-coloured trousers, he burst into the party like a dervish. Shouting to Clive in jangling Greek, kissing Mary extravagantly, he circled around sparking loud conversations, scooping up drinks and draining them before the ripple in the crowd caused by his appearance had completed its detonation into heartier laughter and louder gossip.

He alone seemed unaffected by the humid heat, standing relaxed and squat. At several paces away, his square brown face and sun-dipped hair, as well as his small boyish stature, gave the impression of an improbably youthful figure. Then a group closed around him and the noise level rose again on guffaws, gurgling laughter and snorts of mirth.

Mary was beaming, a sheen of perspiration on her forehead and chin. 'I didn't think he would come,' she confided as Elizabeth brought out a tray of food.

'Why not?'

'He's been in a bad state. His wife died.'

'Oh.'

'We haven't seen him at all this summer – knew he was here, of course, but didn't like to impose, you know. Just thought we might as well put an invitation in the post, he could always ignore it . . .'

'Well, that's good, then, that he's come. Do you know him well?'

'We've seen quite a bit of him here in the summer the last couple of years. Clive and he have mutual friends. He's good company, Julian. And Simone – his French wife – she was fun too. It's very sad.'

A roar of barracking from the huddle around Adie made them both turn.

'Seems to be coping,' Elizabeth said wryly.

'He's unpredictable.'

M ary did not offer to introduce her to Adie, but whether this was out of practicality or protectiveness was not clear. She introduced her instead to a middle-aged couple,

Bob and Netta Cooper, who advertised their recent travels to Goa by wearing almost matching silk kaftans.

Most of the guests were in their fifties or sixties. A smattering of younger guests made their base close to the drinks table, quickly becoming loud. When Elizabeth went over to them, they turned out to be the children and, in a few cases, the grandchildren of the semi-retired academics, writers and amateur painters who were the backbone of the party. They left early, pumped up with free alcohol, to drive down to the bars and discotheques of Ipsos and Corfu Town. Elizabeth declined an invitation to join them. She had no desire to dance, or try to hold a conversation by screaming over loud music. '*I was feeling older than my years, tired, with a stone in my heart. They must have thought I was very dull, and so I must have been,*' she confided to her diary.

Directly below the house, a mulberry tree spread over a lower terrace. Clive called it his 'Tree of Idleness' and had put a low wooden table and some comfortable sun chairs under it.

Elizabeth was sitting there alone, lost in her own thoughts after the younger guests had left, when she heard footsteps cross the brittle grass. A bottle of wine was thrust on the table, and two glasses. She looked up to find a man standing straight in front of her.

In the light of the hurricane lamps behind, his white shirt glowed yellow, cracked by deep shadows. She could barely make out his face.

'May I?' he asked, already pouring black wine.

He held out his hand. 'I'm Julian.'

His palm was firm, warm and dry, Elizabeth noted.

She introduced herself nervously.

He took a seat, and raised his glass before draining it in one. '*Yammas!*' he said to the empty glass.

She felt awkward. Why had Julian Adie chosen her to talk to? Should she start to discuss his work? Was that expected, or unacceptable in the circumstances? She had genuinely admired the books set in Cairo and there was a copy of *The Gates of Paradise* on the bookshelves in the cool low library room which she had picked up and dipped into. Should she offer some praise or would that seem too desperate? What about his wife – should she offer her condolences, or make no mention to remind him of his sorrows?

'I-I like your books – very much. Especially *The Cairo Triptych*. I thought it was . . . mesmerising.'

'It's very kind of you to say so.'

He poured himself more wine and added a few more drops to her glass, which was still full.

'What brings you to Corfu, Elizabeth?'

'I needed a holiday.'

'Why?' He sprang right to the heart of it. 'What had exhausted you at home?'

'I, er – '

'Tell me about yourself.' His voice was exceptionally cultured, but well modulated like a smooth musical instrument.

She still could barely see his features but his presence was strong, and she sensed sympathy. Warmth emanated from him. It was an immediate and compelling sense of intimacy which caught her by surprise.

So Elizabeth told him she had graduated from the Byam

Shaw a year previously, had gone there to study after completing her university degree in French, a condition imposed by conventionally conservative parents. With all the optimism of youth and the glory of Albemarle Street where she had recently recorded the triumphant sale of four pictures, Elizabeth announced herself as an artist.

He asked her to describe her pictures and he listened intently.

Against the dull throb of music from the house above, they discussed art and photography. 'The world is not a coherent story: it is a sequence of events, and glimpses of events, and colours and impressions,' he told her. 'It is light hitting objects and what that represents.'

Hardly knowing what she was doing, she told him about Goethe's colour wheel, and he made her expand on all that she knew.

'The idea was "to marvel at colour's occurrences and meanings . . . to uncover colour's secrets",' she said. 'He was a scientist as well as a poet and novelist.'

'Go on.'

'Do you mean that?'

'I hate party chit-chat.'

She wondered if she could believe him. He said nothing more.

'Well, all right then . . . Goethe arranged the three primary colours, red, yellow and blue in a triangle, each colour taking a vertice. Between them, are the colours that are made when they are mixed, so that – for example – between blue at the apex of the triangle and yellow at the right foot of the triangle, is green. Opposite green on the other side of the triangle is purple: the mix of blue at the top and red at the left foot. The triangular spaces between these then form tertiary colours, further mixtures.

He was interested in trying to interpret human reaction to colour, and its effect on mood and understanding. He linked each colour with different emotions.'

'For instance?'

'OK. Yellow was splendid and noble, making a warm and comfortable effect. It was the polar opposite to blue, which stood for shadow, darkness, coldness, distance, but also emotional understanding and a quiet reflective mood.'

'Red? Danger, I suppose?'

'Not really. More . . . festive . . . and of the imagination.'

'Tell me something more.'

'Goethe called it the sensual-moral effect of colour on the sense of the eye. Different combinations could indicate complex emotions such as melancholia and lucidity, seriousness and serenity . . . He said that the emotional aspect of colour should be considered and taken into account by artists, insisting that it was all part of consciousness.'

Adie stared at her, silent for once. She had no idea what he was thinking. Most likely that she had bored him.

'Tell you what,' he said at last. 'I'm going off to lay my hands on another bottle of this rather splendid wine, but to send me on my way, tell me how long you are staying here.'

'As long as I can.'

'No one waiting for you back home?'

'No. Absolutely not, in fact. I'm afraid I behaved rather badly.'

'How wonderful! Don't move an inch.'

'It wasn't wonderful, it was—'

Adie turned and moved away. He was just a shadow on the rim of light from above.

'—awful . . .' she said to his wake. Then she began to laugh. She was drunk after all, she realised far too late. The novelistic cliché was suddenly funny. She thought he might enjoy it. 'I'm a runaway bride!' she shouted into the darkness after him.

Adie may or may not have run into more wine, but he did not return.

The next day, as she dozed by the swimming pool in the Stilwells' garden, spent by critical self-examination as much as by the long late night (how *could* she have rambled on about colour wheels – what on earth had she been thinking?), a shadow fell over her. Clive was standing, hand outstretched with an envelope.

'Just found this on the hall floor,' he said.

It was a handwritten note from Julian Adie. '*I enjoyed our conversation last night,*' he wrote. '*Come to dinner tonight.*' He named a restaurant in Corfu Town on Capodistria Street, and the time, nine o'clock. The invitation was not extended to the Stilwells.

'Should I go?' she asked Mary.

Mary was chopping vegetables in the cool of the cavernous kitchen. She sliced an aubergine with a deft stroke, exposing spongy, faintly green flesh.

'It's up to you. Do you want to?' she returned the question, smoothly wiping her hands on her apron as she kept her eyes on Elizabeth.

'Well . . .' Of course she did. As soon as she had read the message she had felt a shiver of excitement. But she had to keep that to herself. 'What do you think? You know him.'

'It's not for me to say.'

No, Mary would never say. Whatever was happening in Elizabeth's life was her own business; unless Elizabeth made it clear she wanted to discuss the reasons she had called off the wedding, her current thoughts, her fears for the future, Mary would never pronounce judgement. That was why, Elizabeth realised in a rush of grateful affection, she had felt as comfortable as she did coming to them in the first place.

'If you want to go, do so.'

No mention of him being twice her age.

'I'm assuming . . .' Elizabeth was looking for confirmation of what she hoped would be the case. 'If he hasn't written the invitation to all of us – that it will be just me?'

Mary gave a short laugh, disconcertingly as ever omitting the normal progression of exchanges on any vital subject. She picked up the knife and pierced the mysterious black sheen of another aubergine. A curl at the corner of one side of her mouth might just have been mischievous.

'Julian Adie has a terrible reputation with women,' she said.

II

Shiny-faced and nervous, Elizabeth sat as still as she could in the car. The road wound down and down towards Corfu Town. By her side, Clive drove with his fastidious schoolmaster's style: caution in all matters, especially on foreign soil; a mixture of deference to native custom and the historian's knowledge that events might spiral out of control at any time.

She was sure that he had not had a longstanding arrangement to meet a friend at the Liston, that his insistence that he was going into town anyway was a kindly excuse for making sure she was safe. The travel issue, and her safe passage back, he could control; Julian Adie he patently could not.

Elizabeth was torn between wanting to know more about their famous friend and not wishing to seem overly interested. Most of the journey, they spent in companionable silence.

They drew up at the edge of the Esplanade, where Clive parked, punctiliously observing the marked bays which Greek drivers took only as vague suggestions. She was conscious that she was more jittery than she had expected to be, that she was fiddling mindlessly with her hair.

They strolled across the darkening park, and he walked her to the restaurant.

'You don't have to.'

'I have plenty of time,' he said firmly. 'I shall be at the Hellenic Club from ten o'clock onwards. It's very easy to find, at the end of the Capodistria, opposite the palace. You can ask anyone. I'll be there waiting for you.'

The restaurant was smoky and crowded. Groups of Greek men overpowered most of the tables, so many of them clinging so desperately to the sides of each one that the effect was of a shipwreck with too few lifeboats. Roars of laughter and the clatter of plates cannoned off the walls. It was definitely not what she had been expecting.

Feeling conspicuous in her lacy white mini dress, Elizabeth stopped at the door. She almost turned and went out again, thinking she had come to the wrong place.

Then she saw him, at a long table the length of the wall. There must have been twenty people around it, the party mostly men but including a few women. Behind, a dingy mirror, speckled with brown age spots, reflected his blond head, bobbing as he talked and drank at equal speed and jabbed a finger to emphasise a point. To one side of him was a stocky man with a beard who made him rock back with mirth, to the other an equally cheerful woman with short brown hair and a frisky grin.

Elizabeth was both relieved and disappointed.

'You came!' Adie stood up as soon as he noticed her. There

was no denying he seemed rather unsteady on his feet. 'Come and meet everyone – everyone, this is Elizabeth.' He made a rapid-fire round of introductions, none of which hit home.

A chair was found and she was squeezed in between a Greek biologist and a bald American who said he wrote plays.

Plates of food were piled on the table: bowls of glistening olives, bread, aubergines, fried peppers, and tiny fish. And carafe upon carafe of thin red wine.

The talk swelled over and around her.

'Snivelling malingerers. Never known a day's hard work . . .'

'. . . so to avoid the press he arrives at his own wedding ceremony in the back of a butcher's van . . .'

'. . . A toast to the gods of rashness and misadventure . . . May they keep us and inspire us . . .!'

'. . . it's a form of courage, you see, refusing to give in, no matter what the critics say . . .'

She tried to catch Adie's eye, but he was never looking her way.

The Greek biologist on her right had a sweet manner and a wild mane of dry brown hair. The playwright to her left was prickly. He did not venture his name. Conversation with both was easy in that a few quiet questions set each off on his pet topic.

'. . . when the little bastard gave me a second bad review all it made me think was, what would really ruin his day . . .? Well, it's the prospect of me writing more, and making a lot more than he does, living in his crummy Brooklyn penthouse not an original thought between his ears, the little shite . . .

'Have you met Veronica?' the playwright broke off to demand, nodding at someone over her shoulder.

Elizabeth turned.

An attractive but pursed-lipped woman was now standing behind her chair. A hard, assessing gaze was embedded in her bony face. She held out a hand which slithered briefly past Elizabeth's. In her very early middle age, she had smooth, expensively maintained skin, but with deep lines cutting from nose to mouth and between the shaped, lined brows where she frowned. She was dressed in a neat pink suit, and a girlish scarf tied as a headband over stiff controlled brown curls,

'Are you one of his *daughter's friends*?' The emphasis was unmistakeably rude and she was addressing Elizabeth.

'Sorry, I don't know what you mean.'

'I thought as much.'

Veronica signalled to a waiter to squeeze a chair into the confined space between Elizabeth and the playwright, and wiggled in. A drink was brought for her. It looked like whisky.

Veronica drank deeply, and flicked a glance up the table where Adie was deep in conversation with the woman to his side, managing to make it seem as if she were the only person worth talking to in the room. Elizabeth wondered whether she might not be the only one feeling she had been brought here under false pretences.

Not that it should matter to me, thought Elizabeth. I don't even know the man. But all the same it was disconcerting, realising she was disappointed. Her attempts at conversation with the American woman kept stuttering and failing, mainly because the latter's efforts to keep tabs on Adie were becoming less and less discreet. At one point her glance became a loaded stare. She speared a piece of pepper delicately, allowed it to dangle in a greasy yellow ribbon from her fork, contemplated it with disdain and slight puzzlement, then put it down again untouched. Then she laughed in the back of her throat.

'Word of advice, never believe a word men say. That's the best way.' A crack in her voice hinted at an over-emotional state of mind. But there was an abrasiveness about her that precluded any empathy. 'I learned that from my second husband.'

Elizabeth said nothing.

'Divorced now,' she continued bitterly. 'That's the best way too.'

It was impossible to ignore the woman's compulsion to observe Julian Adie. To Elizabeth it was unseemly, obscene almost, to be that obvious.

'Are you and Julian . . . together?' she asked boldly.

Veronica crinkled her nose. 'Does it look like we are?'

'I . . . well, no . . . ' Elizabeth was stumped again.

Noise levels rose. Always among the top notes was Adie's staccato laugh. His stories inflated into theatrical performances. At one point he got up on his chair to demonstrate the agonising plight of an opera singer with piles and a top C to hit. She was just part of the audience.

He was really something, thought Elizabeth. It was fascinating to see him in action. He dominated the table, even when he was listening rather than speaking. His effervescence was tangible, like a fizzy drink. There was such abandon in his amusement. She had never been this close to anyone like him. The evening was hardly what she'd expected, but that was all right. She was glad she had met him and had the conversation with him at Clive and Mary's party − it would be a story to tell one day.

'You heard what happened to his wife?' Veronica interrupted her thoughts. The harshness in her voice made Elizabeth wonder if it hurt her throat to speak like that.

'Only that she died.'

'He once said she was the only one who could keep up with him. She was such a tiny woman, but she would match him drink for drink. They drank when they were happy and when they were sad. They'd drink brandy together at breakfast and not stop at one.'

The woman leaned in and Elizabeth could smell the fumes on her breath.

'Simone would keep pace with him. Smoking, drinking, fighting, shouting. He threw a plate, she'd throw one back. He thought that was wonderful. Anyone who met them wondered how she could do it. And it seems she couldn't. She got sick at Christmas. They thought she had pleurisy. But by the New Year she was dead. A tumour in one lung and another in the liver. Completely inoperable.'

Veronica nodded as if Elizabeth was doubting her.

'Poor woman,' she murmured.

Poor Julian, too. It was hard to reconcile the show he was giving with the shock of losing his wife like that. But who was to say that there were inappropriate ways of dealing with devastation? Elizabeth was uncomfortable discussing either of them at his table. She tried to change the subject but Veronica was oblivious.

'She was tough, though – make no mistake. She left her husband for him. She persuaded him to move to France and went out to work as a secretary so that he could write all day. She wanted him and nothing was going to stop her.'

Veronica's attitude was a strange cocktail of admiration

and anger. She was drinking rapidly. She could have been trying to emulate Simone. Her words slurred into a hiss: 'He must have been worth it.'

H ours later, Julian was still going strong. He had barely glanced in her direction. Elizabeth slipped out. She could not get round the table to where Adie was sitting with his back to the mirrored wall, and she could not catch his eye, so she raised her hand to say thanks and goodnight. No one noticed.

Just as he said he would be, Clive was waiting for her at the Hellenic Club.

'Thank you,' she said, meaning for all his many kindnesses, not just that night.

He put down the glass of brandy she knew he would have nursed for hours.

'How was it?'

'Interesting. I'm glad I went.'

Perhaps it was the defiance with which the words came out that ensured Clive asked no more. She sat back in the passenger seat of the car. The scene in the restaurant played in her head all through the dark cinema of the drive back to Kouloura.

III

'You ignored me!'

Elizabeth gasped at the injustice. 'What?'

Fat droplets of water rolled out of her hair and down her arms. Still out of breath after her swim off the rocky beach, and the climb up the path, she stopped abruptly and took in the group sitting under the idleness tree: Clive and Mary, a man she did not recognise, and Julian Adie, who had more accusations to fling.

'Never even said goodnight!'

From the soft shade, they all stared at her, exposed in her bikini in the fierce afternoon sun.

'I'm sorry, I—'

But he was grinning at her.

'Here's a wrap for you, dear,' said Mary pointedly, tossing a gauzy garment from the back of a chair. 'Cup of tea?'

Elizabeth accepted both.

She turned to Adie, uncertain what she was expected to say, but he got in first.

'Actually, I've come to apologise to you.'

'Oh?' She was conscious that everyone else was listening. 'There's no need . . .'

'On the contrary. Last night — I simply had no idea until it was too late that my brother and assorted company would take upon themselves to follow me to my favourite restaurant and take over the entire event, completely unbidden, and scooping up undesirables on the way . . . It was appalling, quite appalling. And then I looked up and you had gone — and quite rightly too.'

'Well, I—'

'You will give me another chance, won't you?'

'Another chance?'

Elizabeth did not know what to say. She was not aware that a previous chance had existed.

'You are awfully pretty, and very intelligent too. You might take pity on me.'

He seemed oblivious to the fact that they were not alone. 'Besides, I have a very strong feeling that we could be soul-mates.' His astonishingly blue eyes twinkled, but there was indelible sadness under the charm. 'And I always act on my instincts.'

Elizabeth just caught sight of Mary raising her eyes to heaven.

Early the next morning, she went out with him in a borrowed sailing boat. At the helm of the sloop, he was a different man. Gone was the cocksure repartee, and in its place a seriousness she could relate to.

Out on the wide blue strait, he followed the coast round to the north of the island, past Kassiope, skimming past scrubby headlands and shallow deserted bays of clear green, towards the great brown-bear mountains of Albania lumbering ahead to the east. The wind in her hair, she sat in the prow, exhilarated by the movement and the spray. Her nervousness at being in his company lasted no longer than getting used to the movement of the boat.

At noon they anchored at a wide sandy beach and walked inland to a lake surrounded by white flowers.

Julian stood still for some time, hands on hips, surveying the roll of the hills and the patterns etched by the sun and breeze on the water. 'It hasn't changed,' he said at last.

'Is this somewhere you used to know well?' she asked.

'Several lifetimes ago,' he said.

For once he was still. The extraordinary stinging blue of his eyes rarely fell away from hers when he talked.

'But the trouble with coming back to somewhere like this,' he went on, 'is that it's always the same.'

'Isn't that good?'

'It makes you realise how much you've changed. Where is that other person who used to exist? Drugged on lily scent – embalmed, perhaps . . .'

He unpacked wine and food. They sat and drank. It was odd, she thought, she didn't feel a moment of nervousness in his company. The indefinable warmth she had felt in his presence that night at the party was stronger than ever. He asked all kinds of questions in the direct way he had, and she found herself telling him easily about David, the son of family friends in the village where her parents lived in Suffolk. A handsome boy – she still thought of him as a boy – who was kind and in love with her. How he had waited for her to finish her studies. And how she knew, little by little, that when she graduated from the Byam Shaw, she would not be able to marry him after all, as both families had determined.

How she liked David, but liking was not enough. There was something missing, she confided (faintly astonished to be giving the thoughts form in words that she was speaking aloud), some vital spark that had never quite ignited for her. Of course she regretted the hurt she had caused, the embarrassment to their parents in the village, the wasted expense and the non-returnable deposits, the booked church and London hotel for the reception, but surely it was better, less hurtful, to stop it all before rather than six weeks after the ceremony.

'We should have been coming back from our honeymoon about now. . . .'

Julian laughed. 'I've always taken the opposite view. Never shirked a wedding – but then paid the price!'

They sat in silence.

'There was a baby. I had an abortion,' said Elizabeth.

The sand was hot under their bare legs. Warm breaths of wind played in the air between them.

'I know how it feels, to lose a child,' he murmured.

She had to lean in closer to hear.

His powerful shoulder muscles clenched as he turned to face the sea. The handsome tanned features crinkled in the searing brightness. 'First my Greek daughter, then my Egyptian child.'

'Tell me,' said Elizabeth.

S o he did.
He told her how he had arrived in Egypt heartsick and battered, watching the coastline emerge through a cold white

dawn from the deck of an Australian transport ship that limped into the Western Harbour at Alexandria. Harried through the darkness by the Luftwaffe, the crossing from Crete had been a violent plunge south for survival.

Other less fortunate vessels lay ripped open inside the arms of the docks. The stench of spilled oil, its viscous blackness slicking the still water, permeated every pore.

As the sun rose hot and oppressive, he was directed to an army truck bound for a transit camp. The green flats and reeds of Lake Mareotis were the last landmarks before the desert road struck out into flat nothingness.

'I had lost a wife, a daughter, and my island.'

'Lost?' It was an involuntary interruption of the urgent fluency of his story, but she had been puzzling since the first time he said it. Did he mean they had died?

'She left me, taking the baby. She went back to the bleak homeland.'

Still staring out at the horizon he paused, then exhaled. His voice was so soft, the rhythm so lulling, the words seemed to float on the warm air.

'But then I met Loula and I knew there was no going back for me.'

Elizabeth held her breath, willing him to go on, to confide more. He poured more wine then settled back. A light breeze caught the opening of his white cotton shirt and he visibly relaxed.

'I was at the Gezira Sporting Club in Cairo. A press gathering. She stood a little apart from the crowd, so proud and silent. Loula Habib, they told me when I asked who she was.

'I was hooked straight away. This was no English rose; this was another species of woman, with soft cinnamon breath, skin of golden silk and claws that cut deep. She was wearing a dress of tight scarlet silk, with a darn under the arm.

'The second time I saw her it was at a party where a woman fainted. Loula brought her round so calmly and capably, yet her hands trembled afterwards. I was drawn to her like a magnet.'

Loula was twenty-two years old, estranged from her middle-class parents in Alexandria, and working as a nurse. Her father, a banker, was part Syrian, part French and Spanish, with a strong dash of Jewish blood; her mother was French Alexandrian with Lebanese.

'She had such a strong beautiful face – lotus-petal cheeks, dark burning eyes. Neither of us had any money. The scratching of beetles wore away at the nights in her bed-sitting room. But the way she held her head proudly away from the stench of the drains and squeals from the abattoir a street away . . .

'Then I was seconded to Alexandria to work at the British Information Office and Loula went with me. We took rooms in a Jewish philanthropist's mansion in the Moharrem Bey area.

'At the top of the house, there was a tower rising two storeys from the roof, high above the garden full of banyan trees and ginger lilies and snakes, and a view of Lake Mareotis to one side and the pockmarked shaft of Pompey's Pillar to the other. At last it was peaceful enough to start writing again.

'I picked away at a borrowed typewriter, my mind else-where.'

'Elsewhere?' asked Elizabeth.

'That was where I wrote *The Gates of Paradise*.'

*

Julian lay back, propped up on his elbows. He said nothing. Elizabeth gazed around at the soft green hills and across the lake towards the sea beyond, let the heat unknot the tightness she had been carrying for months.

She felt no awkwardness as the minutes went by, just the warmth.

After a while he resumed his story.

'At the end of the war, I got what I wanted – a return to Greek soil. I was posted to the island of Rhodes to work as an Information Officer for the occupying forces and I took Loula with me. As soon as I finally got my divorce papers from Grace and we could square it with her family, Loula and I got married there.'

'You were happy again?' asked Elizabeth.

'Blissfully. The happiest two years of my life.'

'What happened?'

'Loula fell pregnant – and we were so delighted. The time had come to leave Rhodes, the hand-over to Greece after the war was complete, so we travelled back to England for her to have the baby. All went well, or so I thought. The most ravishing little dark creature was born. We called her Hero. The baby was perfect. But sadly . . . all was not so well for Loula. She tipped down and down.'

'What do you mean?'

'She went mad.'

He said it so matter-of-factly. Elizabeth was searching for the right words to convey her horror, when he went on, this time more kindly, 'There was nothing anyone could do for her – she went down into a spiral of madness.'

'A depression after the birth?'

'I suppose so. It was appalling, shocking. She would rave

and threaten to harm herself. Psychiatrists were called in and retired without helping. No one knew what to do.'

In the circumstances, he took what he considered the best option. He installed Loula with friends near his family home at Bournemouth, while he went to Cyprus to take up a new part-time post and set up home as they had planned. The domestic situation would be taken care of, and all prepared for her. But he was to await Loula's arrival for more than a year.

On Cyprus he found an old Turkish cottage at Bellapaix, a few miles inland from Kyrenia on the northern coast, and for a few sunny months, despite his worries, it seemed he had finally achieved what he wanted so desperately: to free himself to write while living relatively cheaply abroad. He had an idea for a serious and ambitious novel — perhaps a series of novels — set in Cairo and Alexandria.

But again he was thwarted. In order to keep himself and send back enough money for Loula and the child — as well as contributions to his elder daughter Artemis's upbringing, even though Grace had married again back in Britain — he supplemented his part-time government post with a teaching job in a Greek-Cypriot school which ate up his writing hours.

When Loula was at her worst, he looked after Hero alone on Cyprus, with the help of a local nanny. But it was a strain, and he was barely able to fulfil his work commitments, far less do any productive writing.

Loula emerged eventually from her private hell, but she was not the same person.

'She claimed she no longer loved me. We tried, but we never succeeded in living together again. In time, as she recovered, she asked that Hero be allowed to return to her, and I had to agree it was the best way.'

It was a wrench he had to bear with a mixture of sadness and relief. He had not coped well by himself with a young child. The routine of working, writing and looking after his daughter had been punishing.

Elizabeth wanted to reach out to him, past the merry extrovert persona, past the impulsive exhibitionism, to the part of him that was strung tight.

W as it loss, in various forms, that drew Julian and Elizabeth together?

Photographs of her that summer show a pretty blonde woman, hair long and straight in the fashion of the time, wearing short skirts, but with a shy, wary look. Slim and smiling she may have been, but in repose the face was vulnerable and the smile a little forced.

Why did Julian Adie attach himself to her? It was a question Elizabeth asked herself many times. It might have been that he sensed in her hurt a mirror of his own. She recorded his character at that time as tender and vulnerable. The age difference between them was not mentioned, except for once, obliquely. '*We seem to be in a timeless zone. It could be any year; we are simply the essence of ourselves,*' she wrote. It was clear from her overblown tone she had been spending time – perhaps too much time – with Julian Adie.

He may have come close to the truth when he told her, one day up in the hills, 'You remind me a little of Grace.' She took that to be a reference to her painting, and did not pursue the comparison.

She was drawn to him, in a way she had never experienced before.

The purity of the attraction was exciting, but also unnerving. It was there. The indefinable charge that she knew she had been missing with David. Something was going to happen between them.

Elizabeth knew she was out of her depth with him. But wary though she was, she would not have struck back for safety. She wanted this experience, *his* experience, a chance to swim in uncharted territory.

For several days after their confessional, he collected her at eleven each morning in the boat from the little harbour at Kouloura. The days drifted into the same pattern. She would walk down through the olive grove from the Stilwells' house, brown lizards skittering from the dusty path, crickets jumping at her footfall through the brittle grass. One particular turn brought her out of the trees, still high, and presented a panorama of the sea, and the white sails waiting for her below. Great cypresses made long dark curtains between the lane and the sparkling blue as she dropped down, picking up pace. Closer still, the knotted, crumpled stones which tumbled into the sea were amethyst curds under the clear water, as if the land was anchored by fields of submarine crystal. His hand, raised in greeting from the deck.

On the third morning he sailed the boat past Kalami to a place in the sea cliffs where the brutal cracked mesomorphic rocks arched and shattered above a pool of green in the blue water. On the jaw of the rocks sat a tiny stone hut.

'The shrine of St Arsenius,' he announced.

He edged the boat in as far as he could, dropped anchor, and took his shirt off. Then he dived in wearing his sailing shorts. He waited for her in the water as he urged her to do the same. Elizabeth plunged in and swam for the shore, unable to keep up with him. He pulled her up onto the flattest rock.

Elizabeth's heart was beating hard after the swim, yet Adie was unaffected by his exertions.

'This is the thing,' he said, standing gleaming against the sun. 'Here is a piece of rock fallen from a cliff into a sea of extraordinary blue. But to me, it's magical. Look carefully and it's a whole world.'

She sat still, her feet reaching cool water, doing as he asked, feeling the sea's briny kisses on her toes.

He flopped down beside her. Lying back, hands behind his neck, nose pointed up at the sun and eyes closed, he began to talk, voice slowed so it was almost hypnotic.

'Manos, my old landlord before the war, led me here.

'He is always busy. We can hear him shouting on the rocks below, as we lie in our stark white rooms, the light playing in waves on the ceiling. The colours of the sea are inside too, in my wife's vast unframed canvasses. On the table where I write, my diving mask lies next to a copy of Ovid's *Amores*, a flask of Greek brandy and a salt-encrusted, sun-crinkled notebook.

'Manos is a fisherman and olive farmer; our good friend and guide. One afternoon, as the nets lay drying, he called up. We took the small rowing boat towards the bay at Agni, past the flat plate of yellow rock where the fig tree grows in a crack, and a soft carpet of moss leads our feet past submerged boulders and inky starbursts of sea urchin. We pulled past that green headland too, and found ourselves here.

'This was the place they had found the icon washed up, a small dark gilded oil of St Arsenius. He had clearly survived an arduous voyage, apart from some damage to his luxuriant beard, so the fishermen felt it was right and fitting to look after him, in return for favours as yet unspecified. So they built a resting place for him, and once every year the priest was ferried here to hold a short service.

'Manos nudged the prow right into the rock pool, and then lightly as a dancer, for all his sixty years, he leapt out of the boat and helped us scramble ashore.

'We climbed to the door of the shrine. Once inside, he knew exactly where to feel in the darkness for a candle. In a pumpkin glow, we could make out the altar on which the saint was propped against the far wall, a quizzical and somewhat scratched expression on his venerable face.

'A phial of thick golden olive oil was opened and poured into a lamp on the altar. He crossed himself in the Greek way, to us the wrong way round, and we tied the door closed behind us with weathered rope.

'The next day my wife and I came back alone. We bathed naked in the rock pool, then lay eating figs and grapes in the boat. It rocked like a cradle on a blue and gold swell.'

For a long time the only sounds were the smack of water on stone, the call of birds and the tick of cicadas from the hillside.

Then he reached out to touch her for the first time.

His warm mouth tasted of musky French cigarettes.

They made love in the grove above the rocks, on grass soft as hair. He was tender with her, always. She confided to her diary that his skin smelt of honey and tasted of salt.

Elizabeth was entranced by his mind, his body and the setting. 'It was like being locked into a spiritual experience. I could feel the nearness of immortality, the life force of thousands of years, and I was part of it, all senses heightened.

It was like nothing I had ever known before, a great doorway opening to another world.'

A fterwards they dived from the rocks, and he led her to the breech, the secret opening into the cave he called his temple.

'I used to worship in there. A rough statue of Pan I made of clay to sit on the stone shelf. It must have dissolved years ago.'

Play of sunlight flashed jade green into the peacock blue of the water. She had never seen such shifting blues. She wanted to remember every second, every fragment of it, this intense moment. Every sense was sharp and singing. And she was conscious that she was in it, living it now.

He made her adventurous.

Catching her waist underwater, he wrapped her with his arms as if he did not want to let her go.

'Thank you,' he said.

'For what?'

'You've made me young again.'

L ate that afternoon, heading back across Kalami bay he changed direction as if on a whim. Behind the little village, hardly more than a string of houses above the beach, green hills rose steeply in the shape of a bowl. They approached the shore at the near end of the bay where a square white house was set almost in the arm of the headland.

'My old home,' he said. 'I'm going to introduce you to Manos.'

'Manos who first took you to the shrine?'

'The son of Manos my old landlord.'

A young boy ran out on to the jetty in front of the house. The boat shuddered as it slid into place. The boy caught the rope and tied the boat up.

'This is his son, Manolis.'

Julian spoke to him in Greek. Manolis shook their hands with a grin on his wide, engaging face and Julian reached into his pocket for a large coin. The boy whooped with delight as he handed it over.

Elizabeth hung back as a small, sinewy man waved from the wall and then came down.

'Here's Manos.'

He welcomed Julian with a brotherly hug, shook her hand solemnly, and led them to the waterside terrace which was shaded by an acacia tree.

Julian and Manos jabbered in frantic Greek. Now and then he turned to her and translated what had made them laugh.

'Thanks to my phenomenal success,' he said, rolling his eyes to defuse the boast, 'there has been a resurgence of interest in earlier work – *The Gates of Paradise* in particular. Apparently there are tourist boats with megaphones ploughing into the bay here and solemnly broadcasting that this is the very spot where all my books have been written.

'Manos suggests that I take up residence once more in my old apartment in order to greet the crowds, Pope-like from the balcony each day at noon. Then we can all make plenty of money by staying just where we are, drinking ouzo all summer!'

Manos chuckled and shook his head. 'Not ouzo,' he said in English. 'Champagne!' Then, as if the thought made action, he got up and beetled inside. He emerged with a bottle of Greek wine which fizzed when he pulled out the cork.

They watched as he poured the golden effervescence carefully into three glasses.

Julian passed one to her. 'No, wait!' he said. He looked around the terrace with some urgency, then seized on a red flower growing in a terracotta pot. He snapped off a long succulent bud and brought it to her. 'Hold out your glass!' he said.

She did, and he dropped the bud into the wine. Magically it unfurled into a scarlet trumpet with bright yellow anther.

'Hibiscus,' said Julian. He looked deep into her eyes. 'Look how deep red the heart is.'

A pink trail of pigment floated through the bubbles until the wine was stained pink.

'Can I still drink it?'

'Of course! Manos, tell her!'

Manos nodded and clapped his hands. Elizabeth laughed, and tasted the wine over the petals, metallic and herby.

Sunburn still hot on her arms and legs, her mind still adjusting to the newness of what had passed between them, Elizabeth sat sipping in a happy daze. Everything had changed between them. It was as if this introduction to his old life marked the beginning of a new depth in their relationship, or understanding, or whatever it was between them.

When they left, he held her close in the boat, as he edged it away from its mooring. The sun was a crimson beacon on the mountains above. Elizabeth stretched out her legs and leaned back on his shoulder. For the first time in a long while she felt at peace, happy just to be in the present.

IV

For all his grief at the loss of Simone, Julian liked to be surrounded by people. In the evenings following their afternoons in the grove, or at the olive press on the hillside, there were invitations to parties, boat trips, restaurants, and almost every night he would pitch up at one gathering or another. Often, Elizabeth went with him. His friends and acquaintances were eclectic: from the Corfiots he had known as a young man, to expatriate British and Americans, cultured and successful, poets from Athens, Yugoslavia and Paris.

One evening, she recognised the intense American woman from the restaurant among the throng at the Liston Bar. Julian made no effort to speak to her. But Elizabeth saw the expression on her thin, taut face and the same hungry stares she had given him before.

'Who is that?' she asked him.

'Who's who?'

'The woman over there in the yellow. I can't remember her name. She was there that first evening in the restaurant when we ignored each other.'

She was clear still in Elizabeth's mind: the girlish scarf

around her head like an alice band at odds with her tightly controlled face. The barely repressed bitterness released by drink.

'That's Veronica Rae,' he said.

'Veronica . . . that's right. Who is she?'

'What of her? There's nothing to say.'

'She's staring. She stares at you all the time.'

'I haven't noticed.'

'You obviously know each other,' said Elizabeth. 'Why doesn't she come across and speak?'

'I really have no idea.'

But that could not have been true. Surely he wasn't oblivious to the intensity of Veronica's reaction to him.

Adie, for once, kept quiet.

'*I was so bound into becoming whole again myself, and absorbing every second with J that I did not look beyond that,*' wrote Elizabeth on 15 July. '*I allowed myself to sink into this enclosed, exhilarating world of the senses that we had created.*'

It was a perfect fantasia, made more so by the implicit knowledge that it was a temporary retreat for both of them. It could not last. She was too young for him, too inexperienced. The ghost of Simone was always with them. Elizabeth knew that. In barely mentioning his loss Julian ensured she knew how deeply he was wounded. '*This affair is healing balm, for him as much as me.*' It was all about living for the moment, finding happiness where they had least expected.

But less than a week later, she was confessing: '*I am under his spell, completely. This is the real thing, for me. Could it be for him too? Whatever happens, I want to remember this enchantment all my life. I don't care if it means more to me than it does to him.'*

Was that the wistful observation of a diary writer trying to persuade herself, in the teeth of what she knew to be true? She must have known even then that Julian Adie would always be out of reach.

Looking for Julian

Melissa Norden

If I could not see Julian Adie himself, I would search out what he saw: that was my reasoning. I might come to know him better by putting myself in his place, not by looking into his eyes but by somehow seeing out from behind them. And by using other senses: by tasting his words, rolling them around my mouth, writing them by hand on paper, matching them to my surroundings; by feeling the blue water on my skin and the ridged rocks under my bare feet; by taking in deep breaths of wild sage and pine, jasmine and the sharp orange-mustard smell of the marigolds that hung over the lane up to the White House.

In my raw state, I was sensitive to every tiny observation. Sapped by the events of the previous months, I had hardly dared look too closely at my own situation. I can see now that going to Corfu was my own escape from reality, from sadness and shock. It was my way of trying to make sense of what had happened: my mother's death and Richard's betrayal. Giving myself this task, striving numbly for objectivity, was my way of coping.

A part of me had come to the fore, the quiet anxious part that only feels truly safe with files of information and books. In that state, I relate better to people and events reduced to print on paper or screen than with living personalities and present complications. People are less dangerous at one remove. I can rationalise it now; at the time I was dealing with life's blows the best way I could. I was even beginning to feel stronger. As if I was in control.

So I stared at the houses on the hillsides and wondered whether they had been there seventy years ago for Julian Adie to see. I walked through the olive groves and across the headlands looking for clues. This was where Julian Adie set his course: to learn how to look and to feel the spirit of place and to write; to remake himself as the person he wanted to be. In this too, he was becoming my guide.

Adie wrote of the elemental magic of the rocks and sea, but it was always beauty with a dark undercurrent. Even when the island was his paradise found, the threat of war and destruction shadowed even the brightest blue.

His account of his life with Grace at the White House has the quality of a recovered dream. '*On the island we live in the historic present,*' he wrote. Grace stands on the rocks watching as a small boat edges away across fields of sea shimmer, measuring the seconds of its progress in ribbons of glittering light. She dives again and again, for cherries which she drops into the pool by the shrine. Then they sleep in the shade of an ilex, velvety sage for a pillow. They live in a place of charms and spells, and the sea is the enchantress.

There was plenty he missed out, like the physical discomforts of living in Kalami at that time. There were few modern amenities. The house would have been lit by oil lamps. Drinking water came from the spring on the hillside, routinely carried down in earthenware pots by the women. Manos's innovative plumbing was a comic thread which ran through *The Gates of Paradise*. His fisherman-landlord enjoyed inventing his own mechanical systems (including a rare flushing lavatory), ingenious but sabotaged by their own idiosyncratic flaws. This was the man who made an outboard motor for his boat out of an old well pump; it progressed at a stately pace apparently towing its own fountain.

In winter, heat came from piles of branches which smoked in the cavernous stone rooms. Local medicines were medieval, dependent on herbal remedies dispensed by the wise women of the village and hot water which could take twenty minutes to boil on a wood-burning stove. The Adies were soon sending to England for more supplies of aspirin, quinine and antiseptic lotion, which they would dispense as required to their new neighbours. The long dark nights were spent learning demotic

Greek from the village school teacher and the fisherman and his family, learning to pronounce the harsh throaty 'g' sound while the waves crashed furiously in counterpoint on the rocks outside.

But in the Greek landscape, in the great blue eye of the light and the seas, he found a world of possibility, of myth and magic, and of freedom. He ruled a sensuous empire of his own making.

As Adie himself admitted in *The Gates of Paradise*, when you describe something several years after the event, it is already overlaid with nostalgia, sentiment. It has been transformed by time already, and represents another, remade past. Any interpretation I could make of Julian Adie was bound to be based on my own needs and preconceptions.

Now I was peering in, trying to understand, trying to place my mother in the picture too – but I had no clue how she featured. The Corfu that Julian Adie recreated in his book belonged to another era, decades before she could have met him. His words were useful only in that they painted a background picture of him and the place. They cast no light on what came later.

Part Four: Sea Music

I

'You must come!'

Melissa had only been back in the apartment for twenty minutes, still dusty and hot from walking, when there was a battering on the door. Eleni stood there, flushed as if she had run down the hill.

'Where?'

'Come up to the house!'

Her excitement was infectious. Melissa followed her without question, breaking into a run to keep up as Eleni bustled ahead up the lane, past the office and round to the back of the house, then across the vegetable garden to the stone outhouse, lower than a barn but longer and more substantial than a shed. Inside the dust motes played in a sequence of sun shafts through crude windows. Along the far wall stood items of heavy old-fashioned furniture, armoires and dressers. Wooden crates, cardboard boxes, plastic chairs, engine parts around a disembowelled motor, an upright piano, its wood warped and cracking, crockery, jugs, picture frames gave it the choked appearance of a junk shop.

Eleni went to one of the sagging cupboards.

'It was here! I had a feeling I knew where it was, and then this afternoon I thought I would just have a look, and—'

A black leather box, age spotted and partially rotted, stood on a scrubbed table. Next to it was a dented and tarnished brass horn. It was a gramophone, in several pieces. Beside it, standing proudly to attention, was Manos.

'It was his!' said Eleni.

Melissa stared, not understanding.

'His! Julian Adie's!'

The gramophone didn't look as if it had been assembled let alone played for half a century or more. Manos bent over the contraption, clicking his tongue and blowing away dust. 'The needle is still there,' he said, his head sideways, almost on the record table.

Melissa wasn't hopeful. 'Surely it won't play after all these years. . . .'

Eleni dived back into the cavern of the cupboard, until only her legs were visible. She emerged triumphant after a minute or so of inaudible commentary from within. 'Now we will see!' she cried, holding up an ancient disc in a torn and brittle brown-paper sleeve. From the grin on her face, she was having fun anyway, pleased she had been right all along, even if this was as good as it got.

Manos wound the handle, and astonishingly the table turned. He set the horn, and it clicked into place. Eleni clapped her hands in anticipation, wanting to help, offering a heavy black disc.

Gently Manos lowered the crude tall needle on to the outside groove. There was a sudden crackling and the sound of notes.

But in the briefest moment when Eleni and Melissa exchanged excited glances, Manos abruptly flipped the needle up again.

'Hey!'

'What?'

Manos shook his head. 'Not now. Come on.'

He picked up the gramophone effortlessly, belying his advancing years, and carried it like a baby back through the garden, round the side of the house, and down the hill. Eleni and Melissa followed wordlessly in procession.

Outside the boat hire office they halted. Manos said something in Greek to Eleni, and she smiled in sudden realisation before ducking into the office. She came out with a key, and crossed the road to the White House. Up the steps under the marble plaque which announced Adie's long ago residence, she unlocked the front door and motioned Melissa to go in first.

Inside, she was at the head of a long spacious room which ended in the sea and the famous balcony over the sea. Manos set the gramophone on a low table, taking a chuckling pleasure in making this a drama.

There was so much to take in all at once, it was giddying. Light speckled floor tiles set in diamond formation echoed the winking sequins outside. Sea craft of all sorts rippled past. The plain white walls held pictures of Adie (but none of Grace) and the house in the 1930s, a publisher's portrait from the 1980s, photographs of the White House taken from the sea showing its eminent yet nestling position on the rocks.

British newspaper articles were also framed, on closer inspection written as glowing references to the beauty of Kalami and the special interest deriving from the Adie connection. How much of the layout was the same then as now? It was a substantial apartment, bedrooms leading off both sides of the long sitting room, just as Adie had described it. Were the walls, the wooden ceiling, the bookshelves the same as he would have seen every day?

Melissa was overwhelmed by so many questions the words dried on her lips.

Eleni slid open the glass and went outside, beckoning her to follow.

When they were standing silently on the balcony, over the wide expanse of sea as if on the prow of some great steady steamer, a crackling and hissing released the first grainy notes from the gramophone. A familiar rise and fall of soft muffled piano notes began: slow, entrancing ripples of music Melissa recognised as 'Clair de Lune', long-ago touch of hands on a keyboard, preserved under the blanket of scratches, through the kicks and swooshes of the turntable pulling round in regular rhythm, like waves or a baby's heartbeat heard on ultrasound.

The same notes Julian and Grace would have heard, in the same place.

The music died and there were only catches and clicks which slowly wound down.

They stayed still. Ahead and all around the sea was constantly moving, forming patterns of light and dark. The spray thrown up against the far rocks was a wisp of silk.

Melissa turned round.

Eleni and Manos were beaming.

'Thank you . . . that was just wonderful.'

'His table where he wrote his books is here too,' said Manos proudly.

'Really?'

Eleni pointed to a large dining table covered with a colourful plastic cloth, from which sturdy white-painted pine legs protruded. As a desk it would have been enormous, a truly serious expanse on which to write.

'I wonder where he placed it to work,' said Melissa.' By a window, maybe.'

She looked to Manos but he only shrugged. 'Go on, have a look around,' he said to her.

So she drifted from room to room, as Manos, as generous with his thoughtfulness as with his time, cranked up the gramophone again and let the sounds from the frozen, forgotten recordings float on the air once more.

Church pew-like seats crouched against the wall. Ceiling fans in the bedrooms stood waiting for summer when the heat could stifle sleep. All was spotlessly clean.

Another record went on, a jumping ticking version of a great classical symphony. With a jolt of recognition, Melissa remembered a passage in *The Gates of Paradise* describing an obsessive few months when Adie could only work with Beethoven's Fourth blaring through the rooms, played over and over until its symmetries and sequences had burned themselves into every cell of his body.

The possibility that this was one of his records was like being let in on an ancient secret, at the heart of which was Adie's complex hedonism and the clues to what came next. The music combined with the sound of wavelets stroking the rocks below, and filled her senses with a sense of wonder, and profound uneasiness at the extent of all the questions yet to be answered.

A lexandros appeared in the doorway. 'The boys told me you were all down here. Looks like you have a full schedule for your research on Julian Adie,' he said.

'It's amazing,' said Melissa, ignoring his curt tone. 'Thank you so much,' she added, to all of the others.

'I have to go back now,' said Eleni, looking at her watch. 'Will you have dinner with us?'

She accepted with pleasure. So did Alexandros.

It was a relaxed evening. Melissa felt easy with the family's undemanding hospitality. By ten she could feel her eyelids dropping. When she stood to thank them and say goodnight, Alexandros said, 'I'll walk you back.'

He ushered her out of the door with a slightly stiff formality. Melissa wondered what it was he really wanted. His offer to accompany her had been firm, with no option of refusal.

They reached the road. Across it, the dining terrace of the White House taverna was almost empty. Intriguingly, the waiter was posed with binoculars in the same spot where she had seen him that first evening.

She pointed him out. 'What's he doing?'

'Checking out the competition. The taverna on the beach always does better business when the nights get colder. It's not so exposed, and much cosier with the heaters on.'

'Nothing more sinister than that?'

'No.'

'I thought maybe—'

'Just that.'

Further down the main road, a couple of bars were brightly lit, fronted by blackboards announcing dubious-sounding cocktails. Both were quiet, no music, no loud voices. It seemed unlikely that Alexandros had been worried about letting her walk back alone though a rowdy night scene.

Perhaps he wanted to ask her something. At the steps to the apartment he turned to her. He was close enough for her to see the flecks of silver in the curls on his head, catching the cold neon of a night light on the neighbouring building. She wondered what it was he was about to say.

When he did open, there was an edge to his voice again. 'Why are you so interested? What is this really all about?'

'What?' Melissa had not been expecting that.

'Julian Adie. The White House. Why do you want to know all this?'

'I – I told you.'

Alexandros waved a hand dismissively.

'What do you mean by that?' She was incredulous at his reaction. 'You are the one who hasn't been honest with me!'

It was his turn to baulk.

'Why didn't you tell me about the drowning? The woman who drowned at the shrine? That's the story most people around here know – and you didn't even mention it!'

Alexandros looked rattled. 'Who told you that?'

'Does it matter?'

'Have you been down to the shrine again?'

'So what if I have? Why did you tell me all about the shrine, but nothing about the woman who drowned?'

'Because we don't talk about it. Because in any case, she did not drown at the shrine. That's just a story that's taken hold. It was further up the coast.'

But Melissa was riled. She couldn't help pushing it. 'Why don't you talk about it?'

He scrutinised her for a few seconds, long enough for her to feel uncomfortable. 'Why are you doing this? Julian Adie, Kalami, telling me about your mother? What is it *for*?'

She was about to defend herself with some reasoned plausibilities, but none came. How could she have told him the real reason?

So I can focus on something that can't hurt me. So I don't have to think about what's really happening, in my own life, in the present.

In the absence of being able to say the words, she felt the silence like lead. She had no idea why they were arguing. It was just a silly story, nothing to do with why she was here.

When she did speak, her throat felt sore. 'I'm sorry if I've annoyed you. I don't mean to,' she said.

'No . . .'

'I was very grateful for your time yesterday, at the shrine.'

Silence.

'I want to find out about my mother and Julian Adie. Because I don't *know*. It might be too late ever to know. And you're right, the shrine is nothing to do with her story, but was the only way in that I could think of. I had to do something, or . . .' Or I might crack, she thought miserably.

He seemed about to say something, but then looked away.

She went to climb the stairs. 'Well, goodnight then.'

He cleared his throat. 'I, er, I shall be in Corfu Town tomorrow, having lunch with an . . . acquaintance.'

Well, good for you, she wanted to say.

'It's Theodora, the woman I mentioned to you, she knew Julian Adie when he came back to Corfu in the nineteen sixties,' he said rapidly. 'If you wanted to join us, you would be welcome.' He stood awkwardly, not meeting her eyes. A hint of defensiveness was rapidly replaced by self-importance. It wasn't hard to see why he and Christos did not get on.

Melissa could not understand him. He was clearly as irritated with her as she was with him. Yet he was willing to help. Was he playing her along for some reason? It was quite possible. But then, if he was going to lead her to someone who might tell her something new, she had to find out what she could.

'Thank you. That would be . . . interesting,' she said warily.

He bowed his head. 'I have to go now. Theodora and I will be at the Liston at twelve noon tomorrow. I have to be in Kerkyra early, but I could still offer you a lift if you would like.'

'Thank you, but I'll get there myself.'

'Good night, then.'

His diffidence was quite charming in its way; perhaps it was the welcome change from the driven, self-obsessed London men who had surrounded her for too many years.

II

She took the local bus to Corfu Town — or Kerkyra, as Alexandros had called it — excited about seeing the capital, discovering its landmarks for herself: the famed confection of Venetian, French, Greek and British identity that lay behind the sea mists. In her bag was a street map marked with her ultimate destination, scribbled from Alexandros's instructions: the Liston, facing the Esplanade.

The interior of the bus was infused with garlic and diesel fumes, but she was happy enough. Somehow she hadn't felt up to hiring a car, even though the Blue Bay travel office and its functional little white Fiats for rent were easy to find. The idea of the mountain road snaking around Nissiki and down to Barbati was dizzying even without the lorries and buses hurtling around the narrow bends.

From her seat over the wheel arch, Melissa was high enough to see over walls and hedges, and stare into private spaces. Olive trees were being cut and burned. Severed branches littered the road, and they were stopped at one point by a man with a red flag as a farm vehicle cleared the knotty limbs and curling bayonets of wood. The unmistakable scent of bonfires seeped under the rattling, badly-fitting window frames as the bus pitched and jolted south.

In contrast, as if the seasons had become confused, a profusion of flowers bloomed, white-blue solanum scrambling everywhere it could get a hold, and the raspberry and cream of the Marvel of Peru, so delicate-seeming yet hardy, rooted in cracks between road and wall. And above, looming cloud-topped was the great surge of Mount Pantokrator, shrugging off small scattered settlements like so many colonies of white lice.

The bus took the east road into Corfu Town. In the old port, cruise ships were docked as if they had simply pulled up and parked on the seaward side of the road. Italianate arches on the buildings opposite still formed the first glimpse at the town for travellers. Now tired hotels and shipping offices, they must have been the same ones in essence that had once greeted Adie and Grace. A version of the same dust and noise would have set their nerves jangling in anticipation, the smells of the docks pungent in the heat.

The traffic was dreadful. The bus finally stopped with a tired wheeze under the authoritarian blank walls of the New Fortress. Melissa climbed down and followed her fellow passengers. They disappeared quickly, bustling away with scrap-paper lists and baskets.

A market was in progress: stalls on both sides of the street held tumbling banks of velvety figs, red plums, apples, oranges, grapes, prickly pears. Between these, other stands released pungent sea smells where silvery fish caught lustrous streaks of green and lilac on their speckled skin, squid lay milky and spent on marble slabs, streaming tangled black-streaked ribbons, and octopus offered tan suckers to the air. Vegetables were displayed shining as if polished, while others were left still dusted with earth.

It was a while before she realised they were in the dry moat of the fortress, which might have accounted for the vague but uneasy sense of oppression. Further on were a few clothes stalls offering sweatshirts and trainers, aprons and leather coats. After nearly a week in a quiet village, Corfu Town seemed crowded and noisy. Melissa felt more vulnerable here, exposed to the hydraulic hiss of dirty buses, the ill-tempered blares of car horns and the hustle of people on the main pavements. The streets were unexpectedly imposing and sophisticated.

Suddenly uncomfortable in one of the hubs, a square full of shoppers and office workers as well as tourists, she sheered off down a wide emptier street, gambling that it was in the direction of the sea. A pervasive smell of drains counterpointed the elegant buildings from the turn of the last century, and apartment blocks like those found in well-to-do towns on the French Riviera. She passed a museum housed in a villa that must once have been a great symbol of wealth.

At the end of the street lay a sea wall of low stone, and to the left, a fair walk away was framed the intriguing scene she had found on a postcard back in Kalami: a perfect Greek temple on a rocky mound. It took her by surprise, if only because she had thought of trying to find it and had assumed it was an isolated site, perhaps in the south of the island, not here as a centrepiece in the capital. But a glance at the map showed clearly that this was the Old Fortress. She was charmed by the ease of stumbling so effortlessly across something she'd wanted to see. Soon the fortifications above the temple came into focus, and left her wondering how she could possibly have interpreted them simply as rocks between the green trees when she saw the postcard, or even missed all signs that the whole was set on a tiny island.

Opposite was a park with a rotunda. This was the Esplanade she had to cross to get to the Liston, stepping to the side of roller-bladers, families with prams and pushchairs, gangs of organised tourists, drifting groups of teenagers and solitary old ladies in black. Cafés under the trees were noisy and full, the atmosphere sociable.

There were even more people in the Liston. The architecture was unmistakably French, modelled on the Rue de Rivoli: a walkers' boulevard of elegantly arcaded buildings facing the park and the sea. There was no other side of the street, as if the architect had decided the island should not be allowed to have too much of a good thing. Almost all the space under the arches, which would originally have been built to protect the passers-by from excessive heat and light in summer, and the rain and wind in winter, was filled with bar tables and chairs. On the other side of the street were more of the same, this time under canvas and trees.

The broad stone arches were weathered and crumbling in places. In each arch swung a cast-iron lamp, many decidedly rusty and fragile at the joints. Above, slim windows were shuttered and a few narrow balconies jutted on stone brackets.

Melissa found the Liston Bar about halfway down. The place was crammed. Waiters wove with snake hips around the many groups, and shouts and bursts of laughter reverberated slightly under the high vaulted roof. She was just wondering how she would get a table when one of the shouts formed itself into her name. She spun round, and saw Alexandros standing, waiting in the shy, defensive pose that she was coming to recognise.

A lmost the first words she spoke to Theodora were a lie. 'I'm doing some research on Julian Adie,' she said. The words came out glib as you please. She didn't even know why she said it. It might have been aimed at Alexandros, to show he was not the only one who could deal in omissions.

'*Re-eally?*' Theodora's voice was a smoker's drawl, the accent unplaceable.

She was of indeterminate age – in her seventies, maybe. Self-consciously artistic, she sat plumply upholstered in flowing clothes of batik prints. A vast necklace of beads clinked on the shelf of her chest.

Her glass of cloudy ouzo was going down rapidly.

'Well, just beginning, at least,' Melissa said nervously, trying to patch the gaping flaws in this concept. 'It . . . it's still just an idea really.'

It could have been worse. She might have said 'book', and then she would have been stuck with talk of publishers, and invented deadlines and contracts. It was best to press on swiftly.

'Alexandros tells me you knew Julian Adie well.'

He had said nothing of the sort, but Theodora beamed in the light of implied flattery. She raised a gnarled hand, further knobbled by large rings, into her dyed red hair, and smiled with tombstone veneers.

'Yes . . . well, *quite* well, let's say. Lovely man, but perfectly impossible. Great fun though, totally unpredictable. What's the phrase – ? Lust for life. That was him.'

A yapping from somewhere nearby had her bobbing to investigate the underside of the table. A waft of strong musky perfume was released by her sudden dive. Alexandros sat impassive. It was impossible to guess what he was thinking.

'Roger, Mummy's got it for you here . . . yes, she has,' rasped Theodora. 'Yes, she has . . . *good* boy.' She raked through a substantial leather handbag and put her hand under the table.

'Roger . . . my Pekingese,' she said when the whiny yaps had been assuaged.

'Ah,' said Melissa.

'Named for Mr Moore, one of my all-time favourites. Charming man, don't you think?'

'I'm sure he is.'

'And not half bad as an actor either, despite what they say.'

Alexandros took charge at this point, summoning a waiter, and ordering lunch without consultation.

Melissa was riveted by Theodora: the red hair too long for her age, fringe separating on her shiny wrinkled forehead, the lumpy nose – possibly she was a committed drinker of wine and Greek spirits. Melissa would not have been surprised if she had put a cigarette in a long ivory holder.

Roger growled menacingly. Alexandros took a turn at giving him something from his pocket. 'You knew Julian Adie when he returned to Corfu to spend summers here, later on when he was a successful writer. That's right, isn't it?' he prompted.

'Oh, yes, he was well-known by then. The Cairo books

had made his name. He was popular on the island too: he seemed to have friends everywhere, from the Greeks who remembered him from before the war; to the ex-pat set who'd arrived in the intervening years. And he loved a party. Drank like a fish of course, but he was a spiritual person, too. He always wanted to understand, to get on the right wavelengths with people, loved to hear their stories – as well as being a virtuoso teller of his own, of course. The way he would speak . . . you've never heard anyone quite so witty and engaging, and all with such charm . . . but afterwards you could feel quite exhausted with it all, as if you'd been *sandblasted* by the sheer torrent of words that used to come out of him!'

Melissa glanced at Alexandros. Amusement danced briefly in the lines around his mouth. He was certainly not disagreeing with her.

'You also said he was unpredictable,' said Melissa. 'In what way do you mean?'

She paused, gazing into the middle distance with narrowed eyes while taking a drink.

'Well, for a start you never knew whether he'd turn up, or when . . . or with *whom*. Sometimes that could be exciting – he'd arrive with someone quite extraordinary, maybe someone famous and you wouldn't believe your luck, but other times the people he had in tow could be dreadful old bores that only he seemed to find fascinating. He was definitely a *collector* of people . . .'

A few more gulps of ouzo lubricated the process of remembering.

'He was also unpredictable in that you never knew what he would say next. He was pretty opinionated, and he loved to shock. He would say the most *outrageous* things and you

never knew whether he was serious, because he would swear
he *was* but with such a twinkle in his eye . . . And he was the
most dreadful fibber, but it was all so much *embroidery* – just
part of the act of being entertaining, so that most people let
it go.'

'He made up some of his stories, you mean?'

'Oh, undoubtedly. You'd meet someone a few days later
who'd featured in one of his yarns and say how it had kept
a table in stitches, and how utterly hilarious when such and
such happened, and the person would turn to you and say
that it didn't actually happen that way *at all*!'

'So . . .' Melissa frowned, 'people didn't get upset with him
then?'

'No, no. It wasn't unpleasant. He wasn't doing it to *hurt*
anyone, you see. It was only to amuse. Taking something
quite ordinary, and tweaking the details into an account that
could be quite side-splitting. And maybe people expected it
anyway of a novelist.'

Theodora was hitting her stride, and luckily in the direction Melissa wanted to take.

'You see, on that score we trusted him: we trusted him to
make us laugh and be good company. Where you *really*
wouldn't trust him was where women were concerned . . . I
mean, he was married, and very happily so by all accounts,
when he first came back to Corfu in the sixties, but you
wouldn't have known it to see him in action.'

'He was quite blatant about it?'

'*Completely!* He was a rampant little devil – he'd try it on
with any woman he could. And more often than not he
succeeded as well! He was such a short man but no one ever
seemed to notice that when he was actually there. It was as

if all the stories and the cleverness and the laughing made him ten feet tall. His wife was French, I think . . . small and blonde. Lively. He'd met her . . . I don't know, somewhere in the Med after the war. They lived in France, anyway, when I met them. Nice woman – good fun too. Very effective blind eye, she must have had as well.'

Alexandros looked thoughtful. Melissa thought he was going to say something, but he retained his air of interested bystander.

She took the plunge. 'Back then, can you remember ever coming across a young artist called Elizabeth Norden – or rather Milne, as she was then?'

'We were all young then, dear!' Her chuckle turned into a raspy cough.

Melissa smiled, sympathetically, she hoped. It was a trick of time that she thought of Theodora on Corfu as older than her mother. The air of bohemian dottiness gave her licence to play a part, and play it thoroughly. Had she always been like this, more pertinently when Adie knew her, or was this persona her defence against encroaching old age?

'Did you ever meet her, though? Does the name Elizabeth Milne mean anything to you?'

Theodora looked away again, as if trying to recall.

'Why do you ask?'

For the second time, Melissa was less than honest with her. 'I know her,' she said.

'I see.'

Was she struggling to remember a name that sounded familiar – or to hide the fact that she did know it?

'It was all a long time ago,' said Theodora, switching her

attention to her glass, which she seemed surprised to find empty.

It was as evasive an answer as she could have given.

The food came soon after, the tastes a mixture of Italian and Greek cooking, sweetly spiced by the Middle East. Melissa took some rich meat stew sprinkled with salty feta cheese but had little appetite. Alexandros ate slowly but steadily. Theodora seemed more interested in several pitchers of wine.

She was eager to talk, but about herself; how she had been married to a Greek, who had died ten years ago. Leaving her relatively wealthy, it seemed. She chattered about his business – how he had come originally from Crete, where the family made a fortune from sultanas, and he had turned to other dried fruits and packaging. Rarely did she return to Britain.

She touched on life in Corfu when she arrived in 1965 – the voracious bedbugs and mosquitoes, the unspeakable smells and lack of modern drainage. 'Of course I read the *Paradise* book. But despite what Adie wrote, it was never an Eden. He glossed over all the inconveniences and difficulties. It was still primitive when I first came here.'

'You can still find the places, though,' ventured Melissa, glad to be back on the subject. 'It's not as if they've vanished, or been demolished. And the colours are still there, the patterns in the sea, and the sunsets.'

'Only in some places. Development – they went about it all the wrong way at first here. They'd ruined half the island before anyone woke up. Adie hated it. You should have heard him rant on. It was one of the rare times when his sense of humour deserted him. "They've *spoiled* it all!" he'd shout and he'd be in a rage. It made him angry — *really* angry.'

Over tiny cups of sweet coffee, the conversation meandered away again to other topics. Alexandros opened up enough to tell them about a trip he was planning to Egypt for some archaeological research, the grant from Athens University which would pay for it. Theodora asked about Melissa's life in England and Melissa managed to avoid any more unnecessary untruths by telling her she was an archivist by training and had recently been living in Kent. She tried asking her again about Elizabeth, but Theodora shook her head as if a faint recall had slipped away again.

Lunch over, as they prepared to part, Theodora said, 'Come and see me if you like. Villa Krassadikis in Sotiriotissa.'

Melissa doubted that she would, but smiled and thanked her.

A lexandros was thoughtful as they walked out of the café together.

'She's obviously lived quite a life,' said Melissa. 'How did you meet her?'

'I've known her since I was a child.'

The same answer he had given when she'd asked about Adie. It implied long-term familiarity, yet he had first described her as an acquaintance. Melissa had the distinct impression that Alexandros was not being as straight with her as he pretended.

'Are you going back to work?' she asked.

'No.'

'Oh, I thought . . .'

'I have just finished a project. Now I'm doing some research for the next.'

Staring past him she watched a lizard slither up a crack in the stucco building. 'What do you——?' She was about to ask him exactly what he did, but he cut her off.

'You ask all these questions,' he said, 'but you don't answer any yourself.'

'I do!'

'Not really. You tell me one version, and Theodora another. Which is true?'

She hung her head.

'Perhaps neither is true, or you can't remember what you said? It doesn't fill me with confidence that any of this has a chance of fair representation, whatever you are planning to do with it!'

'I'm not planning anything. That's not – '

He stopped walking abruptly. 'What business is any of this of yours?'

'I told you,' she whispered.

'I don't think so,' he said brusquely.

It was a full-blown argument. She could not believe how quickly it escalated. His anger was real.

'Just leave it, OK?' he said.

'But——'

'Forget it all.'

He strode off leaving her in the middle of the street. She stared at his back, watching the way his jacket swung loosely from his tense frame. It seemed a complete overreaction. She was at a loss to understand why he was so defensive.

Furious, Melissa turned into the maze of streets which

sucked the crowds down into the old town. Tall, shuttered buildings rose on either side of the narrow lanes, giving a feel of Venice without the watery lanes.

She had done nothing to deserve the outburst from Alexandros. She took deep breaths and tried to put the conversation out of her mind.

Several shops were selling fancy-shaped bottles of the kumquat liqueur she'd tried with Christos, a viscous orange concoction that might have seemed palatable in small sips under candlelight, but which in daylight, uniformly present in everything from tiny glass citrus fruits, exotic bottles and huge flagons, hinted at cruel poisons, curiously sinister and factory-made.

Skeins of gold jewellery gleamed from windows on both sides of the street, beside kiosks selling fragrant custard doughnuts, leather goods, belts and handbags. Fur coats, suede coats and knitwear filled racks outside, ready for the first chills of winter.

She went into a few shops half-heartedly, buying nothing.

What should she make of Theodora? Had she seemed to recognise Elizabeth's name at first? But then the moment had slipped away. Had she learned anything new? Not really. It was another near miss on the trail of the sinuous truth about Julian Adie. And all the while, looking for her mother was like trying to hold a melody in a minor key while a band is playing in the hard bright blare of C major.

III

In Kassiope the next morning boats were crowded into the harbour.

Melissa passed a couple of hours listlessly wandering and drinking coffee. It seemed a typical resort town on a Greek island, larger and more commercial than Kalami. A ruined castle perched above the town, its broken outline speared by trees. Down on the quayside a few whitewashed one- and two-storey buildings were testament to its past as a fishing port before the tourist hotels were built. In ancient times, she read in the guidebook, it provided refuge for sailors fleeing war as well as storms. The Roman emperor Nero once sang at the altar of the temple of Jupiter Cassius, a god of the seafarers.

In a shop selling video games and DVDs, she bought a cheap compact disc of Debussy's piano music. 'Clair de Lune' was the third track.

Back in Kalami, she played it on the basic player in the apartment, and let the yearning notes pull her to the balcony, watching the light stroke the surface ripples of the sea, feeling the October chill and the sadness.

Her mother was gone. She would not find ways to deal

with that loss here. The evolving patterns in the music tugged at her thoughts. In free fall, she was back in their tiny family – her mother, her father and her – but with the disconcerting feeling that something was wrong with the version of events she had understood to be true but could not isolate quite what that was.

Yes, Elizabeth had always been quiet and reserved, but she had been honest with her daughter; too honest perhaps, when she had been too young really to understand adult problems. At the age of nine Melissa would rather not have known her father's manifest shortcomings as a husband.

Now, of course, she wished she had taken more notice. As a child she had simply closed her ears because it was not information she wanted to possess, nor for it to possess her. She knew now of course that it had, although not in the way she had feared. It was an insidious knowing that undermined her now, as an adult, and made her wary of both separation and reconciliation.

She was back to the unpleasant reality of being betrayed: that you begin to question your own judgement. The feeling swells that nothing was ever as you believed at the time. Your husband is not the person you thought he was. And your hopes and dreams for the future are exposed as ridiculous.

Was that how Grace felt when she found out Adie had been unfaithful for the first time? And when he was caught out, was he sorry for his betrayal, or merely that he had failed to get away with it?

A t about six o'clock a heavy knock on the door startled her.

Melissa wondered if she could ignore it. But the music was playing. Whoever it was would know she was there. Reluctantly, she opened the door.

It was Alexandros, clutching a bottle of wine.

'I'm sorry,' he said bluntly. 'I should not have said all those things yesterday. I was wrong.' He pushed a hand nervously through his wild curls.

There was nothing for it but to invite him in.

Standing inside the door, he came straight to the point. 'Before you arrived there was someone else asking questions. A man – an American. I thought you were connected with him.'

'An American man? Why would you presume we were connected?'

'He was asking the same questions as you were.'

That took her aback. 'Asking about Julian Adie and my mother?' She was incredulous. 'Why on earth—?'

'Not exactly about your mother. But, like you, he was looking for information about all the people who had known Julian Adie in the nineteen sixties. He was also very interested in the stories about the woman who drowned.'

Far too late she seemed to hear something that Christos had said, and that she had let go at the time. He had asked her whether she was another one looking for information about the drowning.

'Why did he want to know?'

'He wouldn't say at first. Then he said he was writing a biography. There was . . . a rather unsympathetic quality about him. He seemed to have some, ah, rather unpleasant theories about Julian and his connections with people here. We didn't give him much help. That is, some people spoke to him but they were trying to make something of it for themselves. Most of us just didn't believe him. He wasn't talking about the Julian we knew.'

Alexandros gave an acid smile and then seemed to loosen up. His shoulders released and there was a glint of amusement as he said, 'He, er, went around the village every morning saying *"Kalamari! Kalamari!"* to everyone. We called him the Squid-Greeter . . . !'

Melissa managed a smile. The news made her feel uneasy. 'You must get all sorts of people turning up here asking questions about Julian Adie, surely.'

'Some, yes. Normally you can tell that it's simple interest or curiosity. In any case, it really is not that many people who come for that now . . . his work has rather fallen from fashion.'

'So when I turned up out of the blue . . .'

He inclined his head. 'It seemed . . . a strange coincidence. So I'm sorry if you found me . . . suspicious.'

'Are you saying that you do believe me then, about my mother? What's made you change your mind?'

Alexandros looked down and reached into the inside pocket of his jacket. He extracted a postcard, looked at it for what seemed too long, and then, almost reluctantly, held it out. 'This.'

It was not a card but a photograph.

It was so similar to the photographs Elizabeth had unearthed that it might have been from the same film. Melissa brought her hand to her mouth.

'You recognise it?'

She nodded.

There was a crucial difference, though. In this picture a group of people was posed on the rocks.

'There's a date on the back,' he said. 'July 1968.'

Melissa held it and peered carefully at the row of faces. Surely ... 'Is that Julian Adie ...? And—' her heart started pounding. 'That's my mother,' she said, pointing at the image of a young woman with long blonde hair.

'That's what I thought,' said Alexandros.

'How could you know?'

'You look so alike. Look at the shape of the chin and the set of her eyes.'

He was right.

'Where did you get it from?'

'I found it in a drawer. It must have belonged to my parents.'

So there it was. Proof positive that Elizabeth had once been in Kalami with Julian Adie. She felt weak, suddenly. She had so nearly gone home without seeing it. But then she was overwhelmed by more questions.

'Why did you wait until now to show it to me?' Her mouth was so dry the words felt sticky.

'I found it only yesterday.'

Her cheeks flushed tight and hot. 'Oh.'

How could he know the extent of her doubts, the awful suspicion that she was chasing air by coming here?

'Sorry, I didn't mean it to come out like that.'

'Would you like to have it?'

'Are you sure?'

He nodded.

'Do you know who else is in the picture?'

'That's Ekaterina ...'

So it was. Melissa had not recognised the slim, willowy woman.

'That looks like Manos,' she pointed at a man in his sixties, 'but it can't be.'

'It's his father, the older Manos. That's Clive Stilwell. He and his wife Mary were friends of Julian's. They lived over by Kouloura. He was a historian, and became friends with my father Nikolaos, who is on the end there.'

Melissa made a note on a scrap of paper.

'Your father – is he——?'

Alexandros shook his head. 'He died five years ago – and my mother last year.'

'I'm sorry,' she said.

'I think it must have been given to my father – it doesn't look like one of ours.'

'You've no idea who gave it to him?'

'My guess would be Clive Stilwell, but I can't be sure.'

He was right. There was no means of knowing.

'You don't need to keep apologising,' said Melissa. He handed over the wine, and she suggested they drink it together.

Alexandros sat down and seemed to unwind a little.

Melissa was relieved too. She understood what had been going on. There had been a reason for the tension in their exchanges, and now it was gone. They could talk properly now.

She fetched a corkscrew and two glasses. She could not help thinking about what Christos had told her, what they had in common, after all. He had married a woman who then left him and went to live in Athens. While his wife may or may not have fallen in love with someone else, what she did know was that he was hurt in the same way she was. How was he coping with what had happened to his marriage, and was it any different for men?

It might be a while before that subject could be broached.

She poured the wine. 'Eleni called you the history man. Are you an archaeologist?'

He took a glass. 'No. I design museums, mainly.'

'Mainly – ?'

'And – and I write books.'

'What are you working on now?'

'A book about Cavafy.'

'I'm sorry, but I don't think I know . . . ?'

'Constantine Cavafy. He was a Greek poet who lived in Alexandria.'

'I see . . .'

'So . . . Egypt.'

No wonder he had been so sceptical about her supposed project. He was the real deal himself.

To avoid showing the blush that she could feel rising, Melissa went to the kitchen counter to fetch some crackers and olives. 'What exactly are you going to do there?' she called over her shoulder.

'A bit like you,' he said. 'Travelling, trying to make sense of—' He hesitated. 'Trying to find some traces, seeing the places that the writer could have known. So . . . that is my research project. A friend has been commissioned to produce a guidebook. I'm going to write some of the historical parts. It's not really my area, but . . .' He was defensive again, as though she had asked him to justify himself.

'That . . . fits in well then,' she said brightly.

From that moment on the conversation flowed surprisingly easily.

Melissa relaxed. He was not boring, nor difficult, as Christos implied. Yes, he was serious, nervous, a little stilted in manner. But the deep laughter lines, the cheeky look when he smiled in confidence, the bitten fingernails pointed to a man who compartmentalised his life, keeping his feelings hidden from all but those closest to him.

He told her how he had designed city museums in Greece and Italy, and exhibitions in London and Tokyo, and his long angular face lit up when he explained how nothing compared to the first time he had remodelled the museum in Corfu Town, the thrill of being able to order the exhibits, to touch carefully what he had only known from a distance, the sense of being face to face with the past.

In turn she tried to convey how she loved the ordering of the past in words and documents, the overwhelming mass of information in a huge national archive that she put into logical sequences, storing it so that generations to come would be able to access it, perhaps find their answers there.

They finished the bottle, and she opened another. Neither mentioned any personal circumstances, but there was a connection between them. She had known it from the start. The weaknesses and wounds were obvious to both of them, too big to be glossed over, the empathy between them unspoken.

But now that he was relaxed, she saw for the first time how good-looking he was. As he talked he looked straight into her eyes, and she could study the sculpted cheekbones and straight brows and tanned skin. Always before, his face seemed to have been lost behind constant activity, the intensity of his speech and the rapid hand movements which accompanied the torrent of information.

There was something else unexpected too. He genuinely seemed to be enjoying her company.

'*Clair de Lune*' was playing softly again in the background. 'I'm glad I've, ah, had a chance to talk to you again,' he said, hours later.

She waited for him to go on, but he said nothing more. He looked serious.

'What is it?'

'You must know . . .'

He reached out tentatively and touched her arm. His hands were different from Richard's: larger and browner and more damaged. There was a sense that they were working hands that sailed a boat and dug the land and used tools with skill.

He put his other hand up to her face, barely letting it rest on her cheek. His deep brown eyes were soft as melted chocolate as he watched her reaction. She held her breath. Neither moved. Up close she studied his strong jaw, his tanned and lightly stubbled chin, the appealing shape of his mouth. He looked so intense, and so sad.

It was years since she had kissed a man for the first time. She had an overwhelming urge to put her lips on his.

Seconds passed.

Then, infinitely slowly, he leaned in.

His mouth was full and soft, then urgent. Under her hands his shoulders were muscled. She wanted him to hold her. There was no doubt that she wanted this to happen.

Her thoughts strayed to Richard and she tried to block them by moving closer to Alexandros. She wanted to live in this moment, her body and his. She breathed the scent of his skin.

It was different. There was no city fragrance of traffic and aftershave. Alexandros wore the tang of ozone and fresh grass. Richard and Sarah. Remember that. She was doing nothing wrong. Perhaps this would even make it right.

Was Alexandros thinking about his wife?

She closed her eyes and allowed him to pull her closer.

Perhaps it was the wine, or the desperate need for comfort and validation. It was certainly the feeling that they were isolated together, sharing a single cell of experience. Nothing beyond that mattered. They were both eager, and taking the risk was something that felt good, for the first time in a long time.

Soon she was not thinking of Richard at all.

IV

The next day was her last in Kalami.

In a pensive mood, Melissa packed up. Then, suitcase left open on the floor, she went out for a final swim at Yaliscary. It seemed far longer than ten days ago that she had first climbed through the olive groves and found the flat velvety rock which let her down into the water.

Her mobile was switched on, but no one had called. There was no message from Alexandros.

As she walked along the village road, she wondered whether she might go up to the farm, leave a note perhaps, but shyness stopped her. The trouble was she did not trust her own judgement. She had trusted Richard, and she had been played for a fool. And this was by someone she thought she understood, someone who shared her cultural references. By contrast Alexandros was a much more puzzling figure.

He had seemed so sincere, but how did she know that he wasn't just as adept at the seduction of tourists as Christos? His murmured endearments could easily be part of a well-worn package. Perhaps that was even why she had been attracted to him, had actively wanted the lack of loyalty, the lack of commitment. None given, none expected. No disappointment or hurt.

In any case, what did she really know about Alexandros? Only what her flawed and damaged senses made of the disparate clues to his personality. That he was as different from Richard as it was possible to be. He seemed so transparently earnest and faithful to what he believed. True, she hardly knew him, but she had reacted to some deep-seated goodness in him. She had wanted him as her friend.

Then she stopped herself. She shouldn't think like this.

But she lay on the rock until long shadows crept over the beach.

On the way back she dropped into the boat hire office. She needed to arrange a time with Manolis to return the apartment keys.

Eleni was there pouring coffee. 'Stay! Drink with us!' she insisted.

Accepting gratefully, Melissa sat down at the desk. A framed photograph of old Manos had appeared, all bulbous nose and deep frown lines and decked in his Sunday best (homburg hat, a grey suit and a black-and-white striped sports shirt). She was sure it had not been there before.

Conversation was of the harvest, the new hotel developments down the coast at Barbati, their elderly neighbours.

'She plays the same music over and over again, like she wears the same clothes for a week, then it's all change – of record and apron,' said Eleni.

'The husband has sacks under his eyes, like a bloodhound,'

elaborated Manolis. 'He judges her mood by what is blaring out of the speakers. There's a band from Macedonia that play very sad music. That's always a bad sign.'

'That and the red apron . . .'

'Ah, yes . . . the red apron. The warning signal.'

'In fact, they are very happy,' said Eleni. 'He's quite deaf – so the music doesn't bother him that much.'

'He's not so deaf in the bar when someone asks if he wants ouzo . . .'

Melissa let her thoughts wander. Afterwards, when she'd said her farewells, she swallowed her pride and walked up the track to the farmhouse, but he was not there. It seemed pretty clear after all that it had only been a fleeting illusion of comfort they had both been looking for.

A nxiety put a fist to her throat the next day. Her spirit was as fragile as the early mist and the air left a chill on her nose and bare forearms.

The escape was over. She was already dreading the decisions that had to be made; the loneliness and the coming winter; the wind howling down the chimneys and the ice to be chipped from the car windscreen in the morning; hardness and brittleness to be dealt with. And always the question: *Will I be able to ride this out, or am I more vulnerable than I imagine?*

The night with Alexandros might simply never have happened.

In feather-grey morning light Melissa walked up to the White House for the last time. It was shuttered, lifeless. There was no sign of activity at the boat hire office either.

She waited a while, then wandered up into the olive grove.

Petals of wild honeysuckle flew on the sea wind, some catching on the black nets beneath the trees. She reached the top of the hill.

As she stood resting, a figure detached from the wooded path opposite and emerged on the beach, skirting the rock where she had sat for so many hours. Melissa stayed where she was, watching the scene. The dark-clad figure bent down, picked a few leaves then carried on in her direction, revealing his height and ranginess as he began the winding path up to where she had stopped. Alexandros.

For the first time she felt nervous about seeing him.

Rooted to the spot, confidence truanting, she listened to his footsteps coming closer around the bend.

'Hello . . . I haven't been following you, I promise!' Melissa forced herself to sound bright when he looked up and saw her.

He managed a shy smile. 'You couldn't have done – I've been on my boat all night.'

'What . . . night fishing?'

'No . . . just thinking. And then I slept.'

He was just as awkward as she was. He put his hands through his unkempt hair in the way she now knew well. His clothes were wrinkled and sea-stained. It looked as though he might even have slept in them.

'Sounds . . . lovely, actually. Do you often do that?'

'Sometimes. When I have something important to think about.'

For a few minutes the sun glinted through a knife slash in the grey and indigo sky. His pupils shrank suddenly in the brightness.

Then all was sombre again.

'Have you had breakfast? Do you want some coffee?' he asked.

'Well, I—'

'Please?'

They walked in silence back down the slope to Kalami, then turned off the road and took the track up to the farmhouse.

'Sorry about the state of . . . ' He waved a hand round the kitchen, the dark wood dresser laden with both plates and books. Papers were strewn over the table, along with a book, in English, of sea myths and maps, and several editions of Greek poetry. A laptop was open, the keyboard a dalmation's pelt of smudgy dark fingerprints.

Producing mugs of instant coffee and soft sweet rolls from the supermarket, he was apologetic for the quality of what he was offering. She assured him she would have been having the same on her own.

'I'm leaving this morning.'

He said nothing.

'I hope you find what it is you are looking for,' he said quietly.

Melissa nodded. You too, she thought, but did not say. She was reluctant to presume anything.

He put down his mug and scribbled on a piece of paper. 'Here's my email address, and telephone number. If you want some more help, then you can always ask me.' Was it only his help that was available to her?

There was still a knot in her chest. 'Thank you. I think you already have my mobile number.'

He let that go without comment.

'Well, you know how to contact me.'

'Yes.'

He opened his mouth to continue, but did not.

T he sea was stained a rich cobalt by the time she left. 'Be happy,' he replied as she said goodbye. 'That's what they say in Greek.'

They exchanged a platonic kiss. But then he gathered her to him in a clumsy, bone-bumping hug. It was a scorpion end, a sting of fear as she walked away from the comforting split seams of his old clothes, his books and the warmth of his presence, and the one night she had felt alive again, back past the wind-lashed cyclamens and towards all the broken promises a thousand miles north.

An hour later she took the keys back to Manolis, and kissed Eleni goodbye.

As she waited for the taxi outside the apartment, clouds lurked in malign umber hues on the horizon, choking the mountain ridges and sucking all freshness out of the air. Cypress trees billowed like sails as they took the wind.

Tucked into her shoulder bag was the photograph he had given her. Proof that Elizabeth had been with Julian Adie in Corfu. But so what? What had she really achieved apart from finding a selfish glimpse into a secret part of her mother's life and an excuse to run away?

Looking for Julian

Melissa Norden

My mother had died. Little by little I was starting to accept that one inescapable fact. I was not going to be able to use Adie as the key to unlocking her failing memory, or to spur her to fight any harder than she did, but I still wanted to understand what she had been trying to tell me. It must have been important in a way that I did not yet understand. So I couldn't let it go.

But neither did I tell anyone at home about Julian Adie, or what had really taken me to Corfu. I knew what my friend Leonie would say, that I was living in my imagination, letting it run away with me as usual. She would remind me that I had a tendency to become wrapped up in research projects in order not to have to think about what was really happening in my own life. It wasn't the first time.

I knew that. Of course I did. But there was something else that drew me to the Adies and more particularly to his first wife Grace: the universal concerns of a woman on her own wondering what the rest of her life would hold after a shattered marriage. Perhaps I was beginning to obsess about Grace. But then, my mother too had attempted to find out more about her, searching for art books that reproduced her paintings and photographs. Why was that?

To all intents and purposes, Grace Heald disappeared from Adie's story when they divorced after the war. His official biography gives a touching account of their departure from Corfu in September 1939, their hands forced by the reality of their island exile. Grindlay's Bank in London warned that they would not be able to guarantee the transfer of funds during wartime, and the prospect of sitting out a prolonged conflict was bleak. No longer able to dismiss the rumours from abroad, they scrambled for tickets on a passage south to Athens, and subdued, they prepared to leave. Village women and children were gathering the grape harvest, while the fish swam free. The men had been sent to the mountains to prepare for defence. In calm waters like slabs of malachite, the viridescence streaked black with weed, mines were being laid. As unseasonable rain slanted down, Adie stood on his balcony watching the green-black sea, '*half-suffocated with grief*'.

In Athens Grace discovered she was pregnant. They

obviously felt that they both ought to do all they could to hold the marriage together, and for a while, in their new city home, it looked as if they might succeed. Certainly Adie tried harder to be an 'old married man', and there was also the practical question to address of how to earn some real money in order to support a family. He achieved this under the auspices of the British Council, which found him useful teaching work as well as a part-time post using his new mastery of the Greek language as a journalist on what was effectively a pro-British propaganda publication.

Their daughter was born in May 1940 and they named her Artemis, after the goddess of the wild and of the hunt. '*She is a sweet darling, quiet and good with search-lights of sea blue for eyes. Grace is very tired but rightly full of her achievement in producing such an angel,*' he wrote to Peter Commin. The same letter hints that he may have been spending more nights in: '*I'm loath to trust the situation enough to send for my books, much as I would like to fill up a splendid array of bookshelves in this apartment. But could you send some of the Elizabethans? I am scribbling most evenings.*'

But he was still a carouser, given the chance. As he settled to his exile, Adie the inveterate talker and drinker soon found sympathetic company among his fellow expatriates and Greek circles opened for old friends from Corfu and Paris. By the summer of 1940, he was often to be found late in the bars and restaurants of the Plaka, the old quarter of Athens, with the rowdier writers and poets to whom he always gravitated. Soon, with his openness and gift for friendship, he was at the heart of a hard-drinking literary set, a meeting of minds between Greek and Briton.

His wife may not have appreciated the resumption of his social life, but the friends he made in Athens would stand him in good stead when Greece fell in April 1941, and no doubt he excused his worst excesses on the grounds that he was providing them both with a security net of contacts.

But it seems Grace disagreed with his methods of assuring their future. In late 1940, she left, taking the baby with her – taking one of the few remaining routes home, via Turkey and Karachi. Evidently she preferred to take her chances on an appallingly difficult journey than remain with the volatile Adie in uncertain times.

His friend the writer and fellow British Council wordsmith Alan Maurice attests in his memoirs that the arguments between them had become increasingly ugly. Adie found Grace too malleable. He liked arguments; the verbal cut and thrust made him feel alive. She did not; discord only upset her. '*I need to feel the blood coursing,*' he told Maurice. '*All she ever wants is for me to calm down.*'

When she turned, sick of his behaviour, it was more unexpected to Adie than it was to anyone else. He still loved Grace deeply; there was no doubt about that. He never spoke a sour word about her afterwards. Grace, on the other hand, vowed never again to read a word he wrote.

It would be ten years before he saw his beloved Artemis again.

What fired me – still – was the end of that marriage, when they had been so happy. Clearly the all-encompassing sensual partnership he described in his book was at odds with reality. Equally clearly, he had adored her. But the problem was that there were only his biographies to go on. Her story went on in parallel but unrecorded. It piqued me that it was never properly explained what had gone wrong.

Adie and his great friend and correspondent, the equally libidinous Don Webber managed to reinvent themselves every few years, with a new wife, a new book, a new location. They seemed to accept the end of marriages with such *sangfroid*. Was this evidence of a capacity to control their emotions, or simply proof that those emotions had never run very deep in the first place? Did they never struggle, these romantic prag-matists, with the loss of hopes, of what had seemed like a future mapped out?

My interlude in Corfu seemed like a dream; but it had made Julian Adie become almost real to me. It was a strange magic, reading his words now I had seen his landscape for myself.

Not everyone agreed Adie was a good writer. Even

at the height of his fame, the critics had their ears tuned to his false notes. 'His polymath's ambition allied to an adolescent need to shock' wrote one. 'His brilliant glibness' was another excoriation. His characters were one-dimensional, they said – all mouths and monstrous egos, with emptiness at their core.

But did his flaws make him a bad man – or a more compelling one?

I made a list of his characteristics as I saw them from my reading of the biography and his own work: Earthy, intense, idealistic, curious, sceptical, cynical, arrogant, engaging, charismatic, generous, funny, brutal and selfish, loquacious, torrential, entertaining and infuriating.

All the critics point out that Julian Adie is an intensely autobiographical writer. He himself claimed his books contained all there was to know of him. Without ever specifying personal revelation, almost every piece reflects his experience or observations, and he can be charming. So much so that it is impossible to like his writing without feeling that you would enjoy his company as a person.

But there's a problem. Behind the charm and the garrulous sociability, the smooth articulacy, enthusiasms and vivacity is a blank. In his work, there is a contradiction between the solid, stocky physical presence and the elusive heart of the man. The more I looked, the more I realised I was looking for what he had left unsaid under the mesmerising lushness of his set pieces. And I came to realise that what I was searching for – his smaller, authentic voice – was frequently absent. He revealed only what he chose to reveal about himself, often leaving the reader to draw his own conclusions. Perhaps this is the secret of Adie's success: the personality which so beguiles – on the page as in the taverna – is a work of personal interpretation according to our own needs, leaving only the impression of intimacy.

What was he to my mother and where did she fit into his story? It was hard to reconcile Elizabeth, so gentle and poised, so cautiously self-contained, with this adventuring cosmopolitan.

Part Five: A Mermaid Singing

I

Corfu, 1968

'I have a disease called islomania,' Julian told her. 'I am morbidly predisposed to love islands.'

And, he made clear, there were times when he needed to suffer alone. He would take the boat by himself and sail around the coast, or set off in his camper van revisiting old haunts. Or even try to work in the rooms above the olive press where he was staying. Elizabeth accepted his solitude as a necessary part of his grieving for Simone, although when she asked him, gently, about Simone he said nothing. If he did speak of his state of mind, it was usually in generalisations.

'I should know by now that unhappiness passes,' he told her. 'When I left here the first time, I'd never known such agony. But it can't last, not at that intensity.

'When I went to Egypt, it was appalling. I'd lost everything, you see. My wife, my child. And Greece. I felt that very deeply, the loss of Greece, like part of myself. And loss was all around, successive waves of loss. I was attuned to it, you see, and I saw it, felt it, everywhere. From the tragedies etched on the monuments, from outpourings from the ancient poets, from the faces of the wounded military as they were hurried on from the desert, to the startled eyes of the refugees as they disembarked in the harbours, astonished to find themselves there, astonished to find they had survived to be anywhere at all.

'All the words, in all the languages, washed over like a tide, leaving their debris, the displacement and the unhappiness. But they were also eroding in infinitesimal ways all the sadnesses that had gone before.'

'Have you ever been back to Egypt?'

'No. Why would I? Ghastly place. Hated it.'

Elizabeth was surprised. 'I think a lot of people would be shocked by that – to know that you hated it there.'

'Why? It's completely irrelevant. What's on the surface is irrelevant. It's the strata underneath that interest me. You don't fall for a place because it looks fine, or hate it because it's a seething anthill of a shanty town, you make what you can out of what it *implies* . . . of the stories it tells, or seems to be telling, and how a place changes a person.

'I had to stop fighting it for the city to appear. I had to stop the anger and reach down to pick up and feel the thick petals of frangipani, taste the grittiness of the cheap black windfall dates picked off the sand by the poor, and smell what was in the air: the sea salt and jasmine, the bruised tangerines and the dung. Then I found my way in.'

She was in awe of him: the way he talked, the effortless articulacy, the way he saw an inner life in geography. But neither was she blind to his faults. He had the habit of issuing an edict, then closing down the conversation when it ceased to suit him, she noticed.

The days on the boat, the moorings in deserted coves, an illicit trip across the water and to his old hunting ground: these would be just the two of them. Her skin was soon baked as brown as his. Elizabeth began to live for the telephone calls that told her to be at the jetty.

His light blue eyes were chips of quartz, hard and bright. *'He is a force of nature,'* she wrote in her journal. *'Quite unlike anyone else.'*

As the summer grew hotter, she came to know and anticipate the tides and contradictions of his behaviour. He claimed he could not write. 'The words come like snails' coughs in February,' he said. Then a few days later he claimed he needed time alone in order to work. He wanted to spend days and nights with her, but always of his choosing.

Elizabeth went on walks of her own into the burning days, first finding different routes down through the olive groves to the sea, and then striking out into the hills over herb-scented scrub. She sketched, she took photographs and wrote on scraps of paper that she would stick in her diary when she returned, hot, dusty and thirsty, her limbs ever browner and tingling with the delicious ache of physical effort.

When they met he always questioned her closely about where she had been, what she had seen, what her impressions were. He had a way of making her feel as if it were a secret discovery between the two of them, the mapping of a world that lay just below the surface, invisible to anyone else.

She was strong and confident again. There was no doubt she was over David and the wedding debacle. It was far away and long ago, and that was due to Julian Adie. Together they inhabited somewhere out of time, out of normal experience.

Evenings together would often begin in the Liston Bar in Corfu Town. Drinks would flow as his friends and acquaintances dropped by knowing they had a good chance of finding Adie there. Tourists would crane their necks wondering whether or not it might be him. Back-slapping bonhomie was his prevailing mood. But Elizabeth had witnessed by now how that mood could switch. While he rarely gave any outward sign of being drunk – his exuberance seemed natural; he was as engaging at eight in the morning after his breakfast swim – he drank continuously. So it seemed logical to blame the wine when blackness cut in as if a light bulb had popped.

On the periphery of several evenings was Veronica Rae. Some nights she arrived with friends and contented herself with her trademark stares from a separate table chosen, it seemed, to keep him in her sightline. Julian would occasionally raise his hand in greeting when she arrived but would otherwise ignore her.

'How exactly do you know her?' Elizabeth asked. She knew she was being persistent on this issue, but the woman was disconcerting.

'I think she came via Don Webber, somewhere along the line – Paris maybe.' He was in a soaring mood after a day rediscovering a near-deserted cove to the north. They had slept through the afternoon there, entangled and drugged on warm wine. 'She's been hanging around a few months. She might have been here in previous years. I can't remember.'

'She gives you such looks!'

'Does she?'

'Of course she does. I can't believe you don't notice.'

'I don't let it bother me.'

Elizabeth tried to do the same.

Then one evening Veronica came directly to their table. She was alone. Her hair was scraped back (in another hair band that matched her dress) in a way that accentuated the boniness of her little face and shadowed eyes. She jutted her chin at Elizabeth as she stopped. It was only six o'clock and the other chairs were empty.

Veronica smiled complicitly at Adie. 'I had a wonderful time, darling. We must do it again . . . very soon.'

Elizabeth felt her stomach clench. She had not seen him for two days. She sat back in her chair, trying to appear relaxed. She knew better than to say anything.

Others arrived. Voices and laughter rose as the company swelled around them. Elizabeth, wearing a smile that now pinched her cheeks and made her unable to concentrate on even the smallest of talk, endured an hour of yachting tales from a bloated ex-businessman followed by a dinner placement between a morose British scriptwriter and the editor of a local English-language newspaper who was a serious admirer of Adie's novels. The evening seemed never-ending.

She waited until they had cadged a lift back to Kalami where he suggested a nightcap in one of the beach tavernas. Then she made the mistake of asking him what Veronica had meant.

His reaction was purely physical. His chest expanded; his broad shoulders locked; and his face changed colour. It was as if the rage was engorged under his skin.

'Why the hell shouldn't I poke her if I want to?'

That took her breath away. She had clearly not understood her position, or perhaps had only seen what she had wanted to see. Either way, she felt the ground shift under her feet.

'Am I answerable to you? Who do you think you are?'

'I – I . . .'

'Possessiveness! I can't bear it. Never, ever try to possess me. It's the kiss of death, dear.' His tone was light and mocking. The surge of rage had passed as quickly as it had blown up.

Elizabeth said nothing.

Julian ordered brandy. He had a jaunty cut-and-thrust conversation in Greek with the waiter, and as if nothing had spoiled their togetherness, covered her hand with his. Its compelling warmth stole down into her bones.

She stood up. 'I'm going now.'

The moon was fat in a clear, star-pierced sky. There was plenty of light by which to walk back to Kouloura.

He exhaled the distinctive smoke of his French cigarette. 'You don't want to spend the night with me?'

'No.'

He didn't try to persuade her to change her mind.

She left.

Fireflies jittered and glowed as Elizabeth struck out briskly. The headland was darker than she expected where the trees blocked the pale light. She shivered but she could not turn back.

She felt sick, and worse. She could see all too well what she was: a silly, naïve girl with a stupidly aching heart. Yet not so silly, she reminded herself; she had always known what she was doing, what he was. Of course there were going to be cracks in the relationship. If, in his mind, it was a relationship at all.

As her strides became looser and her breathing calmer, she thought, so what if he wants to see Veronica too? She had wanted experience, to learn sophistication. There was no way she had a future with Julian Adie; she was just fooling around with him, using him as much as he was her. The thoughts went round and round as she tried to rationalise her feelings and assuage the sharpness of sudden hurt.

I t took a few seconds after she woke the next morning to remember what was wrong. That she had been half-awake all night, irritated by the constant whine of mosquitoes. Why she felt heartsick. Several replays of his callousness made her get up blearily. It was still early — there was no sign of Clive or Mary. Still wearing her nightdress she shuffled into the kitchen for some coffee and took it outside on the terrace. The sun was too bright. It made her head hurt.

'*She walks in beauty, like the night . . .*'

The familiar ringing voice made her jump. Julian was sitting below, under the idleness tree. He bounded up the steps, and thrust a vast untidy bunch of wild flowers at her. His hair was tousled, still wet from a swim.

'I am so sorry I upset you,' he said. 'I behaved like a pig.'

Sorry for upsetting her, she noted. Not sorry for whatever he had been doing with Veronica.

He shrugged with his arms out for her. How can I help what I am, he seemed to be saying. Sometimes I'm bad. The crinkling, twinkling eyes.

She must have hesitated for all of thirty seconds.

The trouble was, she wanted him. His emotional hold over her was like a strong undertow. She would not call it love; that would be too dangerous, would leave her too open to hurt. She knew for certain it would be the kind of hurt she had never felt when she was with David. Even now, just imagining losing it was sharp and intense.

Elizabeth was starting to accept that he meant more to her than she did to him. But that was no reason to forgo the pleasure of being with him.

From then on, when she did not see him she suspected he was with Veronica.

The other woman's catty and dismissive remarks to Elizabeth continued when their paths occasionally crossed, but at least assured her that she was as much a thorn in the other woman's side as Veronica was proving in hers.

She resolved to stride out harder and longer on her walks, pour her energies into her drawings, and to make some new friends. She went out a few times with the young set she'd met at the Stilwells' fateful party, dancing at the beachside clubs at Ipsos, but never felt a hundredth of the excitement she had with Julian Adie.

II

In Kassiope, the dark quayside was transformed. Tents and stalls selling sweets and fripperies jostled for space with nut and melon-seed vendors, and tables and chairs laid out on three sides of the square. Strings of electric lights winked and hummed in the trees.

'The festival of midsummer's eve, and the eve of St John's feast day. A *paneyiri*!' said Julian, leading the way. The entourage trotted to keep up, including Clive and Mary.

Elizabeth felt her spirits lift as she saw how the setting and the anticipation of a Greek feast were balm to Julian's tricky mood. For days he had been alternately quiet and argumentative. None of it had been directed at her, but listening as he sounded off about the world in general, and bourgeois prejudice in particular, had been sapping. Now, his enthusiasm was infectious.

The aroma of lambs roasting on the spit mingled with the smell of oil from boats recently docked and sweet honey cakes and red-hot charcoal.

Church bells rang, and the door to the chapel was open.

In every direction the streets were full, the crowds meandering down to the water and the spot where three fires would be lit, currently ragged wigwams of twigs and branches.

'There!' Julian pointed to the table he wanted to claim. Elizabeth laughed as he pulled her along, and kissed her playfully as they sat down.

The wine began to flow.

The three fires were lit, burning in the middle of the party. 'The same is happening in villages all across the island,' said Mary. 'The fire is supposed to be purifying. It drives out bad spirits and uplifts the soul.'

It certainly seemed to be having that effect on Julian. He was in high good humour, waving at people as they passed and clapping to the music that had started.

'The local men will jump through the fires wearing headdresses of olive branches,' Mary continued. 'They jump through the fires three times calling for the blessing of God from St John.'

Right on cue there was a cheer from the crowd as the first supplicants appeared, heads bowed under rough leafy crowns.

'I'm in too!' cried Julian. 'Spyro, you got the hats? Come on, Clive, you could do with blessing!' He was thoroughly enjoying himself.

After the ritual, they hurled the headdresses into the fires and whooped as they burned.

'It is thought to drive away witches,' said Adie, grinning. 'Pagan, in origin, of course.'

Elizabeth gave concentrated thought to Veronica, then felt guilty.

The scent of roasting lambs grew stronger. Long tables were set out for the feast: bowls of herby tsatziki, spicy kebabs and sausage and colourful salads of red pepper, others of tomato, cucumber and crumbly chunks of feta cheese.

The band was in full flow. Rippling melodies played on the balalaika, guitar and flute were overlaid with mournful singing.

'They're old Corfiot songs. "Sea, you youth-swallower",' Julian translated, ' "all the bodies of the young you have sucked into your insatiable maw . . ."'

'Traditions run deep in Greece. When I was young here no workman would ever take a nap under a tree because he feared the Nereids who waited in the shadows for the unwary.'

He listened, moving his head to the rhythm. '"The boat's ripped sail and the cunning seas, the wind like the breath of Helen as she is snatched away" . . . Despair is never far away. In Greece, songs are history. Lyrics are poems that tell a true story.'

Soon there was dancing around the fire, those who remained seated singing and clapping in time.

At first it was mainly the girls and women dancing.

'Do the men have their own dances?' Elizabeth asked Spyros.

'Traditionally the *paneyiri* attracted the young people who wanted to get married, and these were the dances performed by the unmarried women.'

'A sanctioned flaunting of themselves to attract a male,' said Julian.

Many of the women were wearing a country costume, headdresses ornately decorated with flowers, and tight bodices. Their black shoes were dusty from the several miles of tracks they had walked down from the hills.

When a men's dance started, Julian and his Greek friend rushed to join in the frenzy. Clive stared to explain the *kalamatianos* and *syrtos*, but the music was too loud to speak over. Elizabeth watched as the spiral went first one way and then the other, ever-expanding to allow more revellers to join the line.

Then it was her turn.

'Come on,' said Mary. 'Follow what I do. No one minds if you go wrong.'

Elizabeth allowed herself to be drawn in. She felt young and free. Her blonde hair swinging, she knew she was noticeable and enjoyed being seen. She danced for longer than she had intended. The line went round and round, ever longer, whipping round in a frenzy of music and stomping from the crowds. The lights were whirling above their heads.

When she was finally released she looked around, still laughing, for Julian, hoping he had been admiring her efforts. But she couldn't see him anywhere.

'Has anyone seen where Julian's got to?' she asked back at their table.

No one had. Neither did they seem unduly concerned. She sat down to drink a glass of water. His unpredictability was a given.

Half an hour went by. Elizabeth muttered that she was going to look at the stalls, and slid back into the throng. The band, still going strong, had slowed the tempo to a dirge. The singer wailed, his head thrown back.

She bought a paper twist of honeyed nuts. Still she expected to see his face at any moment bobbing among the dancers, or chatting at another table. But he did not materialise.

Unwilling to return to the party without him, she wandered into the town. Music and light blazed out of shops and cafés. Men called out to her.

A circuitous route took her back to the quay. She was about to rejoin the others at the table when she saw him.

He was with Veronica.

They were pressed into the shadows of the harbourmaster's office.

Elizabeth hesitated, then walked straight up to them.

'Hello,' she said with stiff civility.

Veronica ran a finger down Julian's cheekbone in a defiantly intimate gesture.

Elizabeth turned to Julian, unsure what she expected him to do. He confounded her, though. He gave her a sheepish smile. Then he closed his eyes and clutched on to Veronica. For once, he seemed drunk.

'We were just leaving,' Veronica said.

Elizabeth stared. 'I'll say goodnight, then,' she said to Julian.

He said nothing.

She worked her way round the knots of festoons and raucous groups. Her ears roared; it was like being in an echo chamber: voices from the party boomed and rang in the black air. This time she did mind.

Clive and Mary drove her the few miles back to Kouloura. Stoutly, no one mentioned Julian.

H e might have gone with Veronica that night, but he was still intent on seeing Elizabeth.

The night after that, he telephoned the Stilwells at four in the morning asking for Elizabeth. He demanded that she speak to him. 'Tell her I'll send a car for her now,' he shouted. 'I want to see her right now!'

He did not get his way.

Julian told her to make no demands on him, but then persisted in demanding she carry on with him as before. 'But you are immeasurably more lovely than she is!' he cried, as if that made it all right.

She knew what he was doing; he was playing games with them both.

Still she was drawn to him. The golden aura, the careless manner, his intense interior life, his exuberant insistence on mystery and exploration – it was all a great conjuring trick, one that fascinated her. She could not stop going back until she understood how it worked.

So Elizabeth continued to go out on the boat with him, to lie in the sun on the rocks, to make love by the sea, to listen to him talk, and to learn about his world beneath the surface. She would live in the moment, she had decided, never trying to possess him. After all wasn't this what her generation was fighting for, the right of women to enjoy sex in the same way that men did? Everyone else was doing it, being free and laughing at the old constraints.

Although Mary and Clive said nothing, she felt their

apprehension. And if they did say anything she would tell them she had no need of their concern. She was fine. If they thought she was out of her depth in the undersea world of other people's motives, they were underestimating her. Maybe she had learned more than anyone realised from Julian.

For gradually, Elizabeth was becoming aware for the first time in her life that she had power too. The first time she felt it, it seemed too much for her, like too much horsepower in a car. Now, once she was used to it, she wanted to test out the surge. The ride was spectacular.

III

J ulian speared a piece of white fish with a kebab stick.

'Veronica tells me I should give you up,' he said.

The boat bobbed at the side of the jetty at Agios Stefanos where they had put in for a late lunch. Under the awning of the taverna, glad to be out of the glare of another perfect day, Elizabeth sat as still as she could.

There it was again. Possessiveness. Two counts of it, and neither on her part.

Elizabeth waited for him to qualify this statement, but he did not. 'Please don't think that I have any thoughts about you and her, or you and any other woman, come to that,' she said calmly.

'You're sure about that?'

'Completely.'

He grinned. 'I knew she was wrong.'

Steeling herself not to betray any emotion, Elizabeth met his eyes, playing the game too. He reached for the notebook he always carried, he pulled out the centre pages and started to write.

Elizabeth ate slowly, concentrating on taking in the burning blue of the tiny bay seemingly blocked at the end by the mass of purple-brown hills across the strait. The water glittered and she had to screw up her eyes to see.

'There.' He pushed the folded paper across the table.

'*Darling Elizabeth,*' he had scrawled. '*Whatever idiocies I may commit, whichever stupid woman I might let drink persuade me I want in that irrational moment, know that I adore you. You are the one who has given me this summer and made me whole again. Remind me of this whenever you need to. I adore you. Julian.*'

She kept her eyes down.

'Keep it. Read it when you doubt me, when I'm a fool,' he said.

It was hard to tell if he was mocking or sincere.

T hat night the party was held at a Swiss architect's house, a pink palace above Nissaki, a few miles south of Kalami. A carnival theme had enticed guests to 'Dress with Abandon'. Julian and Elizabeth turned up as they were, straight off the boat. The moon hung huge and low over the smooth black sea.

They climbed the steep steps from the mooring. Voices and notes of music drifted down the dark hillside. A scops owl called. Soon they reached a path lit by torches through the garden. It emerged from trees on the lawn where a juggler was throwing more flames into the night. Moving arcs and circles of orange light hung for a few seconds in the air.

Guests had spilled down from the house. Masked waiters in black dived in and out of the shadows.

At the head of the final flight of stairs up to the wide terrace,

Veronica was waiting at the balustrade. She must have seen them coming.

Her voice cut through the darkness. 'I see you still have your silly little friend with you. She's lasted longer than most of your young meat.'

She was encased in a skintight silver sequinned cocktail dress, in the moonlight she was a mermaid covered in thousands of winking scales, the material tight over her neat hips and flat stomach. Already drunk.

Julian smiled pleasantly. 'And good evening to you, Veronica. How lovely to see you.'

She gave a malevolent squint. 'He's only using you, like all men do,' she slurred in Elizabeth's direction.

He swatted her away like a fly. They went up the steps to the villa, not looking back to see whether she was following.

The conversation at the party was the usual mixture of the inane and the spiky. Costumes were admired. A snatch of conversation floated over:

'Never marry a foreigner. He seemed so nice before I could understand what he was saying.'

She caught Julian's amusement and they both laughed. Through the swirling burlesque of the party Veronica was watching them. She hardly took her eyes off them wherever they were, even as she tilted her head back to tip more drink down her throat. For a few seconds, Elizabeth felt claustrophobic.

A man tried to determine her views on student activism.

Another asked her whether this was her first time in Corfu. The music changed from subtle strings flying lightly on the dusky air, to the more earthbound sounds of the Rolling Stones. Couples had begun to dance, digging at the beat with their elbows, faintly ridiculous in formal evening dress or bizarre creations worn to approximate the idea of wanton hedonism but succeeding only in looking as if they had raided a dressing-up box.

Elizabeth found Julian was no longer at her side. He had been spun off by a succession of acquaintances and strangers, constantly in demand.

She smiled uncertainly at another woman about her own age.

The woman returned the smile and came over. She was dark with an hourglass figure encased in a slightly old-fashioned style of dress, a brightly made-up face and a ready smile. 'I'm Theodora,' she said.

'You're English!' There was no mistaking the flat working-class vowels. 'I thought you were Greek . . . you look—'

'St Albans, originally. Married to a Greek,' she said.

They exchanged brief histories. Theodora's husband considered himself a foreigner too, as he came from Crete originally. Three years ago she had come to Greece on holiday, met Giorgios, and stayed. 'The King of Greece used to spend his summers in Corfu, so that's what we do now,' she giggled. 'It's that kind of family.'

Theodora was good company.

'I'd like to have a go at painting,' she said, when Elizabeth told her a little about herself. 'But I probably won't be much good. Seems like fun though.' Then she added, quickly, 'Hard work, I should think, to do it properly.'

'Yes, well it can be . . .'

'Sorry, is that boring?'

'No . . . no . . .'

'You look uncomfortable – what's up?'

Elizabeth tried to concentrate. 'Oh, nothing – it's just—'

It was impossible to ignore Veronica. The dagger of her glare was between the vertebrae of her spine.

Elizabeth sighed. 'It's that woman. Do you know her?'

Opening a sparkly evening bag, Theodora took out a pair of glasses. 'Can't see much without them – silver sequins, you mean?'

Theodora peered, while Elizabeth wished she hadn't asked. 'Don't think I do know her. Why do you ask?'

'She's always . . . oh, it doesn't matter. Just wondered, that's all.'

Another wave of claustrophobia.

Elizabeth made an excuse and left the room. The note he had written was still in her bag. She found a bathroom and leant against the basin to read it again. A kind of cruelty uncoiled in her gut. It was unpleasant to realise that was what it was.

If a possessive nature repulsed him, she might let Veronica do for herself. The woman was already drunk and behaving badly. All that was needed was to tip the edge. *'Darling Elizabeth.'* Yes, Julian, she was thinking, I have learned such a lot from you.

Elizabeth folded the page neatly. Then she went back to the door of the room where most of the guests were circulating, and stopped a waiter as he went past. Indicating Veronica, she asked him to give her the note.

She rejoined Julian. She slipped her arm around his back

and kissed him affectionately. He played up to it, for the benefit of all.

Veronica put her glass on a Chinese table with the exaggerated movement of the extremely drunk, stepping back to admire her work as if she had arranged and placed a vase of flowers. She stood shimmering for a moment.

A space cleared, as if others sensed the change in atmosphere.

Her dress slashed to the waist and skewed over one shoulder to expose one small well-shaped breast, on heels so vertiginous she could only walk extremely slowly and deliberately, she seemed to take a long time to pitch and roll towards them on her set course.

Finally, she arrived in front of Julian. His eyes were on a level with her chest, 'Ah, Veronica. I'd know those nipples anywhere.'

Veronica swung an arm, and cracked a slap against his cheek.

It rang out. The room fell silent.

Then she turned to retrace her steps, but tripped, breaking a heel of one shoe as she saved herself instinctively. In a parody of dignified retreat, Veronica limped the length of the room.

Julian rubbed his face.

'What the hell was that for?' he asked.

The party noise resumed immediately, louder and more excited than before.

Come on, let's go,' he said. 'I'm not in the mood for this any more.'

He took her hand and led the way.

Elizabeth followed, quietly satisfied, but feeling shocked too – shocked at herself and what she had done, how easy it had been.

His clasp was warm and strong, pulling her down through the groves. The night air was a cool caress on her bare shoulders. They did not speak. She did not ask where they were going. The sea rubbed against the rocks below to their right. He was sure-footed and she followed. The path wound up and down. She barely noticed the walking. She was still astonished at her own initiative, and uncomfortable with the unkindness.

When he stopped, he pulled her to him. His mouth opened hers, soft and compelling. Her body responded.

Not far below them was the pool, black and bottomless before the copper path which led to the moon. She recognised the hut-like building pale above the glittering water.

Lights passed on a ship, silent and alluring, flying through the night.

The dark earth retained the day's heat, baked into the ground. His warm hand was on her stomach. She brushed her cheek against his chest. Then he guided her to the grassy mound on the ground above the shrine.

She pulled off his shirt and tasted the familiar sweet saltiness of his skin. The sea where they had swum was still on them both. She felt a surge of euphoria as he pulled her dress up.

A dry twig snapped only a few yards away.

They froze, listening for more sounds. She giggled, then kissed him again, wanting him more than ever, feeling equal to him.

More cracking in the undergrowth made them both start.

'It must be one of the fishermen,' whispered Julian. 'He'll be going down with his trident and an oil lamp for an octopus.'

All was black and resinous where they lay.

The footsteps were irregular. Was that a voice, muttering low between breaths? Elizabeth held her own. Each crack of the ground cover was followed by a brush of the fine carpet of pine needles. The strange rhythm grew more insistent. The brush after the beat, like the sound of a slow-hand jazz drummer.

She could not help but giggle.

'Can you see anything?' she asked.

'No.'

She began to kiss his neck lightly, expecting him to enjoy the incongruity. But he gently stopped her.

They waited, listening, still stretched out in the undergrowth.

The sound was the same: crack-shuffle, crack-shuffle.

It made her think of Veronica again, and the drunken attempted elegance of her one-heeled walk, and she smiled to herself. She would not mention it. She did not want to go on about it.

'Fuck,' said Julian. 'It's her again.'

The silver dress gleamed in the moonlight. Like a malevolent mermaid, Veronica sat on the rock. She was speaking to herself, in spurts and mumblings.

'I thought that slap had an air of finality about it,' said Elizabeth, trying to inject some grim humour. 'Obviously I was wrong.'

'I'm sick of this,' he said.

Elizabeth shivered. 'What are you doing?'

He stood up as if braced for a confrontation. 'I'm going to talk to her.'

'Shall I come too?'

'You stay here. Probably make it worse if you said anything.'

He started down, then turned and motioned to her to keep out of sight.

Elizabeth thumped the ground in annoyance. The night was really being spoiled. She had a sudden visceral, primitive desire to lash out and hurt the other woman. It was so unlike her, that she was shocked again, this time by her own violent impulse.

These thoughts pinned her to the ground. From the back of her mind, a dread rose. Without being able to identify its source, she felt sucked down by fear.

Minutes passed. She could not hear what Adie was saying to Veronica, only the low murmur of conversation from beyond the shrine. Then louder voices, his then hers, harsh and shrill.

They would have to take her back, Elizabeth supposed. Back to the party, back to wherever she was staying. It was not how any of them would have chosen to end the evening.

Elizabeth stood up as quietly as she could and began to creep closer, wanting to hear what was being said. The monochrome of the pine wood, the cypress spears, the scrubby hillside seemed to close in on her. She was behind the shrine now, in the shadows.

Julian and Veronica must be sitting or standing below, on the turtleback rocks; she could not see them. She picked her way down. She heard a splash, followed by another.

Were they swimming together? Surely not. The dark sea was too powerful, too dangerous for someone in her state.

Elizabeth stumbled out on to the flatter rocks. She could see nothing in the water.

'Julian?' Then she called his name again, louder, across the inky pool.

Silence.

Then he broke the surface, gulping noisily for breath.

'What's going on?' shouted Elizabeth.

Still no response.

'Where's Veronica?'

'Gone!' he gasped furiously.

'What do you mean, gone?'

'In the water.'

'But – she can't swim that drunk!' Elizabeth scanned the swell. Was that a movement further out? 'Veronica!' she shouted. 'Are you there?'

No answer.

Adie dived underwater again. He swam like a dolphin. He was strong. If the woman was down there, he would pull her up. He shot up again, scattering silver droplets.

'What happened?' Elizabeth asked uselessly. She had heard the twin splashes.

'Stupid, stupid woman!' he was shouting. 'What was she thinking of?'

'She can't be far away. It hasn't been long enough.'

He hit the water angrily with a flat palm, looking wildly all about.

'She's not there? Veronica!' shouted Elizabeth.

'What can you see from up there?'

'Nothing . . . nothing!'

They shouted, louder and louder, across the sea. Nothing came back but the faint echo of their own voices.

'What should we do now?' asked Elizabeth, starting to tremble.

'I don't know . . .'

Elizabeth tried to be rational. 'Are you sure she's still in there – she didn't climb out and you didn't see her go? You might have been underwater, not heard anything—'

'It's possible . . . but if that was the case you would have seen something, heard something—'

'I suppose . . .'

'I'm going to get the boat,' said Julian, hauling himself out of the water. 'You run to Agni and – no, wait . . .'

'What? What should I do?'

'Nothing. There's nothing you can do—'

'But—!'

'No. I want you to do what I tell you,' Julian told her. 'Go back to Kouloura. Go up to the tavernas at Agni and call yourself a taxi – better, take the water bus if it's still running. Go home!'

'But I can't!'

'Yes. You can. You must. Look, there's no time to waste.'

'And what are you—?' she cried.

But he had already set off back up the path the way they had come. 'I'm going to get the boat . . . !' he shouted back.

'Should I call someone for help?'

His words floated down to her.

'I'll do it!'

IV

At Kouloura she waited the next morning, watching the sulky water, the sunless currents. A wind beyond the headland ruffled the cypresses. The same rocks, the same trees and scrub moved silently above a grey sea. All had changed.

Julian stayed away. No news came. In a state of suspension, pleading a hangover, Elizabeth sat for hours in the garden. The hills across the strait turned a sullen face to the emptiness, brown turning to a menacing iris-mauve as the day wore on. That evening the colours were too vibrant for her tired eyes, the contrast too reckless.

And all the time, jarring her nerves, making her head ache, was the appalling doubt that everything was as normal as it seemed. Where was Julian, what had happened next? She should never have left. She was furious with herself for following his orders so meekly. If only she had insisted on going back with him. But he had been so decisive when she had had no idea what to do next. In the heat of the moment she had let him override her better judgement. Just like so many other times, whispered a sly voice in her head.

Elizabeth closed her eyes. What did she actually remember of the previous night? Did the two of them, Adie and she, really see Veronica on the rocks? Yes. The mermaid dress was so distinctive. Was Veronica sitting or standing? Sitting. Did she seem agitated or calm? Earlier she had been drunk and truculent. Did she argue with Julian when he went down to her? There were raised voices. Did she threaten to hurl herself off the rocks and he ignored her? Julian was not ignoring her. Did she go into the water? There was a splash, followed soon after by another. Was there a tussle and she slipped into the sea? It was impossible for Elizabeth to know. Did Veronica try to swim? Again, impossible to know.

Had Julian been in time to take the boat out and find her in the water?

Or was Veronica still missing?

The letter. If she was still missing, it would be her fault.

Elizabeth shivered. She should never have done such a stupid thing. Of all of them, Veronica might not have been the most unhappy, but she was quite possibly the one most out of control. Here was a woman, twice divorced and a heavy drinker, become child-like in her need, and unable to imagine the consequences of her actions.

She forced herself to breathe calmly.

Surely the most likely answer was that Veronica had crawled back to the party, dripping wet and crazed. A bed would have been found for her, and she would have spent the day suffering.

Elizabeth fervently hoped that was the case.

There was of course another possibility: that Adie, having found Veronica, had allowed her to persuade him to spend the night with her. Both salt and wound. But in the circumstances, Elizabeth began to think that might not be the worst outcome.

S till he did not appear, or even telephone. By early evening, Elizabeth was in such a state of agitation that she got ready as if she was due to meet him, allowing Clive and Mary to assume this was the case, and took the water bus to Agni. From there she walked up to the olive press. No one was there. Neither was he in any of the local tavernas. She walked over the headland and down into Kalami, even stopping to ask one man outside a boathouse if he had seen Adie that day. Darkness fell, but she did not find him.

Back at Kouloura much later, feeling shrunken and with uncomfortable intimations of guilt, she considered asking Clive for some telephone numbers of Adie's friends on the island but stopped short of doing so. It seemed wrong to alert anyone else to whatever it was that had happened. This was between the two of them; she needed to talk to him without provoking questions.

Mary knew something was wrong. 'You're such a lovely girl,' she said. 'Don't let yourself be hurt by him.'

Elizabeth spent a second sleepless night.

E arly morning the next day, the news spread fast through the villages.

Mary, holding loaves of fresh bread from a shop in Kassiope, told her, 'There's been a drowning. The fishermen at the Forty Winds found a body.'

Elizabeth trembled, hardly able to breathe as she asked, 'Who?'

'They don't know yet.'

'Man . . . or woman?'

'Woman.'

She had been washed up on a narrow beach of white stones. The body was encased in a gleaming skin of silvery scales. The fishermen thought they had found a sleeping mermaid, with her blue-white skin and matted tendrils of dark hair. On the Nereid's face and upper arms were plum smudges of deep bruising.

H e was there, this time, at the olive press. Her first instinct was to open her arms to him, grateful he was safe.

When I heard about the body – I thought it might have been you! You went off into the dark and then . . . nothing! she wanted to cry. But she did not. She knew not to even before he said anything.

In the doorway, Adie was unshaven and shuffling. For the first time, he seemed his age.

'You'd better come in,' he mumbled.

The room was in disarray. A piece of paper stuck up half-ripped from the roller of his old typewriter. The poems he had been working on were litter on the floor, torn, defaced and crumpled.

No mention was made of his avoidance of her. Elizabeth wanted to say that any guilt was irrational. They had not made Veronica follow them, had wanted no part of her silly games. But again she kept her thoughts to herself.

'What happened?'

Adie lit a cigarette. The ashtray on the table was overflowing, the smell from old butts acrid. She pulled up a chair opposite him.

'I sat down on the rock with her,' he said. 'I told her I would take her back to the party, take her home, whatever she wanted. But what she wanted was to sit on the damn rock and give me hell.'

'What was she saying?'

'She just wanted an argument.'

'So you argued?'

He shrugged.

'Why did she jump into the water?'

'She wanted me to swim with her.'

It was only then that Elizabeth realised. 'You'd brought her there before, hadn't you?'

A reluctant nod.

So much for being special, thought Elizabeth. 'So then what happened?'

'I bloody well jumped in after her. She was so off her rocker she had no idea how dangerous it was!'

'Were you still arguing?'

'I'm sure I was arguing with her.'

'They say she had bruise marks all up her arms,' said Elizabeth. The picture was in her head all the time. The silvery body washed up on the beach.

'I was trying to fish her out – she was struggling against me, the stupid, stupid woman. She was far too drunk to know what she was doing.' A vein was bulging on his neck.

Elizabeth hesitated. It was only for a split second.

'You don't believe me!' he shouted, turning on her.

His hand closed on her wrist, pulling her roughly in to him.

'You're hurting me! Of course I believe you. I was there, wasn't I?'

He let her go. 'Sorry.'

In an instant, he was so subdued she wondered if he had slipped back into the raw grief he had only recently overcome. His blue shirt was stiff and stank of stale salt water.

'It was an accident,' she said soothingly. 'A terrible accident that you did your best to prevent. I heard you splash into the water after her.'

He was tossing down glass after glass of foul retsina. It was on his breath as he spoke. She noticed his hands were trembling as he described how he ran back to Nissaki to get the boat. All night he had gone up and down the coast searching for her, torch in hand, outboard motor gunning. The night fishermen had joined him. No one had seen or heard anything.

'So – the police? They know all this?'

'They know.'

There was nothing more to be said. She reached out and put a hand on his broad shoulder.

Eyes deep blue, in the face that now seemed creased, he fixed her with an unreadable gaze. Seconds passed.

Her gaze dropped to the binoculars on the messy table. The strap had snapped and the rough ends were tied.

'We had better not be seen together any more,' he said.

She was aghast. 'Why? We've done nothing wrong. Surely we just have to tell someone – the police – exactly what happened! That she followed us from the party and we know when and where she went into the water.'

He did not answer.

'Julian?'

'No.'

'No? Why not?'

'We can't, that's all.'

She stood astonished. 'But . . . why?'

Elizabeth started to shake.

He stood up. 'I'm leaving tonight. I'm going back to France.'

'I don't understand . . .'

He pushed his hands deep into the pockets of his baggy jeans. 'I can't stick it here now.'

'No . . .' She looked away from him and saw for the first time the tatty suitcase open on the floor, filled with bundled swirls of cotton clothes.

'It hasn't been the best way to—' He rubbed his sticky hair, embarrassed perhaps.

'Will I see you again?' she interrupted. But she would not, could not, say, *Don't go.*

He shook his head. 'Who knows?'

The temperature dropped. He was closed off to her. She had no way of bringing back the man she had known for the past two months. That was not the person standing in front of her, a shrunken man who would not meet her eyes. Her heart was pounding as she stepped back instinctively.

'You want me to go then?'

Silence.

'Let me help you,' said Elizabeth. 'It will be all right!'

'You can't.'

He was dismissing her.

The realisation stunned her. She wanted to turn the clock back. To dive into sunlit water with him. To hold him like before.

'Whatever happens, I will never forget this summer—' she whispered.

But Julian turned his back.

Swallowing her pride, her voice breaking, she reminded him of the name of the gallery in London through which he could contact her. She gave him a brush of her lips on the side of his mouth, and left.

She was empty, numb. Elizabeth did not confide her discomfort to the Stilwells. Not even to Clive, who would have brought his gentle certainties to bear on her distress. To do so would have meant revealing the extent of her feelings for Julian Adie, and by implication, the truth about her affair with him. She was caught: on the one hand feeling too young and inexperienced to have entangled herself in such adult games; and on the other too mature to be seeking a second opinion of the manoeuvrings like an adolescent.

The loss of the baby, of David and the married life that never was, the future that would not be; all returned now, intensified in a swift blow. But far worse was the certainty that the golden summer with Julian was over.

It began that evening, the odd pressing in of fear, like a low-level hum. The bruise around her wrist throbbed. Was it guilt as much as misery that was driving Adie away from Corfu? In any case, shouldn't he stay while there was some kind of official investigation? Had he told her the whole truth about what had happened that night? Elizabeth pushed the suspicion away immediately. But it gnawed at her assumptions.

How angry he had been when he accused her of not believing him. His hand tight as a vice on her wrist.

'You're hurting me! Of course I believe you. I was there,

wasn't I?' she had cried. It was only afterwards, long afterwards, that she realised that only one of those statements was
completely true. The pain around her wrist left the imprint
of a livid dark bruise which took a long time to fade.

E lizabeth left Corfu at the end of August.
   By then she was haunted by images of the pinched face
and the silver dress being swallowed by the blackness. The
strange cruel gods of the sea that always frolicked close to
any haven Julian Adie made from mortality. She missed him
and their dazzling dream world with a wrenching ache.

Julian Adie, Behind the Myth
Martin Braxton

The weather turned suddenly on 20 August 1968. Adie stood alone on the stone jetty, his back to the White House as the storm struck. The sea was a sheet of crow-black sullenness, rippled like mourning crêpe. Darts of cold rain pierced the cotton of his shirt.

For a second time he was leaving this place harried by the knowledge that his paradise had imploded.

He knew what happened when a human drowned. His meticulous and macabre description of a death at sea is the centrepiece of *The Cairo Triptych*. He was intimately acquainted with the physiological process by which water began to enter the lungs, followed by a brief period of laryngospasm – the desperate tightening of the vocal cords – which kept the inrush at bay for a few vital minutes, but then, when the force of the sea engulfed the lungs, the lack of oxygen to the brain and body tissues. In long heady sentences his prose builds and swells as he recreates the waves of panic, the minute composition of the bacteria, algae, sand and microscopic sea life in the mouthfuls of water, the frantic fatal gulps. The terrible suffocation as the body remains submerged, the trauma and collapse of the central nervous system, the stopping of the heart.

Julian Adie's dark side was habitually concealed under the gilt of sociability and laughter. It emerged most often in the work, but it could be unleashed at any time. Since childhood, when he was bullied for his lack of height, he had had a propensity for violence, both physical and emotional.

Surveying the water which, the day before, had carried the body of Veronica Rae before nudging it ashore on Avlaki beach south of Kassiope, Adie must surely have thought back to that other departure, decades before in the teeth of war: south first to Athens, then on to Egypt, alone.

The Cairo he found was a hellhole. The city cowered under the *khamseen*, the hot spring winds that blew up, sand-laden, from the Sahara to the south. The sky was dun-coloured with choking grit that swirled into every weak spot, the eyes, the mouth and nose, the psyche. The traffic was unspeakable, fouled and confounded by animals wandering in its midst.

Life was cheap and brutal. Teeming crowds deformed by disease and poverty snagged on beggars' bony feet as they passed. Shrouds of black flies covered dead bodies in the streets. Goats and strings of camels silted up the streets with defecation.

Yet being alone had its advantages. Adie launched himself day and night into finding work and somewhere to live, calling as ever on contacts and friends of friends, tapping, perhaps more confidently than he felt, into the British Council and diplomatic network. He was still only twenty-seven, and possessed of huge energy, an endless stream of entertaining anecdotes, a capacity for serious discussion too, of literature and philosophy, and a cast-iron head for liquor. It was not long before his powers of persuasion, added to his fluent Greek and brief experience working in propaganda in Athens, landed him a junior post in the Foreign Press department at the British Embassy.

Cairo began to open up for him. At night, lights blazed. Every exotic delicacy was on offer, from the restaurants packed with locals and Europeans, to the plethora of brothels catering for every taste and perversion. Despite the bombing of the harbour at Alexandria, it was an open city and as such did not come under attack. The atmosphere was a heady mix of guilty excitement and seediness, from which death was only ever a few paces away, where stained and patched-up soldiers came in from the desert battlefields to seek oblivion from the fighting.

Adie was a fixture at the Black Mamba club, not far from the smart Shepheard's Hotel, on the terrace of which the supply of pre-war champagne and hock served to those who could afford it, did not run dry until 1943.

'He would stand barely taller than the top of the bar, glass always in hand, mesmerised by the abdominal rippling of a particularly abundantly fleshed belly dancer named Hekmat,' recalled Bernard Bressens, British Council official, would-be poet and one of the new circle Adie met at the Anglo-Egyptian Union, another establishment to promote closer cultural understanding, in this instance through literary debate. 'He was dedicated to the idea of encountering as many women of as many different nationalities as he could, and as far as I saw, he enjoyed unparalleled success. He never spoke about a wife.'

This was a time and a place where beggars with weeping sores shivered outside Shepheard's and offered their sisters for sale, a clash of cultures where anything was available to be discovered by those with money or curiosity, or a taste for human abasement. For the foreigners in the city there were no moral constraints: no rules; no families to embarrass; no past form to live up to. Julian Adie embraced it all: the atmosphere, the license.

It afforded him the freedom to explore a new erotic landscape in a way he could scarcely have imagined on his rock in Corfu. In that sense, he was never to return.

Part Six: Landlocked

I

The *bergerie* was a modest low-slung farm building. It was built into an escarpment so that the hill rose from the first floor at the rear which gave a sense of protected privacy to the stone, barn-like structure that Elizabeth always talked about extending, but never did.

Its land, a couple of acres on a scrubby hillside, was scented by wild lavender, thyme and rosemary baked and dried in the wind and sun. Pine needles and blown olive leaves crunched underfoot. Then the view opened: orange earth, rocks, green slopes and indigo hills.

The key stuck, the way it always did.

The house looked the same as ever. Melissa expected Elizabeth to call out to her at any moment; she felt her presence at her shoulder, at the end of the corridor, outside the kitchen door. This refuge had been a constant of her childhood. Her parents had bought it together a long time ago, so long ago that she had never wondered how they had ever come here in the first place. Long summers had been idled away here, and one hard biting winter of mistral and floods, the year her father died.

Missing her physical presence rather than his, Melissa welled up, not at the sight of the chair where Elizabeth would sit, but at the sight of a geranium straining itself into life on the tiny terrace outside the kitchen, and the sunny patch of garden where her mother had tried so doggedly to cultivate bushes of red hibiscus but succeeded only with pale pink.

Melissa was thrown, and vulnerable. But she knew that coming here was the right thing to do.

'Are you going to keep the house?' Richard had asked when she first suggested making the trip.

It hadn't occurred to her to do otherwise.

In the April after Elizabeth died, the southern breezes were already warm. Wild flowers splashed colour over the meadows. The Languedoc is rough and rugged country: a hard-thorn land where the sun beats with a pulse, heating and rushing the blood.

This is the Roman province, the *Provincia*, south-west of Nîmes, reputedly the hottest town in France, not the tamed expensive land to the east of Avignon most people call Provence. The great aqueduct of the Pont du Gard arches over these valleys, the amphitheatres still used for bull-fighting. True, stark white developments now lured droves of budget holidaymakers to the coast due south, but inland little had changed from the hamlet where Melissa had grown up, summer by summer. There was nothing to entice visitors to St Cyrice, only a homely bar-restaurant, and a small grocery store.

The *garrigue* is all around: scrublands of thorns and wild herbs, scorched grass and holm oaks; dry ochre soil, so pitiful it seems miraculous that any plant could grow here, so barely does it cover the rock it lies on. Where the earth has stuck fast, the ground is cut by torrent beds from the winter rains. The plateau under the high limestone ridge of the Pic St Loup is an imperious presence, its cruel scraped fingers pointing up to the heavens. The landscape is pitted with caves and craters, and deep erosive wounds.

S he had forgiven Richard, it seemed.
He brought the cases in from the car.

'Is everything OK?' he asked. He meant inside the house.

'Appears to be,' she said, meaning everything, and wondering if that could really be true. She turned on the tap at the sink. It spluttered and choked up brown water. She waited until it ran clearer then splashed her face.

It was always like this when they arrived for the first visit of the year. Cobwebs swung from the beams. A scent of dried herbs struggled against the stronger smell of dust and damp and mouse which would dissipate as soon as the shutters were flung out and windows opened. Last year's flies were crispy black corpses on the drainer. Already there was a faint hum from new battalions.

They looked at each other.

'It will be all right,' he said. 'We'll do lots of trips – to the caves, maybe.'

The first time she brought him here they went to the Grotte des Demoiselles. They climbed aboard a funicular railway which carried them deep inside the mountain peak, so cold and far that she was glad he was with her among the stalagmites and stalactites.

Melissa nodded, looking him in the eye, remembering all the good times here together. 'Lots of long lunches . . .'

He took her hand.

'We could go to St Martin.'

They closed together, travel-grimy and safe. He kissed her deeply, and she kissed him back.

Anger stowed away, recriminations suppressed, Melissa had allowed him to hold her during the bleakest winter months. Not to forget, but to take the first steps towards the forgiveness that is supposed to be the purest balm. Her doubts were stilled by the sad certainty that it would be a long journey back.

But the truth was that her emotions were a brew of grief and contradiction where Richard was concerned. There was no point in her friends saying she was grieving for the end of her marriage as well as her mother. She knew the difference, could feel it, and they did not. She had not lost him for ever.

'I know it will take a long time,' she admitted to Leonie. 'I will be suspicious. It will take a lot to get the trust back. But I'm prepared for that.'

She supposed that was natural. It was amazing how it could be possible to carry on in an apparently normal routine, filling the day with practicalities, and not addressing the crisis. They had agreed they should have a serious discussion at the end of three months, and now it had been four, both afraid of what might be said, what might fly out of the box.

They took it easy the first few days. Melissa, alone, told their village friends the sad news and checked the boundaries of the land, the two acres of scrub and trees.

Brown bears and wolves still staked their territory in these parts, according to village talk. Certainly there was wild boar. Early on, a neighbour, Monsieur Lechal, advised Elizabeth against planting a row of hazel near the potager, as they were too much of a lure for the boar.

Melissa had a knowledge of the local customs and lore gathered over the years from their neighbours. The way the farmers cut wood for building at full moon when the sap was high, and wood for fuel at new moon when the sap was low, for example. The way they would only grow Jerusalem artichokes for family consumption, never to be sold at market because people grew tired of them during the war when the Nazis requisitioned French crops for their armies but habitually rejected those mysterious knobbly tubers.

You needed at least two relatives lying in the churchyard before you could be considered a local. But for Melissa it was still a home, a constant, a repository of memories.

'We should put in a better pool,' said Richard. 'And finally do that extension your mother used to talk about, when we get the money from Bell Cottage. This is such a fantastic location – it could be a spectacular house.'

Melissa kept quiet.

'This is when it's a good thing to be an only child,' he continued. 'No one else in the family who has to be bought out or compromised with. We can do exactly what we want and no family arguments.'

Actually she liked it as it was. 'I don't see much point in changing it too much if I'm not going to sell it.'

'Might want to rent it out for some of the summer though. It would be a good income, especially if you don't want to go back to work.'

'I will go back to work. But I need a change. I don't want to go back to where I was. I want to find a project, perhaps on a freelance basis.'

He still did not seem to understand how fundamentally she had been re-evaluating her life this past year, and how far he had prompted that. It was too easy to blame it all on Elizabeth's illness and then her death.

He took himself off happily to swimming pool constructors, and had several local builders come round to give quotes. Over bottles of red wine in the evenings, he grew expansive along with his plans.

Words and plans flowed over her as if she had dived in and was swimming underwater already. They were both trying, but there was still a barrier between them. Melissa was starting to think it was her fault.

In bed one morning, he reached out and pulled her to him. His hand was warm and heavy on her hip.

'Let's go to St Martin today.'

The pressure of his hand, how easily she could shift position and turn it to pleasure. His blue-green eyes were soft, and sincere.

St Martin.

At St Martin de Londres, a village that grew in medieval times from an earlier priory, 'Londres' has nothing to do with London, as she had once thought. It derives from the Occitan word for swamp, which then begs the question whether the French for London is a sneaky Gallic joke.

It is a gorgeous place, with its vanilla stone and cobbled passageways. The Place de la Fontaine is the entrance to an ancient world. When monks first arrived they were looking for hardship and suffering, faith being founded on survival. They chose the rocky barren valleys and inhospitable peaks to prove themselves and their determination to worship, and came in that spirit to the 'swamp', the boggy marshlands which surrounded it. Hardship was the price of heaven.

Richard and Melissa were married in St Martin. First there was a brief administrative ceremony at the Mairie, then they led the wedding party through the vaulted passage up from the square, to the church where the marriage was blessed.

They drove there in quiet good spirits, Richard at the wheel. The way he drove was one of the things she had always liked about him: fast but safe, and with surprising consideration for other people on the road.

In sidelong glances, she reassured herself. He was still the same person she had loved for so long. The tousled light brown hair, the pleasant profile as he concentrated, the iridescent chip of one blue-green eye, the mole on his left cheekbone; he was just the same.

She had a sense of the landscape expanding to cradle all within it: the vast *garrigue*, the perched hillside villages, the region's long-horned sheep, and Pyrenean fawns, beaver and otter in the rivers, all lay beating under the sun.

The Romanesque church of St Martin de Londres was deserted. Melissa felt a stab of sadness as she took in the familiar pattern of arches on the rounded exterior; the porch decorated with a weatherworn relief of St Martin himself that she knew so well; and inside, the clover-shaped floor plan.

Richard put his arm round her waist and they moved up to the altar. Empty space where the pews had once contained their families and friends, all bright silks and hats, and the anticipation of a grand celebration. She knew what he was trying to say.

'Nearly seven years,' he whispered.

She was silent.

He put his lips gently on her neck. A tingle ran along her collarbone. But beneath it was something unsettling. The sensation of a creeping panic. She willed herself to feel the romance of the moment, the vibrations from the past, when they had stood on this very spot with such happiness and certainty.

She felt nothing. She could not let herself go, could not bear to think of the hope they'd once had. It was all too unbearably sad.

'We should have had a child by now,' said Richard.

'But you never wanted children!' The words burst out of her mouth before the thought had been processed. 'You always said—!'

'That was then.'

The silence thickened.

'Say something.' His voice was urgent.

Melissa was so angry she could not speak. Tight with rage and disappointment, she could not begin to explain how he was making her feel.

Shakily, she shook her head.

'It could be just what we need – what do you say, Lissa? A baby? Don't you want to have a child?'

'Do you?' The incredulity was plain to hear in her voice: a voice that did not seem to be coming from her; reedy in the echoing chapel.

'Yes, I do.'

It was a punch in the heart. If he had wanted children, years ago, before it was too late for her (was it too late for her?) then maybe both their lives would have taken different courses. Stupid supposition. Of course they would. Once, right at the beginning, she had nurtured a fantasy that one day their children might explore the garden and splash in the pool at St Cyrice just as she had done, bringing their friends, making new ones in the village. She had come to terms with knowing it was not likely to happen. She had simply become used to the idea that having children was a closed door, for her; blocked it up and accepted that their life together was enough. Only latterly it hadn't been, for him.

Now the idea formed that he could go off and have children with a different woman, a younger woman, and the thought of it tied her stomach in knots as surely as if he had punched her there too.

'How could we have a child now, after all that has happened?'

'Well maybe not *now* – but in a while—'

In a while she would be forty.

'You have no idea what you're saying, do you?'

'I thought we were trying again – I thought it might—'

'Thought? You don't think!'

He made a noise that let her know his patience was threadbare. But if he was offended, then she was doubly so. She wanted to scream at him.

'You have no idea what you're saying, what the reality of a child would mean – providing security, for a start.'

His hands dropped away. He turned and left.

She heard the aggression in his footsteps on the stone, but did not turn round. Heart pounding, she stood alone at the altar.

Was she being unreasonable? Oh God, probably she was. If they were really going to try again, she was going to have to give more ground, engage with him fully again. Run! Run after him! But then she remembered his betrayal and was stuck to the spot.

It was not supposed to happen like this. They were supposed to walk together through the past, and emerge from the church for a glass of champagne, another set of promises – more intimate this time – and order an indulgent lunch. They should have been touching hands, meeting eyes, sharing delicious food and rebuilding. It was not going to happen, and this time it really was her fault.

She could not unbend. She could not forgive, and she certainly could not forget. So much for the wedding vows.

Long, silent minutes after his footsteps had stopped ringing on the flags, she found her way out. Dazzled by the shift in light, she waited in the porch, wondering where he had gone.

He was not in the bar-café on the square which was the obvious place to look. The square itself was empty. On market days it was crammed with people and stalls, a confusion of produce: gleaming purple-black aubergines, wooden pails of olives, tomatoes like scarlet cushions, the cheese lorry, chickens turning on the mobile rotisserie.

She missed her mother, and in another sudden shaft of pain, wondered what it would have been like to have a daughter of her own. Tried – and failed – to imagine what she might have looked like, what her personality might have been, what she would have made of her life.

A bench under the plane trees was empty. Aromas of frying garlic and roasting meat from a nearby doorway were fanned by a breeze that made the leaves rustle high above the little village square.

Around a corner, he was talking urgently into his mobile.

'Who are you calling?' she asked, before thinking.

'Work,' he snapped.

'I see.'

'I might have to go back. Or get myself to a meeting in Paris at any rate.'

She said nothing, felt nothing.

The telephone call came as Melissa was scrubbing the kitchen floor, a penitent scouring at her own failings.

Richard had gone shopping alone where normally they would have enjoyed going together. 'I will have to go to Paris,' he'd informed her as he took the car keys. He left without another word.

If she had not been so sure it was Richard, ringing to say he was sorry, she wouldn't have answered the telephone.

'Hello?' she said, sniffing.

'May I please speak with Elizabeth Norden?' A smooth male voice, the accent American.

Melissa explained.

'And you are?' came his response.

'Taken aback by your directness,' she snapped, in no mood for any conversation. 'Who are *you*?'

'This is Dr Braxton, of the University of Michigan. I'm

currently in France researching a new biography of the British writer Julian Adie.'

That caught her off-guard. She sank down on to a nearby chair. 'I see . . . and why would that—?'

'Are you a friend of Elizabeth Norden?'

'I'm her daughter.'

'Ah. May I know your name?'

Sweat trickled down her back. Her arms ached from scrubbing. The room seemed to darken. She told him because she could not see how she could avoid it. She was also thinking rapidly of how odd it was that a stranger should call out of the blue, and yet who might be the one person who could answer her questions – questions she had spent the past few months trying to dismiss as irrelevant now.

It seemed to be proof, if it were needed, that she had been on to something.

'Well, Melissa, this is a fairly delicate matter – it would be better if I came to see you. Would that be possible?'

'I'm not sure . . . you'll have to give me some idea what this is about.'

A sigh at the end of the line. 'This-s-s really would be better in person, believe me.'

'But it concerns my mother?'

'Yes, it does.'

Melissa hesitated.

'I wrote her last summer,' he continued. 'I don't know whether she got my letter of introduction?'

'I couldn't say.' That made her think, though.

Elizabeth's eyes glittering. Holding the book of poems, waving it upwards to say '*Take it, take it.* You need this.' But no words of explanation.

They made an arrangement to meet the following day, in the café in the next large village.

'I thought we might go down to the coast tomorrow,' said Richard, when he returned. His cold indifference seemed to have vanished. 'Are you on for that?'

'I can't tomorrow.'

He gave her a look as if to say, well, that's just typical of the way you are at the moment. He might even have been about to say it, but stopped himself. Instead he carried on into the kitchen with the shopping bags, shoulders hunched. She heard the crump of fruit and vegetables bruising on the table, the opening of the fridge and the hiss of a beer bottle being opened.

She had fully intended to tell him about Dr Braxton. She wanted someone to discuss it with – about how it was possible none of what she had found out about Elizabeth was by chance, how it might even have been Braxton who, indirectly, sent her to Corfu, by writing Elizabeth a letter. It had come too late for her to answer, but it was important enough for her mother to try to tell her. *Or maybe, to warn her.*

In the event, Melissa kept quiet. Perhaps she wanted her own secrets, as he had his. And just as Julian Adie had been her consolation in Corfu and the awful weeks following her return, so now perhaps his new biographer could provide fresh insights and he would be so again.

She wasn't surprised when Richard made another phone call and told her he would definitely have to get himself to the meeting in Paris. He left that night, with a show of annoyance and apologies. Melissa drove him to the train station at Nîmes and they parted with a dry kiss.

Alone that night Melissa reread Adie's poems. His voice spoke from the page every bit as persuasively as it had done before, evoking the images that seemed so resonant: the vacated rooms still scented with perfume, the lipstick on the drained glasses, the used twisted sheets; fierce passion distilled into austere lines on the page. She took curious comfort in the intimate alchemy of words, and what lay behind them – the proof that a man could behave badly yet still feel anguish at the hurt he had caused.

And the book itself, the *Collected Poems* her mother had given her, which she had brought to France hardly knowing why. Smoothing her hands over its shiny dust jacket, feeling the sharp corners of the pages, staring at his inscription and signature, visualising the man himself touching it, she wondered whether any forensic traces of him were embedded beyond the words: an invisible fingerprint, or an infinitesimal droplet of sweat from the side of his hand as he wrote.

Corfu was vivid in her mind again. It was sharp with colour and pain. She could not help but think of Alexandros. She would have liked to talk to him. To tell him what had happened, ask his advice. Could this Braxton be the same man who had been asking unwelcome questions in Kalami? There was never any doubt she would meet him.

II

The café at Les Matelles was a typical village establishment, with its high wooden bar, brown walls and posters advertising local events. Melissa felt instinctively that she should keep Dr Braxton, whoever he might be, on neutral ground.

For once she tried not to succumb to imagination, deliberately avoiding the temptation to construct a picture of him in her mind before she saw him. In the event, the reality was stranger than any caricature she could have devised.

The other side of a *citron pressé* at a table outside, a pip spit away from traffic rumbling through to somewhere more interesting, and where they were the only customers, Dr Braxton was surprisingly attired in the kind of candy striped jacket worn by a juvenile lead flapping a tennis racket in a nineteen thirties comedy. He was portly, in his late forties. His dark hair was retreating over a domed head, but colonising his lower face in a luxuriantly well-maintained beard. Steel-rimmed glasses framed protuberant blue-grey eyes and a large silver signet ring weighted the little finger of his left hand.

He stood up and they shook hands formally.

'So Melissa, what do you know about Julian Adie?' he opened after a few basic pleasantries. His manner was every bit as smooth as his voice on the telephone.

'Not very much, I'm afraid.'

Dr Braxton shifted forward with an intense look. 'Julian Adie is a gift and a challenge to the biographer,' he asserted as if beginning a lecture. 'Any academic study of his work has concluded, no matter how sorrowfully in the case of his fervent supporters – of whom there are many, including myself – that there was an enigma at the heart of the man.'

A sip of bitter lemon shrivelled the inside of her mouth.

'I have even begun to teach a class exploring the contradictions of his work, and the reversals of previously held viewpoints. To be frank, I am questioning and learning as much as my students.

'There have been many attempts to capture Adie in print, as it were, some more successful than others. He appears in a legion of books, memoirs and other biographies, a direct consequence of his friendships with other poets and writers, and no doubt, his charm as a man who made such an adventure of living.'

Any observation or pronouncement was made in a tone of complete self-confidence. Perhaps this was meant to be reassuring. Melissa suspected he was using the very words of one of his lectures. She wanted him to get to the point. Yet, clearly this was a man used to dictating the pace at which a discussion progressed, and exactly when a new fact would be revealed.

'Wasn't there a serious biography published a while back?' she asked casually. 'Surely it all was in there?'

She knew that was not true. She had proved it herself, inadvertently, frustratingly.

Dr Braxton leaned back, sticking his fine stomach out and pushing his glasses back up his nose and paused, assessing her reaction. 'Is Elizabeth Norden mentioned in th-a-a-a-at book?' His voice rose and a disconcertingly ovine vibrato broke through to give the pronoun a drilling extenuation.

Melissa stared, as if slapped. What had he found out? Was it much more than she knew?

Beads of sweat pimpled his forehead as he continued. 'Why isn't she mentioned? Because he made damn sure she never w-o-uld be mentioned! She could not be associated with him in any way because she *knew*!'

'Who are you talking about – Adie? *Adie* made sure, or the biographer made sure?'

'Adie, of course!'

'And . . . because . . . why, exactly?'

She was fighting to prevent any reaction showing on her face.

Dr Braxton reasserted vocal control, but answered her question only with another one. 'So the nub is, what do *yo-ou* know?' he asked.

'I'm sorry?'

'Do we both know what *I* know?'

The effect of this playground tactic in the circumstances, especially in view of his self-confessed eminence in the academic world and her own wariness, had the effect of making her laugh involuntarily.

Braxton pushed his glasses back to the bridge of his nose again with an index finger and waited intently.

'I really don't know what you are asking,' Melissa replied at last.

Wrists resting on the table, he made a steeple with his hands, then raised the structure to his upper lip. Great thoughts seemed to be accruing inside his domed head. They would have to be phrased to his satisfaction before release.

Seconds passed.

'I sent her another letter last fall. I don't suppose she got it.'

'She might have done.'

'She never said?'

'She was ill.'

Dr Braxton closed his eyes and breathed deeply into the steeple.

She watched him for several minutes, determined that she would give no more away.

At last he sighed and spoke:

'Julian Adie wrote some of the most lyrical, enchanting, life-enhancing celebrations of the human condition. He made personal myths of the places he went, the people he met. But the reality was his life never ran smoothly. Perhaps he wanted too much, too badly. The gifted golden youth of the nineteen thirties gave way year by year to a disillusioned, sour and bad-tempered old man. He had a bad reputation with women, which got worse as he got older. Some said he was violent. He was certainly given to messianic rages, especially when drunk.'

He darted furtive glances right and left, then leaned in to the table.

'So what happened to him – where did the beauty go, the healthy lust for life? Why did it turn to self-destruction? This had been puzzling me for years. Something happened, but what?'

Melissa sipped her drink, never taking her eyes off his. He gave a couple of toad-like blinks.

'Then, last year, thanks to the small reputation I have built up as a student and teacher of Adie's work, I was approached by a woman who claimed she was a friend of his daughter, Hero. She chose the simple expedient of sending an email to me at the university site. Would I be interested, she asked, in some papers which had belonged to Adie's daughter?

'Naturally, I was intrigued. I responded immediately, travelling to London to meet her the following weekend.

'I met . . . my contact in a public house in North London. She explained that the papers had been given to her by Hero Adie the year before she died. The two women had been good friends. Hero had extracted a promise that the package would be kept private until it was judged that Adie's reputation was once more in the ascendant.

'The papers were Hero's journals and diaries. These pages stated crudely – but backed by a mass of circumstantial evidence – that Julian Adie was a cruel and violent man. In fact . . . he killed a woman.'

He stopped there, wanting to see her reaction.

Melissa tried hard not to give him one. 'And this is what you have been investigating? I can see it would make an astonishing new take on Adie's life.'

'Astonishing? It's explosive!' The voice went squeaky again.

'But . . . Hero Adie – she committed suicide, didn't she? She was a troubled young woman. She might not have been making a rational judgement.'

'It might not be true, you mean?'

'Do you have proof?' asked Melissa.

'That's what I'm working on.'

'How far have you got?'

But it was a question too many. He was the one trying to get answers. He crossed his arms and blinked.

'It must be libellous,' she said. 'The dead can't defend themselves.'

'Neither can they sue for libel, that's for sure.'

There was a charged pause.

'I'm not about to write anything that cannot be justified. I am not about to destroy my own academic reputation with some ill-conceived notion.'

'I really don't think I know anything that can help you.'

'You could talk to me about your mother.'

Melissa took a deep breath. 'But why would I want to do that?'

'Well . . .' The tone of his voice was disturbing. Again he pushed the glasses back up to the bridge of his nose with a forefinger.

Her hands were shaking. She hid them quickly under the table. 'Are you trying to say that she knew about a murder? Because that is just . . . unbelievable. If you knew anything about her, you would realise that.'

'But I don't know her,' he pointed out. There was a hint of a threat in his words. 'That's why I would very much like to talk to you about her.'

He stared intently and, heart thudding, Melissa realised how clever he had been. He had never even asked if her mother had ever been associated with Julian Adie. But somehow the fact of it was under discussion.

She had nowhere to go but to say, 'She would not have been party to anything that harmed another person – or even an animal. It was not in her character.'

'I'm not saying that.'

'What then?'

'Simply that . . . she was one of the people who was known to have been with him, the summer it happened.'

Clenching her hands, remembering Elizabeth's gentleness, Melissa stared into his thick glasses. Her own reflection coiled tight in each lens.

'What do you know about the *Songs of Blue and Gold*, Melissa?'

'Songs of blue and gold?' She had never heard of them.

Dr Braxton observed her reaction with fierce concentration. 'Your mother never spoke about them, ever?'

'No.'

He eased back a little, but in the manner of an actor. 'What if I were to say to you that Julian Adie confessed?'

'It would mean nothing to me.'

There was a pause. 'I am going to give you my card. I would sincerely ask you to consider whether . . . there is a possibility . . . you would allow me to see Elizabeth Norden's papers.'

He slid the card across the table. She let it lie there, with its string of academic endorsements and a list of telephone numbers.

It was only then it occurred to her. 'How did you get my telephone number?'

'It was on a letter from her to him, in university archives.'

The number for the *bergerie* was the same as it had ever been. 'And her address here too, I suppose?'

'She wrote him many times when he was living in Sommières. She used to go see him there.'

Melissa felt winded. What else was she about to discover

about her mother? How was it that complete strangers knew more of Elizabeth's life than she did? The questions were profoundly unnerving.

She stood up, cornered but ready to fight. Somehow she managed to sound almost normal. 'You will have to let me think about this. And let me do it in my own time. If I am going to help you, I will contact you not the other way round. Do you understand that?'

He inclined his head. In his beard was a damp pink half-smile like a tiny newborn animal in a nest.

M elissa drove back to St Cyrice, shaken.
Would Dr Braxton appear unannounced at the door of the *bergerie*? He had disturbed her peace of mind, already fragile as it was. She was rattled, and resentful that there was nowhere to hide from him.

He was looking for papers, but Elizabeth did not have any papers, as such. Not in the sense that he meant. As an academic he seemed to have lost sight of the fact that most people were not like the old writers he studied; they did not keep documents of every encounter, correspondence with other old writers, journals and philosophical exchanges. If any of Elizabeth's papers did exist, they would only have been records of pictures sold or designs executed in other people's houses. And these would have been in the house in Kent. But Melissa had cleared the study, the desk with its bulging drawers, the cupboard and the bookshelves. There had been very little of interest to find.

At six o'clock Melissa phoned Richard.

'Are you coming back?'

'Of course. It was only a couple of meetings. You knew it was always on the cards that I'd have to go back at some stage. At least it's only as far as Paris. I'll be back soon.'

He seemed able to act as if nothing had changed, whereas for her, everything had altered.

'Tomorrow?' she asked, dreading the answer.

'With any luck,' he said.

D r Martin Braxton. Who was he, and was he trustworthy? Melissa was used to dealing with facts. She was thrown by the messiness, the probable unreliability of human testimony.

She thought about her own trail to find Elizabeth's connection to Adie in Corfu. Manolis and Eleni; the memory of their unconditional kindness made her smile. She wondered how Alexandros was, how his trip to Egypt had gone – and what had happened with his wife. She wished she could speak to him. She wanted to tell him about her encounter with Braxton – Alexandros might have provided her with some desperately-needed reassurance, but his number and email address were in a drawer back in England.

III

It was extraordinary that she had not made the connection before. She had realised, of course, that Sommières – Julian Adie's last and longest-standing place of exile – was close to Nîmes, but not that it was so close to where she was now.

But there it was on the Michelin map: mid-way between Montpelier and Nîmes, barely twenty kilometres away: the small town where Adie lived for thirty years.

If Dr Braxton was in the south of France, this had to be the trail he was following. Melissa had no idea what she was looking for, only that – for Elizabeth's sake – she had to keep up with him.

As she had managed so many times before, she put all thoughts of Richard out of her head, and got in the car. Taking the main road across the *garrigue*, she was in Sommières in a little over half an hour.

The proud Roman bridge of stone arched across the Vidourle river, each leg with its own elegant smaller arch which reflected in the water as a teardrop. A V-shaped weir broke the water's smooth glassiness.

On the hill above, wearing a rolled sleeve of trees, rose a tall defensive tower, square and strong, as if the old town were flexing a bicep, in a warning not to overlook its strength and purpose.

Melissa turned on to the embankment road and parked.

The river was green and sluggish. Large brown fish drifted fitfully, until they fought for deeper water near the Bar Vidourle, a café-bar with a terrace across the road hanging over the river.

Sommières was not a smart little town made bijou for Parisians and northern tourists. This was a place of crumbling stones and fortunes, of tall narrow alleyways, cool and damp, with the smell of drains, built on Roman walls and ramparts. Some of these medieval passages were buttressed by primitive arches of pitted stone; walking through them was a country dance under linked arms.

These houses had been inhabited for centuries. Generations of families squeezed into damp, angular spaces. In one passage, washing was strung across from an upper window. A history and continuity prevailed, but not the one she was looking for.

At the ends of alleys were bright snapshots of the streets running across: the red awning of a newsagents bearing the ubiquitous masthead of the *Midi Libre*; a kebab shop from which came the aroma of grilling meat. On all sides, sun-blistered plaster cracked into mosaic.

The main square was signposted: La Place Jean Jaurès.

Ice-cream parlours and bars reached out to visitors, but the bustle seemed purposeful and home-grown. Above the shops, plaster facades were patched and peeling. Shuttered windows hinted at mysterious interiors.

Melissa went on through, her eyes drawn upwards. By a church, balustraded terraces rose up to the castle and to the blue ribbon of the sky. Inside, high above, noon's bright hot light pushed and pulsated through intricate stained glass. She emerged blinking. Opposite, a house formed the corner of the alley, its stucco in such a state of decay that a rusting metal strut was exposed, evidence of previous repairs decades ago. A metal street sign, raw and powdery brown with rust, announced the Rue Docteur Chrestien (1758–1840).

A screech came from a blue-painted window. Behind a screen of chicken wire was a jungle of willow and olive branches, in the middle of which sat a huge macaw, green and blue, and squawking out its raucous commentary.

A few steps away hid l'Ancienne Impasse du Paradis. A round sticker of a dollar sign had been smacked on it. Below, a silver spray of graffiti read *Screw You* in jagged psychotic letters. It had competition across the narrow street, where a great devil head in red snarled from a facing wall, with the legend to the side of one jutting cheekbone: *On sort faire des bêtises* – we go out making mischief.

She suspected Julian Adie would have been amused by that.

Then, back in the Place Jean Jaurès, she saw it.

Stuck to the glass of a shop door was a small poster advertising an exhibition of sculpture, currently running at the Espace Julian Adie.

She pushed at the door and it opened with a smooth click and the ping of a bell.

Inside it was a narrow *librairie*, lined with shelves of magazines and books, stationery and plastic toys. The smell of paper and felt pens brought back breaths of her childhood.

'Can I help?' The woman behind the counter wore half-moon reading spectacles perched on her head like sunglasses. Her expression managed to convey helpful efficiency as well as abruptness.

'I'd like a street map, please.'

She indicated a circular stand. 'We have a selection.'

Melissa pulled out a couple and chose the one which had the largest scale.

'The arts centre, L'Espace Julian Adie – is it marked on here?' Melissa asked as the woman handed her some coins in change.

'I'm not sure. May I?' She opened the map, and reached for a pen. 'Here.' She indicated a street near the castle. 'Would you like me to mark it?'

'Yes, please. Will it be open now?'

A brief glance at a slip of a watch on her slim wrist. 'It should be.'

Melissa thanked her and turned to leave. But as there was no one else in the shop, she took the chance to ask, 'Excuse me, do people still remember Julian Adie well?'

The woman pouted slightly, then patted the top of her head as if to reassure herself the glasses were still there. 'M'sieur Adie, he was a famous English writer. He lived here for many years. But he died . . . oh, fifteen, twenty years ago now.'

'But people here still remember him?'

'The older ones, yes.' How could it be otherwise, her eyes

seemed to say. She was on the point of dismissing her, when she added, 'There is a small collection of his books and diaries on display there. If you're interested you should take a look.'

'Thank you. I will.'

A fractious yapping that can only have come from a small, spoilt dog could be heard the other side of an open door at the back of the *librairie*, calling its mistress to heel. 'I'm coming, I'm coming, *chéri*,' she cooed.

Melissa took her cue and left with the map.

Here and there were building works, the restoration of ancient houses, *Chantier interdit au public*, as if the public were there in any numbers to press its collective nose against the slats in the wooden barrier.

On one unprepossessing wooden door was a fly-speckled board showing faded photographs of women wearing feathers and bikinis. It was the portal to an old-fashioned Théâtre-Cabaret, open solely on Saturday nights. The pictures might have been taken thirty years before. The women in the pictures might now be pouchy grandmothers, still bumping and grinding out their routine for the same mechanics and farm workers who had slept with them at eighteen.

Further on, a bar pumped out pungent curls of Gauloise smoke, and strong coffee.

A window far above exuded the faint melody of a song she recognised. Her footsteps padded across stone to its rhythm.

And then, just as she was wondering how much further it was, Julian Adie was right in front of her. A vast banner unfurled his face, half-smiling, down the side of an austere solid stone building. A few steps led up to a cobbled court-yard, where a tall, blue-grey door stood open. Inside that, was L'Espace Julian Adie, the town's arts centre.

Melissa went up.

Through the door was a high vaulted hall in bare brick and stone. The space was filled by metallic sculptures. A thin young woman in a short black tunic stood just inside, by a desk covered in leaflets.

She looked up but did not smile.

Melissa did. 'Hello. I understand you have an exhibition of Julian Adie's books here?' She made it a question, for politeness' sake.

'The permanent exhibition, you mean?' The girl's dyed red hair was pulled into untidy sprays of hair by elastic bands. She could not have been more than twenty.

'I think it must be.'

'Over there, in that room.'

Admission was free, it seemed. Melissa went across the cool floor, past aluminium torsos and agonised zinc corpses. The current sculpture display, she assumed. A small room to the side held a large glass-fronted cabinet, scuffed and chipped at its base where the wood had been pecked out by toecaps over the years.

It held a miscellany of objects. Prominent was a photo-graph of Adie with Anais Nin at the Bar Vidourle, the cafe she had noticed on the river embankment, its setting appar-ently unchanged from thirty years previously. In others Adie was grinning at a blonde woman who looked like his third wife Simone Réjane. Several handwritten notes rather than diaries, in English and French, and a scrawl on a programme for a summer art event in 1975 which stated that Sommières had provided him with the happiest years he had ever known. An edition of *The Carcassonne Quartet* in French translation, the book that won the prestigious Prix de Grenoble, and another of his *Collected Poems*, open at the title page to reveal his signature.

Melissa stared hard, trying and failing to make them tell her something, these bits of paper he had touched or blazed to create. But they were random pieces of paper, nothing more. For about a quarter of an hour, no one else was there. But neither was any sense of immediacy, let alone intimacy.

When she emerged, the girl by the entrance counter had gone. Melissa was alone with the beaten metal torsos.

Had Elizabeth come and stood here too, with her own private memories? For now Melissa knew – surely – it was no coincidence that she had chosen a house in France so close to where Adie had made his home. *When did my parents buy the bergerie? Which year was that first summer at St Cyrice?*

Lost inside her own head, she hardly registered movement at the periphery of her vision. It was the click of heels on the flagged floor approaching that jolted her back into the present.

'Are you all right?' asked a woman.

Melissa started.

It was hard to tell whether the rapped enquiry was an offer to impart information about an artist, or concern for a tourist who had strayed out of her depth and looked uncomfortable. She was not tall – hence the stilettos, perhaps – and wore a laminated badge on the lapel of her tailored blue suit, 'Mme Delphine MASSENET' along with an air of authority.

'Yes,' said Melissa, 'I'm fine, thank you.'

'It seemed as if you wanted to ask something.' Mme Massenet's tone was matter-of-fact rather than unfriendly.

'Well, actually, I would.'

She waited, head tilted. The olive skin across her proud cheekbones was smooth and plump.

'I was interested in your permanent exhibition – Julian Adie's life and work.' Melissa used the grandiose terms the little display had claimed for itself and tried to keep the disappointed edge out of her voice.

'You know his work?'

She nodded. 'I was wondering, as I'm here in Sommières, if you could tell me where his house was?' It struck her as she said it, that had Adie still been alive, the request could well have been received with suspicion. A stalker's question. A deranged fan.

'Monsieur Adie's house? Across the bridge, on the western side of town. Route de Saussines.'

Pointed in the right direction, Melissa had no doubt she would find it easily. When Adie bought the house it was the largest in the village, the *maison de maître*. It was a great shuttered nineteenth-century mausoleum straight from the pages of Flaubert. His family named it the Vampire House. There was a photograph of it in the biography.

'Thank you, madame.'

'You're welcome.'

'I don't suppose . . .' she began, then hesitated.

'Yes?'

'I was thinking . . . obviously Monsieur Adie is remembered here,' Melissa waved a hand around to show she meant the arts centre. 'But I assume there must be people here in the town who remember him as friends . . .' She tailed off, unwilling to say what she really wanted. It seemed too presumptuous.

Madame Massenet visibly raised herself on her heels. 'I knew him.'

'Well, that's marvellous—!'

There was an awkward moment as Melissa's sudden enthusiasm met her equally unexpected blankness.

Melissa opened her mouth to say something, anything, when Madame Massenet interrupted. 'You really need to speak to Annick.'

'Annick,' Melissa repeated. 'Is she here? I mean, could I speak to her here?'

'She's in and out.'

It was not helpful. This was proving an odd encounter. Yet probably no odder than her questions – or did they have hundreds of people each year, sidling in, faintly embarrassed in their British way, of revealing their interest in a compatriot who wrote books, and some of them dirty ones at that? To this woman, Melissa must have been one more in a long line of tourists, crumpled clothes limp and big feet splayed in shoes suitable for pounding the ancient cobbles and climbing steps.

'I enjoyed the exhibition,' she said, trying to reinstate their previous roles.

Madame Massenet nodded, as if dismissing her.

Melissa was almost at the door before she called out. 'We have a literary evening here tomorrow. A French author, Gilles Barreau. Annick will be here if you want to find her.'

'Thank you, madame.'

The girl was back at the counter as she passed. She caught Melissa's eye and held up an index finger to make her wait a second. Flicking through a sheaf of pamphlets, she extracted a simple flyer. '*Une soirée avec Gilles Barreau,*' it announced. 'The time is on there,' she said, handing it over.

A nnick. The name was familiar but just out of reach, like a tune which once haunted and now cannot quite be pinned down. Was she imagining its resonance, mistaking the name of a film star or a parfumier, perhaps, for the answer she wanted?

Excitement stirred. Melissa walked faster and faster back to the car. Now, again, it was just possible to conjure the spirit of Julian Adie, to picture him on that corner, or disappearing down that alley.

Unlocking the car she paused, looking up at the stunted top of the tower rising over the town. She drummed her fingers on the roof of the vehicle, feeling the heat the metal had absorbed. She was warming up herself, infused with purpose.

Within minutes she had crossed back over the bridge to the western side of town, looking out for the Route de Saussines.

Would the new ring road have swallowed his Vampire House? She was looking for a grand *maison de maître*. A peculiar choice of residence for a man who professed to enjoy living as an olive farmer, or a fisherman.

Traffic snarled and smoked around a sharp bend. To judge from the vehicles, this was still an enclave of rusty vans and Peugeots, a France not much changed from Adie's time.

Melissa drove as slowly as she dared, constantly checking the rear-view mirror for anything coming up close behind.

The house, she was certain, was enclosed behind a wall, screened from the road by trees. Its mansard roof would be just visible from the road.

She could not see it. The town ended abruptly after a vast dusty graveyard and the road out was rapidly engulfed by fields. Either she had taken the wrong turning, or she had failed to recognise it.

B ack at St Cyrice, the *bergerie* had an abandoned feel. Richard was not back.

Melissa's spirits dropped, though she was not surprised. It was hardly the first time he had lost days of a holiday due to a difficult deal. She called him, but his mobile was switched off and went straight to voicemail. She hesitated, wanting to leave a message, but finally pressed the button to end the call.

Melissa leaned back against the wall of the kitchen, suddenly weary. But ten minutes later she picked up the phone again.

'Joe? It's Melissa.'

She and Joe Collins did some catching up – his wife was expecting their second child in July; no, Melissa was not sure when she was returning to work, and it was unlikely to be at Kew when she did – and then she asked him. 'Listen Joe, I'd like a favour.'

'Sure.'

Typical Joe: agree first, then ask what the favour was. Whatever else was going on in her life, she told herself firmly, she had some good friends. There were definitely times nowadays when she wondered how different her life might have turned out if she'd taken him up on his several offers to turn the heat up under their friendship. That was before their respective marriages, of course. Why had she dismissed kindness and sincerity so readily in favour of a false excitement which had turned out to be nothing more than uncertainty?

'I was hoping you might be able to do a quick google and then an index search for me,' she said, picturing him at his desk in London's most prestigious library, the computer never turned off on the untidy desk where he could lay his hands on any required information in a heartbeat. 'I don't have my laptop here.'

'Fire away.'

'Dr Martin Braxton.'

It only took a few seconds.

'Only seems to be one – US academic . . . currently at the University of Michigan . . . author of a study of Don Webber. . . . Is that the one you were after?'

'Yes. That must be him.'

'Do you want anything more?'

'Not really, I just needed to check . . .'

'You sure?'

'Well, OK . . . could you try . . . Julian Adie and Annick?' She spelled out the woman's name.

'Just . . . Annick?'

'I don't have a surname. But it's not a common name, so—'

She could hear the keyboard clicking at the other end of the line. She held her breath, fidgeting with the box of matches next to a candle on the dresser.

'No . . . nothing.'

'Nothing at all?'

'No. Are you all right, Mel?'

'Yes . . . fine. No, well, I suppose I am disappointed – I remembered wrong, or rather didn't remember the name at all.'

'What?'

'Sorry, just thinking aloud. Been spending too much time on my own lately!' she tried to laugh it off.

'I thought you said Richard was with you out there?'

'Yes,' she said sadly. 'He is.'

'So . . . how?'

'It's a long story.'

The thought crossed her mind to ask Joe to look up Alexandros on the internet – perhaps there was a Greek telephone directory on-line. Or perhaps she could get the number for Manolis at the boat hire office, and pass on a message that way. But she held back. It felt far too private to be exposed, even to a good friend like Joe.

She thanked him and said goodbye.

On a postcard from Sommières , she wrote to Alexandros: 'Here I am in Adie's last Heaven.' She made sure to print the address in France clearly in the left hand corner where it was least likely to be obliterated by postmarks.

Months had passed since they were last in touch – and then it had been only an email from Alexandria giving little personal information, just a description of a café where Adie used to entertain his friends.

What had happened since to Alexandros and his wife – had they found a way to get back together too? And if so, were they making a better fist of it than Richard and she were? She couldn't help but think of Corfu, how she had sensed freedom and new beginnings there, despite her grief and the defeated anger about Richard. It was now they were back together that she felt closed down.

T he next evening she set out for Sommières and the literary evening at L'Espace Julian Adie. It would be an adventure, she tried to convince herself. With Richard still away in Paris – although due back later that night, according to a message left on her mobile, broken up and snagged during its satellite voyage – she had nothing else to do.

It would do him good to find her out when he got back.

The scent of pine drifted over scrub. Vineyards striped the landscape beneath the Pic de St Loup and the mount rose above the dancing road like a miniature Matterhorn from one side, then lost its spikiness and menace the closer it came. The evening sun was still warm through the car window. Melissa wondered how many times her mother had taken this road, how many lies of omission she had told in order to do so.

As she crossed the bridge over the Vidourle again, the clock on the gate tower opposite showed twenty to seven. She parked close to what seemed the smart hotel in town, the Auberge du Pont Romain. From the outside it looked almost bleak, utilitarian, but round the corner a gate afforded a glimpse of garden, and a swimming pool, cool trees, a life more lush.

With a quarter of an hour before the soirée was due to start, she wandered down to the river and stood looking out at the wide still water. The town was quiet now. A flock of birds flew over in formation against the weakening light.

Melissa took a few deep breaths. What was she doing here? She had no idea what to expect, had no expectations beyond turning up at the event. Neither did she have any knowledge of Gilles Barreau and his work beyond the titles of four novels listed on the flyer, roughly translated as *The Second Day*, *The Vault*, *The Road on Fire* and *Unforgiven*.

She was just going to slip into the back of the room and try to understand as much as possible. A sudden unpleasant thought occurred that Dr Martin Braxton might have had the same idea.

O ther people were climbing the steps into the front court-yard. The building, she now knew, was an old Ursuline convent. Most of the audience were in couples. Any lone women were elderly.

She paid a small entrance fee at the counter inside. Conversations were rising as the audience milled around the sculptures holding glasses of wine or orange juice. She had a moment of panic. Would she talk to anyone? She had never liked walking into parties and pubs alone, feeling exposed and vulnerable. She took a ridiculously long time putting her purse back in her bag and studying the posters and flyers stuck up on the wall.

Wineglass in hand, she made a slow tour of the room looking surreptitiously at the women. There was no sign of Madame Massenet, nor the studenty looking girl with red hair. And which one of them was Annick?

After ten minutes, they were called into a room to the side where a man was sitting by a polished table stacked with books, and a woman was standing. Melissa took a seat at the back and counted. Twenty-six people, all waiting expectantly. None of them was Braxton. The atmosphere hushed as the man – Gilles Barreau, recognisable as an older version of the author's photograph on the flyer – raised his eyes and smiled shyly. It was the woman who spoke first, to welcome the audience, especially, she said, those who knew the author's books well. There was a genial ripple of laughter at this.

She was rail thin, tall and bony. A cloud of dark hair and razor-sharp cheekbones, generous lips, very slightly slanted eyes. A striking woman, still wearing long hair over the age of fifty, but there was nothing hippyish about her.

'We are very privileged to have this opportunity to hear his thoughts on literature and his work in progress. Ladies and gentlemen . . . the writer Gilles Barreau.'

The woman took her place in the audience, and Barreau unwound himself from his chair. He too was tall and thin, dressed in a golden brown corduroy suit and open-necked dark blue shirt, with hair down to his shoulders but retreating from his noble forehead. His face was dominated by a long hooked nose. It was hard to guess at his age from the back of the room. It could have been anything from forty to sixty.

'As those of you who were kind enough to read *Unforgiven* will know, or at least those gracious enough to allow me to talk about it at such length in the Bar Paysanne all those evenings during its genesis and composition,' he began in a mellow *basso profundo,* to friendly laughter at what sounded like a local joke, 'my themes are the small man and the big universe.'

References to part of his plot construction and details from his books followed. They meant nothing to Melissa, but she understood the gist effortlessly, so long as she did not strain after words she did not recognise.

'As the great Julian Adie, under whose auspices we gather for these evenings, once said to me—'

His words were an electrical charge, almost as if she had willed them into sound. She physically jolted.

'—there is a deeper reality where we are all particles of the same time and space, what he called the continuum.'

Melissa sat further upright, concentrating hard, but he said nothing more about Adie.

Her mind wandered during some of the rest of his talk, which mainly concerned the ideas at the core of the novel he was newly engaged on, and the physical practicalities of writing. Then it was over, and she joined in the applause.

The striking-looking woman got up and came to the front again.

'Thank you very much, Gilles, and thank you for coming everyone, as ever,' she said, beaming around. 'For your diaries, the next literary soirée will centre on the work of Jean Giono, to be given by Monsieur Lambert who is coming from Forqualquier.'

'Thank you, Annick,' said Barreau, and kissed her on both cheeks.

Annick.

Melissa stared at her, unable to think what to do next. Was that the end of the evening, or would there be more drinks and a chance to talk? They could all be going off to dinner now. All around chairs were being scraped back and the sound level was rising. Barreau and Annick were speaking confidentially at the desk, while she was gathering up the books he had used during the lecture. Through the open door back into the main space, people were still standing around. The aroma of coffee drifted in. Perhaps she was in luck.

Should she approach Barreau, or Annick? Both were daunting propositions.

Uncertain whether to stay or go through to the main hall with the crowd Melissa tried to assess whether it might be better in here where it was less likely she would be interrupted by some jocular, back-slapping friend who had come to support them.

She made her move.

Annick looked up with a small, quizzical smile.

More composed than she felt, Melissa extended her hand and introduced herself. 'It was very interesting – thank you so much.' Lame, inconsequential words.

Close up, Barreau was clearly older. Fine wrinkles fanned out from his eyes and his ready smile revealed ageing teeth, crossed on the bottom row.

'You are very kind,' he said. The obvious question hung.

'I came here yesterday to see the permanent exhibition devoted to Julian Adie.' There was nothing for it but the truth. Well, some of it. 'I recently read his biography.'

Their twin stares were penetrating.

'It was only then I realised that he had lived in Sommières for so many years. It seemed I was so close, I had to come and see it for myself . . . especially in the light of his famous "sense of place" . . .'

'That's quite right,' said Barreau, reasonably. He tucked some notes into a battered leather folder.

Annick knew there was more. Melissa could tell from the

way she nodded, very deliberately. 'So what did you think?' She was direct, still smiling, but there was definitely steel under her pleasant tone of voice.

'I'm glad I came.'

Here was the chance. 'I asked yesterday whether there was anyone here I could talk to about Adie, and I was given your name. You knew him, I believe?'

'That's right.'

If she was involved in the running of L'Espace Julian Adie, she must have been used to all kinds of people asking about him, from scholarly researchers to the plain curious. She could so easily stonewall any questions.

A spark fired from her eyes, yellow-brown eyes like a wild animal, ringed expertly with kohl.

'Would it be possible to talk to you about Julian Adie?' asked Melissa.

Drawn by the lit tower of the castle, she ventured further into the labyrinth of medieval passages before leaving, intrigued by the layers of history all around, the ancient buttress making near tunnels of some of the smaller alleys. The high walls were studded with the glow of lamps from the rooms behind. Down on the street, the shadows were deep, making masks of passing faces. Her heels echoed on the brick paving, hard as she tried to alter her steps to dull the sound.

At least she was leaving with something: a time and place to meet Annick back in Sommières in two days' time. But how likely was it that she would know anything about Elizabeth? Melissa was clutching at straws. She felt embarrassed already at the prospect of having to explain herself.

On the road back to St Cyrice there was almost no traffic. Yet she drove carefully, feeling detached and yet anxiously sensitive to every movement on the road, or more usually to the side of it. A small reckless animal scurried across the glare of her headlights, and the scrub moved so freakishly at one point that she feared a wild boar or a deer was about to run out into her path.

The *bergerie* was dark and still. Either Richard was in bed asleep, or he had not returned as intended. In the silence after she cut the engine, Melissa could hear only the rapid beats of her own heart. There was no moon. She opened the car door again while she found the right keys and used its feeble pool of illumination to unlock the house.

A red light blinked on the answering machine in the hall.

The metallic impersonation of Richard's voice filled the emptiness: 'Still in Paris . . . taking longer than I thought. Sorry. I'm at the Hotel Delavigne. Out at a business thing tonight — it's about seven now — so I'll speak to you in the morning. Night.'

Melissa glanced at her watch. It was after midnight. She hesitated, then told herself that this was what normal couples did: they called late at night. The display held the number of the last incoming call. She pressed the button and waited, impatient to tell him about her evening.

'Hôtel Delavigne, *bonsoir*.'

'Mr Richard Quiller, please.'

'Just one moment.'

Synthetic strings.

'I'm sorry, Mr and Mrs Quiller have not returned yet. Would you like to leave a voicemail?'

She should have expected it. Perhaps the truth was that she had done, and all she was doing now was confirming her suspicions. Her heart did not lurch. All she felt was anger and resignation.

'No,' she said. 'No message.'

She should have asked how long they were staying, invented some plausible reason for asking when they had arrived, but she had no need of it, not really. She had all she needed to know. And all she wanted to know.

The charade was over.

N ext morning she threw the clothes he hadn't already taken into a suitcase, along with his gadgets, his radio, books, swimming pool brochures with their pencil notes, and his ridiculous plans for the garden.

She didn't even want it in the hall. It went into the stone lean-to shed at the end of the house. Slamming the door on the last evidence he had been there, she stripped off and dived into the pool as if baptising her solitary state.

After a pot of black coffee, she was crackling like electricity along a wire.

Melissa rang the hotel in Paris and asked to be put through to Mrs Quiller.

The same metallic strings soared in her ear.

Then a woman's voice answered. 'Hello?' There was not a trace of wariness. She recognised the voice straight away.

'Sarah?' she asked pleasantly.

'Yes.'

Melissa ignored the icy punch to the stomach.

'Is Richard there?'

'Er, not at the moment. Who is that?'

'It's Melissa.'

'Oh . . . Melissa!' Perhaps she was pointing, pantomiming at the phone for Richard's benefit. 'I was just here . . . going over some paperwork, before this afternoon's meeting . . . how are you?'

'Don't even try it!' cried Melissa. Then managed to pitch at some semblance of dispassionate control. 'Tell Richard . . . *when* you see him . . . that if he comes back to St Cyrice it will only be to collect his stuff, which is in the outhouse, but really I would prefer never to see him again. He will be hearing from my solicitor.'

'But—'

'That's it. Spare me any more.'

She put the phone down.

Twisting the gold band until it hurt, she worked her wedding ring off. For weeks afterwards she was unable to stop probing the bare stem of that finger. Its absence felt strange, just as its newness had been, the first time she had slipped on the precious metal of Richard's promises.

IV

Annick poured the wine.

Below the Bar Vidourle, the river was a glassy green. Sprightly weeds grew on gravel spits further down, beyond the Roman weir which stilled the flow below the terrace where they sat.

'Did you know this was his favourite place for a drink?' she asked, the carafe of rosé poised in mid-air.

Her black-rimmed stare seemed to burn Melissa's face. She was intense company, superficially friendly – and certainly generous in agreeing to talk – but slightly discomfiting. Melissa knew she did not look particularly well. Two sleepless nights had left her nauseous with the realisation of what had happened. But better to do this, than to dwell any more on Richard.

'There's a photograph of him sitting here in his biography – with Arielle Urbain,' said Melissa, making an effort to keep her voice level. Holding a coherent conversation in French in this state felt like catching fish in bare hands, the words slithering out of her grasp.

'You could be right,' said Annick thoughtfully. 'Do you mind?' She waved a cigarette as she was about to light it.

'By all means . . .' Melissa couldn't feel any worse.

Annick took a deep draw and exhaled. In natural light dry lines crinkled her skin under the strong make-up.

'His last great love.' Her tone was dry.

'Arielle?' asked Melissa.

'That's right.'

'Is she a friend of yours?'

Annick paused. 'We speak sometimes.'

'Does she live here?'

'No, in Paris. She is his literary executor in France. She does good work in keeping his books in print here. Julian always said he thought his work sounded better translated into French.'

'The British love all things French.' Melissa managed to smile.

'But they don't know France, and they don't want to.'

'I'm not sure that's always the case.' She was thinking of all the summers here, making friends, gradually becoming part of the village, learning the language and the local stories, the characters and the points of reference.

Annick shook her head and flicked her fingers. 'No one is happy here at the moment. The only ones who are happy are the foreigners. In this region, they like the cheap wine – but do they know that the farmers are getting less and less for it? For some, the price has gone down so much that they have stopped making it. Haven't you noticed how poor the villages seem? That's because they are, not because they are putting on a show for the tourists!'

She drew heavily on her cigarette, and continued. 'The only people who can be happy are those who don't care that we have riots because there are not enough jobs for the young people. So many who are well-qualified are going abroad to work – London! They would prefer to work there. They see there are more opportunities, while France is run into the ground.

'The government says there is not enough money to keep on the old French way, but this is what we want. What is possible and what is not? They always find money when they have to.'

This was clearly a raw nerve.

She was right, though, about the joy of expatriate life: the absence of any political responsibility. The reinvention of the self in each new place, for each new audience: new country; new life. What Adie did.

'You must have been very young when you met Julian Adie,' Melissa steered her back.

'I was twenty-three. It didn't feel so young at the time.'

'How did you meet?'

'It was very close to where we are sitting here, as a matter of fact. I was walking along the embankment. I must have been out doing my shopping. I was not long married, and took pride in my attempts to look after my husband and new apartment. It was that building we lived in, just over there, with the balcony.' She inclined her head gracefully to indicate which one.

'Your husband – Gilles?'

She sucked hard on the last third of her cigarette and ground it out in the ashtray. 'No,' she said in the way Melissa was beginning to recognise as characteristic. It was a simple statement of fact, expressed without impatience or annoyance. She blew out a long stream of smoke. 'A short, silly marriage.'

'But you are married to Gilles Barreau now?'

Her eyes were slits. 'No, we are not married. But we have been together for a long time.'

Finding a friendly line was crucial. But Melissa was making a clumsy job of it by taking this one.

'Sorry. Please go on.'

'Julian was already at his morning *pastis* right here, where we're sitting. I recognised him. Everyone knew him. I had recently read one of his books and went up to tell him I had liked it. That was the start.'

'When you say, the start . . .'

'We began an affair which suited us both. No commitment, only pleasure.'

Melissa was startled that she was telling her so much so soon.

'When was this, what year? Can you recall?'

'I recall precisely. It was 1975. We were together, in our way, for eight years.'

It occurred to her that Annick's openness could be an indication of how used she was to telling this story.

'I can tell what you are thinking,' went on Annick. 'He was married. Or rather he married Marie Basselin during that time. But we continued to see each other. Yes, that was the case.'

But Melissa wasn't surprised. It was Adie's ideal made real: he wrote; he drank; he had a wife; and he had other women.

'His wife knew.'

'Julian never bothered to hide what he was doing.'

'And what about your husband?' Melissa pressed on recklessly, feeling vaguely uncomfortable and intrusive. But Annick was not clamming up, telling her to stop, nor did

Melissa have the impression that she was revealing any secrets.

'He knew – maybe a bit less.'

The husband who had not even merited a name. Melissa swallowed hard. Barely below the surface was her own misery, her own situation. Richard was like them. *I should find out what I can, learn how to survive . . . It was only an affair. Nothing out of the ordinary. Perhaps I could learn a lot about relationships from these people . . .*

Melissa must have betrayed her unease, because Annick shook her head. 'There was no unpleasantness. Mostly it was not serious. It meant nothing.'

Her tone echoed Richard's voice in Melissa's head. *So why do it then, if it meant nothing?* she wanted to ask, but did not. *If only I could be more like these people, perhaps I would be happier.*

The movement of water below was a faint whisper. Melissa felt warm air on her face, perhaps too warm, as Annick shrugged and said, 'There was an understanding, on all sides. Julian and I were happy.

'He was exciting and brilliant, and tender and unpredictable. I loved him.'

O nce again the biography was wrong by omission. By missing out Adie's long involvement with Annick, a whole dimension had been passed over, hidden just like her mother might be hidden between the lines of the official narrative.

'Did you ever know anything about an English woman friend of his, an artist called Elizabeth Norden who had a house over at St Cyrice?'

Was that a flicker of change in her expression? Or perhaps she was picking up on the tension in Melissa's posture.

'I knew about her.'

'What did you think?'

'It was not a good story — for any of us.'

'Tell me.'

Annick hesitated. 'She appeared one day, out of the blue. She did not understand how it worked.'

Melissa kept quiet, willing her to go on.

'When I asked him, he said they had met in Greece.'

A pause.

'That's right,' said Melissa.

'They must have had some kind of relationship.' Annick shrugged expressively. 'But it was all over a long time before she arrived here. He was no longer interested — he did not want to see her.'

'That's all?'

'What do you mean?'

Melissa swallowed hard. 'Was there anything that had happened, in the past — in Greece — that may have involved her?'

Another pause. 'She made him angry for some reason. And he could be . . . changeable, you know. Sometimes he was violent. Threatening. His rage — it was like a compression of all the bad times, the slights, the feeling of being ignored, it just hummed there, heating up — and then the safety valve wouldn't be able to contain the pressure and it would blow.'

'He *attacked* her?'

'No, no. Not her. He would not see her, as I said.'

'So he took it out on other people then?' It was not a nice thought.

Annick inclined her head in a wry admission of it.

'What did – ?'

Annick cut across the question. 'I remember she was pretty. Very English. Blonde hair down to here,' she chopped her shoulder with a flat hand. 'I had no idea that she was going to cause trouble.' She made a little noise in her throat to convey how wrong she was, then narrowed her eyes. 'Funny . . . she came asking about Julian, just like you. Later there were many, but then . . . it was just the beginning of people coming to look for him.'

'When was this?'

'It was . . . sometime in my first year with him.'

'So . . . 1975.'

'I suppose so.'

She frowned and seemed to be looking closer.

Was Annick making the connection? Alexandros, after all, had spotted the similarity.

And she had been so frank, it seemed the only reasonable thing to do. 'She's – she was – my mother,' said Melissa.

Annick received the news impassively. Nothing would surprise her, she implied with a tilt of the chin.

There was something else, though. A dread that had begun growing and curdling in her gut.

'Annick, have you been approached by a Dr Braxton? He's a biographer. He is researching a new version of Adie's life.'

She lit another cigarette and sucked on it deeply.

'Dr Martin Braxton. An American academic from the University of Michigan,' prompted Melissa.

'Oh, yes,' she said. 'He has been here.' Did she sound bored? Unsurprised? Used to answering all these intrusive questions from strangers?

Of course Braxton would have been here. If she had managed to get this far so easily, and speak to Annick, then it was impossible to imagine that Braxton had not done so too.

'Can I ask you . . . when was this?'

'A few months ago.'

'Did he ask you about Elizabeth Norden?'

'Yes.'

'What did you tell him?'

'Exactly what I told you. I know what I know.'

'And what else do you know about Elizabeth Norden and Julian Adie?' asked Melissa in a quiet voice.

'Nothing,' she said. 'I really don't know what it was that made him react like he did. All I know is what I saw and heard.'

'Which was?'

'He turned on his daughter. His younger one – Hero – was out staying with him for her summer holidays. They say he beat her. He was too drunk to stand when I saw him, and incoherent with anger. The housekeeper tried to restrain him, and he lashed out at her too. Then he disappeared, driving into the hills on the wrong side of the road.'

She stared into the distance. They were silent for a short while.

'You know that Dr Braxton is researching Adie's darker side, his capacity for violence, the bad relationships with women . . . He says he has found some scandal – did he tell you that?'

She removed a flake of tobacco from her lower lip with the utmost delicacy. 'He did not tell me that . . . in so many words.'

'The thing is . . .' Melissa hesitated. 'I don't know whether Dr Braxton is to be trusted.' There, it was said.

Annick was unfazed.

'I have always told the truth as I saw it where Julian Adie is concerned. There is nothing to be gained from changing now.'

Traffic noise on the road behind the café seemed a long way away.

'Dr Braxton seems certain that my mother was part of some . . . bad episode involving Julian Adie,' said Melissa.

'Ah,' she said calmly. 'That is always possible.'

'What do you mean – exactly?'

'Only what I say.'

Melissa was trembling. 'Do you know of any precise event that Dr Braxton has in mind?'

'No.'

'Nothing at all that you might have——?'

'No,' said Annick.

There was not much more to say. They parted having agreed to stay in contact, but Melissa left wondering whether Annick had really told her all that she knew. In the end, she had said very little. But she had confirmed what, until now, had only been a supposition: Elizabeth had been in contact with Julian Adie in Sommières. No doubt she would tell Dr Braxton, and with that same disingenuous manner she had just displayed, that Melissa Norden had come looking for her and what was discussed.

On the way back to the car, Melissa stood and stared up at the house Annick had pointed out, where she had once lived in an apartment with her husband. It had a pretty balcony, with a view of the river. Melissa wondered what other stories since had played out within its walls.

This had all been going on during those summers at St Cyrice, and she had had no idea what Elizabeth had been doing or thinking. Melissa felt faintly disembodied, as a tear trickled down one cheek. She was starting to believe that everyone else, even virtual strangers, knew her mother better than she did.

Back at the car, parked close to the narrow street which led up to the arts centre, she unlocked the door, then propped her arms on the roof and stood a while. She shouldn't be driving. She had not intended to drink all that wine with Annick, but now that she had, she would have to wait before getting back on the road.

She locked the car door again, and began walking aimlessly.

A sandwich at a café in the square seemed a good idea, but when the baguette filled with cheese arrived, she had no appetite. She forced down a few mouthfuls, listlessly absorbing her surroundings. Shops were closed for lunch. Shutters were drawn tight. What went on behind them? She felt as if she were floating above the scene, in it but somehow not part of it.

A blur of pink pulled her out of her reverie.

Pink and white stripes.

Melissa chewed faster, then put down her sandwich. That distinctive, ridiculous jacket. Braxton's, she was sure of it. She was on her feet. Then she was running to the corner where she was sure he must have turned.

There was no one there.

Her soles clattered on polished stone as she entered the church. It was dim, and empty. Outside she scanned the steps leading up to the castle. She saw and heard nothing. 'Dr Braxton?' she shouted. No response.

If it was him, what was he doing now – and who was he talking to? What had he found out about her mother that she had not?

A queasiness accompanied her back to the table. Why was it that every man she encountered seemed to have an ulterior motive, be a philanderer or be purely selfish? How could you trust any of them?

But then, it was possible that her trust even in her own mother had been misplaced. If Braxton was right, she had been wrong about Elizabeth too. She had never really known her own mother. Light-headedness threatened to overwhelm her. Melissa fought the sensation that she might black out.

She could never feel certain again. So was it possible? Could Elizabeth really have been the kind of person who could cover up a suspicious death – or worse?

V

'I've been fine on my own,' said Melissa. 'Felt a bit strange at first, but it's all right. Really.'

'So long as you are OK.' Leonie did not sound convinced.

Melissa lay down full length on one of the shabby sofas. She felt exhausted – but grateful that Leonie had rung.

'You sound . . . tired.'

'I am tired. I lie awake thinking at night. That's what I do most – it seems to take up a lot of the time.'

'Do you think you might be depressed?'

Melissa grimaced. 'I've certainly wondered. Perhaps I am. But in fact, what I feel mainly is relief that Richard has gone. That it really is over.'

Now she could deal with the hurt, knowing this time the split was irrevocable. All the compromises, the holding back, the pretending, were resolved.

'Even when you were giving him one last chance, you knew it wasn't right, didn't you? That you were short-changing yourself.'

'You're right about distance. I knew when I was in Corfu

that there was no going back — but then that's exactly what I did.'

'There you are then.'

'But somehow when I was back in England, I let myself be reeled back again. God, how pathetic does that sound! I'm angry with myself. How could I have put myself in that position, where was my self-respect?'

She could just see Leonie in her office in London, rolling her eyes. 'Richard is a great manipulator, you know that. He always was. Even at the start of it, we all used to think — '

A wave of annoyance tipped over. 'What, you used to sit around discussing how awful Richard was? You and who else used to think?'

'It's not like it sounds. But — look, I can say this now. I should have said it long before. Richard played you. He played on your insecurities, knowing that once he had you, you dreaded the end of the relationship. He didn't so much want you as want to be in control of you. All that business with Sarah — what a massive ego boost for him! Both a mistress and a wife ripping her hair out over him! No wonder he wanted it to carry on a bit longer. He's emotionally stunted, wants constant reassurance of his worth. And what did he ever give you emotionally?'

'That's a bit simplistic,' said Melissa. She was not going to have her marriage dismembered with quite such savagery. 'There was more to it than that. Well, in the beginning—'

Leonie butted in. 'That's just it. It never did develop into the marriage you wanted it to be. Go on, be honest. Did you ever entirely trust him?'

Melissa bit her lip, forcing herself to remember the way it really was.

'You didn't, did you?' Leonie said softly.

'No.'

'And did all the rows and fresh deals ever make any difference?'

'No.' It came out as a whisper.

'No one can ever say that you didn't try to make it work, Mel. You are so strong – stronger than you realise. The steel it took to keep it all going – for years! But we are not our mothers. We don't have to stay with a husband for any of their reasons: economics, shame, stigma. Richard, he's—'

'It's not just him.'

Melissa was going to tell her. She had to tell someone, to release the thought that had been choking her for a week, maybe for longer, floating namelessly, wordlessly in her subconscious. 'I think that . . . it's possible . . . Julian Adie was my father.'

She went over how it would make so much sense. How it would explain why Elizabeth had given her the book – and the trail – while she still could, why it was the one important thing she had left to tell her, why Dr Braxton had tracked her down. And back so much further, how her father Edward had always been such a distant entity, how Elizabeth's marriage to him had fallen apart so quickly, its ties to conventionality so threadbare. Leonie was shocked, she could tell. Incredulous, too.

'But your mother . . . she never even hinted at this before?'

'No, but – '

'You and she were close, Mel. I just can't believe she would have kept something like this from you. She was such a lovely person, with a real sense of fairness. I can remember you telling me how she would try to make sure your father saw you and took you for outings even when he wasn't living with you. I just can't . . .'

'She would never show weakness. Look how long it took for me to find out how ill she was. She wouldn't say!'

Leonie was not convinced.

'It's like . . . not knowing my own history, having to revise my own story halfway through.'

'You can't think that way.'

'What if I could prove it?'

'You won't be able to prove it. Mel, all this Julian Adie stuff . . .'

Leonie was clearly uncomfortable.

'It might seem odd, but it's making me feel better not worse. Depression, obsession – I know what you're thinking. But the way I see it I'm not running away from the demons, I'm facing them head on. Trying to find answers. What else would you suggest? That I run back to Kent, picking over the remains and wailing on about how he can't have loved me properly or he wouldn't have done this? Where does that get me?'

It wouldn't quite go into spoken words, but she knew deep down that if she could understand her mother, she would have more insight into everything; and that if she could understand how a man moved on from wife to wife, she might take comfort from knowing that Richard had genuinely loved her, at least for a while.

Biography was important. In the story of another person's life was all the evidence you needed of the courage required to clear the world's hurdles, or even to dare take the new step. You could find out how other people handled bad situations. Whether in retrospect they made the right decisions. The key was in the human love of narrative, of wanting to know what happened next.

For Julian Adie it was documented; for Elizabeth it was not. There was no smooth transition between phases of life and events neatly arranged in chapters, only a jumble of unreliable memory.

She barely left St Cyrice the following week.
One evening, as she was physically exhausted from trying to reinstate her mother's control of the garden, pruning suckers from plum trees and cutting down the ash-grey branches of a dead cherry tree, her mobile shrilled. Caller unknown.

'Hello.' Her tone was flat, she could hear it herself.

'Is that Melissa?'

That voice – surely it couldn't be, not after all this time? 'Yes.'

'It's Alexandros.'

She had never been so happy to hear from anyone. She struggled to keep control of her voice. 'How are you? How's Kalami?'

'Fine, and yes, fine, I'm sure. I – er, I'm not in Kalami. I'm in Lyon.'

'What are you doing there – I mean, are you working there?'

'No. I'm waiting for a train. I flew in this morning. When I got your postcard I had this crazy idea that I should come and see you – but now I'm here, I'm feeling I might have been a little . . . reckless. I should have called you before. Should have given you er . . . more notice . . .'

'Alexandros,' she said firmly. 'I would so love to see you. Please come.'

*

331

There was no one she wanted to see more.

When she saw him, the tension she'd been carrying seemed to melt away. A rush of elation at the sight of him on the doorstep of the *bergerie*, made her taller and lighter than she had been for weeks. More hopeful, too.

'This is a lovely surprise!' She was grinning uncontrollably.

His face had filled out a bit since she was in Corfu. He looked healthier and happier, if a touch travel-worn. The wild hair had been cut too, no longer trailing past his ears, though the curls still fell over his forehead.

Too much staring. 'Come in, come in . . .' she said. She was self-conscious that she must be looking a lot worse than when he had last seen her.

In the dark flagged hall, he dropped his leather bag and looked around, taking in the thick walls of exposed stone and the wooden staircase. It was odd seeing him in this new context, and so unexpectedly. He might well have been thinking the same of her.

The moment when they might have exchanged a friendly kiss in greeting had passed. 'Tea . . . coffee . . . wine . . . ?' she bustled nervously.

He followed her into the kitchen.

Melissa filled the slight awkwardness with talk. 'It's great to see you,' she said. 'How have you been? Did you find all you were looking for, when you were in Egypt?'

Alexandros took his time answering, deliberately slowing down her rattling tempo. 'In a way I did find what I was looking for. But maybe I knew it all along, and I was only proving it to myself.'

What did he mean by that? Did he intend her to read

something into it? She picked up the packet of coffee grounds, and when he nodded, fired up the filter machine.

'Tell me.'

He leaned, apparently comfortably, against the old pine table, filling that corner of the room with his height and presence. She thought he was going to talk about his wife, but all he said was, 'The guide book stuff was relatively easy when I'd worked out how I was going to go about it.'

'What about the Alexandrian women? Are they as beautiful as all the books describe?' she asked, teasingly, hoping to lighten the tone.

'I'm sure they were.'

He was so earnest that she laughed.

'Let's take our coffee through to the sitting room.'

She was unsure what their relationship was – friendship, shared interest, or was it stronger than that? Had that one night in Corfu been a stupid mistake, or the only honest part of a tentative game they were both playing?

All she knew for certain was that she had the same butterflies in her stomach as that night in Corfu she had relived so many times in her head.

'I am so pleased you're here,' said Melissa. 'There's something I really need to ask you. To be honest, it's why I sent you the postcard.'

Was she imagining it, or did his expression suddenly darken?

Calmly and objectively, she described her meeting with Martin Braxton.

'That was him!' There was no hesitation. Alexandros made

an irritated gesture with his powerful brown hands. 'Braxton. He was the one who came to Kalami just before you arrived last year.'

'Greeting the locals with a shout of "Squid!" every morning!' she grimaced, remembering. 'Now I've met him I can just picture it.'

Perhaps a man that cloth-eared might not be a threat after all. She had worried unnecessarily.

'I have to admit, I have been worried about what he intends to write.'

'What are you going to do?' he asked.

'I don't think there's anything I can do.'

His long face was a mask. 'Perhaps not.'

'You know, there is something that has been bothering me. Braxton said he was investigating the drowning of an American woman.' She kept her voice soft and non-confrontational. 'You never did answer my question about the drowning at the St Arsenius shrine, not properly. Why wouldn't you tell me?'

It was impossible to gauge his reaction. The last time she asked she had received a short answer. She still recalled his words. 'We don't talk about it.'

Now, he sighed. He looked past her to the window and out at the sky. 'It seems . . . that other people are claiming they know more about it now that any of us ever did,' he said eventually. 'We were never sure exactly what did happen.'

'So . . . you never discussed it because—'

'—because we did not want to add to the stories about it! No one knew what had really happened – but everyone had a wild theory. The woman was a foreigner, don't forget.'

'Was it out of loyalty to Julian Adie, then – because you knew he had a connection to her?'

Alexandros shrugged. 'Perhaps that was part of it – especially on old Manos's part. He was so proud to have been Adie's landlord. Adie had paid for the enlargement of his house. But I imagine there was also an element of communal self-interest. The tourist industry was really beginning to be developed at that time. It was bringing astonishing prosperity to places that had never dreamed such things would be possible. It was not in anyone's interest to make more of it than it was.'

'Was there ever an official – a police – investigation?'

'I don't know. I was too young to know what happened.'

'Maybe there wasn't.'

'Maybe so. If everyone was satisfied it was an accident...'

'So there was no counterbalance,' said Melissa. 'Anyone could come along and interpret it how they wished, in a way that suited their purposes...'

She was thinking of Dr Braxton, but maybe they were all implicated in the web of supposition.

'Braxton thinks my mother was there.'

Alexandros sat forward in his seat as she told him how she had gone to Sommières, thinking she was finding her own way into her mother's story, only to find it was another trail Braxton had already covered.

'He's spoken to the same people I did in Sommières... but there's not much that's relevant there. Unless Annick wasn't telling the truth when she told me how she knew who my mother was.'

'Or only part of the truth.'

'Do you think it's worth trying her again – see if she'll tell me any more this time?'

'It's getting a long way from the story Braxton is researching.'

'Not if he's set on finding out about my mum, it isn't!' She was amazed he didn't get that. 'He thinks she was involved in this . . . death. He even called it a killing! He's going to write a book saying that my mother was Adie's partner in murder!'

Her heart was pounding. Finally articulating the threat made it horrifying, as well as incomprehensible.

'Why would he think that?'

'I don't know!' wailed Melissa. 'I simply don't know. If you'd ever met her you'd know it was just ridiculous!'

'It could simply be because of the time she was there . . .' It was lame and he knew it. 'Or someone remembered her name for another reason . . .' That was worse.

He had no answers either.

'Braxton wants to see her papers – but there are no papers. He doesn't believe me. He lives in a world where everything can be found in a book or a library. And if it's not written it can be teased out from between the lines.'

'Do you have a number for Braxton?' asked Alexandros.

'He gave me his card.'

'Perhaps we should meet him.'

'Face him head on, you mean? But we know what he intends to write. The only thing we can do is prove him wrong,' said Melissa. 'And how do we do that?'

The situation seemed bizarre. But the idea of having someone like Alexandros on her side made all the difference to her spirits. The way he used the word 'we' was profoundly comforting.

*

She showed him upstairs, to the bedroom she had hurriedly prepared for him. Gauging his reaction to her lack of presumption was impossible. His face was granite as he thanked her.

Quickly she prepared a simple supper and opened a bottle of wine. Bread and olives went in Provençal dishes on the kitchen table. It would be making too much of a statement to have set it out in the more formal dining room, but she lit a couple of candles. They cast intimate shadows across the long wooden table. The mood was cosy.

Neither wanted to reopen the discussion about Braxton for the moment. Melissa asked him about looking for the ancient sites for the guidebook, and he chatted more easily.

'There's nothing left of the great Pharos of Alexandria. It's almost all cleared out. Within folk memory, the two obelisks known as Cleopatra's Needles were shipped to Britain and America. They built a tram station on the spot where they once stood, or rather one stood and the other – the one that went to London – lay on its side. The only ancient monument left is Pompey's Pillar.'

She served the salad. 'Go on.'

'I also tried to find the house where my grandfather was born. I had always wanted to do that. Did I tell you I once had relatives in Alexandria? But whatever traces had once been were under blocks of modern apartments.'

He met her eyes. He mumbled a few words she didn't catch, then resumed. It was possible he was also feeling awkward.

'One early morning I took my maps and Cavafy's anthology, and stood outside the building where he lived, and spoke some lines aloud. Then I walked through the back streets, an archaeologist, but of the imagination, looking for what was there no longer, and perhaps never had been.

'As I say, the . . . ah, place names are all changed. In the end I took some very thin paper and traced an old map to a standard scale. Then I laid it over the new map of the city, and moved it until I found a m-match. I wasn't going to give up.'

'I found the old Rue Lepsius that way – where Cavafy lived. The building is renumbered, and the road is now called the Sharia Sharm el Sheikh. The Greek consulate has taken over Cavafy's old apartment, made it into a small museum, but it was . . . sterile. The walls are white. You . . . er . . . had to look at the photographs to have any idea of what it was like when it was his home, with deep colours on the walls and idiosyncratic possessions jumbled on every space.'

'Were you disappointed?'

'A little. It could have been done with more thought.'

'Did your pieces for the book turn out well?'

He pulled a face. 'Quite well, I suppose. It's hard to say.'

'It's been a difficult time.'

Melissa pushed back the molten lip of the nearest candle from where a wax stalactite was forming. She wanted to reach out to him so much, to assure him he was not alone, but held back, afraid of spoiling it all, of misreading the tension which had been building since his phone call.

'Yes, but in a strange way that has helped.'

She saw him walking the dusty streets, picking his way through the foetid Egyptian air, his wife in Athens, with no intention of returning; looking around intently, in the process of mastering that knowledge, just as she had been coming to terms with being on her own again.

'I do know what you mean,' she said. 'Standing outside your own situation for a while, learning how to be alone again.'

Alexandros looked away. His expression was profoundly sad.

'Did she come back?' Melissa asked awkwardly. 'Your wife?'

For a few seconds it seemed as if he was not going to reply. He shifted nervously in his seat. Then he looked up. 'No.'

'Are you – how do you feel about that now?'

Another long pause. 'I'm all right. Mainly. My friends are kind. I have my interests, my work . . .'

'My husband came back,' she said boldly. 'But so did the problem.'

After eating, they moved back to the sitting room. More relaxed there, they talked for a long time about their separate situations. How you felt you knew someone, and then discovered you had missed the fundamentals, the driving impulses of their personality. It was good to talk. It seemed a long time since she had imagined having this conversation with him in Corfu. But better late. There was so much she understood better now.

'You aren't still hoping it might work out somehow, are you? With Richard?' he had been visibly jolted when she told him that Richard had been with her up until only a few weeks ago. That she had gone back to him.

The moon was silver bright through the window.

'No. I told you. I feel relieved. I might have gone on trying for years, even when I was unhappy. But he gave me no choice. So for that, I'm grateful.'

'But why did you have to keep on trying?'

That was the question she couldn't answer.

'I don't know. I've gone round and round trying to work it out.' She sighed. 'Lack of confidence, perhaps. Things that happened in the past. Family. A need for security. How long have you got?'

'As long as you want,' he said seriously.

She smiled. 'We don't always feel what we are meant to feel,' she began. It felt as if she were pulling the words out against a great counterweight. 'When you've had a way of coping for so long, it's incredibly hard to change the pattern. It's like being one of those bloody dogs salivating at the bell.'

He spoke slowly. 'When we're in the middle of an awful situation, it's never as clear to the one inside as it is to those looking in from the outside.'

'No . . . that's what my friends told me.'

'It's true. It's only after you come through, and there's some distance, that you can see what everyone else could see all along.'

Melissa tucked her feet up under her on the sofa.

'How many years was it just you and your mother?' he asked gently.

'Most of my life. Even when my father was supposed to be with us, he wasn't – not really.'

'So she is the one you learned from.'

'Of course.'

It was so obvious.

At about midnight, she went upstairs to fetch a sweater. She felt confused, scared of making a mistake. Were they just friends? What about the conversation they had just had – was that a clearing of the way, or a trading of intimacies as friends? It was not the same as that night in Corfu. It was more serious now that they were both free to make a move. It was extraordinary that he was here.

She brushed her hair, checked her make-up and sat longer than she intended in her room. Uncertain what she wanted to happen, she stayed where she was.

When she went down, she found him soundly asleep on his chair. He seemed comfortable, so she fetched a bedspread and laid it over him as gently as she could, resisting the urge to touch his handsome creased face.

And part of her was relieved she did not have to take the decision.

The next day was Saturday. The market in St Martin de Londres was swarming, the crowds swollen with the first spring tourists from the north. They bumped through the melee breathing the concentrated scents of the south in the soaps, dried herbs, the oozing cheeses and the barrels of oil and herb-soaked olives, walnuts, olive oil, spicy sausage and wine. They squeezed past baskets loaded with aubergines, courgettes, great misshapen red peppers, cut melons.

At the café Melissa sat down; a sudden pang of loss and sadness locking her chest. Without thinking she had led the way to the spot where she had sat with Elizabeth so often over the years, just as she had followed the familiar trajectories of the old route through the stalls.

The air felt solid in her lungs. A trickle of sweat made its way down her back.

'Are you OK?' asked Alexandros.

She nodded. 'It just hits me, sometimes. Most of the time I don't let myself feel upset. Mum . . . sorry.'

He reached out across the table and put a hand on her forearm. 'It's natural. You need time, you know.'

Tears were clotting, compressed and painful, behind her eyes. She would not let them go, could not. She would rather they ossified, same as the hard bony hurt.

He was so kind.

They drank coffee in silence, letting their own thoughts be carried on the flow of scents and colours, the lines of life etched deep on other faces passing, the stories of survival they would never hear, the shuffle of the elderly men and women in their rough black and dark blue country work clothes, the shouts of the vendors, the parents with young children, the relaxed well-dressed couples in late middle age.

A plane cut across the blue, high and soundless.

'I'm sorry,' he said. 'I think the, ah, travelling had made me more tired than I thought last night.'

They were lying out on steamer chairs in the garden. A susurrus in the olives, hot sun on skin, clear skies above; it could almost have been summer.

Elizabeth felt close by. Melissa could see her willowy shape by the fig tree, breathing in its sweet sensual August scent, and by the wall of the courtyard pulling the destructive ivy from the dry cracks of the stone wall. We can only make assumptions based on the parts we know of the full picture, or believe we can remember, she wanted to say.

Distant hills slumped on the horizon, giving a sense of space all around. They were facing down the slope where wild flowers had colonised clumps of the meadow, splashing blue and yellow on the ringing spring green of the grasses.

He reached out and took her hand. The warmth of his hand was soothing. Richard's had so often been cold. Her heart seemed to expand with hope. That night in Corfu. Then the optimism was rapidly replaced by dread.

Melissa felt panicky. A churning of the emotions that was made sharper by not knowing why she should feel this way.

Alexandros leaned over to her. His eyes were the same melting brown as she recalled. Just like she had rerun in her head all those months since that night. Suddenly it seemed too good to be true that he was here.

She was even more attracted to him than she had been in Corfu. He had lost the pained brittleness she had seen when they first met. He was decisive and confident now. He had come back into himself. Physically as well as mentally, he was stronger. He was more than she remembered, perhaps more than she could handle.

She did not respond when he cupped her face. Or rather she must have done, because he dropped his hand as soon as she looked at him.

'Sorry,' he said. 'I thought—'

She could only look at his shoes, at the grass, and the smooth red-stained wood of the chairs.

'Is it too soon?'

'I don't know . . .'

'I did not know that you had, er, gone back to your husband.'

'No . . . you couldn't have known that . . .' Melissa picked at wood, unable to explain why she was so confused. She was drawn to him, more than ever, and flattered that he had come to find her, but what was his motive in doing so?

'I don't really know why you're here. We hardly know

343

each other.' There. It was said. She regretted it as soon as the words were out. She closed her eyes tightly, wishing this was not happening.

The chair creaked as he stood up. Wind rustled lightly in the walnut tree above.

'I came because – because—' He cleared his throat but did not continue.

A mad notion surfaced that he had not been honest with her. That there was another reason he had turned up. Perhaps that was to do with Braxton and his theories too. She should have been suspicious earlier.

'What did you want from me?' she whispered.

He looked broken. His face was all angles and incomprehension.

'I did not want anything. I was hoping that we could give to each other. I thought about you so much after . . . that night. Thought that if I gave it time, it might be special between us.'

She shook her head.

'I'm sorry, I got it wrong.' He was bitter again, with the old clipped edge to his speech.

Wretched, she began to explain, but was not up to the argument. It was too soon after Richard. It was painful to think of him, of the way he had manipulated her emotions and screwed up her trust and trampled over her judgement. Thinking about the past months made her tense up. Richard had spoiled everything for her. But the ugly truth was that she had let him do so. Her judgement really was terrible. She was angry with herself for being such a sap.

'I will go,' said Alexandros.

She wanted to stop him but could not think how to do so.

He was walking back towards the house, and she was saying nothing. She could not call him back. It was too soon. She was too wounded.

When he came down with his travel bag, he proudly refused her offer of a lift to Nîmes. She clasped his hand, willing him to understand what she couldn't say. It was a stilted goodbye – another stilted goodbye – and then he was gone.

The place felt desolate without him.

VII

Melissa threw every shutter open in a symbolic gesture to spring cleaning, poked into forgotten cupboards and hung rugs outside for beating.

Afterwards, feigning optimism, she went into town to the *agence immobiliere* to find out what rental she might expect, should she decide to put the *bergerie* into their hands for the coming year.

That was the impetus, born out of a renewed sense that she was at last moving on and concentrating on the practicalities, no matter how turbulent her inner life, that sent her into the locked room at the side of the house.

At the far end of the *bergerie* was a flight of six ragged steps to a pale green door from which paint unfurled in flakes. It was a simple cell-like room used for storage. But perhaps, she thought, it would be possible to convert it into another bedroom, which would add to the rental price. It would be a good practical project, satisfying and profitable, to complete her journey back into the present.

The key was in the drawer of the kitchen table, a blunt rusty weight in her hand which left brown-red dust in the palm. Perhaps it would not even turn in the lock. She took a cloth and some oil, hoping that might work. She need not have worried. Once jiggled into position, the key turned easily.

It was dark inside, with a slight scent of damp. In the light from the door, Melissa stared in. Heavy curtains were drawn over the single small window. She remembered the walls as knobbly grey plaster, but now they were whitewashed. A few cobwebs hung down, and there were patches of crumbly dust, and what might have been mouse-droppings perhaps, on the plain wooden floor. But this was no storeroom as she recalled it.

A single bed, with a mean frame of black iron, was pushed lengthways against the far wall. On it were cushions and folded cotton spreads. Against the walls to either side were low bookcases, of assorted sizes, old and cheap, the kind that might have been brought back from a flea market. On the floor was a wide tray, holding several ballpoint pens.

Finally, a small pine table. On top was a radio, three candle-sticks and a half-full box of candles.

It looked as if Elizabeth had been using it as a kind of study.

Wondering when she had done this, and why she had never mentioned it, Melissa went over to the bookshelves and looked closer. Her heart skipped a beat.

Travel books, on India and Greece, the Greek islands, Egypt, old ones featuring Yugoslavia, were crammed against books by Julian Adie. His poetry was there, and his novels too. The Mason biography, much read.

There was a collection of interviews Adie had given, tran-scripts from radio and television programmes catalogued by an academic; critical assessments of his work; volumes dedicated to the study of his Spirit of Place. Then there were the biographies of other men and women who had known Julian Adie. She picked out one at random, and turned to the index, heart beating faster, feeling sweaty, knowing what she would see. Adie's name, underlined, and a string of page numbers.

Most of the books were twenty, thirty, forty years old. Had Elizabeth haunted antiquarian and second-hand bookshops to get them? Melissa worked her way along. Picture books of Greek Islands. A book of photographs by Grace Heald.

And then, when she had barely assimilated the first, another discovery.

An old sketchbook, dropping its pages. A foolscap notebook, lined pages, a white sticky note on the front in her handwriting: 'Precious. My life in parts. Very roughly written.'

Part Seven: Discoveries

Julian Adie, Behind the Myth
Martin Braxton

Temporal conventions are irrelevant in Adie's oeuvre. Time is pulled continuously out of shape; the present distorts the past, and what was once fact is relegated to unreliable recall, even in his autobiographical work.

Adie shows us how memory subtly reorders the past, playing up certain incidents and compressing others by the importance to which they are assigned by the mind. But in his obsession with the tricks of memory, he is highly susceptible to nostalgia in its cruellest form, and this trait is crucial to an examination of his state of mind in the summer of 1968.

This is the turning point of the myth: his descent into the underworld.

In May, still shell-shocked by Simone's sudden death, Julian Adie returned once again to Corfu. He set off east through France in a stink of petrol from the jerry cans strapped to the inside of the camper van. The student unrest in Paris had spread to the rest of the country in a great wave of belligerence, blockades and disruptions. Many filling stations were closed, but nothing would deter him from making this journey to a spiritual home. And for a free spirit, his views on the political situation were surprisingly conservative. 'I would kick them all back into the Sorbonne,' he told Peter Commin. 'They don't know how lucky they are.'

But when he arrived on his beloved island this time, nothing was as it should have been. The rented villa in Paleokastritsa developed a sewage problem. He hated the atmosphere of the tourist town which had sprouted weed-like between the scallop bays. '*The New Costa Brava*,' he called it, writing grouchily to Don Webber of the invasion of unattractive hordes wearing shorts and caring nothing for the history and classical reson-ances. His beloved landscape was despoiled by litter, and worse, building sites in the coastal olive groves from which grew monstrous cheap hotels, ugly and attractive only to an equally unappealing clientele. His old haunts, especially in the south of the island, had to be filtered through an ever-thicker imaginary gauze. The wounds he had come back to lick were deeper and more bloody than he had realised.

He returned to Kalami, refusing the offer of his old rooms at the White House then regretting his deci-sion. He found a couple of rooms above an olive press off the path to Agni, close to his old cradle, the rock pool by the shrine. There, he could look out to a purple-sprinkled sea shielded by trees from all earthly disappointments.

Was he simply glutting himself on his particular pleasures: alcohol, sea and sun, and the cut and thrust of words which reassured him more than anything else that he was indeed alive? Surely he must have thought now and then of Grace, his long-ago wife.

He was an older, paunchier man. His hair was still thick and light although it must have been greying by then, but on a good day the engaging smile was undimmed in the sun-lined face. He was still extremely attractive to women.

To the world at large, Julian Adie was a success. He was still the great catalyst, the man who 'pumped champagne bubbles into the air', according to fellow poet Bernard Bressens. Stir in the hard-won fame and praise for his work, and it must have been a potent brew.

On the other hand . . . strip away the romance of his travels, his seductive powers, his fame – and what was left? A middle-aged man, a nomad in a camper van grieving for his dead wife. Anyone meeting him now, having read *The Gates of Paradise*, would see it clearly for what it was: an elegiac howl of pain for the author's lost youth and idealism.

Drink helped: it enabled him to function relatively normally until he overshot the mark; it was his constant companion now. Words had dried, along with the effervescence and belly laughter. He went through his paces with women, but in a manner which suggested a tired old animal tied to biological habits. For the first time he felt old, and this time no amount of mythology could disguise the torture of his loss.

He could not bear to be alone. He would go to expatriate parties, occasionally behaving badly. His state of mind that spring and summer was impulsive, reckless even. He was alternately morose, roaming the island alone in his van in search of the past, sleeping out close to deserted beaches, or so gloriously drunk that he could steal a donkey and ride it one afternoon right up to the counter of his favourite bar on the Liston in town.

He raged at the state of the island, but he was also battling his own unsightly flaws. With the years, the successive losses, he had become more angry, embittered, and inclined to lash out. The pugnacious undertow of his work was showing up in real life. Julian Adie could be a violent man, and this was becoming more and more difficult to contain.

He had been seeing a wealthy divorcee, Veronica Rae from Santa Barbara, California, who had been introduced to Adie by Don Webber. They had first met when Adie went to Berkeley on a lecture tour the previous year. It is possible their affair started there. When she heard the news of Simone Adie's death, Veronica had seized her chance. They exchanged letters, and he must have offered her enough encouragement to take a transatlantic plane to Greece as soon as she knew he would be there.

But then one evening at a party, Adie meets a young Englishwoman called Elizabeth Milne. She is in her early twenties, compliant and star struck. Pretty, blonde and naïve, she provides consolation and asks nothing of him. She also bears a striking resemblance to his first wife Grace Heald.

And Julian Adie is an uxorious man, always happiest with a wife whether or not he is faithful to her. Some days, crazed by grief, drink and fury at the loss of Simone, he is barely able to control himself. He has alarmed some of the locals who have known him since the Kalami days with his unreasonable demands and embarrassing outbursts. He cries not only for Simone, but for Grace and Loula too.

It seems doubtful that Elizabeth Milne could have had much idea of the nature of the man. Flattered by his attentions, she would have been a stranger to his experiences and preoccupations: the grinning at death in Cairo, the rank, sweet odours of decay and degeneration, the macabre and cruel fascinations. She would have been oblivious to the objective reality which can be seen so clearly by anyone comparing a photograph of Elizabeth Milne with Grace Adie: that, subconsciously or not, he had cast her in Grace's role before the fall from paradise.

His moods swing. One moment he is full of bonhomie, the next the bright blue eyes cloud and narrow. One night he is found sobbing inconsolably at the tourist spot of Kassiope, while fires are burning for a saint's feast. His old Corfiot friends fear he might be close to the edge, that he might be suicidal.

Worse, he cannot write. He is trying, and failing. The fear is constant, he confides in a letter to Don Webber, dated the end of June: the fear that he has dried up, the fear of losing everything yet again. How many more times can he start again, can he 'shuck off his skins like an old snake'?

But there is no doubt the man has courage. In his personal life, he has rebuilt himself time and again. He is certain he will do so again, even though this time his courage is more a kind of recklessness, or madness. After all, he has come back to his beginning as a writer, to those mythic Ionian waves that hold the sunlight in their blue swell. He had forgotten the way the sea changes temperature with the currents, the cruel caress of the undertow as it pulls towards the turtleback rocks, but that is good. He will revisit the start of his story again, and remake it with hard-edged experience.

He has the title already: *Songs of Blue and Gold*.

His two rooms at the olive press are austere. He wants it that way. He wants to live as he did back in the nineteen thirties. But he is no longer that young man in more ways than one. At the woodworm-infested table he uses as a desk, moths butt the stinking paraffin lamp he has placed by his faithful old typewriter, but the words come only as stutters.

According to local lore, Adie was the bringer of riches and was welcomed back like a lord. His landlady, Marina Dandola, supplies him with paper for the typewriter, wine, her own olive oil and the hard black bread he has requested. From her cottage across the path she hears the tapping as he works, his footsteps and the engine of his camper van starting up. Her recollection is of him working from sunrise to mid-morning when he would set off to spend the day elsewhere. She went into his rooms to tidy up and make the bed until he told her that he preferred her not to. He seemed superficially cheerful if a little distracted.

But Yannis Retalas, son of the erstwhile shopkeeper at Kalami, has a different perspective. 'His soul was troubled that year.' According to Retalas, Adie was uncharacteristically silent. But then one night he got into a fight in the bar. A local builder was talking with friends about a construction site he was working on, and Adie staggered up, gave him a torrent of oaths.

He had turned to go, having said his piece, but then whipped round and landed a right hook on the builder's jaw. A scuffle ensued, from which Adie emerged with a cut lip and a ripped shirt. He had to be banned from the bar, which put the owner into a bind because Adie's money had been keeping the till full.

*

Elizabeth is often with him as he revisits the places he remembers. On a boat supplied by a Corfiot friend they sail the coast. They walk the mountain paths. Her presence might calm him a little, but despair is never far from the surface.

One night he takes Elizabeth to a party given by the Swiss architect Ivo Swarbach. It is a bad move. As soon as they arrive they come face to face with a quarrelsome Veronica Rae. Guests have been exhorted to '*Dress with Abandon*' but even so she stands out from the crowd, a bony figure in a column of silver sequins.

At one point, fuelled no doubt by quantities of alcohol, Adie and Veronica engage in a loud argument. It is a classic of its kind; the company falls silent and listens. The public spat is played out in front of dozens of witnesses. A slap rings out – Veronica has struck him hard and humiliatingly. Elizabeth runs to his aid, screaming abuse at her rival. Julian Adie has to be restrained from retaliating. For he would hit a woman, let there be no doubt about that. It would not be the first time, nor the last. A few minutes later, all three of them have left the party.

It is the last reported sighting of Veronica Rae alive.

What happened next has long been the subject of intense speculation. The published facts are few but what is certain is that Veronica Rae's body was found on one of the tiny empty beaches south of Kassiope by fishermen two days after the Swarbach party.

*

When I began my investigations at Kalami it was with the intention of subjecting text to the closest scrutiny, remarrying Adie's words to the landscape as it were. I wanted to see for myself the St Arsenius shrine, intrigued for some time by the fact that after 1968, Julian Adie never wrote another poem or lyrical passage about the place of his iconic rebirth. In interviews Adie gave subsequently, whether in print or in radio and television conversations, this fulcrum of his idealism was never again mentioned. All questions were blanked. Why?

The abrupt abandonment of what had been Adie's thematic heart, so crucial to understanding him as a man and an artist, pointed to a seismic shift which warranted detailed investigation beyond the texts.

It was not long before my enquiries in the locality took a disquieting turn. Not only did people remember Julian Adie but they spoke about him as if he were still among them, as if events which had taken place decades previously were still newly-minted.

I put to them his name, the location and the dates. What emerged from all these separate conversations, with only slight variation of detail, was a single unsettling story. In the centre of it were Julian Adie and a drowned woman.

In the days after Veronica Rae's body was discovered, police interviewed the host and party guests as well as the wider expatriate community. With no evidence to the contrary, they rapidly — perhaps too rapidly —

concluded their investigations with the declaration that the death was not suspicious. Accidental drowning while under the influence of painkilling drugs and alcohol, was expected to be the official verdict, and indeed was reported as such in the local expatriate newspaper, which also – extraordinarily – declined to mention Adie's name in connection with the incident. In fact, the verdict was left open.

Astonishingly, there is no record that the police ever interviewed Adie. Furthermore, he was allowed to leave the island a few days later. Neither was Elizabeth Milne interviewed by police.

My researches, however, have cast serious doubt on the presumption of both Julian Adie and Elizabeth Milne's innocence in Veronica Rae's death. But by the time the body had been released to the Rae family, the two key witnesses had fled, in Adie's case at least, never to set foot on Corfu again.

Elizabeth Milne changed her name on marriage soon after, becoming known under her married name of Elizabeth Norden as a London-based landscape painter (again, in a curious echo of Grace Heald) and relieving herself of any lingering connection to a suspicious death in a foreign country.

On the island, the stories persisted.

The three of them were seen that night on the rocks by the little chapel of St Arsenius.

*

Kosmidis Patronas was a boy of twelve who had been taken out by his uncle, a night fisherman. He has no doubt that the two women and a man he watched from the fishing caique with its acetylene lamps were Julian Adie, Veronica Rae and Elizabeth Milne. He put the time at about ten thirty. His evidence at the time was not taken seriously because of his age and the fact that he was a summer visitor himself – from Thessaloniki – and therefore his grasp of local geography was not deemed sufficiently reliable. It should be noted too, that as a stranger he had no knowledge of Julian Adie nor reason to be gratefully loyal to him as were so many of the villagers of Kalami and Agni.

Now an electrical engineer, Patronas has never changed his story. He stands by his identification of the figures he saw from the boat. The scene was lit by a searchlight moon, and he remembered the distinctive blond hair of the strong stocky man, and the long blonde hair of the younger woman.

But most vividly of all, he recalls the silver dress worn by Veronica Rae, catching the light like the sparkling scales on a fish as it turns in the water. She was upright on the rock. She was not swimming, nor did she show any sign that she was about to go swimming.

They were almost round the headland when he heard a scream. His uncle held the caique on its course. When asked, he said he had not heard anything. After a while Kosmidis thought he must have imagined it.

*

The most important and startling evidence, however, is provided by Marina Dandola. It was she who cleaned the olive press after Adie had left in a hurry and discovered the mess of papers along with the empty bottles and overflowing ashtrays. Some of the papers had been burned. Others were ripped through and defaced. But there remained about twenty that were legible, if stained and screwed up. She could not read them, but she was canny enough to know that Adie's golden touch might make them worth something one day.

After all, Manos Kiotzas had sold several manuscript pages given to him by Adie on his departure from the White House at the outbreak of war. The high price they fetched after Adie became famous had bought the first boats that he hired to tourists.

But these sheets were half-finished, then half-destroyed. No one wanted them. So she kept them, never entirely losing hope that one day they might come into their own to her benefit.

A title page had been neatly typed yet the poems were stillborn: phrases and words that were never published, never carved and polished by Adie into his *Songs of Blue and Gold*. And there was a simple reason they could never be put before the public. As I will show, they can be read as his confession.

Looking for Julian
Melissa Norden

Finding my mother's account was a shock, not least because I had been so certain there were no papers.

The notebook, originally a painter's sketch book with extra papers stuck in, was bound tight with a thick elastic band to hold it all together. The closely scribbled pages of tiny writing were sometimes hard to decipher. It was oblique in places, but for the most part remarkably honest. Some of it was uncomfortable reading for a daughter. But this much was clear: Dr Braxton, for all that his intentions had made me wary, had discovered before I had a devastating episode in my mother's life. In many ways, it was the defining event of her life and one from which she never entirely recovered.

He was right too about the existence of papers, papers of a kind I would never have expected to find. I was astonished, and profoundly discomfited, to find verbatim records – or as near as could be – of her conversations with Julian Adie in Corfu, preserved as if she did not want to forget them, wanted to be able to reconstruct them afterwards. They were dated May to August 1968. Reading these pages was like eavesdropping. The intimacy was unsettling, but my need to know overrode any other consideration. Her observations were raw fragments, like shattered pottery still caked with earth in the archaeologist's hand.

Letters, too. A folder of them, some written but never sent; others postmarked and returned.

The biographer comes to the aftermath like a guest too late for the banquet, to the disembowelled birds and spilled wine and crumbs, then has to find a way of gathering the leftovers and reconstructing them so that all the pieces make sense. It is a delicate business. The memories of those who were there might be unreliable, or coloured by previous slights and arguments. At any rate, the picture built up piecemeal is only ever a construct of the biographer's imagination, even when worked by the purest of motives.

We all want wholeness, for the narrative to have a clear momentum followed by conclusion. But what we are faced with is constant revision and reinterpretation, as subsequent versions of the story come to light. And the writer of a new biography must necessarily find something new to say, must be in the business of recreating a life, for better, for worse, and for his own purposes.

I would not have begun this endeavour had it not been for Dr Martin Braxton. At first I was simply trying to discover the truth about one episode in my mother's life because I thought it would help me to know her better, because she had seemed to be telling me something that she wanted me to understand. Then, later, it became my duty to ensure that she was fairly represented in the light of Dr Braxton's published work.

All successful biographers need a source of new material and a piece of good luck. Dr Braxton had his piece of biographer's luck when he was approached by Hero Adie's friend Megan Venner with private papers which contained the astonishing allegation that Julian Adie had been party to a suspicious death.

According to Braxton's published account, he detected the story in a scholarly manner from Adie's own literary works. He fretted away at the texts, eager to know why Julian Adie never wrote another poem or lyrical passage about the blue sea and the shrine where he was 'reborn', why he would never speak about it after the summer of 1968.

He presents himself as the academic reading between the lines, making his wide-ranging assumptions, becoming the biographer. Decades after the events he describes and distorts, he is peering into the gaps, the evasions, the edited leaps, like a caver shining his torch into the tiny crevices and crinkles of rock, making tiny temporary circles of light deep underground.

What he found in Kalami was perfect for his purposes: a collection of unfinished poems.

No previous biographer (nor Julian Adie himself for that matter) had written about Elizabeth even as an unnamed shadow. In any published account of his life, she was not even a footnote. Gradually the truth of her presence has been established, teased from the dust and rubble of a literary reputation.

Now I am writing her into Julian Adie's story. It is a personal account, of course, but true to her, I hope, and her version of events.

- *1968* -

On her return to England from Corfu in the late summer of 1968, Elizabeth wrote to Adie, care of his publishers in London. She was cautious in her choice of phrasing, but made it plain that she needed him to contact her.

Veronica Rae was dead. To Elizabeth, that knowledge was crushing. The weight of evidence was surely that her death was a tragic accident, caused by her own reckless behaviour and instability. But was Adie's continued refusal to acknowledge Elizabeth a sign that they — as the last people to see her alive — had greater reason to feel guilty?

For Elizabeth did feel guilty. She and Julian Adie were implicated. She had provoked Veronica by sending the note over to her at the party, knowing that the woman was stupidly drunk, wanting to hurt her. Adie had been with her when she went into the water.

He was the only person she could talk to. '*And if he would not, that could only mean that there was something that must remain unsaid,*' she wrote. '*What happened that night that was so much worse than I first thought?*'

Several weeks elapsed before he replied, in the briefest terms. His letter was polite, and claimed pressure of work. He did not suggest they meet again, but asserted he would remember their time together with pleasure. He wished her luck for any exhibition she had in the future. It was friendly but it had the ring of finality about it. He answered none of her questions.

She kept the letter, but tried to forget about it.

Alone in the tiny bedsit she rented in Pimlico with an allowance from her parents (still concerned about her state of mind but relieved not to have to face the social complications of her return to the family home in Suffolk), Elizabeth buried herself in books: psychology, science, history and novels. She was glad not to have been summoned home but she could not paint; her hand trembled too much to hold a pencil to a line drawing. She felt weak when she ventured out and fainted one day on a bus. Her nerves were a constant susurration, never allowing her any peace. She was frightened; but what was she so scared of, all the time? What had happened that night? Could she really have done any more than she did?

She began to rationalise that her present problems had more to do with her sense of guilt at a first, tiny, death – pushed right down inside until it turned rotten.

Elizabeth managed to haul herself to the bookshop on Victoria Street where she bought Adie's books, tearing through them looking for clues, searching for some insight. *The Colossus of the Rose*, his account of Rhodes and his post-war romance with L and their subsequent marriage, was so richly evocative it made her weep. She was too close; she was there with him in L's place as they walked in medieval darkness through the town in the months before the street lamps were restored, into the overgrown garden which holds the Mosque of Murad Reis, and into its deeper blackness, deeper quiet, among the broken Turkish tombstones. And later, in the course of another summer evening incursion, finding the tiny house at its heart, overrun by hibiscus.

She was there with him on the fallen gravestones while sunset trembled over the mosque's dome, rosy as the wine, the dry leaves of the eucalyptus cracking from the branch as they took flight, whirring through the soft scented air. She was L with her generous lips, and dark, darting eyes. She inhaled the musky sighs of flowers and tobacco smoke, a breath away from the dark crumbs of bone.

Elizabeth certainly fell for his literary romanticism there. For Julian Adie misled her, along with all his other readers. He had been a terrible husband to Loula Habib.

The question is: how far was Elizabeth aware of that? The diaries make much of the romanticism, but the slowly dawning doubts about him are implicit rather than set down in black and white.

When, months later, Elizabeth finally found the will to paint, she filled vast canvases with abstract roars of the sea, tumultuous waves and treacherous rocks.

The year following his wife Simone's death was a turning point for Julian Adie. All biographical sources agree on that. His *joie de vivre* was gone, according to reports from many of his old friends and accounts in several memoirs. His long correspondence with Don Webber faltered, and he began the long retreat into solitude at the imposing house in Sommières. He wrote nothing but rambling thoughts for his notebooks; no poetry, no travel pieces. It would be four years before he managed to channel his demons into the next big novel cycle, *The Carcassonne Quartet*.

Long-standing confidants such as Peter Commin and Bernard Bressens who tracked him to his Languedoc lair found the '*bumptious little satyr*' of old much reduced in spirit, and morbidly introspective. '*He had pulled back into two rooms at the back of the house, which remained shuttered and neglected. He claimed this was due to the expense of heating the place, but that cannot really have been the issue, and certainly not in high summer,'* said Bressens in a concerned letter dated October to Adie's literary agent (and their mutual friend) Peter Hobday.

Hobday made a visit himself and was shocked at what he found, including the extent of Adie's drinking and the bats colonising the top floor of the old manse. *'Julian was a deeply troubled and unhappy man,'* he said. *'It was more than just the loss of Simone, dreadful though that was for him. He told me it was the loss of hope, of self, of any cohesiveness. It was shocking because this was a man who had reinvented himself so often before, in a new country, with a new wife, with a new style of writing. I would say it was a breakdown – it was very serious indeed. But he would not accept any help. He was determined to push through it on his own.'*

Adie's plight was reported in much the same terms by a journalist and photographer sent by the London *Sunday Times* when they went to see him in November 1968. The celebrated writer was withdrawn yet prone to sudden rages. He indulged in forensic examination of his own character and motives where previously he had always been more interested in abstracts and other people. He objected vehemently to the suggestion that he spend more time in the company of trusted friends, retorting that he was all the company he needed, and when he was bored of himself he drove down to Aigues Mortes and picked up 'the saddest fishiest-smelling whore' he could find. It was impossible to tell if he was telling the truth or deliberately trying to strike a bum note.

Julian Adie was a survivor, though. So long as he had a sunny landscape away from the prison island of Britain, with a passionate effort he could ride out the bad times. He professed that his love for France was in inverse proportion to his hatred of the old country. If anyone dared to point out that France suffered just as much industrial unrest, and paralysis of the state system, he would narrow his eyes, their colour changed to stainless steel, and decree, 'It's completely different. The British worker downs tools because his life is unbearable – well, he's right there. Only he thinks it's about money and factory hours, not seeing it's the whole grinding wretchedness of the country. The French strike for a *philosophy*.'

Superficially these were good years for him. He had achieved fame, and the books supported him without the necessity of having to find other employment. His gift for making enduring friendships sustained him; there is no doubt his company was relished by a host of fond individuals, from writers and intellectuals to the dustman with whom he enjoyed fruitful discussions of existentialism. Wine was plentiful and cheap. He soaked it up, along with the light, the heat and the respect accorded him.

- 1973 -

When Elizabeth saw Julian Adie again, she was a married woman with a small child.

She and my father Edward were idling in the south-west of France under a benign September sun. Edward was trying to set up an appointment to view a renowned collection of Byzantine art at a private house in Nîmes. Through an ex-colleague at the Courtauld, he had arranged a fortnight's rental of a cottage not far from Uzès, and combined it with a lazy holiday before the start of his college term.

Edward Norden was a lecturer and art historian fifteen years older than Elizabeth. They had met at a private dinner at the Chelsea Arts Club in early 1970 when she was drawn to his self-assurance and wit, as much as his sandy, bluff good looks. Occasionally he wrote pieces of journalism, he said, and he would very much like to inter-view her for a feature on up-and-coming female painters. He adored the seascapes. The resulting article was less a newspaper interview than a whirlwind romance.

He always claimed that he made Elizabeth's name in more ways than one. He had promoted her paintings in a series of serious studies and continued to do so. Even that was beginning to look like selfishness. He loved telling people his wife was Elizabeth Norden, although that marital fact never stopped him pursuing other artists, invariably attractive female ones.

*

That day, in late September 1973, I would have been two years old.

Elizabeth was enervated, not knowing quite why – or at least not admitting the reason to the diary she kept. '*I wanted – I needed – some small escape that morning,*' she wrote. '*I wanted to let him see for himself what it was like.*' By this, I assume she meant her husband, and his propensity even after less than three years of marriage for leaving her to her own devices (and a demanding toddler) while he pursued his own interests both at work and play.

This time, though, Elizabeth, usually so resigned to his behaviour, rebelled. She walked out leaving me with him for once.

She took the car and drove west, aiming on a whim for Carcassonne. But she had misjudged the distance – it was much further than she thought. She was stopped, forcibly, in a tiny fortified village where a market blocked the road. St Martin de Londres, read the scratchy sign. Why go on, she reasoned, if she did not feel like it?

She managed to squeeze the car into a parking space among battered vans and ancient Peugeots, and went in on foot.

The casual artistry of the fruit and vegetable stalls entranced her: the polished red peppers like grotesquely oversized plastic lips, the smiles of split watermelon, the sensuous pink of the fig she pulled apart in her fingers.

An old woman in black sat in a doorway with a single tray of fungi. Stunted men swayed past with rolling gait and the wide chests of fighting cocks.

Elizabeth was dizzy with the colours and textures. She sat down at one end of a café table whose other occupants were a group of middle-aged women discussing their ailments, and those of their families, with the competitive concentration of a contract bridge party. She gave in to her own thoughts, let the scene pass like a film in front of her.

She noticed his hair first. The tanned *paysan* with blond hair. Perhaps there were touches of grey in it. Short and stocky, that expression of secret satisfaction playing about the lips, in the flow of market shoppers but apart from it. The confident swagger, chin jutting up.

It was Julian Adie.

He was poking beadily about the cascades of vegetables; a mean string bag dangling from his wrist contained a few small lumpy parcels.

Her heart was pounding. What should she say? She rose unsteadily to her feet, but hesitated for too long. He had gone past before she had decided what she was going to do. She stood up and called his name, meaning only to be friendly, but he was disappearing into an aisle of stalls, his tracks closed by the other shoppers and browsers.

'*And that is when I began to think of him again. Just that glimpse. It brought it all back when I had almost succeeded in forgetting about him.*'

When Edward suggested buying a property in France, spending summers under unbroken sunshine, eating good food and surrounded by the true colours of the south, she surprised him with her keenness. If she realised that his motives were as much concerned with the buying of a slice of freedom for himself as much as a plot of foreign soil, then she kept her reservations to herself.

He travelled to France by himself several times over the next year, for academic as well as house-hunting reasons. In 1974 they bought the tumbledown *bergerie* at St Cyrice.

It was Elizabeth who made it her choice, finally. '*It was nothing to do with Julian Adie, and it was everything*,' she wrote.

After the first few years, it was just as well she was happy there. She and I were spending most of the summers there alone while Edward pursued his own interests. Gradually they pulled further apart until they were effectively separated. For my sake, I think, they maintained the decencies.

We saw less and less of him. He died before I had a chance to know him as an adult. He was fifty-five when he had a heart attack. A twenty-four-year-old classical violinist was with him in the hotel room in Milan.

- 1974 -

Julian Adie wrote that the past is not fixed. It is always at the mercy of perception, a perspective which changes with deepened knowledge and experience. The act cannot change, but the understanding of how it happened can.

In the Languedoc, Elizabeth tried again to contact him. *'All the questions had rushed back. I needed to know what had really happened, that night in Corfu,'* she wrote in her diary.

But Elizabeth was snatching at air. Adie would have none of it. Several letters survive from this time, rough drafts, or nearly good copies which were spoiled by a nervous mistake. It was important to her to get the words right, especially to him. Desperate for a response, she was *'willing someone to say something that chimes with my own understanding, someone who understands my reference points'*. Again she writes, *'The mind locks — taking pictures one after the other, painting pictures one after the other, hoping to transform it into what one hopes to see. Romance over reason, desperation over reason.'*

Finally there is the letter sent, but returned.

Several times she wandered around Sommières in the hope of bumping into him. But perhaps the Julian she had known on Corfu already no longer existed, just as the adventurous blond youth of *The Gates of Paradise* had long since slipped away to be superseded by the older man. In a newspaper photograph she kept, dated 1976, he was almost unrecognisable. He was drinking so much that his nose had developed into a lumpy purple protrusion, his bright blue eyes were sunk in fatty folds. He was stout, and apparently in disguise under a woollen hat of the type worn by French countrymen.

Finally, she steeled herself and went to his house. She found the only inhabitants were two very young Swiss women in his swimming pool. Adie was not there, they informed her.

Adie was elsewhere a great deal, at this time. He had begun placing advertisements in the personal columns of the newspapers, hoping to meet as many women as possible. This he defined as creative endeavour (and admitted it in a forthright interview in *Midi Libre*): not only was there a good chance of finding some uncomplicated sex, but he was on the look-out for new characters for dissection in his ambitious new sequence of novels.

When Elizabeth found out about this, she wrote: '*He is making a stupid spectacle of himself, but hardly seems to care. It is the talk of the cafés and bars of Sommières.*' The news hurt her; her attitude seems that of a discarded wife (which in reality she was, though not Julian Adie's), a woman who had a vested interest in keeping a scandal at bay that might taint her by association.

She left her telephone number with the Swiss girls at his pool, and again on the notepad by the telephone in the kitchen as she left (in case they forgot or were too high on dope to remember), but received no call. She wrote at least one more letter which was similarly ignored.

Was there an element of deluded romance about her chase? Her own words hold nothing to suggest she would have liked to resurrect the affair at that stage. The romance was all in the past. And why would she have wanted to, given his current activities? For what it is worth, I am sure that was not in her mind, not even to have her revenge on my father.

My mother was an elegant woman not only in her appearance but in the sense that she always behaved with dignity, having been unable to escape the creed of good behaviour ingrained in her since childhood, despite her few notable rebellions. She was self-contained, and averse to taking risks. Adie's behaviour would have horrified her. No, by that stage, I am sure she would not have been interested romantically in Julian Adie.

Yet each Saturday in summer she would take me – at least until I was old enough to want to stay with friends in the village – to the market at St Martin de Londres. There we would sit in the café by the fountain, and we would watch the faces as they passed. It was our game, or so I thought.

She never saw him there again, but the hope persisted that she might.

The following excerpt from her diary shows that her sense of guilt was hardening, compounded rather than eased by the years. Julian Adie was the only person she could talk to about it, but he would not.

She began to blame herself, although not without an appreciation of the irony.

'*We were all playing games that summer in Corfu, and they knew better than I did what the score was. But this one was my game. Did I regret falling for him? Not in the beginning, when it was happening. He was exciting, and generous and kind. I came back into myself under his touch. He was like a healer to me and I will never forget that. But afterwards, yes. In retrospect I understand much better. Perhaps I was stuck with a lingering infatuation, but I accepted that was all it was. That was for Julian as he was in my mind, not as he became.*'

It must be right to see her continuing interest in Julian Adie as obsessive. But it would be a grave mistake to assume that the reason behind it remained unchanged. In any case, she would see Julian Adie again, although it would be several more years before they finally spoke.

- 1975 and after -

When Julian Adie met Annick Plazy on the banks of the Vidourle in 1975, she was twenty-three and recently married. From their first shared *pastis* at the Bar Vidourle, they had an understanding. They began an eight-year affair which suited them both: in Annick's own words 'no commitment, only pleasure'. It was his ideal made real, and did not preclude another marriage for him, this time to Marie Basselin.

Marie was the only one of his wives who knew of him by reputation before they met in Paris; she should have been prepared.

Sophisticated and cultured, she was a green-eyed russet-haired beauty from a wealthy family. He met her through the daughter of a long-time friend. She was only in her thirties, a fashion model and latterly a designer. Excelling himself with his own self-regard, Julian Adie was unfaithful to her the day after their wedding with a tourist he picked up at the Bar Vidourle.

There was no honeymoon. According to Marie, in conversation with Adie's first biographer Stephen Mason, disillusionment was almost immediate. Adie was suffering blackouts triggered by alcohol abuse. 'Like many who take refuge in drink, he was mean and embittered. But he was still clever. He used his words and actions to destroy me. No, I am not exaggerating. He had always to gain the upper hand, to outwit you, to blame you for everything so that he could be absolved. You could not reason with him. It would all be twisted back at you.

'He got angry because here was a woman not falling in with his plan of how life should be and what should happen next! He did not realise how strong I was, and he did not like it!

'But it was hard, because there were times when I would have to question my own judgement, when he justified his behaviour with crazy fabrications: once I refused to come out in the car and collect him from a nightclub in Nîmes at four o'clock in the morning, so it was my fault that he went off with a tart he picked up when they were both too drunk to see. And after a while I would start to feel, even though I knew it was not logical, that it was my fault, that I had made him do it.'

If his writing is any indication, his moods were dark during this time. His playfulness is edged with cruelty, and his creations obscene – sadistic, even. Self-destructive despite his continuing success with a harem of local women, who seemed to care for him beyond all reasonable expectation, he would rage at Marie when she tried to moderate his intake. Construed as criticism, her efforts would make him more determined to drink as much as his body would take.

She would leave for Paris, return, only to repeat the process. He manipulated her. She retaliated. They fought – violently at times.

'It was a mad time in my life,' said Marie. 'He did manipulate my mind, because I loved him and I feared losing him, having to admit the marriage was a disaster. It was only when I woke up and realised he had lost me, not the other way round, that I could regain my self-respect. Now I look back and wonder how it took me so long. But at the time . . . I was too close. I could not see it.'

The shortest and most disastrous of Julian Adie's marriages was over in a storm of recriminations over his women, his drinking and her spending of his money.

The novel he published in 1977, written during the stormy year of their marriage, is even darker and edgier than the previous offering in *The Carcassonne Quartet*. The lyricism is tainted with obscenity. In a radio interview to mark its appearance, Adie sounds short-tempered and sour.

Asked about himself, he growls, 'My life? It's all there in the books. Read them or don't read them. I don't care.' When asked whether his much vaunted theories of 'modern love', sex and marriage brought him, or anyone else, as much pleasure as they were supposed to, he declines to answer.

'He did not age well. There was a suppressed rage all the time, I always felt,' said Sally Commin, second wife of his old friend and bibliographer Peter. 'No one enjoys getting older, but he found it harder than most to adapt.'

He thought of himself as a romantic and a force of nature. Others thought him a self-centred egotist, raging against the serial failures of his marriages and the lack of any genuine appreciation (as he saw it) of his literary gifts in the home country he had always dismissed so vituperatively. He was mired in the kind of bored, dissolute expatriatism that he vigorously despised.

Newly divorced, Adie could be as affably garrulous, intelligent and amusing as ever. He was fizzing with new ideas. But there was a new hardness that was all too easily polished to a gleam by drink. In repose, one newspaper interviewer reported, he had the blank stare of a lizard waiting to strike.

And it is true that his work became progressively darker, more cruel and perverted. Friends who had previously only glimpsed Adie's black side were now offered novel-sized vistas of the inner workings of his mind, and had found themselves shocked as each successive volume of *The Carcassonne Quartet* appeared.

According to Dr Braxton, *The Carcassonne Quartet* contains Julian Adie's 'confession'. Braxton is jubilant to find what he calls the final piece of the puzzle in *Adele*, the third novel in the sequence, published in 1979.

I found Elizabeth's copy of *Adele* in the room at the *bergerie* where I discovered the diaries.

A page was turned down, and a passage marked, or rather roughly scored with red ballpoint pen until the paper had torn.

Within these furious etches, the narrator is describing how he is young again in the water, released from the poisoned watch of advancing age. The sea is black and cold but his limbs move smoothly, porpoise-supple. Under her gleaming fish-scale dress the woman is naked on the rock above, thighs parted, taunting him with the scarlet slash between her legs. He sinks his teeth deep into her, hard enough to draw fresh blood, rejoicing in the viscous oyster taste. His hands are spiny starfish on her white thighs. He looks up, breathless. Then he pulls her abruptly down, deliciously conscious of her pain as the sharp stones rip into her. She cries out as salt attacks the gashes in her flesh. She struggles, protests she cannot swim. He tows her by the hair, wedges her into the angle of a rock and leaves her gasping as he swims back, sleek as a water rat, Poseidon to her Medusa.

The other woman, waiting under the trees, is excited.

The prose is urgent, the images sickening, obscene in places. Braxton would love to claim this as the final confession, he says, but stops short. Even he admits the danger of assuming a work of fiction must necessarily be an insight into the author's own thoughts. As we have seen so many times, Adie was a man who used his experiences in his work, but the result was never the whole truth.

So, in his reassessment of Julian Adie, Dr Braxton asserts that he and Elizabeth Norden were implicated in Veronica Rae's death. He strongly implies (but does not go quite so far as to claim conclusively) that Julian Adie killed Veronica Rae.

His claim that Julian Adie was never to see Elizabeth again after their separate departures from Corfu that summer is, strictly speaking, untrue although in essence, he is correct. Moreover, Braxton's claim that this sudden rupture was due to Veronica Rae's death, indicating some form of guilt, perhaps joint, perhaps individual, cannot easily be dismissed.

'*My life is all there, in the books and poems,*' Adie once

said, and my mother wrote out that quote in her diary for 1979. I cannot tell how literally she took it.

Perhaps this does explain how Elizabeth became the person I knew as my mother, how it squares with what I understood at the time. When I think back to those years at St Cyrice, I have to peel back layers of my own. Most of the memories are of my preoccupations such as swimming and making camps in the woods with village friends, mending my bicycle or finding someone else's father to do it for me. She is there, of course, at the table in the kitchen, or working the garden, but she is at the periphery of the main picture, which is of myself, as a child, coming back to the *bergerie* hungry and dusty, asking what's for supper.

If Elizabeth had been red-eyed or weeping when I returned, naturally I would have known she was unhappy. But she was not. My mother was herself: calm and capable, slow to show annoyance. The *bergerie* was clean and bright. She prepared delicious, adventurous food for us to try, chatting about the markets she'd been to and what she had found there, the people she'd spoken to. She drove off on her own expeditions to churches and cheese-makers, *brocantes* for cheap old furniture which she could sand down and paint. All I can conclude is that, yes, it was possible – in practical terms – for her to have been the person Annick described haunting the streets of Sommières because she had the transport, and the opportunity while I was happily in the company of the neighbours' children. If I were asked whether I recognised that person, I would unhesitatingly deny it. Yet she was. I have her word for it.

It is true, now I think hard, that we were almost always alone in the evenings, and that she could be very quiet. At the time that did not seem cause for concern. She read a great deal.

I never heard the name Julian Adie from her. Not even when the newspapers were full of his name and the terrible suicide of his second daughter Hero, his '*Egyptian child*' who hanged herself in 1985 using a pair of silk stockings just as the character of Adele had done in his novel. My mother never uttered a word when the column inches subsequently poured out, picking over Adie's malign effect on the women who had loved him.

It must have been just as well that she never spoke of him. Imagine how our circumstances might have unfolded if the use of his name had been easy and familiar. It is hard not to conclude that Elizabeth was better off without him, whichever version of his life you wanted to believe. What for her began as a disappointment, many would interpret as nothing less than a lucky escape.

There is another quality she had, which I did not fully appreciate at the time, and that was her quiet determination. It carried her through her marriage to my father to self-sufficiency and a second successful career. It ensured we both held our heads high. It would also ensure she saw Julian Adie just once more.

In 1990 Julian Adie was found dead in his bath, a bottle of rough red wine spilled on the floor, and a bunch of black grapes clinging plumply to the lip of the tub. In his throat, always so busy, always producing words with such brio in life, was lodged a large, whole grape.

For many months afterwards, a rumour ran that a woman had been seen wild-faced and driving erratically away from the house in a small white car at the time of death. The tale was never proved anything but apocryphal although it would have been all too easy to believe.

Before I left France that summer, I did find his house in Sommières. I went on foot this time, knowing I must have missed it first time in the car. Behind high walls it stood, closer to the Roman bridge than I'd expected, the building proud, well-maintained and now divided into apartments. A new road clips the edge of its territory. No longer is there a vineyard to the side, but a municipal football pitch, and to the front, fine wrought-iron gates which open onto the glorious vista of a vast parking lot and a Champion hypermarket.

The picture I was left with was not the golden young romantic on his island, but the gnarled traveller at the end of his journey, and with him only ghost companions. The sensuous pagan who had tried to disengage time had grown old. Not a bad man, but a lost one.

As I stood outside those gates, I thought too of my mother: the summers at St Cyrice and the secret patterns of her life; all those years when I had no idea of her state of mind or intentions. The woman who had come to this great bourgeois house with only the skin and bones of her hopes, was completely different from the mother who cared for me. I had thought it had been just the two of us for so long, I had no concept that there was another person who was with us all the time, informing her decisions, clouding her thoughts and drawing on her compassion. I was there with her, at the time, and yet I did not know.

I knew nothing of the gaps in my knowledge. When I finally realised, and set out to try to fill them, I had to look for Julian Adie first. My search was made all the harder by a poignant imbalance: profound though his impact on her life was, she barely registered in his. It may well have been due to Dr Braxton's approaches to her during the previous months that my mother gave me the book with the inscription. Peraps I misjudged what I should do with it. In retrospect I wonder whether all she wanted was for me to take it away and lose it somewhere, which was what usually happened to books she lent me.

*

Travelling in Adie's footsteps, I pieced together a sad and surprising story which told me a little more about her character than I knew already, although nothing that would alter it profoundly, and a great deal more about myself.

In re-evaluating her life, I discovered a more complex version not only of her personal history but of our joint history. To push the theory further, perhaps that is the point of biography: by reading the lives of others we are only ever trying to find points of reference for ourselves. Their journeys are our own.

Part Eight: Medusa

I

B ell Cottage felt like the inside of a dark cold shell as Melissa went through it room by room. Cupboards and drawers were cleared to bare wood, and furniture labelled for removal.

'So you're really selling, then?'

Leonie came down one Sunday. She said it was to help pack boxes, but Melissa knew it was more than that.

'Yes. It's . . . a good offer. A family with three children, moving down from south London. They're really keen. It wouldn't be practical for me to live here. Especially not on my own.'

Leonie looked around at the long low rooms. The chill of solitude had settled over every surface. 'No . . .'

More boxes from the flat in Morpeth Terrace, their provenance clearly marked, were stacked against one wall in the hall. They had arrived a week before and not been invited further in. Soon they would be sorted and repacked for storage along with all the others.

'The divorce is going through,' Melissa told her. 'I want it done as quickly as possible.'

Leonie gave a sad frown.

'I'm fine – really. It's not great . . . but it's OK. At least now I really know where I stand.'

So many words and actions at odds with each other which she would not now have to disentangle. No more doubting of her own understanding of a promise or a situation. *Never again will I let a man try to control me, blame me for everything so that he could be absolved.*

Leonie hugged her. 'You're doing so well. I'm so proud of you.'

Melissa nodded. She was proud of herself too, though warily so. She should have heard the snapping sinews of the failed marriage sooner – should never have given him the second chance – but had to comfort herself with the knowledge that she had tried her hardest. She had pushed the anger that came with it into a different channel and now she was trying to keep thinking positively.

'I'm going to buy somewhere in London. That's the plan at any rate.'

'What about work?'

'Well, there's a possibility of a contract job at the British Library. You remember my friend Joe Collins? He put me on to it.'

'That's good.'

'It's just a possibility. Meanwhile there's plenty to do here. I want to see the sale through before I commit myself to anything. I can manage.'

Leonie held back.

Melissa sensed what she was thinking, though. The madness of those weeks in France when anything seemed possible, because there was so much she did not know, when the past was a place of excuses and misinterpretations, of disconcerting discoveries, and whispered half-truths, stories and sighs, and being caught in the crossfire.

'Julian Adie – he never could have been my father.'

'No.'

'I was clutching at straws.'

She listened intently, without interjecting, as Melissa told her about Elizabeth's papers, and a brief version of the story they related.

'That's . . . good,' she said at last.

'Yes . . . it is.'

'But?'

As relieved as Melissa was, she knew Leonie was right. She was still holding out. There were issues yet to be resolved.

W hat she missed most of all, now she was in possession of the main story, was the chance of an explanation of all the minor ones; the semi-absorbed stories left hanging in the void in the absence of dates and facts. Who exactly was the great-uncle (or second cousin, maybe) who joined a troupe of actors and made for America, or the one who dropped to his death between two great ships in harbour in New York? Where, exactly, was the obscure ancestral line supposedly come down from William Wordsworth? Now that Elizabeth was gone, there was little chance of joining the dots.

Fighting introspection and in need of his good sense, she met Bill Angell for lunch in a quiet restaurant in Tunbridge Wells.

They had a corner to themselves which accentuated the

private atmosphere. Melissa expanded on all she had learned while she had been away.

Bill listened intently, straight-backed and kindly, and suppressed a smile when she told him about the locked library of books at the *bergerie*, many of which, she surmised, he must have sourced. She expected him to say that he had no idea of the story she had discovered, but he did not. With anyone else she might have asked bluntly whether he had known more than he had admitted, but she suspected she already knew the answer. He was a traditionalist of that generation that sets great store by respecting a confidence.

'I finally found out how she came to have the book of poems, signed to her,' said Melissa. 'It was all there in her diary.'

The main course was cleared and Bill waved a hovering waitress away with polite authority.

'She went up to London to see him. Adie's *Collected Poems* had just been published.'

A slight frown deepened the lines on Bill's forehead as if he was trying to remember something. 'So that would have been – when?'

'Early autumn 1980.'

'She wasn't still seeing him then, surely?' asked Bill, sceptically.

'No . . . It was a book signing at Hatchard's.'

Melissa could recall almost verbatim what Elizabeth had written in the densely packed pages of uncharacteristically jagged handwriting describing how she saw the event advertised in *The Times*: the author would be signing copies of his *Collected Poems*, long-awaited and complete with a lithograph by Barbara Hepworth on the front cover, at two o'clock on 7 October at Hatchard's on Piccadilly.

'There had been reviews in the Sunday papers and a lengthy and serious evaluation of his life and work in the *Observer*,' said Melissa. 'It brought it all back to her. Then she heard him on the radio and she made up her mind to go.'

Sensing that Bill wanted details as much as she herself wanted to go over them again, Melissa set the scene. How Elizabeth agonised over the timing of her arrival (should she arrive early before he tired of all the strange faces and small talk, or wait until the end when the crowd was dispersing and he might be more relaxed?) and how she should dress. She wanted it to seem as if it was a careless encounter, taking her by surprise as much as him.

In the taxi from Charing Cross, she almost asked the driver to turn back. She felt exposed, as if she were going to make a monumental fool of herself. But she had to do it. It was the only way she was going to make contact.

'When she walked into Hatchard's the first thing she saw was a poster with his photograph,' said Melissa. 'It had been twelve years since she had seen him last. Again, she almost turned back then. She had forgotten all the things she had rehearsed to say. There was so much she wanted to ask, it was like a compulsion to see him. But she knew at the same time she wouldn't be able to say any of the important things. It was an impossible situation.'

'But she wouldn't have left it there, would she?' said Bill.

He knew her mother well. Melissa was only beginning to realise how well. In Elizabeth's description of what happened next she was brutally honest about her own apprehension, how she held back when she found where Adie was. She heard his inimitable laughter first. A crowd of people was enclosing a desk where he was sitting. He made some quip, and there were more chuckles. '*What I dreaded was that he would recoil from me – even worse than not knowing who I was. I could imagine those eyes, those cut sapphire eyes clouding to enamel.*'

'No, she wouldn't have backed out, not after everything that had happened,' said Melissa. 'She had tried for years to see him in Sommières and been denied this.'

In her head she could see Elizabeth edging forward, the knot of people pulling apart. And there he was: Julian Adie like a little yacht in full sail, throwing his arms out and laughing. Just like Elizabeth remembered him: irrepressible life-giver, the sensualist, the performer – back in himself again. He had left the gloomy peasant persona behind in the Languedoc.

'She hung back, pretending to examine a book, keeping him in the corner of her eye as he signed and chatted. Then she went forward.' Her body had taken the decision, in the same way she first jumped as a child from a high diving board. Her subconscious made the move. 'Suddenly she was standing in front of him.'

Bill's eyes were misting. 'Did he recognise her?'

'No. He wasn't even looking up properly. He was pulling a book off the pile to sign. "Thank you so much for coming," that sort of stuff. He was giving her the eye and he had no idea who she was.'

Melissa paused, wondering how much to excise from her mother's intimate account. She felt protective of Elizabeth's pathetic whisper to Adie, '*We met once – some years back.*' And the element of farce when she was immediately interrupted by a woman like a well-upholstered barrel who pressed against her back and pushed a book at Adie. '*Do you mind?*' she said to them both. '*I don't have long. Thank you so much. "To Kathleen" if you please. She did like your Egyptian books. Can't say they were my cup of tea, if you don't mind my saying. I like a less complicated story. But Kathleen likes that kind of thing.*'

On the restaurant table Bill clasped his hands as if to re-assure himself. He too seemed upset, feeling empathy with Elizabeth. 'He must have known who she was – that can't have been it!'

'Not quite,' said Melissa. 'Adie signed someone else's book and when he turned back to my mother he seemed to see her for the first time. She reminded him of her name and he gave her a wonderful smile. His eyes creased. The hand went through the hair in the old gesture. He remembered, there was no doubt about it. He told her how attractive she was looking. And she was grinning back, but he didn't say anything more.'

Bill was absolutely still, listening.

'She watched his hand as he signed her book. She wrote that it was tattooed with dark age spots.' Melissa stopped there, sparing Bill the details of how it had made Elizabeth feel to remember the touch of it on her own brown skin, the scent of pines and baked earth. But from his expression, he might already have made the connection.

'My mother started to say how pleased she was to see him but Adie cut her off. His voice was impersonal again, thanking her for her interest. But she could see his pen moving over the title page of the book though she couldn't see what it was he was writing.

'The shop was getting busier. A swarm of book buyers

was pressing in on her with their bags and elbows and umbrellas. '*It's been a long time*,' she said to Adie. And his reply was: '*So sorry you had to wait.*'

'She was so sure it was a deliberate misunderstanding. She thought how subtle he was, and how like him. The tone of his voice – was there a hint of the old warmth and intimacy, perhaps a tiny hint of mischief? He loved secrecy, the thrill of the illicit. It was such a game to him. He was writing more than just his name.

'When he had finished Adie handed the book to her, closed.

'She knew it would be indelicate to read it while she was still in the shop, but he had written her a message, she was sure of it. After all the years she would have her chance to meet him again, and to understand at last what had really happened that night in Corfu.

'The taxi was taking her away down Piccadilly before she opened it and read the inscription.'

Melissa reached down into her bag and put the book in front of Bill. She opened it and they both stared at the ambiguous, contradictory words. '*To Elizabeth, always remembering Corfu, what could have been and what we must both forget.*'

'He would have known who she was as soon as he saw her,' said Bill. They had almost finished their coffee but he was still fretting about Adie's ungallant behaviour. 'She was always so beautiful, with that lovely thoughtful quality she had. He would have recognised her.'

Melissa stirred the melted sugar at the bottom of her cup. 'Perhaps that was what worried him – what exactly was causing the thoughtfulness.'

'But he must have known what a gentle soul she was. There was no need to be so cruel.'

'You're right.'

'I always knew something had happened,' said Bill, with an edge to his normally even voice.

Melissa looked up sharply. 'Did she tell you that?'

His grey eyes were so sad. 'No. She didn't have to. I could tell. Something had stopped her in her tracks, something that she never quite resolved. I just never realised that it was anything to do with Julian Adie. It all makes sense now, of course. The books . . . I thought it was just a passionate interest she'd developed . . . that she'd found an author whose words spoke to her. I promise you this has been as much of a surprise to me – '

She believed him. Wrong yet again, to assume he'd kept a confidence from her.

Bill picked up his spoon and studied it before going on. 'I don't suppose she ever told you,' he said carefully, 'that I once asked her to marry me.'

'No . . .'

'It was a long time ago. She said she did give it serious thought, and I think she probably did. When she turned me down she gave all the usual excuses about being set in her ways. But she did say one thing which I never forgot . . .'

He stopped, as if making sure that Melissa was listening to every word before continuing. 'She said that she couldn't marry again because she wouldn't put herself in the position of having to trust a man again . . .'

Neither of them spoke.

'People make things up and don't even realise they are

doing it,' he said ruefully. 'She got stuck with one version of herself and it was such a shame.'

'Perhaps she lost confidence, in herself as much as in other people.' Melissa was thinking of herself, in the dreadful months after Richard.

'Maybe.'

Melissa gave him a smile. Surely Elizabeth should never have doubted Bill's integrity. Had she missed a chance of real happiness with Bill?

It looked as if she had.

S he gave him a lift back to his house on the common and carried on along the country lanes. Preoccupied by what he had told her, she drove along in a kind of trance. As the road wound down into the valley and she had to brake she gave a shiver because she had no idea how she had driven there. For the first time she had actually experienced being lost in thought. It had been a revelation to find out how deeply Bill had cared for Elizabeth.

What else was it he said? That we can all learn from the lives of other people, especially those close to us. Was it his way of offering her some sound advice about her own reluctance to trust?

It was not only Julian Adie who led many lives, she had finally realised – we all live several lives. The child Melissa and the younger Elizabeth were simply characters who had gone, buried in adult selves. It was as though she could now empathise with herself as Richard's betrayed wife, but she did not have to be that person any longer.

And what of all the lives not lived? The Elizabeth who

might have remarried, to a man who truly loved her? Melissa's own never-were lives, which might have been altered by Joe – or Alexandros.

Alexandros. He was like Bill in many ways: good-hearted and generous, serious yet willing to take a risk. Pictures crowded into her mind: Alexandros on the path down to Kalami, his eyes full of shy compassion, the wind pulling at his billowing shirt. The boat in the bay, and the bitter coffee on the breakfast table. The scorpion end. The sharp sting of longing when he had dared to come to her in France, and then when he had gone too soon, gone away – sent away – again because she could not trust herself to trust him.

So often it's not a single event but a succession of separate incidents that make a belief. Events filter down the consciousness until the mind makes a connection. Perspectives shift. Then, at last, there is conviction.

By the time she drew into the driveway at Bell Cottage, she was sure. She would go back to Corfu. If nothing else, she owed it to him to explain. The prospect both excited and terrified her at once.

B ut during the next few days that conviction faltered. She questioned whether it was too late now. How could she simply present herself to him after the way they parted? Every time they tried tentatively to establish the relationship it came to grief. Perhaps neither of them was ready.

What happened next was so startling that at the time it felt as if fate had intervened.

In one of the last rooms she had to clear, a room under

the eaves, on bare floorboards and squeezed between unwanted furniture, under a patina of dust and a stiff calico sheet, stood several old suitcases, long forgotten. The lid on the last one felt loose on its hinges as she pulled it open. A layer of brown paper crackled with age. Beneath were holiday souvenirs: a Spanish doll, a moth-eaten hat, brochures for various attractions – and a wedding album Melissa had not seen since she was a small girl. A large brown envelope opened as it was moved, spilling photographs into the musty well. A puzzle of black-and-white interspersed with a splash of colour formed from the scattered images. Irritated in a numb, distant way, she reached in to pick them up.

Melissa retrieved handfuls of mismatched holiday snaps. Perhaps these were the rejects, the ones not good enough for the albums, the odd ones sent by friends and never arranged for display. Some were of Edward. A shaky shutter had blurred the outlines of his bluff features so that he appeared to be trying to avoid capture by bolting, making a break for the white deckled edges. No note of when or where they were taken.

At the bottom of the trunk, she found a heavy brown paper parcel, tied with string, and a plain card under the crossover. She sat back on her calves, holding it. The name on the card was Julian.

The parcel was a simple one of folded thick brown paper. Inside was a book, a first edition of Cavafy's poems in English. How long had it been there?

Not fate. The excuse she had been looking for.

*

Stalling, she contacted the British Film Institute in London and booked a viewing of an old television documentary held in their library. Down a side street from the sultry roar of Tottenham Court Road a few days later, she was directed along overheated, biscuit-scented corridors and staircases to the room where she took a seat in a row with four other anonymous researchers, each staring at an identical screen. The stuffy silence broken only by mechanical clicking and juddering from the video machines, she put on headphones.

She wanted to see his image moving on the screen, just once, and to hear whether his voice was anything like the one that resounded in her imagination. The programme, filmed in 1965, began in Corfu with the dawn of his creative life. A shot tracked across the sea. The grainy texture of the disintegrating colour pictures made a veil between the viewer and the water. Adie was a squat man of fifty, hair still blond, bobbing on a boat. Only a few years younger than when Elizabeth first met him. This was, give or take, as he would have looked the summer that changed her life. Melissa leaned forward, arms tightly crossed.

'I always wanted to *live*,' he said to camera. The voice was reedier, tinnier, than she expected, the accent pure Empire. 'To make mistakes, to be greedy, rebellious, scurrilous, insightful, loving, hating, mad, bad, dangerous, kind, selfish, generous, inconsistent, angry, arrogant, assertive, uncertain, immoral, loyal, reckless, considerate, brave, passionate ... because, do you see, that's all there *is*!'

Perhaps it was unfair to judge from a mechanical approximation, from a recording made more than forty years earlier, which like the film, like the man, was no longer in prime condition.

The brilliant peacock blues, emeralds, jades and purples of the sea pulling around the sun-baked caves and jagged cliffs. Over the shifting scenes, he talked fondly, hypnotically, of his sailing boat and the trips with friends, of the blue-and-gold-veined sea. The final part of the film showed him going to a party, on a terrace overlooking the sea. For a moment Melissa strained for a glimpse of her mother among the guests. She even rewound the tape and ran it again when she spotted a slight, blonde woman. But she knew the dates were wrong, and it could not have been her.

Afterwards she walked back down Charing Cross Road, past the surviving second-hand bookshops, through the bumping, scurrying crowds, feeling curiously empty.

That night, she was certain.

II

The last Saturday in August, after hours of rain and delays, the plane climbed through cloud. Somewhere over the Swiss or Italian mountains it broke through into heart-expanding blue. Hours later at Kalami, she stood in the apartment she had occupied the previous year. Beyond the balcony, the sea was a lustrous mirror under a deepening sky.

'I'm sorry I can't offer you the White House,' Manolis informed her when she telephoned to book. 'It's completely full until October.'

Melissa looked nervously at her watch. Eleni, asked discreetly, had told her what she needed to know. Now it was vital to pick the right time. This was the moment when she would truly come back into herself. She had done it in her imagination a hundred times. Now it was real.

If she went to Alexandros to apologise, put herself on the line, it would be proof of how far she'd come. She repeated that to herself. No longer stuck in the past but looking to the future; she was seeing possibilities for happiness she never let herself believe in before. It was easier to repeat than to believe.

What if he didn't want to know? She couldn't think about that.

I'm sorry. I'm so sorry I didn't trust you. I didn't trust myself.

At five-thirty she walked up the road. The boat hire office was closed. The track up to the farmhouse was quiet. As Melissa approached the house there was barely a sound apart from her own footsteps on the dust and pebbles. It was hard to tell whether anyone was at home.

The terrace was in sight now. On the point of turning round, cursing her own idiocy, the ease with which she lived in her imagination somewhere beyond rational hope and expectation, she saw the door open. She steeled herself to see him again.

A woman came out. Pretty and young, with long chestnut hair. Something interrogative in Greek was said. She seemed to be waiting for an answer.

'I'm sorry, I don't understand. Is Alexandros here?'

'He is not here,' she replied in slow, heavily accented English.

'Do you know where he is?'

She shook her head, looking Melissa up and down.

Behind her the kitchen was just as it had been the previous year, with no sign that an enthusiastic feminine hand had cleared his things — the files and books, slides and micro-scopes, propagation tanks and jars — from unsuitable surfaces.

Melissa felt a lump form in her throat. She wanted to ask the girl who she was but knew that she must not. Surely — she suddenly realised what a dreadful thought this was —

surely this could not be Alexandros's wife? Don't say his wife was back in the frame, after all, as Richard had so nearly been when Alexandros surprised her by arriving in France.

Surely not.

'Are you Mrs Catzeflis?'

'Catzeflis, yes. Alexandros.'

It was hard to know what that meant.

Melissa took a step back.

'Thank you – *Efharisto* – ' She raised her hand in a feeble goodbye and left.

At the large taverna on the beach Melissa ordered some food she did not want and some wine that she did. It was early for dinner, but surprisingly crowded. Already the scents of cooking and herbs were pungent and familiar. It was soon obvious she had arrived just in time, for ten minutes later all the tables were full. Hard-pressed waiters were apologetically turning tourists away, although offering to serve them drinks out on the beach.

She had to remind herself that the last time she had been here it had been at the very end of the season. This was Kalami in high summer. The buzz of the crowds made it quite different from the place she had experienced the previous year.

But after a while she realised it was more than that. The atmosphere was expectant, as if something was about to happen. The mystery was solved when one of the girls at the next table, where two British couples in their twenties were trying ouzo, picked up a flyer printed in English and used it as a fan.

It read, *Varkarola. The Sea Festival*.

There was also a picture of a boat and a guitar.

Melissa sighed inwardly. She finished her drink, pushed her plate away, and freed the table.

Outside the taverna's canopy, sunset trembled over the headland. Under a glowing sky, the opalescent sea presented a surface serenity.

She went and sat on the beach, down by the water's edge. Now that she knew for certain that Elizabeth had once been here, and what had happened to her, pieces of the puzzle were fitting at last. And overlaying that was her own experience, the previous October, when she had been so sad and guarded. How far she had come, in many ways. How held back she had been by Elizabeth's experiences.

The sea was rubbing over the stones, eroding them, pulling them into new patterns, crushing the minute carapaces of sea creatures in their salty graves, as waves collapsed at her feet. Perhaps there were particles thousands of years old.

Soon the same hubbub of conversations as in the tavernas was rising on the beach. More people were gathering noisily: mostly tourists but here and there were the authentic craggy brown faces of old women in black, skinny children who had spent the summer outside running and swimming, groups of elderly men leaning crookedly together on sticks.

The sky and water were ablaze as the headlands darkened. The painful rock contortions were being lost to violet shadows.

Faintly at first, she heard a high note. The crowd noise seemed to ease slightly before a ripple of interest confirmed that the music was starting. A group of musicians and singers smartly turned out in black trousers and waistcoats, each with a jaunty straw hat, had begun a jingling song. Led by an accordionist and a guitarist they were strolling along the broadwalk. By the time they had reached where she was the song had changed to a romantic serenade. A handsome tenor was playing up to it, reaching out his arms to the nearest pretty girls.

Melissa shivered. She had the terrible feeling she might cry. She had come to see Alexandros, and he was not here, despite Eleni's assurances. She should have contacted him first. She pinched the bridge of her nose and cursed her own rash optimism. Nothing had changed; despite everything she was still the same deluded idiot, still alone. She could see her attempt at a surprise for what it was now: an escape clause. Because she still could not commit herself to acting on her brave new instincts.

The band reached the jetty at the mid-point of the bay where a wooden fishing boat was tied up. To gasps and applause, a string of lights was suddenly switched on, making an arc over the musicians as they stepped on board and stood swaying but still gamely playing. They rattled off what sounded as if it might have been a traditional fisherman's song. Then the boat cast off, one man at the tiller, and puttered regally across the bay to begin a slow circle from taverna to taverna and the audience on the beach.

Melissa stayed where she was for a while, then feeling tiredness catching her, wandered over the pearly pebbles to the rocks below the White House. The new buildings on the hillside behind had caught the sunset so that their pale render now had a sugared-almond quality, rising in tiers like a celebration cake. She sat on the edge of a boulder and watched, detached, as the boat carried the band slowly along the row of beachfront tavernas. The sounds were pure and strong in the cooling air, travelling across the bay which was transformed into a natural amphitheatre backed by the curving mountains.

Behind her footsteps crunched, then stopped. Too close to her for a stranger. Automatically, she looked round. Alexandros was staring straight at her.

They were equally awkward.

'I was just coming to see you' he said, his expression unreadable.

'I came to see *you* . . .'

A spiky melody was playing faster and faster, intensifying her nerves. He seemed equally ill at ease.

'Are you, er . . . on your own?' he asked.

'Yes.'

'I was coming to see you,' he said again.

'Oh! Well, that's . . . How did you know I would be here?'

'Manolis told me.'

'Of course.'

'The village radar . . .'

'Yes . . .!'

'Well . . . It's good to see you. How are you?'

'I'm fine. You?'

'Yes, yes . . . very well, thank you. So – you are back in Kalami!'

'Yes . . . !'

An awkward silence. Then they both started at once.

'Manolis said—'

'I've got some—'

He laughed and shook his head, looking away. He looked even healthier than he had in France, as if life was good. As if she might well have missed her chance.

The music was growing more and more frantic. There was a loud group of teenage holidaymakers kicking and tangling, trying to perform their version of a Greek dance, their white t-shirts standing out like a puppet show down by the jetty.

'Do you mind if I join you?'

'Do.' Her voice was a croak.

He leaned on the rock beside her.

The moonstruck music ended in a tumult of clashing keys and instruments. Then the mood changed and the serenades and songs sounded like laments.

Lights were coming on up the hillside, illuminating houses peachy pink and several plum-coloured lines of windows from the largest hotel. Occasionally he translated a line of a song he thought she might like, but otherwise they were silent.

Melissa was tight and awkward, sitting in the dark with him. All the while she was rehearsing what she wanted to say. She was close enough to smell his scent, that mixture of warmth and sea tang which seemed unbearably familiar.

The band was still giving its all when fireworks were let off the boat, exploding chrysanthemums and kaleidoscopes in the black above the sea. The unexpected salvo made her jump.

'It's quite a spectacle,' she said, determined to sound positive as the sky whined and cracked, trailing gunpowder scents which overpowered the ozone tang in the air.

The finale erupted, leaving an eerie, smoky moment of silence.

She wanted to tell him why she had let him go. How desperately sorry she was that she had not begged him to stay. What she understood now about her life with her mother, and how it had affected her own way of thinking.

It was too hard to say any of it. The words were stuck deep inside.

Alexandros shifted beside her. Her first thought was that he was going to leave. The second that she alone was now responsible for whatever happened next.

The words spilled like gibberish. 'When I was last here, you gave me a photograph of my mother, do you remember?'

He was standing now. She could not wait for his acknowledgement.

'I've got something for you in return. Can I give it to you some time?'

'Of course.'

Crowds were flowing all around them in the darkness, leaving the beach after the spectacle. She paused. 'I'm sorry for what happened in France. That's what I came to tell you.'

She squinted out to sea in the silence that followed.

'You could give it to me now,' he said carefully, at last.

'It's in the Prospero Apartments,' she said.

The book looked more battered than ever after its latest journey. Alexandros pulled the brown paper away. The tooled leather of the spine was scaling, the edges of the cover rounded with use.

He held it up to the crude light of the balcony, examining it as carefully as an artefact.

'Cavafy,' he said softly. Then, opening it, 'A first edition.'

Melissa fetched a table lamp, stretching the lead outside so he could see it better.

'I – I wanted you to have it.'

A shy smile with the hint of a tease lit up his face. 'You could have sent it in the post.'

'I could have done.'

Their eyes connected.

'But I've always been curious,' she said keeping up the contact. 'I wanted to do the right thing – and to see your reaction for myself.'

'See what?'

She said nothing.

Alexandros opened it to the library plate on which was written, '*Ex Libris Clive Stilwell*'.

'The Englishman who lived at Kouloura,' he said. 'You say it was in your mother's house . . . ?'

'Clive Stilwell was her godfather.'

'I didn't know that.'

'Neither did I – at least, not when I was here last year. I found a card with it – all it said was, '*Julian*'. He must have given it to her to pass on to Adie.'

Melissa was thinking about the diary, and the days after the drowning when Adie was reluctant to see Elizabeth. In the end she must have told Clive she was going over to Agni, or Kalami, and it was possible he had asked her to drop the book off.

'For whatever reason, she didn't give it to him,' Melissa said.

She was wondering whether Elizabeth had wanted to keep back an excuse for seeing him one more time. But it was all pointless speculation.

'Why she didn't, we'll never know . . .' she mused.

'Probably not,' said Alexandros. 'Thank you, it's beautiful.'

Each was tentative, unwilling to presume.

It was too cool now on the balcony but to suggest they went inside seemed like an invitation she was too self-conscious to make. This was not how she had imagined the scene. Alexandros was friendly but too distant. The thought that he was simply being polite, that she had missed her chance months ago, began to curdle in the pit of her stomach.

'Do you think I could see Theodora again?' she asked brightly — too brightly.

'Theodora?' He did a fake double take. 'I'm sure she would happily see you. But what more is there to ask?'

'I found my mother's diaries. She did meet Theodora.'

Alexandros rubbed his cheek. 'But what of it?'

She started to explain about the party the night Veronica Rae died, but he had tensed up. She could sense his irritation from three feet away.

'It doesn't matter,' said Melissa.

His mood had changed suddenly. Desperate to regain their previous minutes of relative ease, she tried to change the subject. 'Are you travelling a lot at the moment? What are you working on?'

'I'm working here,' he said, flatly closing that down.

There could be a reason for his awkwardness. She decided to make it easy for him – for them both.

'When I came to your house earlier, I met a woman there.'

Alexandros was sombre. 'It could have been Lia. I sent her to the house to fetch something for me.'

'Right . . .'

'She's my intern at the museum.'

Relief made her fingers tingle. She wanted to fling her arms around him.

Alexandros stood up. She smiled. But he made no move towards her. Instead he said, with unbearable formality, 'I must be going. Thank you very much for the book.'

Her heart uncomfortably skipped a beat. He couldn't go – not like this! He had reached the sitting room before she made him turn round.

'Alexandros . . . I need to . . . tell you something.'

Now was her chance. But everything was wrong.

He started for the door again. 'I still don't quite understand why you need to do this!' His tone was pure exasperation.

'What – what do you mean?' she asked, feeling desperate.

'It's all . . . the past. You don't let it go.'

The room, already dim, seemed to darken further.

She watched him, unable to believe how badly she had handled it.

'Goodnight,' he said flatly.

It was a complete foul-up. Wretched, she wanted to tell him that she understood why he had left. She couldn't blame him – she had left it too late. Going over it all later, miserably lying alone and awake in the dark, she realised she was being presumptuous again, still trying to decipher symbols and complicated languages, not all of them spoken.

What she liked most about Alexandros was his reticence, his very lack of glibness. If he said something, he meant it.

'I'm sorry I didn't trust you.' That's all that needed to be said.

III

No one asked what had brought her back. They
accepted her presence tactfully. Eleni, placid and
buttery-cheeked, greeted her like a sister, inviting
her to dinner. Manolis, following orders perhaps, let caution
override curiosity and asked nothing.

Melissa drank a late morning coffee at the Prospero
Taverna feeling crushed and tired, thinking about a simpler
time when people did not read so much, and before tele-
visions and computers brought the world crashing into
their whitewashed rooms, and long before that when
memory, individual and collective, was the only tool there
was, to order their society, their understanding and their
myths.

Manolis waved and called down from the road. 'It's here!'
She climbed the steps wearily to where the taxi was waiting.
One more conversation, and she could leave.

Theodora's house was on a hillside at Sotiriotissa, just
north of Corfu Town. The address was in Melissa's

notebook all along, jotted down when she'd thought she would never need to use it.

A twisting drive led up from a shabby gate set back from the main highway, through orange and lemon trees, olives and myrtles. A turning circle in front of what had once been a grand Venetian villa was shaggy with overblown grass. The house itself, once a pale yellow, was porous and in need of repair.

'I like to keep it in a state of nature,' she said with dignity.

Or in a lack of funds, Melissa surmised.

She followed her down a gracious hallway.

'You look well,' Melissa told her. Theodora seemed less made up than she had been at the Liston, and her hair was in better condition. More grey had been allowed to show through.

'Rattling with vitamins, m'dear. Life's not too bad.'

On a terrace of potted geraniums and banana trees, they took coffee and nut liqueur and ate tiny cakes in the shade of a pomegranate tree, its fruit hard, shiny and red as Christmas baubles. Theodora took a fraying rattan chair, armed with a fly swat like an African dictator. Every so often she flapped it viciously at the wall but these bursts of movement caused no break in her conversation.

She had been contributing to a local magazine, was spending more time at the Corfu Arts Club, had taken in a stray cat. An expatriate production of *The Tempest* had come to grief in a welter of recriminations.

Behind her, the house groaned with overstuffed furniture, heavy armoires and sideboards. A collection of framed photographs stood on a baby grand piano, and in the corner a bulky old television buttressed by piles of videos. The

door to the terrace stood open but the windows were shuttered.

'How did you get on with your researches?'
Theodora rubbed her fingers together rapidly, as if
there was some stickiness on them. Her fingernails were
thickly varnished deep red. 'I must say I didn't expect to see
you quite so soon!'

'You were expecting me?'

'Well, yes . . . Alex said there was something else you
wanted to ask me.'

Melissa's mouth was dry. So Alexandros had already called
her. Either he was still willing to help, or he wanted to absolve
himself of any further responsibilities for her. She swallowed hard.

'I asked you last year about Elizabeth Norden. I wasn't
entirely honest with you. What I should have said then was
that I'm her daughter.'

Theodora put her head on one side, assessing.

'Yes . . . perhaps you are.'

Melissa let that go.

This time she told Theodora her reasons for asking,
setting out what she knew of the night Veronica
Rae drowned, as Elizabeth had written in her account. She
even told her about Dr Braxton's biographical investigations, although not – yet – the conclusions she feared he
might reach, nor the precise details of what Elizabeth
claimed happened after Veronica followed them down to
the sea.

'It's a long time ago, I know. Do you remember that party

where you spoke to Elizabeth – and do you remember Veronica Rae being there too?'

Theodora nodded. 'I remember – for *many* reasons.'

'Tell me.'

'I was there on my own. I'd had a *dreadful* row with my husband. Oh, we used to have a time of it in the early days – adjusting to each other, I mean. There was a time when I felt he was a lot nicer when I couldn't understand what he was saying . . .' Theodora looked off into the distance.

'So . . . I suppose what I really want to know is . . .' said Melissa, waiting until she had her attention, '. . . was my mother's account accurate – was Veronica Rae drunk, and did she slap Julian Adie?'

Theodora became lively again. 'Oh, yes. *That* happened all right. A lot of people saw it – and gossiped about it for weeks afterwards, as you can imagine. I'd forgotten about the shoe breaking, but that was true. The way she walked out of the room and we all made way for her, like the parting of the waves. I can see it all up here,' she tapped the side of her head. 'The silver dress, too . . .'

'Did you see Adie leave with Elizabeth?'

'I can't remember that. Just the set pieces, you know.'

That struck a chord. It seemed more likely that whatever Theodora was about to tell her would be the truth.

'Did you stay longer at the party?'

Theodora grimaced. 'I stayed till the end. I was trying to punish Giorgios.'

'In her diary, Elizabeth wrote that the last she saw of him that night was when he ran back to Nissaki saying he would raise the alarm. But did he? Did you see whether Julian Adie came back at all?'

She was thinking of the passage in *The Carcassonne Quartet* – the man and two women at the rock pool. How upsetting she had found it because it might have been true. Elizabeth must have thought that too, else why would she have marked the passage so furiously?

'Oh, yes. Adie came back.'

'On his own? My mother – Elizabeth wasn't with him?'

'He was on his own.'

'You're sure?'

Theodora nodded vigorously. 'He *burst* back in, all puffed out – shouting for help: the *bloody* woman was in the water! We all knew without asking who he was talking about, not Elizabeth. He was going out in his boat to search, and he wanted to get the fishermen out looking too. As far as the party went, it was a dramatic ending – and after we thought we'd already had the fireworks . . .'

'But it was too late by then . . .'

'He didn't give any indication that's what he thought. He was trying to organise everyone. We streamed down to the jetty. Those with boats started them up. Others took the path. Make no mistake – we all did as much as we could.'

'Did you ever think there was anything suspicious about the way he was behaving?'

'No.'

Melissa smiled. Relief released the tightness across her shoulders.

'Well, not at the time,' said Theodora.

'Not at the time?' Melissa's heart sank again. She had been so sure that her mother had been right to believe in Adie, that she had not been such a terrible judge of character after all.

Theodora shrugged. 'Well, all sorts of things came out about Julian Adie after that, didn't they?'

Melissa was leaving when she remembered to ask. 'Do you know the local Medusa myth?'

'Now you're asking . . .' Theodora demurred. 'Why?'

'Adie referred to Poseidon and Medusa in something he wrote later.'

Theodora rearranged the baubles hanging from her neck. 'I can't remember. But I know where you can find Medusa in Corfu, though – in the archaeological museum. Why don't you ask Alex?' she asked. 'He'll know.'

Melissa shook her head sadly. 'I've asked him quite enough.'

'Go and see the Medusa then.'

Melissa walked slowly down the drive to the taxi waiting beyond the gates. Seeing Theodora again really was the end of the trail. But then, on a whim as she got into the car, she asked the driver to take her into Corfu Town.

The Archaeological Museum was on the waterfront.

As she walked through the great doors Melissa felt enervated, coshed by too much coffee and yet more information that never quite yielded an answer. Inside the museum the atmosphere was hardly less close than outside. Few other visitors drifted through the high-ceilinged rooms.

She asked for directions, but the mother of the Gorgons was easy to find.

The Medusa was enormous. Squat on furious taut muscled legs, the stone monster was more than life-size;

the central motif, flanked by two supercilious lions, claws drawn, of a great stone pediment from the Doric temple to Artemis dated 570BC. Angry hissing snakes formed a belt around her waist and swung from her hair. But time had amputated her hands and eroded the menace of her expression. The face, with its bulging eyes and mad grimace, the wrecked, pitted mouth and obscene poking tongue supposed to turn a man to stone was now a diminished mask, its bite and horror blunted.

Melissa stood back, taking it all in.

'You asked about the Medusa myth.'

She spun round. It was Alexandros.

'How did you—?'

'The Medusa has several histories,' he said, 'and no one can say for certain which is the true story. One is that she was the victim of a ritual murder, fully, er, sanctioned by the gods on Mount Olympia, the ghastly deed carried out by Perseus using the helmet of invisibility from Hades and a scimitar to slice off her head.

'In another version, it is Athena who ordered her death, because she wanted the powerful head for her own purposes. Same method, however . . .'

His voice was soft, confiding the fables like secrets, the sense of time passing, of improbable tales, beating heat and brightness. The air between them seemed charged.

'But you might like this one better. According to a poem by Hesiod, she was entranced by Poseidon's waves of blue-black hair, and allowed him to . . . seduce her in the dark depths of the sea. One of the children of this union was Pegasus the winged horse.'

'Why are there so many versions?'

'No one knows. Perhaps they are all parts of the same story, incoherently understood.'

'Maybe . . .' she murmured.

'Or perhaps, the ancients knew how to look beneath the story, and to understand that the Medusa was a lunatic, and the fear she inspired was the fear of losing one's own mind.'

The crazed rictus grin. The great bug eyes. The sinister snakes poised to attack on her chest where the pressure builds. Now Melissa could see it. She felt the skin over her own face tighten.

'So . . . the severed head then . . . ?'

'Emphasises where the problem lies, and how its effects must be cut from the body. Yes, that could well be the most plausible explanation.'

A figure of pathos, then; instead of a laughable ogress.

'In all the ancient beliefs, snakes were the symbols of renewal for the skin they could shuck off and regrow. So now the serpents are no longer weapons primed for attack but an emblem of hope.'

'We see what we want to see,' murmured Melissa.

They stood quietly for a few minutes.

'Are you all right?' he asked as they walked out of the room.

Melissa nodded, exhausted suddenly. 'Thanks, that was kind of you. But how did you know I would be—' She stopped as she worked it out, feeling stupid for being so slow. 'Theodora.'

His eyes softened. 'She called me. I had already spoken to her – she knew I was here today.'

'She told me to come here,' said Melissa.

A pause.

'I'm driving back to Kalami now. Would you like to come with me?'

'Yes, please.'

In the car, he was as quiet as she was.

'What are you going to do the rest of the afternoon?' she asked eventually.

'I'm going to take my boat out. I might want to swim.'

The thought of cold water on her body made her long for the sea.

'Could I come too?'

Alexandros collected her at the jetty on Kalami beach. His boat was sharp and sleek, an old-fashioned cutter with a scrubbed wooden deck.

Out on the water she could see the fabled indigo and gold of the Ionian, sparkling on the swell. The lush greens of the headlands. The brown smudged hills of Albania. You could half-close your eyes and imagine the scene had never changed.

He was using the engine – they would not be going far. On the edge of Yaliscary bay, she mentally saluted the flat yellow rock where she had sat for so many hours the previous year.

'Do you want to stop here?'

'No . . . go on further.'

Alexandros waved as they passed the little row of tavernas at Agni. A figure on the forecourt of the middle one waved two wide arcs in return.

'I know where I'd like to go,' she said quietly.

He was expressionless. He understood, though. 'Are you sure?'

'Yes.'

The boat cut through the water, its roll long and smooth.

She sat at the prow as they passed the rocky headlands where the tides nibbled and fretted at the stony land. And there it was: the shrine at the base of the cliff, perched on its strange frozen waves of rock. She remembered with a pang how she felt when she had driven herself in Manolis's hire boat. The shrine was just as it had been; it was as if the year might not have passed. It was just a funny little hut. But where then it had been charged only with her curiosity and longing to understand, now it was full of meaning, new layers of experience and knowledge.

Melissa did not care if the water was deep and cold at the base of the cliff. She was going to swim. A new, expensive snorkel mask would ensure she saw it all clearly. She had done this so many times in her imagination.

Alexandros anchored about five metres away from the rocks.

'Will you come in?' she asked.

'I'll wait here. I like sitting in the boat – it's good thinking time. Take as long as you want, I don't mind.'

Any embarrassment she might have had about exposing herself in a swimsuit in front of him was overridden by the intense need to do this. Besides, she was grateful he was there, for many reasons, not the least of them practical. Splashing into the water would be easy, but it would be hard, maybe even impossible, for anyone to grapple their way back up into the boat alone.

She lowered herself into the water, braced for iciness. It was warm as a bath. Buoyant and comfortable, she struck out for the green shallows ahead. Black ribbons of seaweed were satin caresses on her legs as she swam over them.

Inside the pool of jade and turquoise, the water was clear as glass. Six feet down, the floor of white pebbles sparkled. She could see the blood-red cherries pulsing on the stones, and Grace Adie's sudden graceful dive, effervescence on her brown outstretched arms as she swooped down to harvest them. And Elizabeth, decades later, young and euphoric in her fantasia, kicking her legs while Adie flicked and turned like a fish, splashing sea sequins.

Somewhere to the left of her was the cave with the shelf where the statue to Pan once stood – perhaps it stood there still.

Now the pool was hers. There was nothing bad here, only the silky salt of the sea on her skin. She had no idea how long she floated there. It was a whole world, a real world and a dream world. The sea that rocked a child to sleep. There was a fleeting moment, like a sudden play of light on the sea bed, when she felt she understood it all: how we all brought our past to present experience; how chronology is irrelevant to our own tiny histories. The past mattered. It manipulated and controlled us, just as the ancient gods once did. All was clear, just as Adie had said.

B ack in the boat, Alexandros was waiting.
She swam back, reinvigorated yet calm. High on the bobbing boat he was impassive. When she reached the ladder he bent forward and took her hand, pulling her up smoothly despite their slippery connection. Suddenly waking up to her near nakedness with him, she grappled for a towel.

But while she was in the water he had stripped off his shirt.

There was no inequality between them. So she let the wind dry her, as the boat tipped gently at anchor.

'Thank you – again. That was wonderful. Do you want to swim now?'

'I have done.'

She hadn't seen him, not a splash or ripple.

'I didn't notice.'

'I called to you but you didn't hear me either. Are you OK – do you want to go back?'

She shook her head. It was perfect. It was the present, the vibrantly alive and happy present and she wanted to stay in it.

They sat for a while in silence, watching the light dapple the swell.

'I love it here,' he said. 'When I'm away this is what I miss.'

The sea sighed and crumpled on the pebbled rim of beach.

'I've become a fatalist,' she said. 'Since I found that book.'

Citrus-scented, a breeze danced lightly in the air between them. His voice was soft and low, barely rising above a murmur. She had to lean in towards him across the boat to catch the words.

'Good decision.'

It was too soon, their bond was too newly born and fragile to say what she now believed: that happiness is simply a feeling that anything is possible.

The coast burned red and orange, then the sunset left the boat adrift in a purple luminescence. Under the magic lantern, the sea seemed black. They rocked on darkness. Neither suggested going back to shore.

Wavelets sucked at the hull. In the quiet, suspended in a vast cloud of colour, the hills all around rose protectively.

'I've thought of you often,' he said.

'I've thought of you too.'

'But then . . . I could do nothing. I – it seemed too difficult. There was never a good time for us. It seemed it was not meant to be.'

Birds wheeled above. The scrubbed deck was bone white in the strange light, the wood still warm under the backs of her bare legs. She did not feel cold, just faintly shivery.

She was shy of putting into words the way he had saved her from herself and the constraints her mother's story had so subtly imposed on her choices. How, after he had left her at St Cyrice, she had wanted him so ferociously that every olive tree, every crumb of red earth, every black hill crinkling in the distance was a reminder of Corfu, by which she meant him, Alexandros. How she had so gradually built up her own understanding on the bulwark of knowing that a man like him existed, even if she carried him only in her mind. So faint was the hope that she hardly knew it was there.

Melissa moved closer and put one hand over his.

For a few seconds, as they touched, she could feel the unheard creak of rock as layers settled, the shiver of the cypresses so close on the rocky shore, the soft hollows of the dimpled hills, sense the ripe grapes popping on the vine, see the nacreous sheen in the white morning sunlight, hear the clock of the sea.

This was when it was hard, being older, wary of taking a risk. Being too full of other stories.

He took his hand away, and it felt as if the tide had receded, leaving her stranded with burning cheeks. Then his touch on one shoulder, tentative yet infinitely reassuring. It was too dark to see the colour of his eyes, only the contours of his face. She leaned towards him and felt his breath in her hair.

A sigh and he pulled her in, his hands warm and solid on her back. His mouth brushed hers like the touch of a feather, then was confident and serious. In the dark and secret interior land of a kiss, its surprising new contours and rhythms, the intimate exchanges and growing understanding, they were holding fast together, part of the metronomic rock of the boat.

All was brought alive in the intimate universe of their mouths and hands. The boat at anchor was an independent island, unearthly sky above and the busy sea below.

Reluctantly they pulled apart.

Wordlessly, she opened her eyes.

All around, the sea was patched with low green and gold lights.

He clasped her hand and took it with his as he pointed. 'Look!'

Dipping over the side, he lifted jewelled strings of emeralds. 'Phosphorescence.'

He was laughing as he dripped the magical skeins of gems over their bodies. The water and the ribbons seemed to marble the deck.

'Imagine you are in a sea of green,' she murmured. 'Beneath you the boat is rocking gently . . .'

This was the ancient tale, which we always want to hear again. At last she understood, that she had been searching for this place – the only fixed element in the story – not to relive the story but to find her own version of it.

'It's our time now,' she said, reaching out for him.

SUGGESTED FURTHER
READING

The inspiration for this book came one gloomy winter afternoon when I rediscovered *Prospero's Cell* on the bookshelves of a bedroom at the top of the house. Opening it and starting to read was like injecting the grey with vivid blues and emeralds. A richly evocative account of Lawrence Durrell's life in Corfu in the 1930s, it was first published in 1945 and purports to be a diary in which he is a serious young writer living blissfully in the sun, deeply in love both with his new wife and with the idea of Greece. Durrell states that *Prospero's Cell* is a 'guide to the landscape and manners' of Corfu but it never quite becomes this. It is a lyrical personal notebook, and what he leaves out is as poignant as what he includes.

Its content is almost unrecognisable as the same ground his younger brother, the zoologist Gerald, covers in his famous Corfu book *My Family and Other Animals*, in which 'Larry' lives with the family (which he never did) and is the 'diminutive blond firework' by turns pompously literary and hilarious. And by the time he wrote *Prospero's Cell* Lawrence and his first wife Nancy had separated. He was already sadder and wiser, and living in wartime Egypt with Eve Cohen who would become his second wife.

I was intrigued. Further researches and a reading of several biographies soon revealed a complex and contradictory character. His work, over a period of nearly sixty years – most famously in *The Alexandria Quartet* – was concerned with duality: love and hate; truth and fiction; memory and misinterpretation. And running through it all, the transfiguring effect of time.

Lawrence Durrell wrote beguilingly, drawing constantly on his own experience and his many subsequent moves across the shores of the Mediterranean: to Rhodes (*Reflections on a Marine Venus*), Cyprus (*Bitter Lemons*), the former Yugoslavia, and finally to the South of France (*Caesar's Vast Ghost*) where he settled for thirty years. Interwoven with this background were his many loves and four marriages. He seemed to pack so many different lives into one! And while he was a comet blazing, what of the women he collided with along the way, I wondered? How did their stories end? And what of those he met, whose lives he changed but who did not rate even a footnote in his biography? Soon, I was busy inventing Julian Adie and Elizabeth.

SELECTED BOOKS BY
LAWRENCE DURRELL (1912-1990)

TRAVEL

Prospero's Cell
Reflections on a Marine Venus
Bitter Lemons
The Greek Islands
Caesar's Vast Ghost

NOVELS

The Alexandria Quartet
Justine, Balthazar, Mountolive, Clea

The Avignon Quintet
Monsieur, Livia, Constance, Sebastian, Quinx

POETRY

Collected Poems, ed. James A. Brigham
Selected Poems, ed. Peter Porter

BIOGRAPHICAL AND BACKGROUND READING

Ian MacNiven, *Lawrence Durrell, A Biography*.
    This is the official biography, exhaustively researched with
    Durrell's full cooperation in the years before he died.
Gordon Bowker, *Through the Dark Labyrinth*, *A Biography of
Lawrence Durrell*.
    The unofficial version and no less admiring of Durrell as

a writer, but with a less restrained investigation of the darker episodes in his life.

Edmund Keeley, *Inventing Paradise, The Greek Journey 1937-47*.

This and the following are more academic volumes examining Durrell's literary influences and setting his work in context.

Anna Lillios, (ed.), *Lawrence Durrell and the Greek World*.

Michael Haag, *Alexandria, City of Memory*.

A fabulous book, wonderfully written, which reveals the Alexandria of E M Forster and C P Cavafy as well as Durrell. Haag's own photographs such as that of the now-derelict Ambron Villa (where Durrell lodged), as well as unusual ones missed by other biographical works, make this special.

Hilary Whitton Paipeti, *In the Footsteps of Lawrence Durrell and Gerald Durrell in Corfu (1935-39), A Modern Guidebook*.

This slim volume, packed with photographs and quirky facts, is as enjoyable for the armchair traveller as for the visitor to Corfu.

The Art of Falling

Deborah Lawrenson

In wartime Italy, a love affair changed Tom Wainwright's life. Fifty years later, the repercussions echo down the years to his daughter . . .

In 1944 Tom Wainwright, a British soldier, arrives in the small Italian town of Petriano. The war is nearly over, and in the lull before the Allied troops move further north to capture Florence Tom forges a friendship with the Parini family – and in particular with the eldest daughter, Giuliana. When the war ends he chooses to stay in Italy, planning to build a life with the woman with whom he has fallen deeply in love, but in the tragic fallout of the end of the war his hopes are dashed.

Fifty years later Isabel Wainwright, Tom's daughter, sets off for Petriano herself, to attend a ceremony naming a pizza in the small town in her father's honour. But Isabel isn't so much going to represent her father as to try and find him – for she and her mother have heard nothing of him since, nearly twenty years earlier, he went out one day and never returned. She doesn't even know whether her father is dead or alive, but hopes that by discovering something of his past, she can build a picture of the man she hardly knew.

'A superbly crafted novel that deserves to be called the new *Captain Corelli* or perhaps the new *Birdsong*' Daily Mail

arrow books

Pursuit of Happiness

Douglas Kennedy

Manhattan, Thanksgiving eve, 1945. The war was over, and Eric Smythe's party was in full swing. All his clever Greenwich Village friends were there. So too was his sister Sara – an independent, canny young woman, starting to make her way in the big city. And then in walked a gatecrasher, Jack Malone – a U.S. Army journalist just back from a defeated Germany, and a man whose world-view did not tally with that of Eric and his friends.

Set amidst the dynamic optimism of postwar New York and the subsequent nightmare of the McCarthy witch-hunts, *The Pursuit of Happiness* is a great tragic love story; a tale of divided loyalties, decisive moral choices, and the random workings of destiny.

'A compulsive read'
Kate Atkinson, author of *Behind the Scenes at the Museum*

'This is the novel against which the rest of the year's output demands to be judged'
Express on Sunday

'Kennedy cannot help but write grippingly, and he weaves threads of love and betrayal into a thrillingly masterful ending'
Observer

arrow books

The Marriage Proposal

Célestine Hitiura Vaite

A delicious tale of big dreams on a small island.

Materena Mahi likes movies about love. And after fourteen years with Pito, the father of her three children, she wants a ring on her finger and a framed wedding certificate on the wall. But Pito does not like movies about love. He likes movies with action and as little talking as possible. Pito thinks that when you give a woman a ring and a wedding certificate she's going to start acting like she's the boss. 'Eh,' he insists, 'it's the rope around the neck.'

So when a drunken Pito finally proposes, Materena thinks she wouldn't mind becoming a *madame*. Before long every relative is giving her advice and Materena is finding it hard to juggle her family, her job and the plans for the wedding. And it doesn't help that the groom-to-be seems to have forgotten his proposal. Suddenly, she's not sure that she really wants that ring on her finger after all . . .

Praise for Célestine Hitiura Vaite:

'What a gorgeous, evocative novel! It charmed me from beginning to end' *Sophie Kinsella*

'A feast . . . busting with vitality and charm' *Sydney Morning Herald*

arrow books

The Editor's Wife

Clare Chambers

When aspiring novelist Christopher Flinders drops out of university to write his literary masterpiece, his family is sceptical.

However, when he is taken up by London editor Owen Goddard and his charming wife Diana, it seems success is just around the corner. Christopher is captivated by his generous and cultured mentors – but on the brink of realising his dream, he makes a desperate misjudgement which results in disaster for all involved. Shattered, he withdraws from London.

Twenty years on, Christopher has buried himself in rural Yorkshire, with a career and a private life marked by mediocrity. But then a young academic researching Owen Goddard seeks him out, and Christopher is forced to exhume his past, setting him on a path to a life-changing discovery.

'Original and addictive . . . reminds us of the rare pleasure that an intelligent tale with a happy ending brings' *Daily Telegraph*

'A great read with a fantastic twist at the end . . . thoroughly enjoyable and very clever' *Sunday Express*

'Engrossing, romantic and well-observed – not to mention exceedingly amusing – this is a perfect holiday read' *Daily Mail*

arrow books

THE POWER OF READING

Visit the Random House website and get connected with information on all our books and authors

EXTRACTS from our recently published books and selected backlist titles

COMPETITIONS AND PRIZE DRAWS Win signed books, audiobooks and more

AUTHOR EVENTS Find out which of our authors are on tour and where you can meet them

LATEST NEWS on bestsellers, awards and new publications

MINISITES with exclusive special features dedicated to our authors and their titles

READING GROUPS Reading guides, special features and all the information you need for your reading group

LISTEN to extracts from the latest audiobook publications

WATCH video clips of interviews and readings with our authors

RANDOM HOUSE INFORMATION including advice for writers, job vacancies and all your general queries answered

Come home to Random House

www.randomhouse.co.uk